Milly Johnson is a joke-writer, greetings card copywriter, newspaper columnist, after-dinner speaker, poet, winner of *Come Dine With Me*, *Sunday Times* Top Five author and winner of the RNA Romantic Comedy of the Year award both in 2014 and 2016.

She is obsessed by nice stationery, cruising on big ships and birds of prey. She is partial to a cheesecake or twelve but hates marzipan.

She was born and bred in Barnsley where she lives with her fiancé Pete, her teenage lads Tez and George, a spoilt trio of cats, Alan the rescue rabbit and now Bear the Eurasier pup. Her mam and dad live in t'next street.

Find out more at www.millyjohnson.co.uk or follow Milly on Twitter @millyjohnson

Also by Milly Johnson

The Birds & the Bees
A Spring Affair
A Summer Fling
Here Come the Girls
An Autumn Crush
White Wedding
A Winter Flame
It's Raining Men
The Teashop on the Corner
Afternoon Tea at the Sunflower Café
Sunshine Over Wildflower Cottage
The Queen of Wishful Thinking
The Perfectly Imperfect Woman

eBook only:

The Wedding Dress
Here Come the Boys
Ladies Who Launch
The Barn on Half Moon Hill
Now available as an audio collection called *Petit Four*

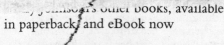

The Birds and the Bees

Romance writer and single mum Stevie Honeywell has only weeks to go until her wedding when her fiancé Matthew runs off with her glamorous new friend Jo. It feels like history repeating itself for Stevie, but this time she is determined to win back her man.

A Spring Affair

'Clear your house and clear your mind. Don't let life's clutter dictate to you. Throw it away and take back control!' When Lou Winter picks up a dog-eared magazine in the dentist's waiting room and spots an article about clearing clutter, she little realises how it will change her life . . .

A Summer Fling

When dynamic, power-dressing Christie blows in like a warm wind to take over at work, five very different women find themselves thrown together. But none of them could have predicted the fierce bond of friendship that her leadership would inspire . . .

Here Come the Girls

Ven, Roz, Olive and Frankie have been friends since school. They day-dreamed of glorious futures, full of riches, romance and fabulous jobs. Twenty-five years later, things are not as they imagined. But that doesn't mean they have given up.

An Autumn Crush

Four friends, two crushes and a secret . . . After a bruising divorce, Juliet Miller invests in a flat and advertises for a flatmate. Along comes self-employed copywriter Hattie, raw from her own relationship split, and the two women hit it off. Will they help each other to find new romance?

White Wedding

Bel is in the midst of planning her perfect wedding when disaster strikes. Can she hold it all together and, with the help of her friends and a mysterious man she meets unexpectedly, turn disaster into triumph?

Eve has never liked Christmas. So when her adored elderly aunt dies, the last thing she is expecting is to be left a theme park in her will. Can she overcome her dislike of Christmas, and can her difficult counterpart Jacques melt her frozen heart at last?

It's Raining Men

Best friends from work May, Lara and Clare are desperate for some time away. So they set off to a luxurious spa for ten glorious days. But when they arrive at their destination, it's not quite the place they thought it was ...

The Teashop on the Corner

Spring Hill Square is a pretty sanctuary away from the bustle of everyday life. And at its centre is Leni Merryman's Teashop on the Corner. Can friends Carla, Molly, and Will find the comfort they are looking for there?

Afternoon Tea at the Sunflower Café

When Connie discovers that Jimmy, her husband of more than twenty years, is planning to leave her for his office junior, her world is turned upside down. Determined to salvage her pride, she resolves to get her own back.

Sunshine Over Wildflower Cottage

New beginnings, old secrets, and a place to call home – escape to Wildflower Cottage with Viv, Geraldine and Stel for love, laughter and friendship.

The Queen of Wishful Thinking

Lewis Harley has opened the antique shop he always dreamed of. When Bonnie Brookland walks into Lew's shop, she knows this is the place for her. But each has secrets in their past which are about to be uncovered. Can they find the happiness they both deserve?

The Perfectly Imperfect Woman

Marnie has made so many mistakes in her life that she fears she will never get on the right track. But when Lilian, an eccentric old lady from a baking chatroom, offers her a fresh start, she ups sticks and heads for Wychwell. But her arrival is as unpopular as a force 12 gale in a confetti factory ... Will this little village in the heart of the Yorkshire Dales accept her as one of their own ...?

milly johnson

The Yorkshire Pudding Club

**SIMON &
SCHUSTER**

London · New York · Sydney · Toronto · New Delhi

A CBS COMPANY

First published in Great Britain by Simon & Schuster UK Ltd, 2007
A CBS COMPANY

This paperback edition, 2018

1 3 5 7 9 10 8 6 4 2

Simon & Schuster UK Ltd
1st Floor
222 Gray's Inn Road
London WC1X 8HB

Simon & Schuster Australia, Sydney
Simon & Schuster India, New Delhi

www.simonandschuster.co.uk
www.simonandschuster.com.au
www.simonandschuster.co.in

A CIP catalogue record for this book is available from the British Library

Paperback ISBN: 978-1-4711-7629-6
eBook ISBN: 978-1-84739-483-5

Printed and bound by CPI Group (UK) Ltd, Croydon, CR0 4YY

Simon & Schuster UK Ltd are committed to sourcing paper that is made from
wood grown in sustainable forests and support the Forest Stewardship Council,
the leading international forest certification organisation. Our books displaying
the FSC logo are printed on FSC certified paper.

This book is dedicated to three generations of my family:

To my beloved sons – Terence and George. My darlings, may all your friends be as wonderful as mine.

To my late Nana Hubbard, who made my birthday cakes and loved to read, and my Granddad Hubbard, a poet, who made the best Yorkshire Puddings this side of Mars and a man who appreciated a well-built woman.

And to my mam and dad – Jenny and Terry Hubbard – who haven't a clue what a strange creature they raised, but who love me all the same.

Prologue

The previous September

They took a day off and went with her because in the three million years they'd all been friends, it was the first time Helen had ever asked them a favour. That was how Elizabeth came to end up carrying a picnic basket in a grassy middle of nowhere, watching one of her two best friends wriggling out of her drawers and about to sit on the giant appendage of a club-bearing man carved into an alien county hillside.

'Hels, are you actually right in your head?' she asked.

Janey said nothing but her equal disbelief showed in the dropped-open jaw as Helen stuffed the discarded pants in her handbag and then sat down squarely and triumphantly on Mr Big's phallic enhancement.

'Now if I had told you what I wanted to do, would you have come?' she said. 'I don't think so! You would have tried to talk me out of it, wouldn't you?'

'Too bloody right I would,' said Elizabeth, whilst thinking, She's lost it.

'And this is the something you needed to do that

is really, really, really important then?' Janey asked, her eyebrows raised as far as they could stretch. 'Dragging us halfway across the bloody country to see a chalk drawing?'

'Aw, come on, we're here now. Just sit down and have a sandwich,' said Helen, straight-backed and sitting there as if she was waiting for something extraordinary to happen.

'Where are we, like?' Janey looked at the surrounding countryside, dominated by the thick white outline of the naked man with the enviable asset. 'And more to the point – why?'

'Oh, I'm having a sarnie, I'm flaming famished!' Elizabeth decided. She was almost brain dead with tiredness, even though she had spent most of the long, *long* journey snoring on the back seat. She threw herself onto the grass next to her knickerless friend and dragged the picnic basket purposefully over. Janey huffed in a 'can't beat 'em, join 'em' sort of way and grudgingly followed suit, muttering something about them all being bonkers.

'He's an ancient fertility symbol,' Helen explained.

'I'd never have guessed!' said Elizabeth, ripping so hungrily into a giant sausage roll that the chalk man almost winced.

Helen went on, 'Well, I was watching this programme a couple of weeks ago about how all these women who hadn't been able to conceive came here as a last resort and sat on his . . . well, here, for a while, and seventy-eight per cent of them – *that's seventy-eight per cent of them* – became pregnant.'

A dramatic silence ensued in which Helen waited for the others to be impressed.

'Well, I have to say it and I hope you'll excuse the pun,' Elizabeth spat through a flurry of pastry flakes, 'but that is positively the biggest load of bollocks you have ever come out with.'

Janey laughed derisively at the same time. 'Oh Hels, come on!'

'I know what it sounds like, that's why I didn't tell you where we were coming,' Helen said, her voice fighting off a wobble, 'but if I don't get pregnant soon, I'll die. I want a baby so, *so* much. Believe me, you two have it a lot easier not wanting children, but I don't care who laughs at me any more, I just Want. A. Baby.' Then she turned her head suddenly skyward, blinking hard, a little ashamed at her outburst but more than that, hurt that they of all people were mocking her.

Janey and Elizabeth exchanged the slightest of glances but each knew what the other was thinking. *She'd always been so light about the fact that she hadn't caught on. How many times had she led their joking about it?* Neither of them had had the slightest idea that her pain ran so deeply.

Elizabeth plunged her hand into the picnic basket again, in a brave effort to break the heavy silence that had descended upon them like a thick, depressing cloud.

'So, let's have a good look at this lot. What have you made us then, Hels? What feast have you concocted this time?'

'There's egg and cress, beef and horseradish, goats' cheese and tomato . . .' Helen began to reel off, dabbing at her eye, trying to make it look as if she had something in it '. . . sausage rolls, spicy scotch eggs, chicken filo parcels, lemon Swiss roll, banoffee tarts, Victoria sponge, crisps, Twiglets, there's a red hummus and onion dip, strawberries dipped in dark chocolate and there's some Diet Coke and wine.'

'That all?' said Elizabeth and Helen blurted out a laugh and the mood was lifted once again.

Aw bless, thought Elizabeth, as she spotted all the little flags on the sandwiches; everything was home-made. Who the chuff could be bothered making real puff pastry these days but Hels? If she did have kids, their sandwich boxes would be the envy of the school. That little thought bubble gave her another taste of her friend's desperation and how very severe it must be to trick them into travelling so many miles to do something as ridiculous as this. How had she missed this before?

'Pass me an egg and cress, would you, please,' Helen said, all tears abated.

'When are the fish and Disciples arriving?' Elizabeth asked, rummaging deep before handing over the cling-filmed triangle bearing an egg and cress sticker.

'I know you're a pig . . . I didn't want you moaning that I'd dragged you all this way and I hadn't fed you,' Helen said, managing a little smile.

'I'll have a beef, please, and pass the plonk seeing as I'm not driving,' Janey said with a deep sigh. 'Tell me you haven't forgotten an opener.'

'It screws,' Helen said.

'That's appropriate!' Elizabeth snorted and got her usual disapproving look from Janey.

The latter then gasped suddenly and said, 'Oy, I hope we'll be all right, sat here on this bloke's genitals. I can't afford to get pregnant.' She looked worriedly down at the segment of chalk line disappearing up her skirt. 'My Head of Department is about to peg it – I'm in line for his job.'

'Oh nice!' Elizabeth said, batting back some disapproval for a change.

'Cough, cough, cough – I'm sick of listening to him,' Janey went on. 'That's a lifetime of fags for you,' and she nodded a warning in Elizabeth's direction. 'I think they'll get rid of him in an early-retirement swoop – he's been with them for about four hundred years so he'll get a good pay-off. Mind you, he'll probably spend it all on Bensons, knowing him. It's only a matter of time before the vacancy comes up; he's always flaming off ill and I'm running the place as it is so I don't want any surprise sprogs knackering up my career hopes, thanks very much.'

Helen tilted her head. 'Well, all I can say is that not all of those women on the TV programme took their pants off when they sat on him.'

'Oh great!' said Janey, shifting her bottom off the white line. Not that she believed in stuff like that, but it didn't hurt to make sure.

Elizabeth poured herself a glass of the wine and reclined to let the gorgeous September sun shine down onto her face. She was too comfortable to move from her position on the ancient willy. Mumbo jumbo crap, she thought inwardly, but she was here now and might as well enjoy it, as it really was a cracking day for a picnic.

Chapter 1

The following February

Her arms and legs spasmed outwards, she let loose a very loud scream and then Elizabeth awoke to find herself *not* on a nose-diving plane but on the seven thirty-six to Leeds and the focus of half a crammed carriageful of 'glad that wasn't me' faces. However, not even their cold-water stares, the probability that she had been snoring and two mega-strength coffees slopping around her digestive system could keep Elizabeth's eyes from shuttering down again – she was exhausted. She was last off the train and, in fact, had the fat, sweaty bloke sitting next to her not caught her with the hard edge of his briefcase as he heaved his carcass out of the seat, she might well have slept through to Barnsley again on the return trip. She had better buck up for later; she was hardly going to be the life and soul of Helen's birthday party face down and asleep in her minestrone.

As usual, the train station was full of suits zipping in straight lines to their destinations clutching a laptop case in one hand and a grabbed breakfast bag in the other. As usual, there were a few early shoppers making a leisurely way up to the main city stores and managing to get in the way of the rushing executives, who did not take too kindly to having lumpy human obstacles on their own personal work paths. And as usual, there was a large contingent of big-bellied workmen staring at women's breasts from the scaffolding as their more industrious colleagues worked on extending the station, yet again. The train used to dump Elizabeth right in front of the ticket barriers, but these days it deposited them all so far away on one of the new platforms that she almost needed to catch another train from there to the exit. That morning, it felt a particularly long way.

At least the ten-minute walk in the crisp February air served to startle her brainwaves into some activity, and by the time she had reached the great, smutty-bricked offices with the giant blue *Handi-Save* sign above the entrance she felt considerably more human and less like a dormouse again. It was an old, weary-looking building in the middle of a sea of younger, more dynamic structures, with its exterior reflecting the majority of the people on the inside – dull, tired and uninspiring. She pushed open the giant stiff revolving door that had given everyone who had worked there for any length of time a deformed bicep. It was easy to spot a long-timer at Handi-Save for they all had one arm bigger than the other, like a male Fiddler crab. Yep, she felt decidedly better for the walk.

'Flaming Norah, you look rough,' said Derek the security man. He, being ambidextrous, had two massive arms. 'Good night, was it?'

'I was in bed for nine,' Elizabeth held up her best shushing finger as his mouth sprang open, 'and before you say it, yes, I was alone. I don't know what's up with me at the moment. I think I've been bitten by a tsetse-tsetse fly.'

'Tsetse-tsetse? Going round in pairs now, are they?' grinned Derek. 'Maybe you're coming down with something. Mind you, in a place like this someone's only got to say "cold" and everyone gets it through the air conditioning.'

'I feel all right in myself, just tired,' she said, hunting in her bag for one of her menthols. She proffered the packet to him. 'Want one?'

'Do I chuff!' he said, warding them away like a vampire who had just been offered a garlic bulb. 'If I want mints I'll suck a Polo, if I want a fag I'll have an Embassy, thanks for asking.'

'Please yourself then! Right, now, I better do something with my face then if I look that bad.'

'I've a carrier bag behind Reception. I could poke two eyeholes in it for you.'

'Thanks a lot, Ras.'

He nudged her playfully. 'Ah, you still look bonny!'

She turned away, mock-insulted. 'Nope, sorry, the damage has been done, you can get stuffed,' and though she could hear him laughing behind her, the smile slid off her face as if it had been greased with three pounds of melted butter. Not that she had taken offence, for it took a lot to wind Elizabeth up – at least it had done until recently, when this infernal tiredness threatened to turn even her cool disposition to something as brittle as the toffee she used to get as a kid that snapped off into artery-severing shards.

Derek, or Rasputin as everyone called him, would have been mortified even to suspect that he had upset her because they went back such a long way. He had only been at Handi-Save a week himself when she had turned up at the Reception desk aged sixteen, all wide grey eyes, smashing blouse buttoned up to the neck and her dark gypsy curls tamed into a ponytail. She had been half-fearful, half-excited by her important-sounding destination – 'the typing pool' – to where Ras volunteered to escort her. She'd had a picture in her mind of lots of typists working around a pool full of warm, blue water and was critically disappointed when it turned out to be just an airless office full of women with perms and frumpy frocks banging away on word processors. Ras was string-thin back then, with a number one haircut and a moustache like Ron from the pop group 'Sparks'. He ended up getting them both hopelessly lost which caused a standing joke that was still running.

Twenty-two years later, they were both still there, crossing paths in Reception each morning, though Elizabeth had long since left the pool and was now the Managing Director's secretary. Ras, on the other hand, had concentrated his energies over the years into evolving physically into a heavyweight wrestler who would fail a Roy Wood's Wizzard audition for being too hairy. He'd had four kids, three wives, two motor-cycle crashes and a steel plate in his head. The only things that seemed to have stayed constant about him were those friendly facial features and the warmth in his morning greetings. He alone these days put a smile on Elizabeth's lips at work, or as she preferred to call it, 'the Hammer House of Handi-Save'.

The worrying part in all this was that if Ras thought she looked rough, then Julia definitely would – and the only reason Elizabeth had pushed herself out of bed that morning was because Julia and Laurence had made it perfectly clear that being absent on a Monday was tantamount to admitting to a hangover. So ironically, there she was dutifully turning up but looking as if she had been on a weekend ciderfest. A picture of the pair of them flitted across her mind, which made her growl inwardly. She was wound into the ground before she had even set eyes on the Gruesome Twosome and it was *so* not like her to feel this way. Hardly anything ever got to Elizabeth and even if it did, she never showed it.

She grabbed a coffee from the machine and slid into the tiny and horribly smoky room that the militantly anti-tobacco Laurence had 'allowed' the smokers to have and, as he said 'pollute as their own'. The rebellious air in there usually calmed her down before she had even lit up, but that morning it felt thick and unpleasant, and welded itself like glue to the back of her throat. She sat on a table in the canteen instead, gulping back the luke-warm gritty coffee whilst pitter-patting with her finger-tips at the fluidy swellings under her eyeballs. She didn't dare risk another look in the mirror in case it threw back a worse reflection than the passable one she ima-gined was there before making her way to the lift.

She pressed the button (only four times that morning) before it started to shudder and rattle upwards at a pace that a snail with a weight problem could beat – even the machinery didn't want to work here! She hadn't always felt like that, for there had been a time when she used to belt up the staircase in the mornings, glad to get to her desk. Obviously that was before the days of that well-known double act Laurence Stewart-Smith, a name impossible to say without hissing, and his wonderful side-kick, Julia Powell – Powell as in the contraction of 'power crazed troll'.

Laurence Stewart-Smith: also known as 'Eyebrow Man' on account of the long furry caterpillar which ran the width of his forehead before scuttling into his hairline to hide the *666*. Laurence Stewart-Smith: in the opinion of the City, *The Man* – business genius, whizz-kid, darling of industry, multi-millionaire man-of-the-people, demi-god of the hoi polloi – but in the opinion of anyone who really knew the man behind the title: total plonker.

Julia did not lift her head as Elizabeth walked past her desk, which had long since failed to surprise her. Julia could not communicate with females on a lesser grade unless it was by email, even when sitting two metres away as Elizabeth did. There were bagfuls of evidence to substantiate the theory that Julia was threatened by other women, who were creatures to be ignored, or destroyed. Men, however, were a different kettle of fish. Then she would start flirting and sticking out her chest and batting her eyelashes in the general direction of the flirtee – the number of bats being directly proportionate to the quality of his suit.

Sometimes, to be controversial, Elizabeth would open a mail and shout across the reply to Julia as it really seemed to annoy her, but this past week or so she was just too tired to play the dissident. Was this the onset of old age, she wondered. Was she about to start dribbling and nodding off after a morning Rich Tea biscuit and exchanging her cappuccinos for a nice cup of cocoa? She was only eighteen months off being forty, after all.

Laurence's first visitors arrived early and hung about the entrance foyer in nervous anticipation. They were the ladies from the Blackberry Moor council-house estate and he kept them waiting an extra quarter of an hour for no other reason, it seemed, than because he could. A gum-chewing photographer from the *Yorkshire Post* announced himself at Reception and Elizabeth collected them all and escorted them up. Jolly poses ensued, in Laurence's open-plan meeting area, with the great man himself, who did not manage to fully lose that uncomfortable look on his face which seemed to say, *Ooh, I've touched a council-house person! Which way is the de-louser?* Then the photographer departed with his PR snaps and the three women perched awkwardly on the ends of the big squashy seats, blushing and stuttering like 1970s teenagers who had just been granted an audience with Donny Osmond. Elizabeth could never understand the effect Laurence had on such visitors. Half the time she expected to have to go and find a mop to clean up excited puppy-like puddles at their feet, but on that occasion, so far so good.

She scribbled some notes down as Julia and Laurence both held their heads at the same angle of sympathetic tilt as they listened to babble about how grateful the Blackberry Moor estate was for the support of Handi-Save. Julia flicked through the folders the ladies had brought full of Before and After pictures of dreary communal dog-toilet areas, which had been converted impressively into playgrounds and thoughtful squares of garden thanks to donations and fundraising. Laurence sat, fingers templed in front of him, head nodding in all the right spots, his one long eyebrow managing to both crease in all the appropriate places and hood a pair of eyes that showed a mixture of boredom and disgust.

'So hif you could . . . er . . . just continue to let hus have that turkey or something at Christmas for hour raffle,' said the lady with the crocheted hat, trying desperately to stuff a few posh aitches in.

'The money mainly goes for the kids' benefit,' butted in another as if it were in some dispute.

'We don't want much, just a few bits a couple of times a year, to raffle hoff like.'

'We're just starting to get some community spirit going, you see.'

The great Laurence Stewart-Smith nodded regally, and as if his head was attached to his assistant's by an invisible puppet-string, it set Julia's off as well. Neither would have looked out of place on the back parcel shelf of Elizabeth's old Vauxhall.

'Of course,' he said. 'I'm sure we could fix you up with a little more than that.' He scribbled something with an important flourish on a piece of paper and handed it to Julia. The ladies' eyes followed the handover of the note with great anticipation. They could not have been more thrilled if he had just written down the secret of eternal life.

'That would be just marvellous,' said the one who had the pencilled-on eyebrows, and her face lit up so much they were in danger of melting.

'Good, good.'

Laurence smiled, raised his watch hand theatrically, flicked his eyes towards it, and then stood to signify their audience time was at an end.

'Well, I'm sorry it's been such a short meeting but I do have another appointment, albeit not as entertaining, which I regret I'm a little late for,' and he flashed his charming smile again and added, 'My assistant Julia will show you out.'

The ladies twittered their way out of the door and as Laurence and Julia made to follow them, the piece of paper twirled to the floor from Julia's file. Elizabeth picked it up. She just managed to sneak a look before Troll snatched it back rather hastily.

Let's just give these old scrubbers some money and get out of here quick, it said.

Elizabeth was disgusted but not surprised. She watched the smiling little trio from Blackberry Moor meander down the office to the temperamental lifts, blissfully ignorant of what their hero Laurence Stewart-Smith was really like. So long as he flung them a few tombola pressies every so often, they would continue to idolize him as a local saint, although Elizabeth knew that one did not get to be in his position by being a nice bloke. Somewhere in mid-management, they cut out the heart and replaced it with an axe. And once a man held power, she had found, he was almost certain to misuse it.

Chapter 2

Janey snapped around the room, tossing tissues and lippy into her handbag, occasionally stopping to rub her stomach.

'What's up with you?' said Elizabeth, watching her.

'Dodgy Chinese last night.'

'Get stuffed with your dodgy Chinese!' said Janey's hubby George, twisting round from watching the preamble to the big match on the television. 'I had half hers and I'm right as rai—'

'In fact, if it hadn't been Helen's birthday I'd have cried off,' Janey cut in.

'You couldn't have done that, we haven't seen each other since Christmas!' said Elizabeth.

'Yes, well – that's another reason why I'm making the effort,' said Janey. 'Anyway, I'm not drinking so no point in us getting a taxi. Sod it, where's my purse?' She shoved George to one side to see if he was sitting on it. Not that he would have known, even if it had been full of razor blades, the dozy sod, she thought. Now what was that other something else that was bugging her to remember it?

'Don't be so wet!' said Elizabeth.

'Ring a taxi and get a few gins down your neck, that'll sort you out,' said the Bagpuss-like bloke, taking a slurp from a can of beer.

'I might have known you'd side with her!' said Janey, thumbing at her butter-wouldn't-melt-faced friend.

Elizabeth grinned at her and looked, for a moment, just like she did at school, give or take a couple of sunrays at the eye corners.

'Oh damnit – flowers!' Janey threw her hands up in despair and blamed George. 'I told you to remind me not to forget the flowers. You'd have let me walk out without them!'

George smiled indulgently, taking her in his stride as usual and sighing like an inflatable shire horse that had just sustained a fatal puncture.

'Flowers, Janey, don't forget!' he said, clicking his fingers as if it had just come to him. Janey hit him with a cushion, although flowers were not the 'something' that was buzzing around in her head, refusing to be pinned down.

'How's work then?' George said to Elizabeth.

'Oh don't ask!' she said. 'The latest thing is' – and she did a fair impression of her arch enemy – '"Would you please ask permission if you're going to be longer than five minutes in the loo?" Can you believe?'

'Never! What did you say?'

'I smiled sweetly and said that I wasn't in the habit of timing myself. I'm forty next year, for God's sake. I stopped sticking my hand up to ask to go to the loo twenty odd years ago. Honestly, that woman. *Heil* Julia!'

She gave a Nazi salute and started goose-stepping up and down on the carpet in front of the television.

'Dear God!' belled Janey from the kitchen, she'd always imagined that at this age they would be mature and talking about the news and what charity Bob Geldof was collecting for these days. George chuckled and Janey thought, He's got a lovely laugh. They had somehow fallen out of the habit of laughing together these days.

'Didn't I read somewhere that you lot were getting taken over?' said George.

'There's been talk for a while,' said Elizabeth, dismissing it. 'Just the Job, the DIY chain, was supposedly interested in buying us out. Laurence loathes the bloke who owns it though and is standing firm. Not that I get to know much, being a mere pleb.'

'Is it really that bad, working there?'

'Worse. Well, the place is okay – it's just her, Camp Commandant. As for him, I just can't find the words. Hang on, I've just found some – he's a tosspot.'

'Aye, it's tough working at the top,' George teased, and smiled at her fondly. He loved Elizabeth like a sister, funny old thing that she was. In her he saw a vulnerability that a caring soul like him could not help but respond to, despite her frosty independent ways and her fruity language. He might have had plenty to say if Janey had been as free with her expletives, but with Elizabeth, it was just part and parcel. Not that anyone would think she had a mouth like a sewer to look at her, all little and slim with lovely, dark gypsy curls and startling grey eyes that his Janey had always envied, but in a nice way. She wouldn't swap what she had for what her friend had in a million years, she'd assured him tenderly, even if Elizabeth *could* eat a double chicken korma and half a chocolate cake and not put an ounce of weight on.

'Do you think there is something going on between those two at work then?' asked George.

'Shouldn't think so,' said Elizabeth. 'Laurence is too smart for that. He's got his eye on "higher things" and he needs to be squeaky clean, though it's not for the want of trying on her part. Office politics! I tell you, Georgy boy, they're worse than political politics!'

'I can imagine,' said George, nodding, although he had never really understood what could be so complicated and difficult about going into an office and sitting on your backside all day typing and answering the phone.

'It just galls me how everyone thinks he's some sort of hero when I know what a really horrible bloke he is. I mean today, right, we had these women in from the Blackberry Moor estate. Honestly, you would have thought they were meeting the Pope! One of them even had her autograph book. Prostrating themselves they were for a couple of boxes of Milk Tray and a Christmas turkey.'

'Blackberry Moor? Where's that? Sounds nice,' said Janey.

George sucked in a long whistley breath. 'Nay, you must have heard of it, Janey love. It's always on the news for drugs raids. The only time any of that lot will have seen a blackberry is if it's been drawn on the back of an acid tab! It's a massive council estate, pet – a right dump as well.'

'But, give them credit,' Elizabeth butted in, 'a few people who live there have got together to get a bit of community spirit going. Laurence linked up with it for the free publicity, but you can tell he doesn't give a toss. He's too busy sending stupid emails to Julia about how fat and ugly people are, which is rich considering he's one step away from being a werewolf and she's got legs you could drive a bus through!'

George stared at her in amazement. 'Here, grind your teeth on these before you give yourself a jam-tart attack,' he said, lifting his bowl of peanuts out to her. 'I've never seen you in a stew before, Elizabeth.'

'Yes, I know,' said Elizabeth, refusing the nuts. If other people were noticing the change in her, it was not in her imagination then.

'Eh, I've just thought,' twinkled George. 'If this takeover thing goes through they could call the company "Hand-Job"! Geddit? Hand. Job.' A great snort of laughter came down his nose and joined Elizabeth's loud and dirty laugh that fed his own even more and so it snowballed, then Janey's laugh added to it, despite her pretending to disapprove. When George and Elizabeth got together, they bounced off each other like a comedy double act. Like they used to.

'Ready!' announced Janey.

'Hang on a mo, I need the loo,' said Elizabeth.

'Again? You've been once.'

'Oh no! It's Julia, she's got to you!' said Elizabeth, pretending to scream as she disappeared to Janey's downstairs bathroom, wondering why she seemed to want to go every five minutes these days.

Janey leaned over the back of the sofa for a habit kiss from George.

'She'll be bloody forty by the time you get there, never mind thirty-nine!' he cracked.

'Oh, get lost, George,' Janey said, but she was smiling at him.

'Bye, Georgy,' said Elizabeth, soon after, and ruffled up his sandy hair with both hands as she passed him. She followed Janey out and they jumped into the car quickly to escape the freezing night air.

They drove down the lane and joined the long-drawn-out curve of the main road that took them past the park and St Jude's Church and the two big secondary schools that had united to become one huge one in recent years. Within five minutes, the redbrick houses had given way to a sprawling grey council-house estate, then five minutes after that, all buildings dropped away and they were in the country outskirts of the town. They passed the local Scout Camp wood and a garden centre with its quaint café by a duck-popular stream in the centre of semi-rural Maltstone. The village was the unofficial warm-up act for the next one: Higher Hoppleton, with its beautiful park and country house set in the grounds like a square exquisite jewel. Higher Hoppleton was the Barnsley Beverly Hills; a Higher Hoppleton postcode had the kudos to make people raise their eyebrows in admiration – which is why Simon, Mr Swanky High-Flying Advertising Exec, had decided that he and his wife Helen would live there when the right property came up on the market.

Four years ago, the Cadberrys had bought a long, impressive bungalow with its own black iron gates, a small, separate office building, and plenty of parking space for their his and hers black BMWs. Although '*they* bought' was stretching it a bit, as Elizabeth had always suspected that most of the money came from the Luxmores' coffers. It was a show-house, the stuff of high-class glossy mags: cushions perfectly arranged, pictures spirit-level straight and yet bizarrely, in the midst of it all was their guest room – a chaos of Simon's old junk that he refused to deal with *yet*. Their old house in quieter, gentler Maltstone was far prettier than this pretentious pile, in Elizabeth's opinion, though not in Janey's. She said the same thing then as she always did as her car crunched up Helen's gravel drive, 'I wish this was mine, isn't it gorgeous?'

Elizabeth didn't answer her; she would rather have had Janey's half-finished warm, friendly house than this big, fancy thing anytime.

When Simon answered the back door, Elizabeth could have sworn that he and Helen had just snapped off an argument. Janey never noticed, she was too busy turning into her usual puddle of drool when in the presence of her friend's husband and his dazzling toothpaste-advert smile.

'Only us,' she announced and they both went into Helen's gleaming high-tech kitchen. They gave her a big birthday kiss and a hug and then they handed over their birthday presents and cards. Elizabeth had made hers and it featured a little watercolour of a tabby cat. Simon hated cats.

'Good evening, ladies.' Simon smiled at Janey. The smile made a grand arc over to Elizabeth where it died on its feet.

Janey smiled back, aware that her heart-rate had increased as it usually did in the presence of this gorgeous man with his wavy golden hair and toned physique. He had blue eyes that could undress a woman at fifty paces and, in her imagination, she had often pictured that woman as herself. She bet he was fantastic in bed, a master of special tricks and foreplay that went on for hours and would make a girl scream aloud, and he would know exactly what to say to make her spine turn into runny oil – like a Mills & Boon hero. Alas, these days, she and George, when they could be bothered to do it, were more of a 'scratch an itch' couple. Then again, they had been together fourteen years and exciting sex was usually a casualty of a long relationship.

'You just caught me telling Helen to keep clear of the gin – she's been feeling a bit off,' Simon said in his plummy posh voice. He reached over and gave Helen's hair a stroke and Janey tingled for her.

'You as well?' she began without thinking. 'We had a dodgy Chinese last night and I'm . . .' She stopped herself just in time before she launched into a full rundown of her confused digestive system in front of Love-God Man and showed herself up totally 'er . . . better now, thank goodness.'

His little sneer wasn't lost on Elizabeth, but Janey

missed it. She was too engaged in watching him move fluidly over to the coat-hooks on the wall through her rose-tinted spectacles. He slipped on a brown leather jacket which looked butter soft, not like the cheap one George had that was so stiff he needed five minutes' notice to bend his arm. The CD-player in the background was oozing out Sade's 'Smooth Operator'. Appropriately so, thought Elizabeth, watching Simon shmooze back across to his wife.

'Right, darling, I'm going and leaving you girls to it.'

'Off to watch the football?' Janey asked.

'Football?' He said it like the word was not in his vocabulary. 'Not really interested in it, to be honest.'

'What's cooking? Smells gorgeous,' said Elizabeth to Helen, thinking how very pale and wispy she looked.

'Prawn cocktail, scampi and Black Forest gâteau,' said Simon.

'Ooh, lovely!' shrieked Janey.

'He's joking, it's just a pasta thing,' Helen replied, flashing him a look. Janey nodded but would have preferred Simon's menu, especially the Black Forest cake. It never got any easier fighting the urge to indulge her sweet tooth.

'I'm going.' Simon kissed his wife quickly and whispered something in her ear that had a bit of an odd effect on her. She looks like she's just had a bucket of cold water poured over her head, Elizabeth thought, wondering what *that* was all about.

'Enjoy yourselves, ladies.'

'Oh, don't you worry, we will!' Janey trilled, sounding

just like the crocheted-hat woman of Blackberry Moor in the presence of Laurence.

'I wish George was like that,' she sighed as the door closed behind Simon and puffed the wake of his expensive aftershave in her direction. 'He's so romantic, just like Mr Darcy.'

Elizabeth fought back the desire to stick her fingers down her throat. Whatever he had just whispered to Helen before he went out didn't look like flaming sweet nothings to *her*.

Helen didn't comment; she just reached for three glasses and said, 'Gin, girls?'

'Oh, go on then, just a treble,' said Elizabeth keenly. If she was going to be running to the loo all night, she might as well make it worth her while. Janey shook her head then thought better of it and relented, asking for a small one – so long as she had plenty of slimline tonic in with it.

'"Just a small one",' mimicked Elizabeth. '"With minus calories, no fat, and a no-carb tonic, please!"'

'I don't care; you can take the mick all you want. I have no intention of putting all that weight on again after it took me all that time to get it off!' said Janey, taking the glass.

Helen thought Janey had put a little weight on since she last saw her at Christmas, although she didn't say that aloud. Janey looked nicer with a bit of flesh on her bones. She had always been a big, red-haired girl with a great curvy body and a round friendly face, and she looked scrawny and pinched now she had become a diet convert. She was built for 'comely' and used to exude a sexy earthiness that she had somehow lost with the lard. Elizabeth thought the same. Not that either of them wanted to start World War III off by telling her so.

'So how's work?' asked Helen. Before Elizabeth could answer, Janey butted in with, 'Oh, don't get her on that subject; she'll depress the backside off you.'

'Thanks, you!' said Elizabeth with an indignant laugh.

'Honestly, I don't know why you don't leave if it's so bad.'

'Because, Smartarse, if there is to be a buy-out and they don't want my excellent services, I might miss out on a redundancy package, for one thing. Plus, I wouldn't give them the satisfaction of driving me out like they have all the other poor sods.'

'You could get a job with less money that'd make you happy. I mean, it's not as if you need the money for a mortgage,' said Janey.

'I might not have a mortgage but I've still got bills and my loan for the kitchen to pay off and important stuff, you know, like food and shoes,' she retorted.

Yes, there were other jobs, as Janey was always telling her, but she had been there so long, it was the devil she knew. Change scared Elizabeth to death.

'Work is crap as usual, Hels, thanks for asking. So now that's out of the way, let's talk about something jollier, like world famine,' said Elizabeth.

'Okay then, how's the house coming along?' asked Helen to Janey.

'Oh, slowly but surely,' said Janey. 'You know George – he might take his time but whatever he does is spot on.'

Elizabeth nodded in agreement, wishing quietly that she had someone like George to come home to. *You did, though, didn't you?* her head threw at her and she quickly fought the rogue thought back into its cage and doubled the lock on it.

Helen filled up her own glass and Elizabeth noticed she had only put tonic water in it and felt duty bound to point this out.

'What's up with you not drinking on your birthday?'

'Honestly! You miss nothing you, do you?' said Helen with amused exasperation. 'Anyway, it's not my birthday till tomorrow.'

'So?'

Helen kept her eyes down and she shrugged. 'I just don't feel like one, that's all.'

Helen was rubbish at lying. Elizabeth looked at her, *really* looked at her and though it sounded stupid, there was definitely something different about her. And Elizabeth instinctively knew what that something was.

'Stop staring, you!' Helen said. She had a laughing sparkle in her eyes.

'I don't believe it; you're pregnant, aren't you?'

'What – 'cos she hasn't had a glass of gin?' Janey scoffed, but Helen was not denying it and looked very much like a woman trying to keep in a secret that was in danger of bursting out her seams.

'You're not?' said Janey her jaw opening wide with surprise and shock and joy. 'Are you? *No?* Are you?'

Then suddenly they were all bouncing around the room.

'You're not, are you? *Embarazada*? Do you remember that "embarazada"?' said Janey, who remembered everything. The three of them launched into giggles at the memory: Janey telling that Spanish waiter that she was too *embarazada* to go off for a drink with him in Lloret. She thought it meant shy until they looked it up in the Harper's phrasebook trying to work out why he ran off so fast that smoke was coming from his heels. The fact that it actually meant *pregnant* probably had a lot to do with it.

'Christ, you've still got a memory like an elephant, even if you haven't got the figure of one any more,' Elizabeth said.

'Ha flaming ha,' said Janey, hands on her thin hips.

'I'm not supposed to tell you!' said Helen, swinging between nervous fear and explosive joy like a metronome gone berserk.

'You didn't tell us – I guessed,' said Elizabeth, with a Cheshire cat grin.

'Simon will go nuts if he finds out you know,' Helen whispered, flicking a frightened-rabbit pair of eyes towards the door as if he were there listening.

'Why the hell should he?' shrieked Elizabeth. 'We're your best mates and as such we should have known before him!'

'Oh, he told me not to tell you until I was twelve weeks', because a lot of people miscarry before then.' Helen squeezed them both tight. 'Oh God, I've been dying to come round and see you. I had a feeling I was pregnant when I was late, because as you know I am *never* late. I wanted to be sure, though, and I knew if I saw you I would not be able to keep the secret.'

'When's it due?'

'Well, by my calculations the twenty fourth of September but I'll get a scan to confirm that in a few weeks.'

'Oh, that's fantastic!' Janey laughed. 'I suppose Simon's dead chuffed.'

'Yes,' Helen said without elaborating, which Elizabeth thought was a bit odd for someone who could gush more than a burst pipe about the milkman leaving an extra pint.

'So sitting on Chalk Man's willy worked then,' said Janey. 'Just so long as he doesn't come through for me, that's all I can say.'

Elizabeth thought the same, although she didn't say it aloud. Not that there was any reason why she should be worried about anything like that, since she always made Dean wear a condom however much he pro-tested, plus they hadn't had any penetrative sex since before Christmas. Plus her periods had been present and almost correct.

'I couldn't believe it when I did the test.' Helen's chirruping brought her back into the real world. Now the secret was finally out they could not shut her up – not that they wanted to anyway.

'What did you think?' said Janey.

'I can't put it into words, honestly I can't!'

Elizabeth smiled. She knew what she would have

said, had it been her, but Helen swore less than Anne of Green Gables.

'I thought we'd eat in the kitchen rather than the dining room if that's okay with you guys,' said Helen.

'Fine by me,' said Elizabeth, who liked her friend's long, thin, cold dining room marginally less than her minimalist, masculine, cold kitchen.

The kitchen table had been laid out beautifully though, with a green table cover and matching place mats and linen napkins rolled into golden rings. There was freshly grated parmesan waiting in a dish, and a huge polished wooden saltmill and an enormous pepper pot which Elizabeth could never resist picking up and twisting whilst saying in a saucy-Italian-waiter accent, 'Beautiful laaaady like the big one, nice and grindy grindy and plenty of it, ah?' The others expected it and then groaned afterwards. Helen's kitchen was very different to Elizabeth's cosy little den in Rhymer Street. This was a room straight out of *Homes and Gardens* but it wasn't Elizabeth's idea of a dream cooking space – and she damn well knew it wasn't Helen's. They shared chintzy tastes, displays of cottagey teapots, big squashy sofas and pictures of cats, not stark white walls and flaming horrible abstract paintings with squares on. This room reflected nothing of Helen's personality and everything of Simon's – hard-lined and clinical and, until the news today, Elizabeth would have added 'sterile' to the list.

'So when do you reckon you caught on then?' said Janey, when they were seated and eating.

'New Year's Eve,' said Helen without any hesitation as she knew this for a fact.

'Ooh, George and I had a bit of an evening then too,' said Janey, remembering how George had managed to rev up his engine with gusto that night. He'd even taken her from behind and he hadn't done that for years. 'You went to a party, didn't you, Elizabeth?'

'Yes.'

'Oh yes – I remember you said you were going. How was it?'

'Not much cop, really. Came home early. This is delicious,' said Elizabeth, shovelling a mouthful of food in so she couldn't talk any more.

'So what happens now? How far on are you?' asked Janey.

'Well, they count it from the date of your last period, so that means I'm nearly seven weeks' pregnant. I start antenatal classes when I've missed my second period.'

'That can't be right!' Elizabeth said. 'That would make you about two weeks' pregnant before you'd even had the fateful bonk.'

'Trust me, it's right,' said Helen.

Janey gasped, 'Jeez, seven weeks! That's like being nearly two months' pregnant!'

'Yes. Well done, Carol Vorderman.'

Janey stuck her tongue out at Elizabeth then turned back to Helen. 'Are you feeling sick then?'

'Yes, I'm afraid so, but even worse than the nausea is the sensitivity in my chest. If you've ever had your nipples rubbed with sandpaper, that's what it feels like.'

'Well, I haven't – *she* probably will have had,' and Janey thumbed towards Elizabeth.

'. . . and tired,' Helen went on. 'I'm so dreadfully tired all the time.'

Elizabeth's ears pricked up, although she was being silly. She'd had a period since New Year – a light one, but a period all the same, thank God.

'Is that a symptom then, being tired?'

'Apparently so, at the beginning. And at the end, obviously.'

'I thought you got sick and fat and that was it,' said Elizabeth, who had never had any reason to read up about what happened during pregnancy.

'No, no, no!' said Helen. 'My gums won't stop bleeding either and I feel like I need the loo every five minutes.'

'I think you must be pregnant as well then,' laughed Janey, nodding her head towards Elizabeth. 'Sounds a right laugh so far, Hels.'

'It gets better later on. When I get to twelve weeks some of the nasty things, like the nausea and the tiredness, should all have gone. Actually, I don't feel too bad this evening for a change,' Helen said brightly, 'but in the mornings I could just crawl back into bed. In fact, I did today.'

'These part-time workers!' said Janey, stretching out for more parmesan, and then withdrawing her hand when she remembered its calorific value. 'I'd love to crawl back into bed some mornings, especially at this time of year.'

'Well, you know what to do – get pregnant.'

'Drop dead!'

'I always thought you would have children, or at least one child,' said Helen.

'We've left it a bit late now,' said Janey, wriggling like a worm on a line anxious to change the subject before they started talking about what a great dad George would make. She was forever batting away the guilt at denying him the chance to be a daddy, even though she knew that it was what he wanted more than anything.

'I really liked working fulltime,' sighed Helen absently, 'but Simon put his foot down. He hates coming home to an empty house. Silly thing is, he works such long hours I could have done a fulltime job and still have been back in plenty of time for him.'

Selfish swine, thought Elizabeth. However had someone as lovely as Hels landed up with a prat like him? Well, she knew the answer to that really; he had nipped in when she was at her most vulnerable and taken her over, just like the evil spirit in *The Exorcist* took over Linda Blair. She had wondered for a long time whether Simon was just hanging on in there until Mrs Luxmore snuffed it and Helen inherited the whole of the family fortune, but such thoughts were hardly a conversation-starter with Helen. She was a suspiciously closed book about their relationship, even to them – her best friends.

'So what if you give birth to a chalk outline with an enormous willy and a club?' Elizabeth said, stabbing a piece of chicken and nodding appreciatively.

Helen brightened. 'I'm quite prepared to believe it could be coincidence, but it does make me feel less of a nutter if I believe he worked for me, and less guilty for dragging you two all that way.'

'We'll never know if it was the magic of the Chalk Man then,' said Janey, although really, she knew better than to believe all that rubbish.

Helen had made the most enormous chocolate cake for afters.

'You *sure* you're not Doris Day reincarnated?' said Janey.

'She'd have a job on, she's not dead,' Elizabeth said. 'Having some?'

Janey hesitated. 'Re-educating her stomach' hadn't happened, and whenever it was within grabbing distance of foods like this, it never failed to loll its greedy tongue out and cry, '*Gimme gimme gimme*'. Working for an international cake and confectionery company hardly helped, with offers to go on market research food-tasting panels left right and centre. She would turn them down every time whilst trying hard not to sob.

'I'm full to busting,' she fibbed. 'Just a teeny tiny piece and I *mean* a teeny tiny piece.'

'I think I must have two stomachs,' declared Elizabeth. 'I'm full to busting with pasta but I'm starving for pud.'

'It's called being a pig!' said Janey, and Elizabeth snorted at her and tried to eat her hand.

The cake looked delicious – but then everything Helen did turned out to be impressive, Elizabeth thought, unless you count marrying Slimy Simon, that was.

'So . . . *fortuna dies natalis, Helena!*' said Elizabeth, lifting up her glass in Helen's direction.

'Wow, Miss Ramsay would be proud of you,' said Helen, giving her an impressed clap.

'So she bloody should be after what she started to put me through twenty-three years ago, is it?' Elizabeth totted up the years. 'Chuff me, it's more than that, it's over twenty-six!'

'How time flies when you're enjoying yourself,' said Janey dryly. 'Anyway, we've suffered far more than you have since that day. I was quite happy sitting with Brenda Higginthorpe.'

'Glenda Higginthorpe, wasn't it?' said Helen.

'Aye, she was such a great mate you can't even remember her name,' scoffed Elizabeth, but Janey was too distracted by the mighty cake to want to reminisce over that particular historical school-day any more.

'Not sticking any candles in that?' she asked.

'I haven't got any,' said Hels.

Elizabeth rooted in her bag for her fag lighter and flicked a flame out.

'This'll have to do then, Norma Jean. You've got to blow it and make a wish on your birthday. It's bad luck not to.'

Then they sang 'Happy Birthday to you, Happy Birthday to you. You're a big smelly tar-rrt, and your bum smells of pooh', despite having a collective age of almost 120. Then they clinked their glasses together and made their own wishes. Elizabeth spent hers willing that Helen would be happy. Later she was to regret not saving the wish for herself.

Helen felt her smile make its exit with her friends. If she tidied up quickly, she could be in bed by the time Simon came back, because he would *know* she had told them. He had so strictly forbidden her from saying anything to them about the baby.

'Why not? Why can't I tell them?' she had asked.

'Do you realize how many babies are lost before twelve weeks?' he had said. 'Do you want to look a fool, announcing you are pregnant only to lose it?'

She tried to make herself believe he had her best interests at heart. She also tried to fight off the shameful suspicion that he wished she *would* lose it and their lives would carry on seamlessly with no one around them being any the wiser.

She was just putting Janey's flowers in the pretty vase painted with sunflowers which Elizabeth had bought for her when Simon came in.

'What are you so jumpy for?' he said, immediately smashing the shell of composure she thought she had built around herself.

'I'm not jumpy,' she said tremulously.

He noticed what she had in her hand. 'And what's that thing?' he said, as if she were holding a rotting fish.

'My birthday present.'

'It's cheap and tacky-looking,' he sneered. 'I suppose Elizabeth bought it.'

'As a matter of fact she did, yes.' He never missed an opportunity to get a dig in at Elizabeth, although they had seemed to get on in the early days. He said it was because he had not realized she was such a tart back then.

When she took it into the dining room, he followed at her heels.

'You surely aren't thinking of putting it in here, are you?'

'Yes, of course I am,' and she set it down on the table. 'Why not?'

'Because, as I said, it's cheap and tacky, *that's why not*. If you haven't any vases, I'll go out and get you one tomorrow.'

'It's a nice vase!'

'It's disgusting,' Simon said, his nose screwed up as if the vase affronted his sense of smell as well as sight.

'It's only a vase. Please don't get so worked up about it!'

'I'm not getting worked up, Helen,' said Simon with increased annoyance. 'I just can't see the point in spending a fortune on a room and then making the centrepiece something like that. The curtains alone in this room cost me eighteen hundred pounds, for Christ's sake!'

'You're being ridiculous.'

He leaned against the stanchion of the door and started staring at her.

'What's the matter?' she asked. He did not answer, just continued to stare at her, in a silence that seemed to chill the room.

'Simon? What are you staring at? Stop it, will you.'

'I know why you're nervous. You told them, didn't you, Helen?'

'Told who what?'

'Oh, don't play the village idiot, you know what I mean.'

'No, I did not!' Her voice was convincingly strong but her cheeks betrayed her by flushing red. She fiddled with the flowers. Simon walked around the table, rested his hands on it so he could lean over it and look squarely into her face.

'Why did you tell them when I expressly told you not to?'

'I didn't, Simon,' she said in a voice that was shaky and full of gathering tears now. 'What is this? What have I done wrong now?'

He shook his head slowly from side to side, despairing of her. 'You know what. You told them you were preg-nant,' he said quietly.

'No, I—'

He slammed his hands down on the table. 'Stop lying!' and his shout brought the silence it demanded. He was staring at her in a way that would burn her eyes if she were to look back at his. Her body language screamed the weakness of doomed prey: her shoulders were slumped, her head bowed and she could not trade eye-contact.

He stood back and raked his fingers through his fair wavy hair. Very quietly now, but icily he continued, 'I really don't believe you sometimes. I asked you not to tell anyone. You agreed – *swore* that you wouldn't – and then you just go right ahead and ignore me.' His eyes were opened so wide they were more white than blue. She hated it when that happened; he looked like some mad twin of himself.

'You just can't keep that mouth of yours shut, can you? Pleasing them is just so much more important than pleasing me, isn't it? Never mind about me, I'm of no importance!'

'Please, I—'

'Oh Helen, just . . . just fuck off. I don't know why I bother trying to look out for you when all you do is throw it back in my face!' He turned away from her; she stretched over and touched his arm but he shook her off.

Where had all this come from? thought Helen, who ten minutes ago had been laughing with her friends – celebrating a birthday and sharing the most wonderful news she would ever have to tell. She just wanted whatever this was to be over, so she confessed.

'Simon, okay, I'll come clean. I didn't tell them, they guessed.'

There was a terrible heavy silence and then he laughed wearily.

'Oh Helen! You are only seven weeks' pregnant – how on earth could they guess? If you could only listen to yourself sometimes. Lies, lies, lies. You'll strangle yourself with them one day. Do you know, you make me sick sometimes, physically sick.'

He looked down at her again, shaking his head from side to side as if she were a disappointing child.

'I'll sleep in the spare room tonight.'

'Oh, please don't sulk. I can't stand it when you sulk.'

'And I hate it when you lie, Helen!'

The spare room was at the end of the long hallway, a small, cold space. She watched him walk slowly down to it and open the door. Then he turned back to her, his face suddenly losing that mad mask and assuming another, a softer one, one full of quiet concern.

'Go to bed, darling. You should not be getting yourself upset like this, it's bad for you. Go on, you're tired and it's late. I'll see you in the morning.'

He smiled a big blue-eyed-boy smile and yet he remained impervious to her hurt and huge eyes that were spilling such great watery drops they would have shamed other men to swift apology. His beautiful, lean body disappeared into the bedroom and he shut the door quietly behind him, which somehow seemed more of a rejection than if he had slammed it in her face.

Chapter 3

Barnsley School for Girls, 1977

Latin was most categorically not *a dead language, but in the past few moments Gloria Ramsay had most definitely heard it contemplating suicide. It was not so much 2F's collective declension of the noun* urbs *with the let's-try-it-on omission of the genitive plural 'i' which turned the correct pronunciation of* oor-be-um *into a very relished* HER-BUM, *it was more that it was delivered in a broad Liverpudlian accent which would have had Caesar spinning in his tomb.*

Her mental harrumph! *was almost audible, but in fairness to the girls, Mr Walton had been their only source of intonation before he was held at Customs on his way back home from holidaying in Turkey. Yes, this confirmed her theory that Latin was not the sort of subject young men with regional accents, flared trousers and hippy shoulder bags who consulted the* I Ching *in the staffroom should be teaching. It belonged to those whose respect for the language was reflected in the sobriety and gravitas of their personal lives. These young male teachers were too much of a distraction to the girls and should never have been allowed into her school – as she thought of it. Old-fashioned and 'past it', oh yes, she was quite aware that this new wave of trendy teachers labelled* her 'Miss Rameses', but surely here was the proof – as the class pronounced men-sas MENZ-ARSE – that her theories were grounded in intelligence and not prejudice.

She shuffled the girls like a pack of cards, breaking their social suits, splicing the good hearts and the diamonds into the black groups of clubs and spades, sending the knaves out to the four corners of the room.

'This is where you will sit from now on,' Miss Ramsay announced to the sea of disgruntled faces and accompanying whingeing ripple of, 'Aw, Misssss.'

'Again: men-sa, men-sa, men-sam,' she encouraged in her ripe and rounded tones.

There was more than a cheeky hint of over-pronunciation from Elizabeth Collier, but even that was an improvement. Little monkeys like her were no match for Gloria Ramsay with her forty years' teaching experience tucked under her brown plastic belt. Elizabeth was a very bright girl, though a little unruly – too much of her older sister Beverley in her, that was the problem. She would benefit from being seated with the gentle influence of Dr Luxmore's daughter, Helen, quietly intelligent, if a little scatterbrained, and Janey Lee, for steady, deliberate ballast – a consistent 'A' for effort if not achievement. Together they made a very suitable triumvirate, although not a popular one, if their three faces, oddly similar with their masks of displeasure at this new grouping arrangement, were anything to go by . . .

Chapter 4

Cleef was around Elizabeth's legs as soon as she had got in the house after Janey had dropped her off, a black silky shape mewing for attention, his tail a velvet curl of a question mark that asked: *Where have you been? Where's my loving?*

'You'll break my neck one day, you will!' she tutted at him, but with an affectionate smile, then she heard the snoring upstairs and her heart sank. Why did she ever let him have a key? Although to be fair to herself, she didn't really, she just lent it to him one day and he never gave it back. Then *things* started to appear, as if by osmosis, from his house to hers: CDs, smelly trainers, dirty washing.

She picked up Cleef and they did their obligatory head-rubbing thing, then she plonked him in the big furry circle that was his bed and went upstairs. However careful she was not to wake the snoring form when she pivoted herself gently into her own bed, it didn't work and *it* awoke, leaned over and immediately started fumbling with her.

'Gerroff, Dean,' she said.

'Oh come on, we haven't had it for ages,' he said.

She did not want it then either. She did not want to feel anything inside her, so she took the short cut through all the pleadings and whining and relieved his frustrations a different way. Then he went back to sleep and Elizabeth stayed awake and stared ahead of her in the dark.

'BUGGER!' said Janey, finally landing the elusive 'don't forget' that had been flitting around in her head. She had to tell Elizabeth who she was sure she had seen in the Co-op, who she *had* seen in the Co-op because there was no mistaking John Silkstone, even after seven years. She would have said hello, had she not been stuck at the only checkout with a good short queue and a till operator who did not click her 'help' light on every five seconds. She noted there was a little more grey in his still mad, dark hair and he looked even bigger than she remembered him to be, unless she had shrunk in her thirties. He stood head and shoulders above most people, like a big friendly giant holding a loaf – no, it was John Silkstone all right, there wasn't anyone else it could have been. Janey made a positive mental note to ring her friend in the morning and tell her, although it was possible she would forget again. Just lately, her memory was getting terrible.

Nocturnal sleep? What's that then, because I can't remember, thought Elizabeth with some frustration. It must have been three o'clock when she eventually got off and then wished she hadn't. She had one of those muddled dreams that seemed to open up all sorts of cupboards in her head and dredge everything out: Auntie Elsie was in it and Sam barking at her; Julia, Laurence and his one furry snake of an eyebrow chasing her up Rhymer Street whilst she tried to run away from him in big tartan slippers; Bev holding a really ugly baby; Helen crying because Janey was having an affair with Simon; Lisa laughing at her with *him*. She was glad to wake up – or at least she was until ten minutes later when she felt exhausted again.

I'm turning into a chuffing owl! she thought. A day off sick tempted her but spending it in bed with Dean set her feet in her slippers and off downstairs to put the kettle on pronto. She left him snoring in bed; he would get up at some point and make a messy breakfast no doubt. At least he would not be home when she got back from work, for the 'Victoria' called him like a Siren at five. That was one lady he would never disappoint with a surprise appearance.

The rumours about the Just the Job takeover had the whole building on edge, and tension hung in the air like a bad-egg smell. Julia 'I don't do good-mornings' was sitting at her desk when Elizabeth walked in. The sight of the pouty vole-like face was enough to set the hairs on the back of her neck bristling so hard she could barely get her coat off over them. Her desk was invisible under a pile of new filing and an explanatory email waiting for her from Julia. It was such a far cry from the days of the late MD Mr Robinson, who breezed in with a, 'Good morning,' charm and warmth billowing behind him like an invisible cape. His presence warmed up the whole building; people smiled more and moaned less. Then he was sent out to pasture so that Eyebrow Man could move in to replace him. He died not long after, which was yet another reason to hate Laurence, should she need a spare. Robbo had managed quite adequately without a power-crazed, email-reliant 'ass-istant' who was supposedly a languages graduate. Universities must be taking anyone in these days, Elizabeth had thought when she first heard that one, for as far as she could make out, there wasn't a lot of furniture in Julia's attic. However, there was an enormous chest on the floor below that might have had something to do with her ascension to the seat at the side of Laurence's throne.

It wasn't hard to work out what Julia's 'sparkling potential' translated as for a man who hadn't worked out yet that bras didn't have pupils, for the woman was a walking bouncy castle. What size her breasts were was anyone's guess, but they were too big for the regular alphabet and had entered the realms of another – possibly 42 pi. They looked ridiculous on her baby-bird frame; her little bony legs were bowing under the weight of them, but there was no doubt that the Ice Man of business and the doe-eyed skinny runt with the overflowing cups enjoyed a rapport that lesser mortals would have killed to share with him. It was quite an achievement to connect with Laurence, seeing as his own PR department called him 'the Prince of Darkness', but whatever it was that was needed, Julia had it by the bucketload. Overnight, as holder of the 'King's ear' she acquired status and power and she relished it like Lucrezia Borgia on PMT week.

Somewhere, though, in all that cloud of Über-confidence was a big insecure hole, because every potential office junior who came into the department and showed any sign of popularity or nous suddenly found themselves back in the temp agency they'd come from. Pam had been very outgoing, Jenny was very industrious, Catherine was very clever, Leonora was just lovely, Jess had initiative, Lizzie was ambitious, Cindy was enthusiastic, Sally was efficient . . . and yet all of them were rejected as unsuitable within three weeks of their placement. They were now without an office junior – again – which left Elizabeth grudgingly holding the teapot. Even though Julia's ethnic-cleansing process had so far only been limited to the young, colourful and dynamic, Elizabeth figured her own days were very much numbered too.

She took a late lunchbreak that day, reasoning that it would make the afternoon session seem a lot shorter that way, and decided that she really ought to eat something if only to try and combat the relentless fatigue. There was a tempting prawn cocktail on brown in the bakery across the road. She bought it, determined for once to take her fully allotted hour. First, she would nip back up to her desk for her book and then return to scoff in the canteen, which would be peacefully empty at that time. It was the nearest to heaven she was going to get that day. Yep, it sounded good.

She snagged her tights on her heel crossing the road

back to Colditz and just managed to miss making a total prat of herself in front of the middle-aged suit, already in the lift, by almost trapping her other leg in the door as it closed. The lift pulled upwards, juddered, made a few weird rattles and then sighed to a halt. The lights flickered on and off indecisively then finally decided to choose off, and what seemed like 2-watt emergency lighting took over. Elizabeth made some polite quip about it being lucky that she'd had some carrots the night before, which obviously registered as a zero on the suit's humour clap-o-meter, although, in fairness, he didn't appear to be listening as he was too busy pressing himself backwards into the corner and showing off the whites of his eyeballs. She smiled empathetically at him.

'It'll be all right, you know, it's always happening,' she said with a frustrated tut, but the suit had progressed to perspiring and his breathing was getting more raspy and desperate with every fall of his chest.

'Oh God, help!' he said suddenly, sliding down the wall, clawing at his collar, his tongue lolling out.

Oh, marvellous, thought Elizabeth. This is all I need, to be trapped in a lift with Michael from sodding *Ryan's Daughter*.

Up to this point, her first-aid experience had been limited to applying plasters and administering tape-worm tablets to Cleef, but being an avid fan of *Casualty*, she had seen her fair share of hyperventilating to diagnose it now. She fell into an inspired automatic pilot (hoping he wasn't having a heart-attack, in which case she was probably about to kill him) and struggled with the Suit's windmill-like arms, trying to loosen his tie and collar. Then she turfed her precious sandwich out of its paper bag, gathered up the neck and made him blow into it slowly, to inhale his own breath, all the while talking like super-nurse Charlie Fairhead and getting him to focus in on her eyes, although she did wonder afterwards if she had that bit mixed up with *Crocodile Dundee*. Anyway, it seemed to work and after what seemed like three months, he started to breathe like a normal well person. She tried to take his mind off the fact that they were stuck in a metal coffin by babbling on about anything and everything: *Coronation Street*, Cleef, her penchant for prawn sandwiches . . . just to fill the dark, claustrophobic silence and nip enough edge off his fear to stop him slipping back into lift-nightmare land. She even surprised herself with the flow of bull she managed to keep up. She had just got him to his feet when the lift jerked upwards, the lights came on and the lift juddered up to the eighth floor, where Suit apparently wanted to get out at as well. He did not want a fuss and said he felt perfectly fine although he still looked pretty vacant to Elizabeth. After bog-all thanks and not so much as a 'Ta-ra, then,' he meandered off in the direction of Laurence's office.

Thank you so very much for saving my life. Oh, it was a pleasure. We must do it again sometime. Oh yes, we simply must. Let me take your address and send you a Thank You card. Certainly, it's ten Rhymer Street, Barnsley, but really there's no need. Oh please. Oh, I couldn't possibly. Oh, you must. Oh, go on then, she chuntered to herself whilst heading off to the toilet. There was no paper when she got in there either. What a day this was turning out to be! She just couldn't wait to see what else was waiting for her in the wings. She found out the answer to that one three seconds later when she dived into her bag for a couple of tissues and felt something wet and runny. She had forgotten about the prawn sandwich which, turned out of its paper bag, had fallen to bits and coated everything with lettuce and fish and butter and pink mayonnaise. Scooping the bulk of it out, she flushed it away, washed her hands and walked back to her desk. *Grrrrrreat!*

She was starting to feel pretty shaky now and thinking back, it was no wonder, because she hadn't had any breakfast either. Luckily, there was still time for a read, a coffee and something dreadful and inedible from the canteen that would give her a well-needed top-up of energy, at least.

'There you are!' said Julia, setting her teeth on edge just by breathing the same air. 'Laurence needs a tray of tea for two. NOW.'

'I'm on lunch, I'm just going to get one myself,' Elizabeth snapped, because if she did not get something a) caffeiney and b) chocolatey in her system, like now, she would: a) keel over or b) kill someone, like: a) Julia or b) Julia.

Julia tossed back her long dark straight hair with an arrogant flick of her head. 'He has an important visitor.'

'Julia, I'm on my lunch. You get it for him, you're his assistant.' Lordy, where had that come from? Elizabeth wondered.

Julia did a few rapid blinks but any loss of composure was quickly recovered. 'Yes, I am. But you make the tea.'

Something wordy and eloquent formed in response in Elizabeth's head. Unfortunately, the filter at her voicebox was a little brutal and what came out was, 'Go and bollocks.'

Where had THAT come from?

'I beg your pardon?' Julia's voice was so quiet with rage that Elizabeth wasn't sure if it was audible at all and she had merely read her lips. Either way, some tired, weary part of Elizabeth's consciousness, pushed to the very edge of reason by a whole cocktail of events and emotions, registered that this was the point of no return. Her mouth disengaged from the rest of her body and ran ahead like Red Rum with a little fat stable-boy 300 furlongs behind shouting, 'Stop, stop! For goodness' sake, stop!'

'What I mean is, why don't *you* take your bandy little legs into the kitchen, switch on the kettle and when it's boiled, stick it up where the sun refuses to shine?'

From the way the open-plan office fell into a stunned hush, Elizabeth sort of gathered that this had not been delivered in a whisper. Even the air conditioning seemed to drop in volume.

'W . . . What?'

Whoosh. A tidal wave of adrenaline rushed through her system with such velocity that she started visibly to tremble with it as her mouth came up to Beecher's Brook.

'Then, when you've done that, why don't you take

my job and stick it up there as well to keep it company.'

Behind Julia, Laurence's door pulled violently open, but not even he and his one long foreboding eyebrow could stem Elizabeth's flow.

'Do you know, you're a nasty, vicious little bitch, a bullying, sycophantic talentless little turd and I can't stand to work here with you for one more nano-second, so, if it's not yet sunk into that minuscule little brain, I'll say it in monosyllables for you. I. Quit.' Silence.

They stood facing each other like two gunfighters, hands itching for their Colt 45s. The only movement was Julia's left eye twitching spastically. Then, as soon as she detected Laurence's presence at her shoulder, her lip started to wobble and Elizabeth watched in amazement as she squeezed on every facial muscle she had to bring water sucking up her tear ducts. God, she was Oscar nominationally good.

Elizabeth gave her a slow clap and said, 'Bravo. Now please give the crocodile those tears back before he misses them.'

Laurence hoisted her up with his eyes, chewed her up and spat her out again.

'Get out, you're sacked,' he said in a whispered scream.

'Sorry, I've already resigned,' she said, then stabbed a finger at Laurence. 'As for you, you've gone through more staff in this department in the last six months than the average family goes through bog rolls in a year. You should be ashamed. All those decent kids turned away for no reason at all.'

'If you had a problem you should have come to me to discuss it *privately*,' Laurence said, his voice a covered growl, aware of the unwanted attention. With his eyebrow in a deep V in the middle, where on humans there would have been a gap, he looked very much like a big bad wolf. But Elizabeth was Red Riding Hood with attitude.

'Oh yeah?' She laughed with a mix of bitterness and amusement. 'Would you truly and honestly have listened? I think not! You're as bad as she is. You can stick your precious job, Mr Stewart-Smith. I saw what was on that note you wrote about those women being old scrubbers, so don't you tell me you'd listen to what *I* would have had to say! Twenty-two years I've worked here, without anything but positive feedback. Suddenly not only do I need a "supervisor" but I'm back filing and making coffee for a living and having to ask permission to go to the toilet!'

'Well, doesn't that tell you something?' said Laurence, his mouth twisted in a half-smug, half-furious curve.

'Yes, it does. It tells me that I should have exchanged my brain for a big pair of knockers!'

'Get out!' said Laurence.

'It will be an absolute pleasure!' She grabbed her coat and bag and stormed forward with her head lifted in dignified defiance. Julia and Laurence parted for her like the Red Sea did for Moses, and eyes everywhere glittered with hungry excitement although no one in the office spoke or moved. Every single second seemed as sharp as if the scene was being played in slow motion, and the only sound was Elizabeth's stomps across the super-bouncy executive carpet. She felt like Neil Armstrong walking across the surface of the moon as she strode on.

She looked straight ahead, ran down the swirl of back stairs (down which she had often fantasized about kicking Julia), swept past Rasputin, out of the rotating door and into the busy Leeds street. There in the cold, unforgiving air Elizabeth did something she hadn't done for many years – she sobbed her guts out.

Chapter 5

The train journey home was a blur. Elizabeth was only conscious of one point between getting on the train at Leeds and picking up her car at Barnsley station, and that was when the conductor asked her for her ticket. She wanted to ring Janey but she would still be at work. Helen would have finished now, but she didn't think it was fair to worry her in her condition, and on the actual day of her birthday as well, so she sat with a cup of tea at her kitchen table and let the events of the day whirl around in her brain. Bits were starting to warp already and even though she was sure she had not sworn at Laurence, her distorted recall implied she had let loose at him with a peal of choice language. Then she tortured herself by imagining she had turned to go and tripped up and everyone had started laughing at her. Her head flung unwanted questions at her. What would people say about her when they got home? What would Laurence demand they write on her personnel record? Would she ever be able to find work again after this? If she didn't speak to someone soon, would she go totally bonkers?

She tried Janey's number as soon as the clock had

crawled around to the time when she usually landed home. Thankfully, she was in.

'You've done what?' was Janey's response, but she didn't wait for an answer. 'I'll be there in about five minutes,' she said and put the phone straight down.

True to her word, within a short space of time, a car had pulled up outside Elizabeth's neat little end terrace with the shiny, postbox-red door and the iron cat for a door knocker, but to Elizabeth's surprise it was Helen's black sleek number and not Janey's ancient Volvo. Both women got out.

Janey had intended to storm in there and ask, 'What the bloody hell is up with you!' until she saw how red Elizabeth's eyes were. She never cried, so this was serious. Consequently she kept her trap shut and let Helen soothe the way first with fussy comfort and much putting on of kettles, and exuding her usual golden air of calm. Although in the end it got too much for her, and she burst out: 'You silly cow, whatever possessed you?'

Elizabeth's head swung slowly from side to side. 'I don't know,' she said. 'It was like someone else was at the driving wheel to my mouth.'

'Aye – Stevie Wonder. You can't talk to people like Laurence Wotsit-Wotsit like that and get away with it.'

'Well, I didn't, did I? I lost my job.'

'Yes, you did, you daft bat!' said Janey, although her tone was more concerned than exasperated.

'Tea or coffee?' said Helen.

'I'm easy,' sighed Elizabeth.

'Yes, we know,' Janey said, loosening the button on

her work skirt. Either it had shrunk in the tumble drier, or she needed to cut even further back on her carbs.

'You've moved your coffee, you naughty woman,' said Helen, foraging in vain around in the cupboard where it was usually stored.

'Oh sorry, I ran out,' said Elizabeth, who had lost the taste for it recently and not replenished her stocks. 'There's plenty of tea-bags though. Look, Hels, this isn't right, you being here on your birthday, and in your condition. I thought you were going out for a meal anyway?'

'I'm pregnant, not ill, so don't you worry about me,' said Helen. She was not going to admit to feeling less than sparkling. She had just called in at Janey's en route home from work on the pretence of saying, 'Hello and thanks for the flowers.' In truth, she had felt quite nauseous and wanted to use her loo. Nevertheless she had insisted on driving them both down the road without a second thought.

'Anyway, the table isn't booked until nine and I doubt Simon will be home before half past eight,' Helen continued with a soft smile. Even on her birthday, she didn't expect to take precedence over Simon's workload.

'Okay, so what's done is done,' Janey conceded. 'So what are you going to do next?'

'Christ knows. Get another job, I suppose, and hope they don't need references.'

'Mmmm, that could be a problem.'

Helen was swirling the teapot behind them to hasten

the brewing process. 'Surely they won't just let you go like that after all these years?'

'Oh yes they will,' said Elizabeth with an accompanying pantomime laugh. 'I mean nothing to the likes of Laurence Stewart-Smith. I upset his "baby" and that's tantamount to treason. He'd have had me beheaded if this was the sixteenth century. Slowly, with a blunt sword.'

'Yes – well, it's not, thank goodness. Can you go on the dole for now?' Helen suggested, adding a wry: 'I presume you don't have thousands of pounds-worth of savings to rely on.'

Elizabeth shook her head quickly. 'I wouldn't get dole. And to be honest I don't fancy going up there and announcing to all and sundry at the DHSS, or whatever they call themselves these days, what I've done to make myself jobless.' Elizabeth made a strange animal noise of frustration. 'I don't believe it! I mean, how could I let a little bitch like Julia Powell burrow into my marrow, eh?'

'You tell us!' said Janey, who was just as puzzled.

It was unheard of for Elizabeth to get screwed up over anything, especially over making a flaming pot of tea. Elizabeth was the coolest person she knew; in fact, she made the Ice Queen look like Ma 'Darling Buds' Larkin sometimes. That wild streak was obviously still lingering in there somewhere, and there they were, thinking that Elizabeth had settled down nicely these past few years, despite the fact she still could not pick a decent bloke to save her life. Then when one picked her, she sent him off packing. However much she and

Helen both thought of Elizabeth, they could have taken turns in wringing her neck sometimes. She didn't need enemies, not when the worst of them all was herself.

'Can't you just say you resigned?' suggested Helen, as she poured.

'She definitely wouldn't get dole then,' said Janey. 'There's always temping, of course.'

Elizabeth sighed. 'I don't *want* bloody dole. But I'll be honest, I'm scared. I've been at Handi-Save since I left school. I've never worked anywhere else.'

'There you go then,' brightened Helen. 'That shows your loyalty and tenacity.'

'Not very loyal telling the boss to shove your job up his arse, is it?' Janey added with a grunt. There was a short silence and then, despite the seriousness of the situation, they all burst into a loud bout of some well-needed laughter. Then Janey clicked her fingers as an idea came to her.

'Do you know what I would do if I were you? I'd take a couple of weeks off and give yourself a break. I don't know – do some of your arty stuff or decorate your bedroom or something. God knows it could be doing with it!' she added in her straight-talking Janey way. 'That'll give your mind a chance to wander and relax. I've never seen you so wound up. In fact, I've never seen you wound up full stop, come to think of it. You're run down, Collier. Maybe you should go and see a doctor?'

'Naw, he'll only say it's my hormones. Don't they go a bit loopy at this age? Don't we start growing moustaches and buying Tena-Ladys?'

'Can you afford a couple of weeks off?' said Janey, serious again.

Elizabeth nodded. 'I should have some holiday money to come. Bloody witch wouldn't let me take my full allowance last year. They can't deny me that, surely?'

Janey sipped at the tea, even though she had gone off drinking it recently. It had started to taste 'tinny'.

'Look, don't fret, I'll be fine. Really!' Elizabeth gave a positive little laugh. 'Now I've had the chance to talk things over with you two I feel a lot better. At least there's no mortgage to pay so I won't get chucked out of my house, and there's just me and Cleef to worry about.'

Big black Cleef, sleepily occupying the fourth chair around the table, acknowledged his name by lazily opening one eye. Helen gave him a fond stroke; she would always think of him as hers.

'Look forward to the moment of karma,' Helen said.

'There won't be any,' said Elizabeth. 'Types like them always drop into horsecrap and come up smelling of roses.'

'Not always,' mused Helen. 'Sometimes they get their just deserts.' She looked to Janey for affirmation, but Janey didn't say a word.

'Okay, then, here's to karma!' said Elizabeth, raising her mug in the general direction of where she imagined karma might be hanging out, but not believing in its existence for a second.

Helen got home minutes after Simon, it appeared, as he still had his overcoat on. He'd had an extremely profitable day and was looking pleased with himself. Last night was all forgotten, and they were friends again.

'You're early,' she said, with a big pleased smile.

'Where have you been then?' he said, kissing her on the forehead.

'Elizabeth's. She's a bit depressed.' She didn't tell him why. She always felt very disloyal telling Simon anything about her friends. He seemed to enjoy any misfortune that befell them. Especially Elizabeth.

'Like I care,' he said, wafting the subject away with a wave of his hand. 'Anyway, never mind about her. I've bought you an extra present. Sorry it's not wrapped, didn't have time.'

He held a large box out. Helen took it from him, put it on the table, opened it and lifted out the long, beautiful vase inside.

'Isn't it gorgeous? Should be too – cost a fortune and I got these to go in it.' He presented her with an enormous bouquet of flowers. He took the new vase from her hands, marched into the dining room and set it on the vacancy where Elizabeth's sunflower vase had stood.

'Happy Birthday, darling.' He smiled proudly and gave her an affectionate hug and she daren't spoil the rare moment by asking where the lovely vase and flowers were that her best friends had bought her.

In bed alone, Elizabeth found there was nothing remotely delicious in the mental recall of telling Laurence and Julia where to go. The whole day had soured like milk in her head and made her feel physically nauseous. She made sure she would not be plagued by unwelcome visitors by texting Dean and telling him not to come over as she was feeling sick, and then she snuggled down under the quilt with a book and some Horlicks, suspecting she was probably set for another sooper-dooper night of insomnia.

Helen found her lost presents the next morning, when she was taking a black bag of rubbish out to the wheelie-bin. Elizabeth's vase was buried under Janey's flowers; miraculously it wasn't broken. She lifted it out and wrapped it in some newspaper from the nearby recycling bag and put it in the secret place in the garage along with all her other favourite things that Simon didn't like displayed in the house, but that her heart would not have her throw away.

Chapter 6

Elizabeth woke up on her first day of being unemployed, feeling that she had been properly asleep for no longer than five seconds in the whole night. She dressed, went downstairs, made a long job of a forced piece of toast and then went back to bed again where she slept solidly for three more hours. She felt a lot better for being able to give in to her bodily demands, but she wasn't used to sitting around doing nothing, and once she was up she was soon twiddling her thumbs and trying to think of something more positive to do than watch reruns of *Quincy* on the telly. Janey's suggestion that she decorate her bedroom was becoming more and more attractive by the minute. At present, it was boring magnolia with an old, past-it beige carpet. It needed warming up and some interest of colour – maybe a nice strawberry carpet and creamy pink walls, she thought. She had seen a room decorated like that in a recent magazine and it looked lovely.

Screwing her unruly hair back tightly into a scrunchie, she changed into an old T-shirt and a pair of baggy black leggings, which were going along the inner-thigh seam but were perfectly adequate for painting in. Then she went hunting for sandpaper in the small storehouse in the garden, which had once been an outside loo. Halfway through roughing up the skirting boards, she had to go and change her bra for an old comfy one because the one she had on seemed to be rubbing her raw in strategic places. She put it down to the new washing powder and carried on priming the bedroom, then when it was done, she set off into town to buy some paint.

It was unexpectedly relaxing, wandering up and down the aisles of the decorating giant's store 'Just the Job', and her head emptied of everything but the task in hand – buying brushes, white spirit, undercoat, non-drip gloss and masking tape. It was as she was deciding between the nuances of *Candy Floss* and *Lollipop* emulsions that she saw *him* cross the top of her aisle. Commonsense told her it couldn't possibly be him because he was in Germany, but her eyes were seeing the indisputable evidence for themselves and there was no mistaking who it was, even after all this time. The sight of him winded her. Her whole body locked. She didn't know what to do. Yes, she did. She had to get out and find some oxygen to breathe. She pivoted around so sharply that she went the full 360 degrees and ended up back where she started. It appeared the small chemical factory that had blown up inside her had temporarily disabled her ability to co-ordinate.

From time to time, she had wondered what she would do if she saw him again, and presumed she would be totally indifferent to him after all these years, maybe even ignore him or at best give him no more than a second glance. Yeah, right! Her head was swirling, memories were bombarding her as fresh as the day they were made, and the overwhelming effect of it all was making her stomach so jittery that she wanted to vomit.

All the things she had told him. Everything . . .

She edged round for a second look but he was gone. Where? She dumped her trolley and crept across the top of the aisles, checking down each one like a crap actor in a cheap spy film. Where the flipping heck was he? She felt someone come up behind her and she jumped back, flattening herself against the Black & Deckers, but it wasn't him, just someone who looked at her as if suspecting she might have escaped from a secure mental hospital. She doubled back, looking out for the sight of his black leather jacket and hoping that no one was watching all this on CCTV. A pulse was throbbing in her ears that totally drowned out the tinny tones of the Musak that was struggling out of the overhead speakers. *Where the bloody hell had he gone?* She did another thorough check and decided he must have left the store. Her heart was bouncing like a mad ping-pong ball inside her and she needed the loo again – and fast.

It then occurred to her that she was nearly forty, not twelve, and that at this age she should have the maturity to bypass such a ludicrous scenario. On the offchance he did not ignore her, what on earth was wrong in saying a normal, 'Hello, how are you? What are you doing back from Germany then? How is Lisa?

Does she still cling to you like a brain-damaged limpet?'
Therein lay the problem with 'normal'. Not only did
her indifference gland need a major tweak, but having
felt the Full Monty effect of how her body reacted
to a mere flashing sight of him, she knew there was
no way in heaven or hell that she could act 'normal'
with John Silkstone in a face-to-face encounter. Not
in a million years.

There was still no sign of him as she stealthily re-
collected her trolley and wheeled it slowly towards
the checkout. She wasn't in touch with her own feelings enough to know if the adrenaline coursing through
her inner motorways was sourced in excitement or
relief or fear. What she did know was that she just
wanted to get out of there and to the safety of her
car as soon as possible. Satisfied that he had left the
building, she joined a queue and allowed herself to
relax a little. She was halfway through paying for her
goods when up he popped again, two tills down,
faffing about with his wallet. Her heart started galloping
again, but it didn't look as if he had seen her. *So far
so good*. She whipped out her Switchcard and signed
her name on the receipt quickly before pushing the
trolley victoriously out towards the exit. *Done it*. Then
the metal arch thing at the door went off, didn't it,
because Mr Efficient Just the Job till operator hadn't
swiped something properly. Then the customer two
tills down lifted his head at the commotion and saw
her at the centre of it.

Elizabeth didn't know what was making her blush
more – the fact that she'd alerted the stares of everyone

in the shop when the spotty stringbean cross between Sebastian Coe and a Los Angeles cop rushed over, or that *he* saw her in her finest gear – no make-up on, a Barnes Wallace bra and crotchless decorating gear. He hung around until Harry Callaghan had cleared her for bombs and drugs and reswiped her non-drip gloss, and then she waited for the inevitable.

She did a really bad acting job of pretending to spot him for the first time as she watched him out of the corner of her eye slowly approach her.

'My goodness, it's you! How are you?' she said with a pathetic attempt at casual, whilst pulling the back of her T-shirt down over her bottom. There was an incredibly awkward exchange of plastic smiles and head-nodding of the like that was only to be seen between animals squaring up against each other in Chester Zoo.

'Elizabeth,' he said. 'How are you? You look . . . good.'

The pause before the complimentary word was telling, she thought.

'Oh yeah!' she said. 'A regular catwalk queen in my decorating gear.' Pleased to get that in just in case he thought this was her normal garb these days and that she had gone really downhill.

'So, how've you been?' she said.

'Good – and you?'

'Smashing,' she said. 'And you?'

'Good. And yourself?'

Flaming hell, this loop could go on for years if she didn't break it.

'Holidaying?' she said.

'No, I'm home for good.'

'Oh, both of you?' She tried not to sound nosy. Even though she was.

'Both? Lisa, you mean? No, we aren't together any more.'

'Oh, I'm sorry to hear that,' she forced herself to say. 'So . . . er . . . how will you cope without German beer then?' *Ha, you prize-winning conversationalist you, Elizabeth Collier!*

'I think I'll manage,' he said.

She tried to think of something witty and incisive, but was already desperately scraping around the bottom of her mental barrel of 'things to say to a bloke you haven't seen for seven years' and he wasn't helping, standing there like a mountain range just looking at her. If she did not get away soon she would faint, she felt uncomfortably h-o-t.

'Well, I best get on,' she said, doing a nervous little dance-step as she started to trundle out the trolley.

'What are you painting?' he said, looking at her wares.

'My bedroom,' she said.

'You still at Rhymer Street?'

'Yes.'

'On holiday from work, are you?'

No, actually, I told my boss to stick his job up his jacksey.

'Er . . . yes. So what are you doing these days then?'

'Me and the bank have bought some land. I'm knocking up some houses and hoping to sell 'em off.'

'Oh great,' she said, as the danger alarm on her bladder started to throb red.

'Well.'

'Well.'

'Well.'

'So, this is . . .' she said, trailing off because she had absolutely no idea of where the sentence was going.

'Yeah. It's been nice seeing you,' he said, looking as if he had just snapped out of a trance. An interesting silence followed in which he might have said, 'We could catch up and go for a drink or something,' to which she wasn't sure how she would have reacted. Not that she got the chance to find out because what he actually said was, 'Well, 'bye then, take care,' and he was off without so much as a backward glance.

Her knees were knocking across that car park. She was as wobbly as the trolley wheels. *John Silkstone.* It felt like November the Fifth in her head, with his name all lit up in fireworks, which was pretty ironic really considering the last time she saw him, she told him to piss off and leave her alone for ever because she hated him.

As usual, there were no interesting jobs on the *Situations Vacant* board. Janey was vaguely aware of some man hanging behind her looking over her shoulder but she presumed it was just some hopeful other, like herself, looking for his overdue chance to shine. It was not though, it was Barry Parrish, the Head of Personnel, and he had been waiting for her to finish reading before interrupting her.

'You've saved me a trip, Jane,' he said in a silky voice that belonged to James Bond. 'I was coming up to see you this afternoon.'

'Oh?' she said, taken aback.

'Have you time for a coffee?'

'Y . . . yes, of course,' she stammered, suddenly wondering if the excitement building up in her boots was misplaced and this was actually P45 time.

He bought her a cappuccino from the machine and they went to sit behind a big plant.

'I'll come straight to the point,' he said. 'There's a vacancy to be posted on the board in the next couple of days and I think you should apply for it.'

'Er . . . oh?' she said, hoping the position wasn't Head of Devastating Wit, judging by this performance so far. It was not, though – it was much, much better.

'Manager of Customer Services,' he clarified.

It was a good thing she didn't have a mouthful of coffee just then, because she would have spat it all over him. There she was, waiting for a step up the ladder courtesy of Old Coughing Lungs, and all the while Personnel were sending her up in a gold-plated lift to the top of the Empire State Building.

'I . . . I . . . don't know what to say,' she said. Well, she did, but she didn't think all those Fs would have gone down too well.

'You could do it, Jane. You have just what that Department needs – stability, maturity, efficiency and organization. I – that is, *we* – happen to think you're our girl for the job.'

He pulled a sheet out of the folder he had with him and set it on the table.

'Here's the job description that will go up on the board. By law I have to advertise it but I'm taking it as read that you'll be called up for interview. The salary is commensurate with the position and there's a car, private health insurance and profit-sharing at that level.'

Janey read the sheet. It sounded fantastic, and yes, she knew she could do it. This was the chance she had been waiting for all her life to show what she could do. 'Slow But Sure' was what it said on all her reports – not 'Natural Clever Clogs' like Elizabeth and Hels. Not that it had done them much good: Elizabeth might have moved through the secretarial ranks at Handi-Save, but she had enough brains to run the place if she wanted to. As for Helen – part-time legal secretary after quitting a Law degree at University? What a waste! Janey had always followed what her mam and dad told her: she took care over everything she did, she did not make mistakes, she watched and learned and she had worked hard. Now it could all pay off.

'Yes, I want to be considered, Barry,' she said calmly, even though her heart was as busy as a drumkit on a Cozy Powell LP.

'Good,' he said, and the Head of Personnel himself lifted up his coffee to her and said, 'Cheers!'

Chapter 7

Over the years, each of them had found their own individual ways to unwind. Helen had always been into photography and was official recorder of their various hairstyles and gallivanting. She owned bulging albums that would have been worth millions in blackmail money if any of them ever became famous, especially 'the perm years' for Janey, and Elizabeth's Mod phase in which she turned up to all things in a parka and a long, dangerous pair of winkle-pickers. Janey liked to sew and was an absolute whizz with a needle or a machine, even though it almost constituted a domestic chore. Not that she was dirty or would have had a germ-ridden house had George not been so handy with a duster and a Dyson, but she didn't get the same sense of achievement that Elizabeth did from scrubbing a floor or polishing a room until it shone.

Janey had always been a big girl – tall as well as broad – and in the days of their youthful exploits, the fashion industry seemed to be under the impression that women of a certain size might prefer to cover up their substantial attributes in shame rather than decorate them. Hip, funky clothes for figures like hers were very thin on the ground so the only solution was for her to make her own, especially during the New Romantic era. She was the appointed dress designer when they went out in frilly white shirts and dandy satin cummerbunds to dance to Ant Music, and when full circle skirts were in vogue, she had run them all up matching grey ones for school. They had gone around together looking like three rejects from *Grease* and Helen had the picture to prove it.

For Elizabeth, her number one way to relax had been with a quiet place and her artbox, especially when she felt the need to escape from the world. At school, Art had a secondary place on the curriculum as a useful hobby but was never afforded the same respect as the more 'serious subjects' like History or Latin. Then, when Elizabeth was twelve Miss Fairclough arrived as a new teacher and saw in Elizabeth a real flair for the subject and she nurtured her like a precious plant. The residing Head of Art, Mr Pierrepoint, was bored and unenthusiastic and ticking off the days to his retirement but Miss Fairclough was a passionate teacher. She set up an after-school club for interested parties, for which Elizabeth was first in the queue. There, Miss Fairclough showed them all the finer points of perspective and shading, as well as enthralling her students with lively tales of the great artists and their wild and wicked ways, and how the various phases in their lives would reflect in their drawings. The example that always stuck in Elizabeth's mind had been one of Picasso's later works, *Grande Maternité*. She would never forget the flowing lines, the serenity of the picture of a mother feeding her baby at the breast that told of the inner contentment of the artist. Miss Fairclough might only have been at the school for a year, but it was at a time when Elizabeth had needed a safe and quiet expression for her confused emotions. She was to find what she learned with Miss Fairclough useful for the rest of her life and she would always be grateful to her old teacher for it.

Before she went up to tackle the bedroom, Elizabeth relaxed with a glass of juice and a sandwich in her bright little kitchen. She'd had it done up last year after one of the ancient units fell off, taking half the wall with it. Now it was bright and yellow, more so in the afternoons when the sun streamed full in through the large window, which framed the neat little back garden like a pretty picture. Cleef was gently snoring on the seat next to her, one leg sticking out like Superman mid-flight. She had the sudden urge to draw him and reached behind her to the drawer where she kept her pencilbox and sketchpad. She would need a new one soon; most of the pages had been torn out of that one. She used a 3H pencil for a delicate outline and it moved quickly over the paper to capture Cleef before he shifted into a more conventional position, although there was a fat chance of that unless a mouse-flavoured bomb went off under his nose. His paw twitched a little and his claws made a brief appearance as if he was dreaming of an adversary. Then he was still again and allowed her to finish. Elizabeth had never kept a diary, but in the forgotten pictures stored up in the loft was a graphic record of her young life.

Unlike the picture of Cleef, there was no delicacy in them, only great outpourings of emotion in thick, black, angry strokes, as in the recently ripped-out pages of her sketchpad.

As Elizabeth entered her bedroom, she saw the room for the first time through Janey's eyes and it was just like she said, in desperate need of a makeover, although it was faultlessly clean. In comparison to the bright pink paint in the tin the present beige walls looked extra dull and boring and tired, but not for much longer. She climbed the ladder, dipped her brush and started the job off. The problem was that painting walls gave Elizabeth far too much time to think. It was all very well 'letting her mind wander', as Janey put it, but it wandered straight over to John Silkstone and stayed there, wondering. *Had he actually got divorced or was it just a temporary split from Lisa? Did they have any kids? Was he courting someone else? Did he ever think of her?* God knows, she had tried not to think about him these years past. There was little point, for she didn't imagine they could ever be friends again. When you hurt someone like she had hurt him, you didn't deserve the privilege anyway and Lisa, for all her fluffy dolly looks, had been head over heels about him. He had deserved some good loving; Elizabeth had missed her chance and that was that. Still, that knowledge did not stop the image of all he had once meant to her start to reconstitute itself out of the ashes in her head and rise up slowly like a great big black-haired Phoenix with massive builder's boots on. Her mind wondered about him a bit more and then the phone rang.

'It's me, I can't stay long, I'm still at work,' Janey said. 'You all right?'

'Yeah, I'm painting like you said,' Elizabeth said. 'Lots of pink. Then I'm going to go down and pick a nice new red carpet.'

'It'll be like sleeping in a flaming womb!'

Elizabeth laughed.

'Oh, by the way,' Janey said suddenly. 'I meant to tell you, guess who I saw in the Co-op?'

'Elvis?' said Elizabeth.

'Give over.'

'Shergar? Lord Lucan?'

'Aye, them an' all.'

'The *Picnic at Hanging Rock* girls?'

'I'm being serious!' said Janey, being serious.

'John Silkstone?'

'How the bloody hell did you know that?'

'I saw him in Just the Job when I was picking up the paint.'

Janey gasped. 'Did you talk to him?'

'Briefly.'

'And?'

'And what? We said hello and how are you, end of story.'

'You must have got something more out of him than that!'

'Flaming hell! How long have you been in the Spanish Inquisition?'

'Oh come on, spill the beans, woman!'

Elizabeth sighed. 'He's living back here and it sounds like his marriage is over.'

'Oh, really now,' Janey said lasciviously.

'Don't say "Oh, really now" in that way,' said Elizabeth, knowing exactly what she was thinking.

Elizabeth was right in her assumption. Janey's mind had romped ahead and was seeing a second spark of hope for Elizabeth and John now that he had split up from the wad of cottonwool he had married. She had never liked Lisa, she had always thought of her as vacuous and dull as ditchwater, and believed that John Silkstone had only taken up with her on the rebound from Elizabeth; any idiot could have told any other idiot that.

'Do you think you'll see him around?' Janey asked.

'I don't know. Probably, if I hang around do-it-yourself shops and building sites,' she said.

'He didn't ask you out for a drink or anything?'

'No, of course he didn't!'

'Oh well,' said Janey, disappointed that her news was so anti-climactic, 'that's all I rang for, really. Helen's vomiting for England, by the way.'

'Oh dear, poor love. I'll ring her later. Are you all right then?' said Elizabeth.

'Fine – more than fine, actually. I had a coffee with the Mr Big in Personnel and, guess what, he wants me to apply to be Manager of Customer Services.'

'I hope you're going to then!'

'Too flaming right I am. Anyway, I'll have to go because I need the loo. I think I must have a bit of an infection, you know, because I can't stop going. I'm nearly as bad as you.'

'It's probably a mix of cold weather and us being old bags.'

'Thank you for that. See you later then,' said Janey, putting the phone down, thinking, *Funny*. She thought Elizabeth would have been a lot more affected, bumping into the man with whom she had once been so totally and utterly in love, according to that letter anyway. But then you never could tell with Elizabeth what was really going on in her head.

As Helen leaned over the toilet bowl for the five-millionth time that afternoon she wondered why they called it 'morning sickness' when she didn't get a wave of nausea until at least lunchtime. Mornings were reserved for being so tired that she did not feel she had slept during the night, and then for the rest of the day she felt so sick she hardly dared step out of the house.

Her work colleagues were very sympathetic – thank goodness. The office was full of clucky old hens in early grandmotherhood who suspected she was pregnant and gushed over her, deluging her with helpful tips, although the ginger biscuit anti-vomit idea made her heave so much at one point she felt she was turning inside out. The only things she was managing to keep down were lemon juice and small baked potatoes covered with tuna and vinegar. She found she had even gone off tea and coffee – they left a really odd taste in her mouth, as if she was drinking them out of a tin can. Even her alltime favourite meal, grilled sole, had her clamping her hand over her mouth and aiming like an Exocet missile for the nearest cistern.

She would be so glad when that stage of things was over – touch wood – in another five weeks, earlier if she was lucky. At the moment, all she could think about was the pulsing headache in her temple and she felt terribly guilty that she could not fully concentrate on what Janey had just been telling her on the phone about an interview, and that John Silkstone was back, and that Elizabeth had met him somewhere. Not that she knew him as well as the others did, but he had been very sweet when he came to take the little black kitten away from her for Elizabeth. She had made a total fool of herself by crying buckets and he had given her his hankie, which had been roughly the size of a double quilt cover. However, she did think that what happened between him and Elizabeth had been such a stupid shame, even more so when they read her letter. Helen loved her friend dearly but sometimes she wished she would open herself up more and let people in. Then again, who was she to say that, really?

Elizabeth had to stop painting to take a nap and then she woke with a blinding headache, which served her right for going to sleep in a room full of fresh paint. At least it gave her the perfect excuse to text Dean and tell him not to come over, as there was nowhere to sleep. He sent one back saying WE DON'T HV 2 SLEEP!!!! She fired one back saying I M REALLY TIRED. One came back straight away with his intelligent spelling: YUOR ALWAYS BLUDDY TRIED.

It was not a relationship; it was just a habit and one that needed stopping. Dean was a casual labourer who had lingered too long after doing a job next door and he had knocked on the door and bothered her for a cup of tea. She could not tell where the job ended and they began, but he had stuck his feet quickly and firmly under her table. Then again, Elizabeth wasn't exactly renowned for her judgement of character. Funny, that – all the people she ever grown fond of she had taken against when she first met them: she thought Janey was thick, Helen was a stuck-up cow, George was a lump and she thought her Auntie Elsie was the Wicked Witch of the West with her flaming boiled ham and over-diluted orange juice. As for John Silkstone, dressed from head to foot in black leather with that stupid cowboy hat on, thinking he looked cool and interesting! She really did not want to like him, but he sneaked up on her heart over the years and so she did the only sensible thing in the end for Elizabeth – she got rid. She sent him away to another woman and another life, yet Dean and his snoring and his mess and his laziness and his revolting habits were there taking up space in her existence. Now really where was the sense in all that?

The job vacancy went up on the noticeboard Thursday and they interviewed Janey on the Tuesday following, three of them: Barry, Judith Booth – the HR woman – and Barry's second-in-command, Tony Warburton. Janey had crossed paths with them all in the past and they had seemed very fair, capable and decent people. The last Customer Service Manager had left quickly and suspiciously, despite having been young and supposedly dynamic, and Janey knew they needed to fill the position as soon as possible. They called her after lunch and asked if she would be available for an impromptu meeting and thank goodness, she'd had the foresight to come to work especially smart and prepared, just in case they sprang something like this on her.

She was a little nervous, but not so much that it made her give daft answers to their questions. All in all, she thought she had done quite a good job and they nodded a lot at what she had to say and seemed quite impressed at how she conducted herself. The stress of it told later though, when she walked out of the interview room with her head held high and went straight to the Ladies, where she threw up the contents of her stomach and three other people's besides.

As Janey was composing herself in the loo, Elizabeth was standing back to admire her handiwork in her new, nearly finished bedroom. It looked so different from the old look that it could almost have been a new extension rather than a revamped space. Even the window looked twice the size with a pair of new pale-pink curtains at the window instead of the old heavy tapestry drapes. She had thrown out the bulky bedside cabinets and tugged and heaved the furniture about, experimenting with a different arrangement, and was surprised at how much larger and lighter the room felt. As she was cutting up the old carpet into strips for the Council to take away, she knew that she did not want Dean staying in this fresh, clean space and that she must now finally end this non-relationship they had. Then she drove into one of the trading estates on the outskirts of town and picked a carpet – a soft strawberry red with a lovely thick pile. There was plenty of it in stock so it could be fitted the following Monday.

Had she picked a blue carpet, things might have turned out not quite the way they did. *Funny how the turn of life can hang on something as simple as that*, she would later come to realize.

Chapter 8

It was the end of a lovely day for Helen. Today she was eight weeks and one day pregnant, and Simon had grudgingly given her permission to formally announce the fact at work – because the denials were becoming embarrassing. She had been warmly fussed over and Teddy Sanderson, her boss, had gone out and bought her a huge box of chocolates. It was the first night for a while that her nausea hadn't totally wiped her out and she lay on their long white leather sofa, listening to a play on the radio with her Adonis at her side. He was reading the financial pages of the newspaper and sipping periodically from a glass of whisky, whilst she contented herself with lemonade. Her hand lay flat on her tummy and she wondered if the baby could sense the warmth in it. She felt calm and serene and totally blissed out. Then it all went wrong again.

She reached over to open the chocolates but as she opened the lid, Simon manoeuvred them out of her way.

'Ah, ah, ah. Don't want you getting fat now, do we?'

'Simon, it's only a chocolate!' she said, laughing and

trying to bring down his arm because she thought he was joking.

'This is the time you have to watch out for,' he said. 'Despite the old adage, you shouldn't really be eating for two, you know.'

'There are probably more calories in this lemonade than there are in five of those chocolates,' said Helen.

'You should be drinking water then,' he said, and he actually took her glass away, tipped it out and brought her some mineral water from the fridge. She laughed because it was so ridiculous and because she could not think what else to do. Surely, he wasn't being serious?

'What's the matter with you?' he said as she stared at him.

'What are you doing?' she asked.

'I'm trying to help you, isn't that obvious?' He tossed the remainder of the whisky down his throat, his good mood gone.

'It was one chocolate and a glass of lemonade!' she said, her mouth still formed into a round of disbelief.

'What's that they say? "A moment on the lips, a lifetime on the hips"?'

'I think so,' Helen said, trying not to sound as indignant as she felt because the last thing she wanted was all this to end up in another one of those stupid rows that blew up from nowhere like a sandstorm to choke their whole evening.

He yawned, folded up his newspaper and said, 'I'm going to bed, goodnight,' and Helen jumped up eagerly, because she so needed him to make love to her and show her he was happy with her and thrilled about the baby, because she suspected he wasn't. He had procrastinated about starting a family since they married, and at four years younger than Helen, he could afford to delay a little. When she argued that she was in her very late thirties, he argued back that women today were having babies easily in their mid-forties and so they had plenty of time still. Helen knew the chances were that she didn't; her mother had gone through a terribly early menopause and apparently, that was hereditary. Of course, her father would have known the facts about that, had he been here to ask.

Whoever said that all top executives were animals in bed were very misled, in Helen's experience. More often than not, Simon was always too tired to make love after a hard day at the office. Each time her date chart and temperature aligned on the optimum time to get pregnant, Simon was either away at a conference or exhausted and unwilling, and her window of opportunity closed for yet another month. She had been pretending to take the pill for three years now, hoping for a happy 'accident', but on the rare occasions they did make love, her punctual-as-ever period came and snuffed out the small flames of hope that dared to dance in her heart. So when her chart told her that New Year's Day was *the* day, she pulled out every stop in the book to seduce him and it worked. Champagne cocktails, over-laced with brandy, oysters, lobster, scented candlelight, smooth music on the CD, giving him an erotic massage in her tiny red Agent Provocateur undies . . . Then whilst he slept, Helen sat with her legs up in the air like a porn star willing the little tadpoles to go find her egg, taking care not to spill one precious drop of them.

She *knew* she was pregnant; doing the test was just a formality for her. She held the pregnancy wand in her hand and watched the blue line appear like magic then she screamed with joy and sank to her knees, thanked God and cried and laughed. She couldn't wait for Simon to get home that night and, as usual, he was late. But when she excitedly announced that he was going to be a father, his congratulatory hug was slack and robotic. She had initially put his shell-shocked demeanour down to the magnitude of the news. Then she realized it wasn't that at all when the questions started: *How could this happen? Did she forget to take her pill? Didn't he tell her they should wait?* Helen blamed a recent tummy bug for upsetting her pill's efficiency. It was a well-known fact that that could happen, and she got away with the lie.

They showered, separately, and then she climbed into bed and snuggled up to him, stroking his chest. He took her hand, kissed it and put it away to the side of her.

'Can we make love?' she asked.

'Not tonight, darling, I'm so tired.'

'But we haven't made love since New Year!' she said, trying not to sound as desperate as she felt.

'It's bad for the baby anyway, until twelve weeks at least.'

Helen lay in the dark for a while, holding him close, though he felt a million miles away. She tried to take heart that he had actually mentioned the baby. She rather thought it was the first time he had.

'Simon,' she asked eventually, 'aren't you happy about being a daddy?'

'Oh, Helen, don't be silly and just go to sleep,' he said, shuffling away from her as if her body against his was an irritation.

Janey and George went through their usual after-curry routine (hers a half portion of a tomato-based one obviously). They went to bed; he made sure she was satisfied then he slipped on a condom and climbed aboard for the missionary position. Then they cuddled up and Janey talked about that interview, again, and twittered on for a bit and he listened patiently and stroked her back until he dropped off and she studied the ceiling for a while listening to his gentle contented snoring.

It might not have been Virgin and the Gypsy stuff, but it was warm and affectionate, easy and familiar, and he knew exactly where to touch her to make the bells ring on the rare occasions these days that they decided on a bit of 'how's yer campanology'. They had never been swinging-off-the-chandelier types and now, even though they were in a sexual rut, it was a comfortable one. Neither of them felt the need to spice things up with sex toys or dress up as Vikings or apply gels that made private parts tingle with desire. George seemed happy enough with his lot and wild dangerous sex wasn't all it was cracked up to be, as Janey had discovered.

She had presumed that when she had lost all her weight, she would feel sexier, more confident, and totally liberated, but she did not – she just felt thinner and hungrier. George never said anything, but she knew he missed her curves, especially her boobs that the diets robbed her of first. He'd always enjoyed having something to grab hold of and warm and soft to snuggle into. He was a bit like her granddad in that way, was George.

'Eeh, you're looking bonny, love,' her granda' would say, and by that she knew she had put on weight. Not that he was one of those blokes who would feed his missus pork pies until she couldn't move, but he had liked to see a good, well-built woman. Her nana had massive boobs and hips that could have launched the *QE2* and they had still been bonking in their eighties.

George loved Janey – big boobs or small – and she knew that all she would have to do is say it and it would be hers, whatever it was. She wished she could offer him the same, but she would never dare ask, because she knew that all he wanted from her was a baby. He never pressed her because he appreciated how important her career was to her, but it never left her conscience that she had not been fair to him. At first she had suggested they wait until they had finished decorating the house before they tried for a baby, then she wanted to wait until she had landed that big promotion or until they had more money to spare. She had made sure there was always something to wait for. Then it just got too late.

She cuddled up to him and kissed him in his sleep.

She did not deserve him, she really didn't. Not after she had almost destroyed him.

Dean was making so much noise at the front door that Elizabeth felt obliged to let him in before he disturbed the neighbours. He was obviously lying when he said he hadn't received any text message telling him not to call up because he had already replied to it with an OK. He was full of Friday-night ale and burping bhuna smells, and he tried to dance with her, edging her towards the stairs to persuade her up to bed. Grudgingly she told him he could stay, but in the spare single bed at the front of the house as her room was not finished yet. He made all sorts of promises on the way up the stairs of what he was going to do to her but luckily, by the time she had come out of the bathroom he was snoring on top of the duvet, like a pig with a chronic adenoid problem. She dragged a pillow roughly out from under his head and headed downstairs for the sofa, berating herself for opening the outside door in the first place. She was just a girl who couldn't say no. Unless that someone she was saying 'no' to happened to be someone decent who deserved a 'yes'.

Elizabeth did not think she had ever enjoyed sex. Even if she was lucky enough to be satisfied, by luck rather than design, she just wanted them to shove off straight afterwards and leave her alone. She had never snuggled up to anyone in that post-coital afterglow, not even to Dean in that 'blink-and-you'd-miss-it' honeymoon period, and once the 'act' was over with, she got as far away from him as possible in bed. It wasn't normal, she knew that, but it was normal for her; she'd had no different experience to prove otherwise. She never consciously wanted to think what going to bed with John Silkstone would have been like, but occasionally something slid under the thought barrier and she would find herself imagining how gently he would have kissed her, how warm his great big body would feel against hers and how he would pull her right into his side after it was done and cuddle her to sleep. She would shake the fantasy away in a panic. It scared her witless.

She really would have to get firm with Dean; he had started to make her skin crawl long before Christmas arrived, but it wouldn't have been fair on him to finish it then, so she had decided to do it after New Year. Then New Year came and she had found herself clinging to him instead. It was all her fault that he was still around; she owed him for being there when she had needed someone familiar with her in the night, anyone who stopped her from being alone and scared in the dark.

Sex, for Elizabeth, was currency and power. Sex was anything but love.

Chapter 9

It suddenly flagged up in Janey's subconscious diary that she should have had her period by then, and when she checked her actual diary, she found she had not only missed it but her next one was due soon. She was not unduly worried because George always used protection and they had never had an accident yet, plus maybe some job stress had held things up a bit. Still, she would feel better when it landed. A woman might hate her periods coming, but she hated them not coming a damn sight more.

Mr and Mrs Hobson had a low-key but sweet romantic evening that Valentine's night and George cooked, because he liked to and he was miles better at it than Janey. He bought her flowers, they settled down in front of the fire with DVDs – an Alan Rickman for Janey then a Jackie Chan for George, and they shared a nice bottle of sparkly vino, which they drank from long champagne flûtes. Then they went to bed, kissed and cuddled for a bit, and he eagerly fondled her breasts which was great until he said, 'I'm sure these are getting bigger, chuck.' And she froze.

In a brave moment, Elizabeth picked up her mobile, tapped in Dean's number but then clicked it shut again. I can't finish with him on Valentine's night, can I? she thought, although five minutes later she was fast revising her opinion as the late-night unexpected visitor banged on her door. She could have used the excuse that he had not bought her a card to lever him out of her life, not that she wanted one from him for this tired liaison had no truck with romance. She let the staggeringly drunk Dean in out of the cold, furious as much with herself for not ending it yet again, as with him for thinking he could buy a bonk with two cod and a giant carton of peas. She knew also that she was partly misplacing her childish anger at not getting a stupid card from *him*, even though common-sense told her this was a ludicrous line of thinking. 'Grow up, Elizabeth,' she told herself, and put up with the sight of Dean trying to co-ordinate the meal onto two plates, a task he was finding pathetically difficult in his present state. The smell of fish was making her retch; all she could think about was the fish being raw and slimy inside the batter. She got herself a glass of water to combat the nausea and then her brain started to run with thoughts of fish swimming in that very water and doing their business in it. She threw up all over the kitchen floor, right into Dean's smelly trainers. They had a convenient row about that in which he threw them in the bin and stormed out to find a taxi in very evil socks.

Elizabeth would have raised her head and thanked God, had she not had the distinct impression that this

was part of a much bigger joke that He was playing
on her.

Helen spent Valentine's night alone with her huge
bouquet of red roses, a two-litre bottle of diet lemonade
and a Jane Austen DVD because Simon was at a charity
dinner event.

'On Valentine's night? Saturday as well?' she had
cried when he told her where he was going.

'Yes, well, they planned it mainly for couples,' Simon
had explained. 'Trouble is, there will be lots of alcohol
and standing around, and I think it will be too much
for you.'

'But I'm fine,' Helen said, trying to stop looking
green. 'Why didn't you tell me about it sooner?'

'I told you about it weeks ago – you must have
forgotten.'

'Won't you feel a bit odd if everyone's in couples?'

'Of course not. It's a business meeting more than a
social event, as far as I'm concerned.'

'Wouldn't you rather be here with me?' she said,
more tearfully than she intended.

'It's important I'm seen there, Helen, for God's sake
– please understand that. It's just another day unless
you're a love-struck teenager or happen to own a card
shop!' he said wearily, as if she were being totally
unreasonable. He kissed her forehead, though she had
raised her lips to him, then he went off in his tuxedo
and told her not to wait up.

Helen watched him go from the window; she waved
but he was already on his mobile and didn't look back.

Of course he was right. Why did they need cards and romantic meals on Valentine's Day when her tummy was full of the proof of their love? She concluded that she really must try to be a better, less pathetic and more attentive wife.

Chapter 10

First thing on Monday morning, the men arrived to deliver and fit Elizabeth's carpet. They were nice blokes who helped her put the furniture back in its new formation and she slipped them an extra tenner for their trouble because she did not like owing anyone. Then, when they had gone, she collapsed on the bed, fell to sleep for two hours, and dreamed about Sam and Auntie Elsie looking around and admiring what she had done. She woke up with the wonderful sensation of Sam pawing at her face, only to find it was actually Cleef who had come to tell her that she was thirty seconds late with his food. As she was getting out his Whiskas, her eye fell on the large 'P due' on the calendar above the cat-food cupboard. Her period appeared to be over a week late, though usually she was a day or two early. At least it came last month, thank goodness, when she really needed to see the cleansing evidence of blood, although she had noticed it was distinctly on the light side.

She felt slightly sick but slotted a slice of bread in the toaster because her stomach was creaking like an old ship with lack of food. By the time it had popped up out of the toaster, she would have thrown it up, had it so much as touched her lips.

What the hell is up with me? she thought, not even opening her mind to options other than a local virus.

When Barry Parrish rang to tell Janey that they were offering her the job, she would have danced on the desk had her head not been cluttered up with other stuff that needed dealing with first. There would be time for celebrations later. She had gone into Tesco the previous day specifically to get a pregnancy test but chickened out in the end because getting one had somehow made the potential nightmare more of a real possibility. She wandered around the store in a fog with all the other Sunday shoppers and bought fifty pounds' worth of foodstuff she didn't need instead.

Janey rang George on his mobile to tell him the good news about the job and he whooped enough for them both and promised to cook something special for tea from the provisions in the overflowing fridge. Janey did not feel like tea, she felt like staying close to a toilet with something nice and cool on her forehead. She went to Boots in her lunch-hour and picked up a test, stuffing it down into the bottom of her bag as if out of sight equalled out of mind. Then she got off early with a pretend migraine and went round to see Elizabeth, who looked worse than she did.

'So what brings the pleasure of your unexpected company then?' said Elizabeth, forcing herself to sound jolly despite feeling like death warmed up to just below chilled.

'Don't ask,' said Janey, sailing past her into the sunny kitchen and putting her bag down on the little circular dining-table in the middle of it.

'Tea?'

'Got any juice or something? I don't feel like tea or coffee.'

'Yeah, course,' said Elizabeth, going to the fridge for the big carton of cranberry juice. 'This do you?'

'Yes, fine. Are you feeling okay? You're very pale.'

'Bit of a headache,' said Elizabeth, rubbing her forehead. 'Probably paint-induced.'

When she turned around, Janey was looking at something she had taken out of a paper bag.

'What's that?'

'What's it look like?'

Elizabeth took it out of her hand. 'A pregnancy test?'

'Yep.'

'Who's it for?'

'Who do you think? My mam's dog?' said Janey impatiently and downed her juice in one, wishing it were a brandy.

Elizabeth didn't know what face to present as instinct, on this occasion, did not encourage her to say 'Wow!' and dance around singing 'Congratulations,' like they had done for Helen.

'You're not, are you?' she said finally.

'I bloody hope not!'

'Well, what made you buy it then?'

'My boobs are getting bigger and I've been feeling a bit sick. It's just a precaution. I'll do this then I can put it out of my mind. I know I'm not pregnant – I can't be,' Janey said decisively.

They opened up the package; there were two tests in it.

'What do you do with it?' said Elizabeth, noseying over her shoulder.

'I haven't a clue – I'll tell you in a minute,' replied Janey, as she unfolded the leaflet inside. She read the instructions twice aloud to make sure she understood them, then she disappeared up the twisty narrow staircase into the bathroom whilst Elizabeth poured out some more juice. Soon after, Janey came back downstairs holding the pencilly thing as if it was something contaminated with the plague.

'Right. Now, apparently, I wait for three minutes,' said Janey. They sat at the table, propped the test up against the salt pot and watched it, Janey with her hands clasped as if in prayer, just wanting to get this nonsense over with so she could go back to normal life. They waited for hours, or so it felt.

'Does a blue line in that box mean you're pregnant or not pregnant?' Elizabeth said as it materialized slowly in the second box. Janey didn't answer; she was too busy going corpse-white and saying F words, which Janey only ever said in the most extreme of cases.

'I can't understand it,' she kept saying over and over and over. She looked as stunned as if she'd just been hit with a sledgehammer, which metaphorically she had. Elizabeth wafted herself with the instruction leaflet; she was burning up whilst Janey was shivering.

'How? I just don't understand!' said Janey tightly, shaking the indicator as if to make it admit it had made a mistake and erase the blue line. 'We never took chances. Ever.' Then she swore again as her head slumped forward into her hands.

'Do the other test – that one might be faulty,' encouraged Elizabeth.

'What's the point,' said Janey. 'It says they're about three million per cent accurate. It's right, I just feel it. Oh, bloody hell!'

'What will you do?' Elizabeth said eventually, taking her friend's hand and gripping it hard.

'What can I do but have it?' Janey said with an unpleasant laugh. I'm totally trapped, she thought, wishing her conscience about abortion was not so strong. She did not want it but she couldn't *not* have it. There was no way she was capable of killing it, for that's what she would feel she had done if she went for an abortion. George certainly would never forgive her if she were to do that, and she could never keep it secret from him – the one secret she had kept from him was bad enough. How, *how* had this happened? It just did not make sense!

'George will be happy,' Elizabeth said tentatively, because she couldn't tell if Janey was on the brink of going berserk like the Incredible Hulk or about to start sobbing.

She did neither; she just got slowly to her feet, lifted up her bag and her keys and said, 'I best go tell him then, hadn't I?'

'Do you want me to drive you?' Elizabeth said, thinking Janey didn't look fit to drive.

'I'm all right. I just need to be by myself for a while,' Janey said, thinking that Elizabeth didn't look fit to drive her even if she had wanted her to.

'Will you ring me when you get home then?'

'I'll ring twice – don't pick up and don't panic if it's not in the next five minutes. I need to circle the block and think for a bit.'

When it rang almost half an hour later, Elizabeth did not pick up. She was too busy drinking more juice and staring at the second testing kit in the bag on the table.

Janey's house was only a couple of minutes up the road from Elizabeth's, but it took her twenty more to pull up outside the substantial Victorian stone-built town villa with the front aspect overlooking the park. She walked up the path, collected herself and opened the door to the rich aroma of lamb cooking.

'Hello there, Power Lady!' George said, coming out of the kitchen in an apron with inflated pecs and six-pack that Elizabeth had bought him last Christmas. His welcoming smile slid as he studied her sad, pale face. 'Ey, what's up, love? I thought you'd come in bubbling over about your job.'

Janey wanted to be excited about her job, except the job was at the other side of a mountain in her head and she couldn't see it at present.

'I'm pregnant,' she said quietly.

George said nothing because he could not take it

in. He was hearing the words he had most wanted to hear in the world but it took him a while to accept that it was not his ears playing a great big fat trick on him. Then when his brain allowed the information entry, his face did not light up like 300 Bonfire Nights, nor did he leap up in the air or make any strange animal noises. He pulled her quietly towards him and cuddled her gently as if he was thanking her. Then he started crying. Then Janey started crying.

A baby, thought George. My baby. Our baby. He wanted to scream the house down. He wanted to lift Janey in the air and spin her round like couples on the telly did. But her face said it all. George's stomach dropped like a stone and he said to himself, *'What have I done?'*

Elizabeth didn't know how long she stared at that paper bag. All she knew was that it was showing light through the window when Janey had left and it was dark grey outside when she picked it up and took it upstairs into the bathroom. She sat for ages on the stool in the corner before she got a grip on herself. She needed to know if this was why she kept being sick and felt tired and irritable, and why every bra she had made her chest feel sore. Knowing would not change the facts, and at least if it was negative, she could finally and forever bury that night. And if it was positive . . . well, it needed dealing with, but hopefully she wouldn't have to cross that bridge.

Remembering the instructions Janey had read out, she stuck the stick into her stream of urine then she took it downstairs, as Janey had done, and sat on the kitchen chair, staring at it so hard that she thought she had imagined the blue line at first, but she hadn't. It was definitely there, as she knew deep down that it would be.

'*Stupid STUPID bitch that I am!*' she screamed aloud at herself. '*Why didn't I go for the morning-after pill?*'

Her brain mocked her: '*Because it was all over in seconds. Because he didn't come inside you and you can't get pregnant if they don't.*'

How many times had she scoffed at the anonymous women on problem pages for believing they could not get pregnant during periods or if they did it standing up or if a man said he had only put it in an inch?

And then I go and beat them all into second place in the Miss Stupidest Cow World Contest by not sorting this out the morning after when I had the chance, she thought. Why didn't I, just in case? Why didn't I? Why had she – sensible, practical and old-enough-to-know-better Elizabeth Collier – stuffed this problem away like a cat in a box and not expected it to scratch and claw its way out?

This could not be allowed to happen: she couldn't have a baby. She wasn't like the others. Janey would come round to the idea of her pregnancy because her lovely family and in-laws would rally and her life would jiggle about, resettle and adjust. George would put her on a pedestal and bring her cups of tea every five minutes and love her . . . love *them*. But her? People like her shouldn't have babies. People who never learned what proper love is, whose mams buggered off and left them, whose dads took family to mean something different to what it should be. Only people with nice blokes at their side should be looking at that stick watching the blue line come out, then go off snuggling and laughing and discussing names and flicking through the Argos catalogue for ideas as to what they might need. It should not be like this; she had nothing to give a child.

She got the Yellow Pages and looked up *Abortion Advice*, shaking so much she nearly scribbled down the number of the abattoir, which was almost the same thing really. *See Clinics*, the entry said, so she saw *Clinics*, expecting it to say *See Abortion Advice* and land her in one of those circular living-nightmare dreams where you never get a straight answer until it's too late. It didn't though, and there was a number. She took it down. She would ring them in the morning and in a couple of days, it would all be done with. She held tight to that thought and kept it in her sights like a runner keeps the finishing line in his focus and nothing else. Nothing.

George and Janey both took a day's holiday off work and stayed in bed and talked. He looked more radiant than she was supposed to, and somewhere in the middle of all that rabbiting, they made love. On Janey's part, it was not so much desire as diversion; on George's part it was guilt and desperation. There did not seem much point in putting on a condom and their orgasms were a particularly intense escape for both of them.

George stroked her hair afterwards and said, 'It'll all come right in the end, you know,' which is the sort of thing George said and, more often than not, it usually did. Janey doubted it would this time, though. How could they live on his pitiful wage for thumping out bits of plastic moulded on a big machine day in, day out, whilst she was meant to give up the career chance of a lifetime? How could this mess ever 'come right in the end'?

Oh God!

Somehow, Elizabeth got to sleep but she woke up at an unearthly hour and killed time with terrible television programmes until 9 a.m. She telephoned the clinic, made an appointment and then rang around some employment agencies, making arrangements to go and see them early the following week when it was all over, and for good this time. She was totally cool and calm and collected. It was surprisingly easy. So long as she didn't think, it was easy.

Chapter 11

After putting the phone down, Elizabeth badly needed to get away from the house and despite it being a freezing, frosty morning, she grabbed her scarf, gloves, and big coat with the furry trim, and headed for the park. Just along from Janey's house were the first lot of entry gates, but these were locked so she had to walk round to the other set on a road where infinitely more expensive houses than Janey's enjoyed the park view. The grass was iced and crunchy underfoot, cobwebs shivered in the hedges like delicate, intricate necklaces and the air was just what she needed – cold, sharp and cleansing.

She took herself along the path and down the twenty-six 'alphabet' steps to where the old stone lion had lived, before he was vandalized and replaced for the last time. This was her favourite bit of the park where, in summer, great banks of flowers flanked a winding path that led to a large, ornate fountain. It used to have water in it when she was a child and kids would paddle in it, but now it was full of soil and little sprouts of early spring flowers. She walked on past where the birdhouses used to be. They had been shabby pens, as she remembered, and it must have been a boring existence for the little things.

The park café was closed, which was to be expected at this time of morning and of year, although its window in the month for opening had always been the same narrow gap as that for ovulation in the menstrual calendar – and about as difficult to catch, unless you were one of the lucky ones like she obviously was. She had a few nice memories of eating Funny Face ice creams bought from there by her Auntie Elsie as they took Sam for a walk. Elizabeth dropped onto an old damp park bench, the same one they would sit and rest on when they were throwing a ball or stick for him. They always got fed up of the game before he did because he would have let them play that until their arms wore off.

There was a mum pushing a little girl on the baby swings nearby as their old terrier sniffed around tree trunks and overmarked them with his own scent. Elizabeth tried to put herself in the mother's place but she couldn't do it. She could imagine herself on a yacht in the Bahamas, or sitting behind a big executive desk with a power suit on, or holding an art exhibition in a top London gallery, but she couldn't imagine herself pushing *her* baby in *that* swing in *this* park. The dog made her smile a little as he was a sturdy old gent with a serious expression, but she wasn't looking at the woman with a soppy, 'Aw, isn't that sweet?' face. There was no emotional content in the scene for her at all; she was seeing just a woman with just a baby. The little girl was holding her arms out for her mam to lift her out of the basket seat. She was a bonny little thing in her pink furry ensemble but there were no twangs going off in Elizabeth's heart, not even when the little girl started kissing the woman's face. Not one.

Soon, the cold became uncomfortable, even though she was wrapped up like the Michelin Man on a Polar expedition. Her nose felt as if it had been frozen off, and there must have been a small hole in the bottom of her boot as her foot felt damp. She walked around the bowling green and wended her way back to the park exit. She didn't feel any better for the fresh air, but neither did she feel any worse for sitting watching a nice mum-and-daughter thing going on, knowing it would not be her and a kid one day. Indifference was a preferable state.

She planned to stay away from the known world until the end of the week, until her appointment, until it was done. Over the next couple of days, she fobbed both Helen and Janey off with the lie that she had caught a bug and so they must keep away from her in their respective conditions. She told Dean the same. He had a bit of a phobia about vomiting so she laid it on thick about how bad that particular aspect of the virus was, which nicely did the trick.

Intending to keep busy during her self-imposed isolation period, she took out her artbox and sketched a few studies of Cleef, but the pictures were dark and she had him so out of perspective that he did not look like the benign animal that he was. She made him longer and dangerously sleek with predatory eyes, and she hated the look of the cat she had drawn, so she ripped the paper out and put her artbox back into the drawer. It frightened her sometimes, what darkness could conduct itself down her pencils. Instead, she watched crap television and read books and started stencilling a line of roses twisted up with ivy across her new pink bedroom walls whilst trying to ignore the answering machine messages from Janey and Helen saying that they were thinking about her, and that if she wanted anything getting from town shopping-wise, she was to ring them straight away . . .

Two days later, as she pulled off the last stencil, she looked down at the clock on the little table at the side of her bed to check the time. In another twenty-four hours she would be back at home, the mess forgotten and dealt with, and then she could pick her life back up where she had left it at the beginning of the week, thank God. She would ring Janey and Helen and say she felt better and they would have an ordinary chat, about ordinary things – she so craved 'ordinary'.

Elizabeth ran herself a deep bath before bed and lit a cigarette – her first for ages because she had totally lost the taste for them with all the changes that had been going on in her body. She slipped into the perfumed water and propped her book up on the wire frame that rested across the bath and which held her soap and flannel and the hard sandy thing that she used to attack the ruthless advance of cellulite. As she took a long drag of the cigarette, guilt blindsided her, hitting her hard as she imagined *it* drawing the cool smoke into its tiny lungs. She batted the picture away but it came back at her with revenge force.

'Bugger,' she said in defeat, and dipped the lighted end of the cigarette into the bath where it fizzled. She was hardly going to enjoy it with those sorts of images flashing in her head, even if it wasn't a formed thing yet anyway but just an unfeeling mass of cells, something tadpoley that would not even be in there the same time tomorrow. Millions of them were lost or taken out every day; it was no big deal in the great scheme of things. Besides, she was doing it a favour in the end.

The water was so hot it was turning her skin pink. Gin and hot baths – that's what they used to do in the old days, wasn't it? If she lost *it*, that would be perfect – problem solved, end of story. She could forget the whole sorry saga without any residue of guilt from having forced the issue at a clinic.

It was then she saw the red blob bobbing and dipping elusively under the surface of the water and she went rigid; surprisingly, it was fear that gripped her, not relief, when she saw more red blobs dancing with it under the Radox bubbles. It *knew* she didn't want it – it was dying, slipping away from her before it was forcibly removed. *Unloved.* She gulped, then leaned slowly forward, wafting a parting in the suds and cupped her hand under the red clots, delicately draining away the water by slightly opening her fingers. *She should get out of the water. Ring an ambulance.* But she remained, statue-still, looking at the red in her hand. It didn't look like blood at close scrutiny, but what the hell else could it be? It seemed to have some sort of fibres. She poked tentatively at them.

What the . . . ? Not clots, but threads from the new bedroom carpet. Just threads. Her feet must have picked them up when she got undressed in her room.

'You stupid, stupid cow!' She laughed hard at herself as cold relief washed over her. Her bairn wasn't dying. *Her bairn.* She did not want to think of this. *Half mine as well as half his.* Stop – STOP. *More than half, because it was growing in her, feeding off her, living in her.* Her laugh at mistaking threads for a miscarriage grew hard and hysterical, and slid without warning into a sob. A long, shoulder-shaking, snot-making, face-reddening, eye-puckering sob – for suddenly, ridiculously, because of a red carpet, her life had been hijacked and locked onto a different course and there was not a single damned thing she could do about it.

Chapter 12

Dean came round the following night with a bottle of rubbish wine that still had the £1.99 price label on. Elizabeth had not expected him and did not want to see him but now he was here she was determined not to delay the Big Goodbye any longer. He was randy as hell and tried to kiss her on the mouth with yeasty, beery breath. Elizabeth did not kiss. She shook him off three times but he still kept trying it on.

'Gerroff,' she said, pushing him hard but he came back at her as if her reticence was exciting him.

'Why should I? Why don't you want to shag any more?' he said, trying to kiss her neck and squeeze at her breasts.

'Because I just don't.'

'That's not an answer.'

'Okay, try this one then – *Because I'm pregnant, that's why!*'

She hadn't meant to blurt it out like that, she just wanted him to stop. Stop he most certainly did. In fact, what she said sobered him up enough to drive a Sherman tank along a tightrope.

'Jesus H Christ,' he said, his face blanched with shock.

He slumped on her sofa and started scratching his head through his number three haircut.

'What are you going to do about it?' he said eventually.

'I'm keeping it,' she said, and her hand unconsciously curled round over her stomach as she heard her intentions aloud for the first time.

'Jesus H Christ,' he said again.

Words were gravitating to his head at an alarming pace: paternity, maintenance, CSA . . . Elizabeth just wished he would go; she did not want to see him again.

'I don't want it,' he said, almost apologizing.

Elizabeth's eyes rounded in shock. Stupidly, it hadn't occurred to her that he might think it was his. She nearly laughed; the idea of having his baby was almost worse than the reality of having this one.

'"I don't want it"?' she quoted him in disbelief. 'It's not yours to want!'

'Eh?' he said.

'I said it's not yours.'

'Not mine?' He got to his feet. 'What do you mean, it's not mine?'

'I mean you're safe. As in, "Who's the daddy?" You aren't!'

He didn't want to be the daddy, but his testosterone levels reacted to this information with affront rather than relief.

'Not mine? It's not mine? Well, whose bloody sprog is it then?'

'Dean, just go,' she said, walking to the door to open it for him, but he gripped her arm and pulled her back roughly.

'All this time you've been making me shove a johnny on and you've been shagging somebody else without one? You . . .' He pulled his other hand back and it hovered trembling in the air.

'Don't you dare EVER try and hit me,' said Elizabeth, with a force behind it that made her shake as she delivered it. He shoved her back against the wall instead of hitting her and snapped open one of the plastic carrier bags she kept stored behind the kitchen door.

'You fucking slag,' he said.

Her heart was booming and her hands moved to cover up her stomach as if to shield the baby's ears from the shower of expletives he rained on her as he loaded up several carriers with his detritus: trainers, socks, his CDs that were spread all over the downstairs, all the while working his way through the Roget's *Thesaurus* entry for 'whore'.

'Here, you can keep the Supertramp,' he said, throwing the CD case at her.

The plastic corner of it caught the bone above her eye and she yelped in pain. By the time her hand had come to it to check for blood, it had already started to swell up to a small egg. Then something spiralled up inside her and she launched herself at him, tiny as she was. *No one hits me in this house.* In her Auntie Elsie's house, she was safe, always had been and always would be.

He was quite a bit heavier than she was, but he was half-drunk and she had the advantage of surprise. She pushed him out onto the street, and the force of it propelled him forward right across to the houses at the other side, where he tripped and fell over the corsey edge, which bought her extra time to throw out his carrier bags after him and deadlock that big strong door behind her before he had the chance to get up. She heard him chuntering on outside for a bit, for the benefit of the neighbours, but he couldn't touch her behind the door that had kept her safe from the evils of the world that lay outside it for twenty odd years. She would not let it in again.

She stood there, eye throbbing, lungs panting, as if she'd run a marathon, when he started banging on the door, those same chaotic feelings coursing through her as they were on that day long ago, when she ran away from home to her Auntie Elsie. Auntie Elsie, who had her every Tuesday for tea and gave her boiled ham and over-diluted orange juice and was strict and stern and was always telling her off about her manners and who told her to sit up straight and to pull her socks up. Auntie Elsie, whom she only visited because she had a huge Alsatian that was as soft as a black sheep. Auntie Elsie, whom she hated. Auntie Elsie, at whom she screamed that day to lock the big door behind her as she crawled into the dog-basket with Sam. To keep her dad away from her.

All three women sat in Janey's big spacious farmhouse kitchen with a Saturday-morning fruit tea and biscuit untouched on the table in front of them. All three of them pregnant. Janey's mouth was open more than Helen's was at the news Elizabeth had just delivered, but only just.

After all these years and all those men, the daft cow gets caught on now, Janey was thinking, her head unconsciously moving from side to side. At this age, and her with no job, and no man.

Helen said nothing; she just sat there stunned into silence.

'I'm keeping it, before you ask,' Elizabeth said.

'Oh, Elizabeth, have you thought this through?' said Helen.

'Just a bit,' said Elizabeth with a hard laugh. 'I thought about . . . getting shut, even booked an appointment, but I couldn't do it in the end.'

The inevitable question came from Janey.

'What about that Dean? What's he said?'

'It's not Dean's.'

'Eh?'

'Pardon?'

'You don't know the bloke,' Elizabeth said, heading off the questions before the big flow started. 'I was supposed to meet Dean at that party at New Year,' she went on, not looking directly at either of them. 'He didn't turn up and I was angry and drank too much and things just went too far with someone. I'm not proud of it, but it happened and I don't really want to talk about it because it's done now. I can't even remember what he looks like, and he was from some-where down south anyway so there's not much chance of tracing him even if there was any point in me doing that, which there isn't. Okay?'

She exhaled and it felt like an extra big full stop on the speech. Janey nodded although something about the story didn't fit but she said no more then because Elizabeth looked so little and pale and she noticed that her friend's eye was swollen and purple, when she nudged her long fringe out of her eyes.

'What happened to your eye?'

'Oh, er . . . Dean threw his Supertramp CD at me,' she said, half-laughing. 'It was an accident.'

'Eh? How can it be an accident if he threw it at you?' Janey said, puffing up with anger on her friend's behalf.

'He threw it at me intending to miss. I think,' Elizabeth said.

'Bastard!' said Janey.

'I never liked him!' said Helen.

'Neither did I,' said Elizabeth.

'So why on earth didn't you tell him to bugger off before now?'

'I dunno. You know how thick I am where blokes are concerned.'

The other two did not need to acknowledge that. For an intelligent woman, Elizabeth would have failed her Key Stage One in Men.

'He's gone now though,' Elizabeth added.

'Good riddance. I never liked him either,' said Janey.

'You never liked any of the fellas I went with.'

'I liked one of them,' said Janey. Elizabeth didn't need to ask her which one that was. 'Are you *sure* it isn't that Dean's?'

'One hundred per cent positive.'

'Well! I don't know what to say, which is a first,' said Janey, shaking her head.

'Look, Janey, it was a horrible, stupid accident. I didn't for one minute think I could have got pregnant, otherwise I'd have gone for the morning-after pill. I can't understand it – I didn't even miss my period last month,' said Elizabeth.

'What? You had a full period?'

'Well, looking back it was a lot lighter than usual.'

'It was probably just your body letting go of some old blood,' said Helen.

Janey was less intellectual and groaned, 'Oh, you stupid daft cow! Well, at least that explains why you were so agitated and told old Laurence to stick his job; your hormones must have been all to cock.' She sounded cross and exasperated but bounced over and gave Elizabeth a hug, even though her friend didn't want one and pulled back in that 'gerroff' way of hers.

'How will you manage?' Janey went on.

'I don't know, I just will,' Elizabeth said. 'If sixteen-year-olds on the dole with rent to pay manage, then I'm bloody sure I will.'

'Yes, if anyone can, you can,' said Helen, with a wide, supportive smile.

'Yes, well, that's not in question,' said Janey, who had always felt sorry for Elizabeth being left alone at eighteen whilst she'd had a full complement of lovely family members looking out for her.

'I've managed so far by myself,' said Elizabeth.

'And us two will be here for you, won't we?' Janey

said to Helen, who nodded her agreement and smiled, with a friendly sort of envy at her tall red-haired friend.

Janey was already filling out, her chest bumping out of her blouse, her cheeks pink and glowing like a country maid's. In stark contrast, Helen was pale and drawn; she had lost weight and her breasts looked smaller, if anything. Her hair was lank, even though she had only washed it the previous night, and her face was dotted with pimples – retribution, she supposed, for having such beautifully clear skin all the way through her teenage years. She didn't care though, for when Simon was moody and quiet or interrogating her about what she had eaten and how much she weighed, she would curl up with her Miriam Stoppard book and read how her baby was growing every day, even if those days were full of bleeding gums and nausea and spots and grease. Each one brought her closer to her baby being born, and that thought alone could make her cope with anything. Except that it made her miss her father, more than ever.

'What do I do first then?' asked Elizabeth, over more tea. 'Do I have to ring the doctors?'

'Yes,' Janey and Helen said together.

'You'll start antenatal classes straight away, I would have thought, and the midwife will tell you all about which benefits you'll be due—' Helen continued before she was rudely interrupted.

'Benefits my backside! I'll be up and working as soon as I can,' said Elizabeth indignantly. 'I'm not sitting on my arse sponging off the state and watching flaming *Trisha*. I'm off to see some agencies on Monday in Leeds.'

However much of a mess the rest of her life was, at least there would be no complications in getting a job for a hardworking woman with experience. Or so, in her naivety, she thought.

Chapter 13

During the large family celebratory meal they held for her, Janey smiled for everyone's benefit and tried to be happy about being pregnant, really she did. She forced thoughts to the forefront of her mind of how much George had wanted this to happen and how fate had eventually intervened and made it so. Everyone was thrilled about it – her mum and dad were over the moon, so were her in-laws Joyce and Cyril, who were never away from the house with either fruit, knitting patterns or pans full of homemade soups and stews to keep up her strength. At the rate they were fortifying her, she could have gone for a WWF title by the end of her first trimester. She knew she should be adoring this attention and revelling in the fact that her husband was treating her even more like a queen than he usually did, but all she wanted to do was sit and cry. It was nothing to do with her hormones, but plain and simple resentment that in fulfilling everyone else's dream, she was losing grip of her own. The guilt she carried for feeling like that told her she must truly be a selfish, self-centred bitch, which only fuelled the tears more.

Elizabeth set off early on the Monday morning, parked her bright yellow Old Faithful at the train station, and headed off for the familiarity of Leeds with the company of a glossy mag and a bag of Midget Gems. It felt good to be back in the echoey city train station, even if it was the usual three-mile hike to the ticket barriers. She loved the buzz of Leeds with its beautiful old architecture, impressive new architecture, big bookshops, old-fashioned arcades, large hip designer houses and tiny Jewish jeweller shops happily cohabiting in the bustling centre. For once, she enjoyed taking things at a slower pace and dodging the rush of executives locked on course for their offices. She had plenty of time to kill before her first appointment and called into a small Italian coffee-shop for a minty coffee whirled with cream, which was more like a pudding, and a toasted, heavily buttered ciabatta. Out of the window, she watched the world of power suits and laptop cases go by without her.

The door to Golden Door Recruitment was old, peeling and a very ill shade of brown, and was squeezed in between a large card shop and a downmarket men's clothes store. The office itself was at the top of three flights of stairs, which Elizabeth climbed to find a surprisingly large, but empty, reception area at the top. Distressed wooden furniture, bald rugs and once-trendy PVC chairs spewing yellow foam from various splits had been placed there to create an ambience of shabby-chic, alas achieving all of the former and none of the latter.

Elizabeth allowed herself to be greeted and seated

by a woman sporting shoulder-pads sized somewhere in between Joan Crawford's and a Chicago Bear's, and was given a form to complete with all her personal details whilst she waited until 'Frances', who was running late, could see her. It would only take a few minutes, Joan Bear said, returning to her desk where she tapped efficiently away at a keyboard, leaving Elizabeth scribbling on top of a badly polished glass table patterned with dried-up coffee mug rings.

A good half an hour and a selection of thrilling magazine articles such as *We only had three teeth between us, but we fell in love* later, just when Elizabeth was about to lose the will to live, Frances emerged from the office with her name on it, smiling and pouring apologies. She looked about twelve and as if she had been at her mother's make-up bag. Underneath the three-inch thickness of her Judith Chalmers shade of foundation, the weaselly arrogant look was more than reminiscent of Julia, and a sparking current of instant dislike arced between them. Frances showed Elizabeth into a well-equipped hi-tech office, took her place behind a computer-topped desk and drank the remnants of her coffee before making a three-minute intense study of Elizabeth's 'résumé', not that it said all that much.

'Ah, you've just worked at the one place, that's fantastic. Why's that?'

'I liked it,' said Elizabeth, which she did until Eyebrow Man and Bow-Legged Troll came along.

'So what made you leave then?'

'I felt it was finally time for a change.'

'After twenty-two years? Interesting!' Frances said, in a *Yeah right!* tone of voice. She studied her client for a hard few seconds, referred to the sheet again and said, 'What was your leaving salary again?'

'Nineteen thousand, two hundred.'

'Oh!' Which was obviously Frances talk for, 'You'll be lucky to match that'. 'And are you looking for temporary or permanent work?'

'Either, but I'll mention it anyway: I'm pregnant.'

'Oh!' Frances sighed as in 'Dear, dear me'. 'Well, let's have a look anyway. You never know.' She pressed a few buttons on her computer and looked hard into the screen, muttering away absently.

'Data-inputter, shiftwork, eleven thousand five hundred, suit school leaver . . . oh, maybe not . . . ha ha – administrator for busy office, blah blah . . . seven thirty to six but you do finish at half past three on a Friday. Oh, sorry, that's in York. Where do you live again? Bradford, was it? Sorry, Barnsley . . . fantastic. Here's one – Halifax, wages clerk. Did you say you did wages? Fifteen thousand with BUPA pro rata . . . oh no, they're looking for someone with SAGE. Let's see Temporary . . . Here we are . . . *flick, flick* . . . oh maybe not. No . . . no . . .'

The phone rang. Frances picked it up. 'Hello? Yes . . . yes . . . Oh, she'll have to wait . . . Well, it's not my fault she got sacked, is it, so fob her off till the morning. Tell her we'll get back to her . . . Yeah, I am with someone . . . Okay. *Ciao.*' She tutted. 'Some people!' she said, with an impatient click of her tongue. 'Now, where's my pen? Oh God, where have I put it? Oh, what am I?'

'*A gormless bimbo?*' Elizabeth answered to herself. She would have laughed but it would have made a very hollow sound. This was useless; she felt it in the pit of her stomach like a big heavy ball. This was not going to be as easy as she had thought; the market seemed geared for youth and blank canvas rather than age and experience.

'I'm sure there'll be something, eventually,' said Frances in a tone that doubted it very much. 'What was your typing speed again?' she asked, but Elizabeth could have sworn she wasn't really listening.

'Seven hundred words per minute,' she tested her. She was past caring.

'Mmmm. Fantastic.' Frances was staring hard at the screen. She could have been playing *Grand Theft Auto* for all Elizabeth knew.

'And what qualifications did you say you had again?'

'Fifteen O levels, seven A levels and a degree in Japanese.'

'Ooh now, Japanese is very business commercial. I think if you leave it with us we will sort you out in no time.'

Christ, get me out of here!

As if Frances read her thoughts, she stood, swept her eyes curiously down to her client's midriff and held out her hand to give a very thin, limp handshake that gave Elizabeth the shivers.

'Well, it's been fantastic to meet you, Lizzie . . .'

Elizabeth bristled. She hated anyone calling her that, although the diminutive version of Frances's name – Fanny – seemed to fit her well enough.

'. . . Here's my card and don't you worry, we'll be in touch as soon as we can. All right?'

'Fantastic,' said Elizabeth, stretching her mouth into a long line of rictus insincerity. By the time she had reached the dysentery-brown door, Frances's business card was an eighty-one-piece jigsaw.

Outside, the clouds were casting an ominous grey light over everything and the sky looked as depressed as Elizabeth felt. In the city she knew so well, she suddenly felt lost, vulnerable, almost agoraphobic as the space seemed thick and oppressive. A wave of nausea engulfed her at the same time as a ravenously hungry sensation, and she could not tell if it was baby or anxiety. What she did know for definite was that she just could not face traipsing off to Branways Office Temps and Angels of the North, repeating this hopeless rigmarole; not today anyway. She was on the scrapheap at thirty-eight and now she just wanted some magic to teleport her home to find herself in front of the fire, with a packet of Gypsy Creams, some bilberry tea and Cleef curled up on her knee. If she hurried, she could catch the next train back, pick up the car from the car park and be at home in an hour. A big soggy snowflake landing squarely on her nose confirmed that this was the most sensible thing to do, so she headed back to the train station sharpish.

She boarded the busy train and moved down in search of a seat, although all three carriages were full, so she paused by a young man whose haversack was planted on the window seat next to him. Any other time she would have had no hesitation in asking him to shift it, and a few years ago she would have rammed it up his backside for daring to be so bloody rude when people were standing. She was tired and weak, though, and not up for a fight, and she just wanted someone to notice that she was pregnant and needed a seat, but unless they had X-ray specs, that was going to be a no-no. She thought she had cracked it when the bloke behind her politely asked Haversack Man to move it, but only so he could slide his own carcass onto the seat. Chivalry was dead, it was official, and she was forced to stand in stiff and stoic British silence for twenty minutes before collapsing wearily into a vacant seat for the last ten.

When she got off the train at Barnsley, it was like walking into a snow globe. Fat flakes were coming dizzily down and she huddled into the little warmth her entirely weather-inappropriate suity-type jacket offered. She dashed across the road to the car park to where her bright yellow car, customized with the outline of a big pink flower painted over the back, was waiting for her. Quickly opening up the door, she climbed gratefully inside and stuck the key in the ignition. The engine turned over, shuddered a bit and then died. The second turn resulted in a cough and a click and nothing else. Elizabeth had that cold sweaty panicking thing that reduces one to 'What do I do? I know nothing about cars!' level, and then she noticed that the button for her lights was turned to 'on'. She had never, *ever* left her lights on before.

'Please, not today of all days!' she cried mournfully aloud to herself.

She ferreted through her bag for her AA card, only to remember that she had left it in her 'ordinary' bag, as opposed to this 'smart interview' one, along with her mobile phone apparently. She sat back, her numb hands on the steering wheel, feeling hopeless, hope-less, tired, pathetic and angry at her own stupidity. *Stupid, dozy, stupid, stupid hormones!* She was never disorganized, never forgot anything. *Is this what pregnancy hormones made you into – a stupid, pathetic, stupid jelly?*

She hadn't cried in years and suddenly here she was, starting to blub yet again, the rate of tears accelerating as she watched the snow fill up the windscreen, making her feel like she was being buried alive. Then a thought hopped into her mind, to kick her whilst she was down, that there was no one at home to say, 'Where's Elizabeth? She should be home by now. I'm getting worried so I think I'll go out looking for her.' No one. How long could she sit there before someone came for her, she wondered. Cleef wouldn't even miss her, only his tea. He was a cat and would just go and find another house and be as fed and as warm and not give her a second thought, just like he had not given Helen a second thought when she had given him away.

Elizabeth did not have a job, she had bog-all prospects of getting another one, and inside her was growing an alien that she could not find it in herself to get rid of, but did not really want. She twisted the key again and again and again in an angry frenzy.

'Start, you bastard thing!' she cried, and when that didn't work, 'Please, nice car, start for me, *pleeeease . . .*'

Then someone knocked on her window and opened her car door.

'You okay?'

It was *him*. John Silkstone. He had turned up like Clint Eastwood did when a town was in trouble. Thinking back, he always had been the human equivalent of a Swiss Army knife.

'Won't it start?' he asked.

Her throat was too constricted to answer. She just shook her head and stared at him with huge, watery, grey eyes. She felt the indignity of her situation deeply. She had seen him twice in seven years – once dressed like a tramp, and now trying to drown a steering wheel with a good eye and a black one. He was the only one who had ever seen her cry.

'I don't know! Come on!' he urged.

'No, it's all right. I can manage.' Why on earth did I say that? she thought, when it was blatantly obvious that she couldn't. Not that he was having any of it, anyway.

'You don't change, do you, Independent Mary? Come on, shift yourself!'

He pulled her out of the car by her sleeve and led her unresisting, like a child, to a Land Rover nearby with an engine purring, as hers should have been. Then again, he wasn't a dozy pregnant beggar who left his lights on. He stripped off his coat behind her and plonked it on her shoulders and she almost buckled under the weight of it.

'Good job you're still driving the same car, isn't it?' he said. 'I knew that daft pink flower would come in handy one day – remember?'

She remembered. He had been with her when she had bought it at the garage. She had taken him along to suss it out because she had trusted him in all things. She had fallen in love with the crazy Battenburg colours and he'd laughed and said, 'Trust a woman! But at least you'll be easy to spot in a crowd!' Then he had disappeared inside to press buttons and levers and rev up the engine and then get underneath to inspect the chassis.

'Here, give us your keys and get in.'

She opened her mouth to say something brave but her weary body overrode it and, instead, she climbed into his passenger seat to find the heater was on full blast and it was lovely and cosy. The radio was on but the wipers were not and the snow-rain slashing against the windows gave only a blurred image of what was going on across the car park. The tears popping out of her eyes did not help; it appeared there was a washer off in her ducts.

Minutes later, the driver's door opened, letting in a fearsome reminder of the freezing outside world, and big John Silkstone in a thick checked lumberjack shirt clambered in and blew some life back into his hands.

'No, your car won't start,' he said, his black hair glittering with melting snowflakes. 'What did you do? Leave your lights on or something?'

'Yeah,' she said, waiting for the 'women drivers' tirade to start. Not that he was ever like that.

'You picked a good day to do that. It's a nasty one, all right.' He clipped in his seat-belt, slipped off the handbrake and started driving.

Silence reigned, unless you counted 'Una Paloma Blanca' playing out from Radio Sheffield.

'Shopping, were you?' John asked at the traffic-lights.

'Went to Leeds,' she said, slipping into monosyllabic mode.

'I saw you coming off the train when I pulled in to get a newspaper from the shop. You know, the one in the bus station.'

'Yes, I do know where the paper shop is,' she said. It was the one she had stood shivering outside all those years ago, waiting for some bloke wearing a flower to take her out for a drink, although she didn't remind him of that.

'Didn't buy much in Leeds, did you?' he said, noting the distinct lack of carrier bags.

'No,' she answered flatly.

'You banged your eye?'

'Yes,' she said, self-consciously pulling her fringe down over it. She had put three pounds of thick make-up on the bruising, but it must have started wearing off. God, she must look a sight!

'Nobody banged it for you, I hope,' he said, his voice tight.

'Don't be daft. I had an argument with a cupboard door.'

The wipers had to go full pelt to shift the snow. She snuggled down into his coat and caught a cocktail of old, shockingly familiar scents: leather and the bottom notes of aftershave and building sites and aromas that had no names but were just *him*.

'I don't know, I've only seen you twice since I came

back and you were skiving off work both days,' he said.

'I decided to change my job,' she said, stiffly and with all defence mechanisms fully activated. 'I went into Leeds hoping to find another.'

'Any luck?' he asked.

'No,' she said, and then the tears started leaking out again, much to her annoyance.

She saw him looking at her out of the corner of his eye but she kept staring straight ahead at the road and the weather. He did not say anything else until he pulled up in front of her house, which was just as well as any sympathy would have dissolved the dam wall holding the motherlode of those tears back.

'Well, thanks for the lift and could I have my keys, please,' she said, slipping out of his coat and handing it back.

'I'll hang onto them and get your car started for you. I told the car-park bloke I'd be back later so you don't have to worry about getting clamped either.'

'You really don't have to bother. I've got AA cover,' she said haughtily, hating herself for being so improperly independent sometimes.

'Oh, Elizabeth, bugger off inside your house and get warm,' he said and leaned right over her. Her heart boo-boomed because for a moment there she thought he was going to kiss her, but it was just to open the door.

'Sorry, there's a knack to this handle,' he explained. 'Your car might take me a couple of days to sort out. I'll try and have it back for Thursday for you.'

'Thank you,' she said with a reticence that suggested he might be doing her a disservice rather than a favour, then she got out of the car. He pipped goodbye on the horn and she gave him the briefest of waves before going into the house, deliberately not giving him a backward glance.

What *was* it about that man that always made her feel so angry and mixed-up and confused, when all he had ever done wrong was love her?

Chapter 14

Elizabeth hopped from foot to foot, partly from the cold, partly from nerves. She'd never been on a blind date before and, at twenty-four, she would not have been on that one either but for the begging and pleading of Janey to make up a foursome with George Hobson, who had asked her out in the pub the previous week. She was too nervous to go by herself and so, in her eyes, there was only one solution – a double date.

'Please – I'll owe you favours for the rest of your life,' she had said, crawling after Elizabeth on her mam and dad's front-room carpet.

'No chance!' said Elizabeth, shaking her away. 'Absolutely none. Wild horses wouldn't drag me.'

So there they were then, waiting outside the newspaper shop in the bus station whilst Janey chewed on her nails and felt delightfully on edge, and Elizabeth just longed for the whole ordeal to be over. She stomped some warmth back into her feet. George and friend were late; with any luck they'd stood them up.

'What do they look like again?' Elizabeth asked, breathing a huge sigh of relief as two beanpoles with spots came up to them, gave them the once-over and then walked on.

'George is quite tall, just normal brown hair, and I don't know about John.'

'Oh well, that should make them easy to spot then,' Elizabeth huffed. She was hating this idea more and more by the second.

'Oh – and they said they'd be wearing flowers so we could recognize them.'

Great, thought Elizabeth. Details like that made it very hard not to run off there and then.

It was at that moment that the Millhouse bus pulled in and amongst the alighting stream were two very tall men with four-foot-long plastic sunflowers pinned to the front of their clothes. One was plumpish, grinning and rosy-cheeked, like a young cleanshaven Father Christmas. The other was black-haired, unsmiling, dressed entirely in black leather – cowboy hat to boots – with a stupid pencil-thin moustache underlining his nose as if it was important. The Good, the Bad and the Ugly theme tune welled up inside Elizabeth's head as he slowly walked towards them, thankfully devoid of spurs. She blinked and rubbed her eyes, but alas he was still there.

'Chuffing hell,' she said to the beaming Janey. 'Please don't tell me Lee Van Cleef is mine!'

Chapter 15

George knew exactly where to find Father McBride on a Thursday lunchtime. He nipped out of work and crossed the road to the George and Dragon pub and there, in the warm corner seat by the fake log fire, with a cigarette, looking at the horseracing and sipping from a half, was the old priest. He had led the services in church when George was a lad. He was a tough Glaswegian who had travelled the world, a good bloke who had taken up the cloak to wear with pride, not to hide behind it.

'Father, can I have a quick word?' said George tentatively.

Father McBride scrutinized him through his little rectangular spectacles. 'I know you, don't I?' he said, giving him the once-over.

'I doubt you'd recognize me,' said George. 'It's been well over twenty-five years since my last Confession.'

'What kept you?' said Father McBride gruffly, but his eyes twinkled as he folded up his newspaper and indicated for George to sit down. 'Is this an informal chat or should we be in the confessional?' he said.

'Probably,' said George, 'but I'm on my lunch and

if I don't talk to you now I'll go mad and probably do something stupid that'll break up my marriage.'

William McBride took a slow sip of his beer and sat forward. 'Go on,' he said.

'My wife's pregnant with our only bairn and it's my fault.'

'I should hope so,' he replied. 'And the problem is . . . ?'

'She didn't want bairns, but I did. So . . .' George stopped.

'So . . .' the old priest coaxed eventually.

'I poked holes in our condoms.' George cringed. It sounded worse out than it felt in.

Father McBride did not flinch when he heard the word 'condoms'. He had been around and he knew people were not saints, and a lapsed Catholic was better than no Catholic at all, he reckoned silently. Had he been Pope, he would have been more lenient on the use of contraceptives, for he had seen too many unwanted babies born in the world, sick and diseased, their mothers unable to cope.

'This is really one for the confessional,' he said, starting to get up. 'Look, come back with me now and—'

'Please, Father McBride – please,' said George, and something in his voice made the old priest throw up his hands and sit back down again.

'An informal chat it is then.'

'Should I tell her what I've done, Father?' said George.

'You know your wife better than I do. Do *you* think you should?'

'I think if I told her, my marriage would be over and my baby would be born into a big mess, that's what I think.'

'Is it a good marriage you have?'

'It's the best,' said George, almost in tears. 'I'm so sorry, I'd never thought any of it through and she won't stop crying. I feel like I've ruined her life. Every time I see her I want to say I'm sorry.'

'Well, when anyone who isn't God tries to play God there's usually a fair amount of damage,' said Father McBride.

George wished the priest would give him a good kicking. It would hurt less than his words. He was right though; he had taken Janey's free will and controlled her. He *had* played God.

'What a mess I've made,' he said. 'I just wish it would all go away.'

'You're not telling me you'd get rid of this baby, are ye?' said the old priest.

'No, no, that's not something we'd do,' said George, looking horrified. 'I just meant, I wish I could turn the clock back.'

'Well, time travel, alas, isn't an option, son.'

'I'm so sorry, so very very sorry.'

Father McBride had another couple of sips from his drink whilst he thought.

'Are you really fully repentant?'

'I am, Father.'

'Will you be there for this family that you wanted so much? Will you bend over backwards for them, keep them and love them?'

'You've no idea how much. Oh Father, what do you think I should I do?'

'I don't feel it's up to me to decide that for you. What do *you* think would be the right thing to do for you and your wife?'

For once George didn't need to ponder, for now the answer seemed blatantly obvious. He knew the burden of this truth should be on his shoulders alone, that it was up to him to carry it, no one else.

'I don't think confessing to her will help anything but my conscience.'

'I think confessing all to God might help you. Properly – in church.'

'I will, Father.' He would too. He needed God on his side to help him and keep him strong enough not to open his big gob to Janey about the horrible thing he had done to her.

'And I hope to have the pleasure of seeing the wee chappy in church one day. With his *family*,' Father McBride added, with a fair bit of weight behind it.

'Thank you, Father McBride. I will. And I'll be there for 'em always.'

'George . . . George Hobson, are ye not? You were my altar boy once. Nice singing voice, if I remember rightly.'

'You remember?' said George, feeling honoured to have stayed in the mind of this good man. 'That's me, Father. I can't thank you enough for listening, helping.'

'I'll pray for you, George Hobson, and your family.'

'Thank you, Father. Can I get you a pint?'

'No, I just have a very slow half these days,' Father McBride replied. 'I don't want to be showing myself up like Father Jack in this corner, now do I? God bless you, my son. A packet of cheese and onion wouldn't go amiss, mind.'

George got him his crisps and a half in for the next week anyway and went back to work with the snow pelting down on him, although he was thinking too hard to feel the wet of it. He continued to think things through for the rest of the afternoon, slowly but surely, as was George's way, and by the time he handed over his machine to the night shift, he thought he just might have worked out how to make some of this right for Janey.

Elizabeth was booked in for her first antenatal at the surgery, although she did not see her crusty old Irish doctor but a midwife called Sue Chimes. She was weighed and consequently discovered that she had put nearly half a stone on already, although how, with all this vomiting and only a two-inch baby twizzling about inside her, she didn't know. Most of the weight increase could have been explained by her chest, she supposed, for she seemed to have developed 'six boob' syndrome. Her nice normal bra that usually covered everything adequately now had two extra boobs popping out of the top and a pair pushed sideways under her arms. She looked like a 'Ye Olde Tavern' bar wench when she was stripped off.

She got forms for free prescriptions and dental treatment, and vouchers in a blue folder labelled

Primigravida, which she remembered meant 'first pregnancy' from her old Latin lessons, and she and the
midwife together filled in a booklet with all her details.
Apparently, she was ten and a half weeks' pregnant,
which sounded quite a lot. Had she been taking folic
acid? asked Sue, and explained that it greatly reduced
the chance of having a baby born with spina bifida.
Elizabeth had her multivitamins in her bag, which she
had taken consistently for years, and checked quickly
to find that she was stoked up with the magic ingredient, albeit unwittingly.

When they got to the father question, Elizabeth
expected the midwife to look at her with disapproval
when she said, 'He's not around,' but she didn't.

Sue Chimes just wrote *not involved* on her notes,
gave her a kind, supportive smile, and said, 'Doing this
on your own is very hard. I hope you've got a good
support network?'

'Aye,' she lied, although it was not really a full lie
because Hels and Janey were in the same boat so she
supposed she wasn't entirely on her tod.

Sue sent Elizabeth off with a small bottle to fill
with urine, then she tested it, recorded her findings
and strapped a freezing blood-pressure wrap around
Elizabeth's arm, inflating it until she thought her arm
was going to burst open.

'Lovely,' Sue said, writing down the result. 'Nice and
steady. Now you keep that up!'

'I'll try,' Elizabeth joked, and they laughed gently
together.

Sue then told her all the things that were probably

starting, or would start, to happen to her and how she could combat them – headaches, cramps, hormonal weeping, tantrum fits, constipation, tiredness, nausea, increase in mucus production, more frequent bladder emptying, bleeding gums . . . the list went on and on. Then she gave Elizabeth an empty sample bottle for next time and a handful of pamphlets to read through.

'There's a lot to take in, but don't be scared,' said Sue Chimes, squeezing her hand and giving her a big smile, but Elizabeth came out of the surgery in a daze. It suddenly felt very real and she was lump-hammered by the enormity of it all. She was just about coping with what was happening to her now; she had not even started thinking ahead. If she did, she might just run off, except the thing making her run off would have come with her, because it was inside her. She did not hate it, she was more afraid of it than anything. She had never had anything to do with babies ever, never even held one, and now she would have the responsibility of one for the rest of her life.

She suddenly wondered if Bev had kept hers.

Helen woke up crying, following a bad dream in which her baby was really ugly and handicapped and would never grow up. Simon impatiently snapped out a man-size tissue from the box on his bedside cabinet for her and told her to pull herself together. He made her feel as if she had just acquired an unsuitable toy that was interfering with his life, which in a way it was. His back in bed was a cold punishment for having to pull out of the dinner date with his boss because she felt so drained and sick.

He had stomped off alone and blanked her when he came home to find her sitting up waiting for him in their long white dining room. She was reading her Miriam Stoppard book at the table with a cup of peppermint tea and a couple of Digestive biscuits on a saucer. He took one look at her and laughed in an 'I don't believe it' sort of way.

'If you were well enough to wait up for me, then you were surely well enough to support me at dinner with Jeremy and Fen,' he said, jabbing a finger in the direction of a half-eaten biscuit, 'and I thought you said you couldn't eat anything?'

'This is the only thing I've eaten all day!' she protested, but it was obvious that he thought she was lying.

Helen could not even say, 'Sushi,' at the moment, never mind dine out on it, and the doctor had told her to take things easy as her blood pressure was a little high. None of this was judged to be as important as diverting some wife so their husbands could talk business, apparently. Simon then accused her of milking her situation for sympathy whilst he took off his tie and threw it over the chair. She watched him, remembering the night she had conceived, when he had stripped off his tie and by the time it had reached the floor, she was in his arms, preparing to seduce him. They had not made love since then and, despite the sickness, she wanted – *needed* – him to touch her so much, to run his hands over her rounding stomach and feel their baby growing.

'The baby, the baby,' he mocked. 'That's all you ever say these days. Look – you're even reading about it again! You really are becoming a huge baby bore!' Then he announced that he was going to bed and flicked off the light behind him, leaving her to cry alone in the cold dark dining room, before she made her way across the hallway to the even colder, darker bedroom.

The table was set when Janey got home, but with candles and the best tablecloth and a small Christmas tree (a last-minute decorative addition). There was chicken in white wine, grapes, and potatoes in their skins bubbling away in the kitchen, mixed vegetables boiling in a homemade stock for extra taste, and a cool bottle of non-alcoholic wine stood uncorked on the table. George was waiting, like a patient butler, to hand Janey a glass of it when she came downstairs from changing out of her suit. The house looked even more shiny than normal.

'You were born with a pinny on you, George,' she often joked. Not that he was a wimp; he once floored a bloke for being horrible to Elizabeth in the pub when they were courting with a right hook that Tyson would have been proud of. John had been in the toilet at the time, which was lucky for the remainder of the bloke's neck. She hadn't told George that Dean Crawshaw had given Elizabeth a black eye because she knew he would have thrown his coat on and gone straight out to the Victoria to give him a taste of his own medicine without a second thought, and Elizabeth wouldn't have wanted that. Just because his heart was soft didn't mean the rest of him was.

'Hiya, love, had a good day?' he said, suddenly noticing how drawn she looked. 'Not feeling sick, are you, sweetheart?'

She plastered a smile on the outside for his benefit, even though she wasn't smiling inside. She had spent the last hour of her working day drafting out the letter that would decline her dream job, knowing that she would probably never be offered this chance again, ever. She would be written off as a baby machine with 'female priorities'. Oh yes, she felt sick all right.

'I'm okay,' she said. 'I'll have to go shopping for something stretchy though, this weekend. These tight waistbands are killing me. I can't fasten the top button at all.'

She had been a steady size ten for three years and had thrown all her 'fat' clothes out. She needed some bigger bras as well because her boobs were inflating like weather balloons. Unlike the others though, her nausea and fatigue had luckily been very short-lived symptoms.

They were both quiet over the main course and, delicious as it was, there was a lot left on their plates at the end of it.

'What's the occasion then?' said Janey, as George planted a crème brûlée in front of her for afters.

'Janey . . .' he started. She waited another five minutes before prompting him.

'I don't know how to say this right, so bear with us,' he went on.

'Okay,' she agreed, putting down her spoon. Reluctantly so, because George's puddings were exceptional.

'Don't be offended or anything, will you? I'm not saying this because I'm lazy or owt . . .'

'Oh, for God's sake, love, just say it, will you?'

'Right then.' He took a big breath. 'You know my job's not up to much . . .'

Bit of an understatement, thought Janey. 'Yes, I know you hate it,' she said.

'Well . . . Well, er . . .'

'George! You're doing my head in! Will you just say it?'

'Okay then' – *here we go* – 'what if I jacked it in and became a househusband and looked after the baby, and you went back to work.' There, I've said it, he thought and waited for her reaction.

She stared at him with her jaw open roughly south of the Equator.

'You big Northern lump!' she said eventually.

He downed his head. 'It was just an idea, sorry,' he said. I can't put this right, he thought. This was my only chance.

'No, you don't understand me,' said Janey breathlessly. 'You big, gorgeous, fantastic, Northern, beautiful lump of a man. You'd do that for me?'

He snapped his head back up. 'Well, course I would. I want to. Oh Janey, I feel terrible about being so bloody thick I can't do anything better than work in a factory making chuffing plastic cogs. Hardly the great provider, am I?'

'George, *I* feel terrible about not having your tea on the table every night when you come home. You do all the house stuff, the things I feel I should be doing . . .'

He knelt on the floor beside her and took her hand. 'I love making your tea. I love cooking. I love being at home and working on it.'

'And I love going out to work,' Janey said, and then she snogged his face off. 'Why haven't we had this conversation before, George? What took us so long?'

He stroked her hand. 'We're having it now, that's all that counts.'

He wished he had been brainy and could have got a job like Simon and set her up in the lovely house she deserved. Dyslexia had not been taken seriously in their schooldays; he was just pigeon-holed as slow and thick, and ignored so he didn't hold the rest of the class up. He could make anything with his hands though; he had a natural flair that had never been harnessed or encouraged because spelling and sums were all that counted when he was a lad. He should have done joinery after school, but he just got channelled into a factory knowing no better and found the rut too bloody impossible to climb out of.

'You do work hard, don't you do yourself down. You provide enough for us to live on; it's me and my fancy ideas that's the problem,' Janey said.

He had tears in his eyes, her big, comfortable, pair-of-slippers husband with the hugest, softest, best heart in the world – one that put her cheating, selfish, unsacrificing one to shame. She did not deserve her luck in having him.

'So, when the baby's here, I'll jack me job in?' he reiterated for confirmation. 'I'll leave it till the last minute and get as much overtime in as I can. I'll work every Saturday from now till then and get the double time.'

'Oh yes, George, jack the bloody thing in,' she said, and her arms swallowed him up, well as much of him as they could. He squeezed her back tightly, wiping at his eyes.

Soft sod, thought Janey. My big, beautiful, soft, gorgeous sod.

You could keep all the fancy flowers and cars wrapped up in bows and surprise helicopter trips that millionaires and film stars gave out to their paramours. Nothing could compete with this moment for either of them. This was *love*.

Chapter 16

All the way home from the surgery, Elizabeth was hoping that John had delivered her car and put the keys through the letterbox so she would not have to see him. Then, when she got home and found the car wasn't there yet, she was relieved that she had not missed him after all. How nuts is that? she thought, although she had long accepted that she wasn't the full shilling as far as her emotions were concerned. She could have hidden them behind a spiral staircase, they were that twisted, or so a disgruntled ex had once told her.

A fat splash of rain landed on her and she hurried into a house that was cosy, warm and welcoming. She had only been in ten minutes when there was a knock on the door and she knew who it was. She opened it up to find him standing there in the pouring rain, jangling her keys at her. She felt obliged to invite him in for a cuppa and he did not refuse.

'That's never the same cat?' he said, pointing at the sleepy black shape on the kitchen chair.

'Yes, it is,' she said. 'That's him.'

Seven years ago, one of Helen's workmates had

given a kitten to her, but Slimy Simon had told her
he had just ordered a leather suite and if she did not
get rid of the creature, he would. Elizabeth stepped
in and said she would have the kitten and John volunteered to go and pick him up for her. Poor Hels. John
said that she had broken her heart handing the little
animal over. She loved cats, did Helen; she should have
kept him and thrown the other animal out. Elizabeth
had thought it then and still continued to think it.

John gave the cat a stroke on the head that woke
him up and Cleef sniffed him, got up, and started
purring, as if some old memory had been prodded
into life.

'What did you call him in the end?' he said.
'Guinness, wasn't it?'

Oh flip. 'I changed it.'

'What to?'

Oh, double flip. 'Er . . . Cleef,' she said.

A slow grin crept over his lips. 'Cleef, eh? As in Lee
Van Cleef? You used to call me that.'

'Did I?' she said, trying to look as if she didn't know
what he was talking about.

She faffed about with cups and teabags, unconsciously
slipping back into that once-familiar routine of milk
and two sugars if she wasn't stirring, one if she was. It
wasn't lost on John that she remembered. She squeezed
past him to get to the fridge. He took half her kitchen
up with that big arctic coat on and he wasn't that much
smaller when he took it off. She sat opposite to him
across the kitchen table and he kicked her accidentally
with one of his big meaty giraffe legs.

'Sorry,' he said. 'Clumsy as ever, eh?'

But that wasn't what was causing the pained expression on her face. She had noticed that the pamphlets the midwife had given her were by his elbow and if she tried to move them, she would only draw attention to them.

'So, any luck on the job front yet?'

Not for a pregnant woman galloping towards forty . . .
'Not yet,' she said. 'I've bought a *Yorkshire Post* though and it's full of jobs on Thursdays. I'll have a look later.'

'What do you fancy?'

'Same as,' she said. 'I'm too set in my ways to try anything else, plus I like working in offices. So what made you come back to Yorkshire then, after living over in Deutschland for so long? Didn't you like it over there?'

'I loved it,' he said, 'especially the south, although most of the work was up north, but . . . well, my dad's got Alzheimer's and my mum will need help.'

'I'm sorry to hear that,' she said, meaning it.

'So am I, but I want to see a bit more of him and my mum now. I can't talk to him on the phone like we did, which is a shame. I've been ready to come back for a while, to be honest. I just had some business ends to tie up first.'

'Sorry to hear about you and Lisa as well,' she said.
Ha!

'Oh, that's all history. In fact, I think she'll be married again by now.'

'Oh?'

'She went off with a German. Called Herman,' he said, poker-faced but with a twinkle in his eye.

'No!' Elizabeth battled with a grin.

'Straight up. He was a nice bloke too. I hope she has better luck this time.'

'You have any kids?'

'No,' he said. 'I hardly ever saw her, to be honest. I used the excuse of working hard so I didn't have to go home, and that's not the recipe for a happy marriage, is it?'

Her breath caught in her throat as he slid one of the pamphlets absently aside so that he would not put his drink down on it.

'Did . . . did you manage to stay friends?'

'She was angry and frustrated with me, so no, I don't think I'll be on her Christmas card list, but I wish her well, really I do. I didn't give her enough love. We shouldn't have got married so quickly. We both did it for the wrong reasons.'

Elizabeth didn't comment. She didn't want to open up that can of emotional worms again – the whole John/Elizabeth/Lisa thing. He drained his mug in one. She didn't offer him another. She wanted to get him out before he saw what was in front of his face.

'Right, I'll get off,' he said, to her enormous relief. 'You leave the lights on that car again and I'll be round to smack your backside. Your battery was kaput though. I put a new one in for you, by the way. And before you start, you don't owe me for it, Elizabeth Collier; it was a spare I had knocking about. Good little car that, considering it's eight years old. Don't do a lot of miles, do you . . . ?'

His voice trailed away as his coat knocked off a leaflet about *Healthy Eating During Your Pregnancy* and he went to pick it up and put it back with the rest. Then his eyes fell full on the titles of all the other pamphlets. He looked at her, then back at them, and she knew he had forged the link between them.

'Yes, I'm pregnant,' she said, mounting an early attack in self-defence. 'That what you want to hear?'

He stared blankly at her; she saw his Adam's apple rise and fall as he gulped, and she could not stop herself from reacting to that look.

'If you must know, I lost my job because my hormones went so crackers that I told my boss to stick his job up his rear end. I'm not with the father, don't actually know who he is, screwed him at a New Year's party and I'm not brave enough to abort it so I'm stuck with it. You see, John, getting away from me was probably the best thing you ever did, so don't *ever* try to convince yourself that you made a mistake − I haven't changed a bit.'

Then she ushered him, unresisting, out of the door, closed it firmly behind him and then slumped to the floor, curling herself into the same shape as the little being inside her.

Chapter 17

The next morning, a letter arrived for Elizabeth, from the Personnel Department at Just the Job. It asked her to attend an interview on Monday at the head office in Leeds, with some bloke called Terry Lennox. Crikey, she thought. Golden Door actually came through for me in the end – and so quickly? Unbelievable! She stuck it in her pocket to show the others the following day when they were due to meet for a scout around Mothercare and have Saturday-afternoon refreshments afterwards.

'How'dja get on in Leeds then?' Janey asked her when they were all seated in the pretty Edwardian Tea Rooms holding menus that were as tall as the little old lady waitresses in their black frocks and white aprons. Elizabeth relayed the saga, stopping short of her meeting with John Silkstone. She knew what they were like; Janey especially would question her like the Gestapo and Helen would get all fluttery with Mills & Boon-type excitement. Then she told them about how Golden Door had fixed her up with an interview and showed them the letter from Just the Job, which the others both thought was a bit strange.

'They wouldn't have contacted you directly in any case, surely?' said Janey. 'The letter would have come from, what was it again . . . Golden Door?'

'It's very quick as well, isn't it?' said Helen sceptically.

'Listen, the last time I applied for a job I was flaming sixteen! I don't know what goes on.'

'Terry Lennox has signed this!' said Janey with a little gasp.

'Yeah, so?'

Helen and Janey exchanged glances and pulled impressed faces at each other.

'What?' demanded Elizabeth.

'Haven't you heard of him? He's the MD,' said Helen.

'Well, if it was this Golden Door lot, they've come through for you big time,' said Janey, crossing her arms over her fast-expanding bosom. It had grown an inch since they had opened their menus.

'Well, it has to be them. It can't be anyone else, can it?'

'I'm very surprised, that's all,' said Janey.

'You can't be more surprised than me,' said Elizabeth. 'I thought they were a bunch of farts.' She suddenly hoped that Frances had not really told them she had a degree in Japanese.

A stoop-backed Mrs Overall-type waitress arrived and took Elizabeth's and Helen's order for strawberry tea and big choux Elephant's Feet. They looked over at Janey, expecting her to go for her usual sawdusty wholemeal scone with a portion of lowest-of-the-low-fat margarine, but she surprised them.

'Make that three,' she said, and got a big cheer from her friends.

'How did your first antenatal go yesterday?' Helen asked Janey.

'Okay,' she said, smiling enigmatically. She had gone for her appointment with a completely different mindset after having that talk with George. His enthusiasm for the baby was extremely infectious and she had found herself thinking that, with the recent turn of events, things just might turn out all right after all. She had not seen him smile like that for a long, long time and never mind the whys and wherefores, she *was* giving him his baby at last. He was so thrilled about it that any of her remaining tears were dried up by his happiness. In fact, she had virtually swaggered out of the surgery feeling quite proud of herself, and it was so good to be free of that ever-niggling gremlin that she was being unfair to him. They had gone to bed early last night and made love – shock horror – with the lights on. Her orgasm had been mindblowing and, to her surprise and delight, she was up for a repeat performance not long after. George had been quite happy to oblige, especially when she went for a different position to their usual one. Then this morning she nudged him awake, ready for more.

'What's the matter with you, woman!' he said, trying to get away from her but giggling too.

'I don't know, but service me, husband!' she said, and made him late for work for the first time in his whole life. She was thinking about that when Elizabeth poked her with a teaspoon and hoisted her out of her reverie.

'Oy, Mona Lisa. What are you smiling like that for? And what about this antenatal? Is that all we get? "Okay"?' And she did an impression of Janey being very elusive.

'Sorry, I was miles away then,' said Janey, and got out her blue folder that the midwife had given her. 'I brought this to show you. Did you get one of these as well? Loads of vouchers and info and a free pants liner.'

'I got the folder. I didn't get the pants liner,' said Elizabeth dryly, 'which is just as well because I'm not sure my heart could have stood the excitement.'

'Can't see me ever using this,' said Janey, picking up a voucher for a free jar of coffee. 'It just makes me feel sick these days.'

'You'll get your taste for it back eventually,' said Helen. 'And tea. Once the baby's here.'

'I hope so. I used to like my Yorkshire tea,' said Elizabeth.

'You're sure you're doing the right thing keeping it, aren't you? You've really thought this through?' Janey asked Elizabeth, softly for her. She knew Helen had been thinking the same but would not dare say the words aloud, whereas she would.

'I'm sure,' said Elizabeth. 'We'll work it out some-where along the line.'

'There's always adop—' Janey started to say but shook her head before she had finished. She doubted even Elizabeth, with her hard heart, could carry a baby for nine months and give it up at the end. There were no options open other than keeping it. She just felt sad that Elizabeth's bairn wouldn't have the family life her bairn would. It was history repeating itself.

'Look, I know it's early days,' began Helen, putting her hand over Elizabeth's, 'but if I'm not in hospital myself, I'll be your birth partner if you want.'

'Or me,' said Janey. 'You know I'd do that for you.'

Elizabeth nodded and her eyes went all glassy, so she started studying the ice-cream menu and getting fidgety on her seat and they said no more on the subject. Even when her dog had died and then two weeks later she had been at her Auntie Elsie's funeral, she had not broken down in front of them. At least she'd had the grace to look shocking though, because when her father had died she hadn't turned a hair. That had always secretly disgusted Janey, although she had never said so aloud.

'Why do they test your urine?' Janey asked.

'For IQ,' said Elizabeth. 'So your kid's got no chance with you two thickies for a mam and dad.'

'For protein,' said Helen, being sensible.

'Who are you having as a consultant?' Janey asked.

'Willoughby-Brown,' said Helen.

'I suppose he's private,' sniffed Janey and Helen nodded meekly. It had been her mother's idea to have one of her father's old medical colleagues, although her father had never believed in private medicine. Or schools, for that matter.

'I'm having Greer,' said Elizabeth.

'Me as well,' said Janey.

'The midwife told me, unofficially, that he was better than Falmer,' said Elizabeth.

'Barry the Butcher is better than that piss-head doctor!' Janey laughed, but as soon as her words were out, she wished she could have dragged them back into her mouth and swallowed them whole.

'God, I'm sorry!' she said to Helen. Her apology made it worse and Elizabeth rounded hard eyes at her.

'Don't be silly,' said Helen, with a smile that didn't quite cancel out the wounded look.

Then the waitress came back with a big tray of buns and rescued the atmosphere from suffocating them all.

It was Janey's first cream bun in three years and it was almost worth the wait; the pleasure of it was certainly up there with the recent night of marital lust. Helen was a bit jittery whilst she was eating it and ended up abandoning most of it.

'What's up with you?' said Elizabeth with a jokey laugh. 'Scared of being seen scoffing?'

Helen laughed back, but it was a very odd laugh.

When Elizabeth got home, there was a note pushed through her letterbox: *Elizabeth, please phone me when you get in. John.* And there was his number.

She crumpled it up and threw it in the bin and got on with feeding Cleef. What on earth could they have to say to each other now?

Chapter 18

Elizabeth wore her new maternity skirt for her interview on Monday – not that she looked very pregnant at eleven weeks, but it was certainly roomier and moved when she breathed out, unlike her normal skirts that were starting to constrict her like hungry boas. She drove down to the station, checked that she had not left her lights on in the manner of an obsessive compulsive disorder syndrome sufferer, and then she got on the train. It had always been far easier to travel to Leeds that way as the few available car parking spaces outside the Handi-Save building tended to be taken up by the keen boys and girls who arrived at unearthly hours, and the overflow car park was miles away in a dodgy, dark area that was a serial killer's paradise. Plus she liked relaxing on the train far more than battling through traffic jams.

She arrived with plenty of time to spare so she spent a hundred million pounds on a coffee in Starbucks and then set off for the day's main event. Just the Job headquarters were a leisurely five-minute stroll from the station down by the waterfront. They were one of the new family of buildings, with lots of glass and an adjacent massive three-storey car park that seemed to cater adequately for its staff numbers, judging by some empty spaces that Elizabeth noticed as she passed by.

She arrived on the dot to report at a very funky and impressive Reception desk that made the one at Handi-Save look like a funeral parlour. The entrance was so lofty and vast that it was more like an airport than an office block, and the blue-suited glossy Reception staff looked like its air-hostesses. A very short wait later, a young smiley girl called Nerys led Elizabeth upstairs on an escalator, chirping on about how awful the weather was. Terry Lennox was running late, she explained, leading her into a room full of squidgey leather sofas.

Elizabeth smiled and said, 'That's okay,' but inside she was thinking about Laurence and his 'I'm important so I'm going to be late just to annoy you – ner ner ner ner ner!' ploys, and her brain went automatically into, 'Here we go again!' mode. Nevertheless, Nerys seemed nice enough and fixed her up a coffee in a real cup with a saucer, not a plastic one that threatened to burn her fingerprints off.

Elizabeth sat quite comfortably in the lovely plush corner room with the massive windows framing the view of the river, happily sipping in the atmosphere of the place, which seemed lighter and more dynamic than Handi-Save ever did, even in its finest hours. Providing Terry Lennox, whoever he was, turned out not to be a total Laurence. Elizabeth was already thinking, Yes, I could work here.

She had just finished the coffee when Nerys put in another appearance.

'Mr Lennox is so sorry,' she said, with genuine apology. 'He hates being late for anything and he was a bit worried you might be getting hungry, so he asked me quite specifically to get you one of these.'

She set a knife, fork and serviette down on the table in front of Elizabeth and then a plate with a delicious-looking soft brown bap bursting with prawns, salad and pink dressing.

'Oh thanks,' she said, thinking, Crikey, is this how interviews go these days? She had expected a Digestive at a push, but lunch-while-you-wait? She wasn't looking the sandwich gift horse in the mouth though, because she was starving, and so she stole a fat prawn that was hanging out at one side. Then she ripped off a bit of bread, then she thought, Sod it, and cut the sandwich into four, and before she knew it, she had wolfed the lot. She was just licking her fingers when a man with a craggy face and rolled-up shirt-sleeves breezed in.

'So sorry, young lady. A thousand apologies – how are you?' He came over with his hand extended and shook hers so firmly and vigorously that he almost pulled her arm out of its socket.

Well, if this was Terry Lennox, Elizabeth thought, he wasn't one of those smooth, slimy executives like Laurence. He had a face she had seen somewhere before, but she couldn't quite place it. Probably on the financial pages of a newspaper, if he was as prolific as Janey and Helen said he was. According to Helen, Terry

Lennox, MD of Just the Job, had been born on a council-house estate that made Blackberry Moor look like Chelsea. He had been written off at school and could not read a word before he was ten. He left school at fourteen to start work in a local brush-making factory that he owned fifteen years later. Through a mix of natural acumen, hard graft, unsentimental ruthlessness, and presumably some luck and black magic, he was now the owner of the biggest DIY chain in Britain, which was fast expanding into Europe and gobbling up the competition for breakfast. He made Laurence look like a choirboy.

'You took some tracking down, you know,' he said in a very deep and broad South Yorkshire accent.

'Pardon?' she said, wondering if he had mistaken her for someone else because this wasn't making any sense.

'Your old Personnel Department were a bit on the reticent side to divulge any info about you – now why do you think that was?' he went on.

Now Elizabeth was totally lost. One of them had a screw loose and she was pretty sure it wasn't her. *'And where* have *I seen him before?'* she pondered. Her thought processes were busy trying to work it out but having no luck so far.

'Are you anything to do with Golden Door Recruitment?' she tried, but his blank look answered that question adequately.

'I thought the prawn sandwich might have given it away for you when I knew I was going to be late. Mischief on my part, I'm afraid. I told Nerys to get you one.'

Whaaaat? It was like being trapped in a game of Cluedo. Mr Lennox, in the office, with a prawn sandwich. Then suddenly she got it.

'You're the man in the lift!' She pointed at him.

He clapped in a 'By George, she's got it!' kind of way. 'Yes, unfortunately that *was* me, and I owe you a huge apology. Why I didn't use the damned staircase that day, I'll never know. Well, I do – I was in too much of a rush, if that isn't the irony of it all. I have terrible claustrophobia, which is why I've always given myself an office not too many stairs up and plenty of room in which to faint,' he said and smiled. 'Anyway, I've been looking for you ever since, to say a big thank you.'

'Oh right,' said Elizabeth, still totally nonplussed. 'Well, thanks for the thanks.' *Was that it then? All this way for a sarnie and a thank you?*

'I found out eventually what had happened to you,' he went on. 'I thought I might have made a contribution to your downfall.'

'No – er . . . not at all.' She felt herself getting hot. Did he know the whole story then? Obviously not or she wouldn't be here. He held up his hand as if Caesar was in the room and he had just hailed him.

'I'm pretty sure that if we could replay the whole day without me flopping all over the place, you just might not have exploded.'

Oh hell, he did know the whole story!

'Maybe I was the straw that broke the donkey's back, eh? So my first reason for inviting you here was obviously to say a huge, huge sorry for that. My second is to ask if you want a job to replace the one you lost.'

Elizabeth's eyebrows shot up so far they almost had to call Maintenance to get them down from the ceiling tiles.

'I did get to see your personnel file in the end,' he went on. 'Quite impressive. I like that sort of company loyalty. It must have been something pretty monstrous for you to jack in your job like that after all those years. Or someone, perhaps?'

'It was,' said Elizabeth without elaboration. She was professional enough not to take the opportunity to slag off Teenwolf and old Bandy Legs, however deliciously tempting it was to do so.

'I haven't got a secretary at present. Mine recently got bitten by the travel bug and is rescuing koala bears or something in Australia so I've been surviving on temps, and every last one of them is useless. Now, let me lay it on the line for you, Ms Collier: I'm an old-fashioned kind of boss — I like a cup of coffee brought to me every two hours without some woman yelling at me that I'm being sexist, although I have been told I am. I may, from time to time, ask you to nip up into town and get me things, although that won't be in your job description, and I shall probably whip you out to lunch occasionally, although I won't be trying to seduce you. I'm very happily married to my Irene and have been for centuries, and no doubt you'll be putting many calls through to me from her because she rings up to talk about our curtains on a regular basis, or so it seems.'

Elizabeth stifled a giggle. She liked him. His rough-edged bluntness was charming.

'I'm not as easy as I like to think I am to work for, but if you give as good as you get and don't go off crying in the toilets like Miss Last-Week, I think we'll get on marvellously. Although, after hearing you in full flow, I don't think I need to prompt you on that front.'

Whoops! thought Elizabeth.

'Now here's the deal. I can't offer you a company car straight away, but if you ever get stuck, we've got pool cars. What I am offering is twenty-four thousand, bloody good pension, profit-sharing, life insurance, private health scheme, staff discount, tax-free Christmas bonus, birthday appraisal and thirty days holiday a year, including your stats. Well?'

Elizabeth's mouth moved soundlessly. Someone up there was having a laugh, she thought. She should grab it with both hands and not mention the obvious. Legally he didn't have a right to ask about her child-bearing plans, it was discriminatory and she could have him for it. 'Keep stumm about the baby,' her instincts screamed at her. 'Anybody else would.' Except Elizabeth was not anybody else.

'It's only fair to tell you that I'm pregnant,' she said. Ah well, that was that then. Easy come, easy go. She did self-destruction so well.

'Oh!' said Terry Lennox, clapping his hands together, interweaving them and bringing them to his lips as if he were preparing to pray. 'Well, do you want to have a word with your hubby and see if he wants you to work?'

She cut him off. 'I don't have a husband. Or a partner.'

If he was an old-fashioned man, as she suspected, that would probably just hammer the last nail in the coffin. Feisty, unmarried and pregnant. Should she just go now, or did he want Security to escort her off the premises?

'Well, I admire your honesty anyway, lass,' he said. 'You'll need a job more than ever then, won't you? So, Miss Collier, when can you start?'

John's Land Rover was parked outside her house when she got home and her heart annoyingly started to Riverdance when she saw it. She tried to pretend she hadn't seen him, got out of the car and stuck the key in the lock, but he was behind her by the time the door swung open and neither of them said a word as he followed her in.

Chapter 19

'I hear your friend has lost her job!' said Simon, with enough relish to coat a pub full of Ploughman's lunches.

'Oh, where did you hear that?' said Helen, stopping the examination of her nicely rounding tummy profile in the full-length en-suite bathroom mirror.

'In the office, of course,' he said. 'You know that one of our accounts is Handi-Save.'

'Yes, I do know that,' she said, 'but I didn't think you were on gossiping terms with anyone there.'

'Not usually,' he said smoothly, 'but she left rather dramatically, didn't she? Hardly the thing to do if you want to get another job, is it? Although I can't say it surprised me.'

'Well, she would have had to stop working in a few months any . . .' Helen stopped herself; she had said too much already and cursed herself for it. Several slow seconds later, Simon appeared at the bathroom door.

'Go on,' he said.

'Go on what?' She tried to wriggle out of it, but Simon could smell when she was covering something up and he moved in on it like a vampire smelling a virginal jugular.

'No, go on. You were saying that she would have had to stop working in a few months anyway. Why would that be then?'

'Nothing. Let me get changed.' She tried to squeeze past him to get to her clothes in the bedroom, but he blocked the way.

'Tell me,' he said. 'Why would she have to stop working?'

'Simon, I'll be late. My mother will be waiting. The play's starting shortly.'

'Why would she have to stop working?'

'Stop this, Simon.'

'Why would she have to stop working? Why would she have to stop working? *Why would she have to stop working?*'

He asked the same question repeatedly until the words drove a painful groove in her head.

'Because she's pregnant!' Helen cried, and pushed again and this time he let her past him and into the bedroom. Behind her he was laughing in delighted disbelief as she threw open her wardrobe door and dragged a top off the hanger. Her mother would be wondering where she was.

'Good God! Who's the father?' he asked.

'I don't know,' she said.

'Of course you know, Helen,' he snapped impatiently.

'I really don't know. She . . . had a fling, that's all I know.'

'When?'

'I don't know. New Year, I think. A party – she didn't tell us much.'

She buttoned up her blouse and slipped on her skirt quickly. Behind her, Simon stood, his brain whirring.

'She was seeing someone at that time, wasn't she? That labourer?'

'Yes . . . no. Yes, but it wasn't him,' said Helen. She displaced the anger she felt at her own weakness by slamming the wardrobe door, snatching up her bag, stamping her shoes on. She felt ashamedly disloyal to her friend.

'This is getting even better,' said Simon. 'So he's not the father?'

'No – yes . . . I don't know,' she stammered. When Simon was like this, she became confused and could not tell what was actually true and what he wanted to be true. He tied her up in psychological knots and made her feel like a professional liar and deceiver.

'You must know who it is!'

'I don't!' Helen said, attempting to leave the bedroom but he stood in her way again. She reached for the doorknob and he slapped her hand away from it.

'Ow! That hurt, Simon!' she said.

'It's very simple. Tell me then I'll let you go out.'

'I don't know. She . . . she was drunk – she doesn't know herself. Why is it so important you know?'

'That isn't the issue here, Helen. What is important is the fact that you keep things like this from me! These are things that affect me as well as you, don't you see that, you stupid cow?' Simon snarled, then he laughed with bitter amazement. 'My God, and you say she's not a slag!' He shook his head slowly and went into the bathroom.

Helen silently slipped on her jacket, the evening spoiled before it had begun, and had just opened the door to go when she heard him say, 'You aren't to see her any more.'

'What?'

'I don't want our child associating with her little bastard,' he said with quiet menace. 'End the friend-ship. I don't care how you do it, but by the time that baby is born, you will not be in contact with her any more. It's time you dropped those friends, anyway. You outgrew them a long time ago, but you can't see it, can you? People are defined by the company they keep, Helen, and you associate with tarts and thickos! How do you think that reflects on me, hm? This really is the final straw.'

He came out of the bathroom, smiling gently, smelling of clinical mint and kissed her on the cheek.

'Have a nice time, darling. Give my love to your mother.'

John sat down on the same chair he had always sat down on whenever he used to come to the house. Elizabeth put the kettle on; it was always the first thing she did when she came in through the front door – well, apart from lighting up a cigarette, but that habit was no more.

'So, where've you been all dressed up?'

'Job interview,' she said.

'How did you get on?'

'I start next Monday.'

'Where's that then?'

'Just the Job Head Office in Leeds.'

'Good for you. So, how's the car?' he said, and she laughed mirthlessly at his continuing effort of small talk.

'What do you want, John?'

'I just wanted to see how it was running.'

'Great, thank you, but what do you really want?'

'I don't know,' he said, using his hand like a big comb through his black hair that had lots of stray grey ones coming through these days. He'd had it freshly cut, just after the point where it started to curl. It made him look younger somehow, and his brown eyes seem larger and darker.

'I just want to be friends again,' he said. 'We're so awkward with each other and we were never like that, so I suppose I'm here to sort it out. We were always good friends and couldn't you use one of those right now?'

'I've got enough friends,' she said, not understanding why she had to be so snotty with him all the time. She hated herself for it, yet couldn't seem to stop it.

'You needed a friend the other day in the car park.'

'If you hadn't come, do you think I'd still be sat there?' she snapped.

John got up and strode towards the kitchen door, and then he stopped, took a deep breath, counted to three and swung back to his seat at the table.

'No, I won't let you drive me out,' he said. He looked cross, but there was his hand, stroking Cleef, gently as you like.

'Who's the baby's father?' he asked calmly. 'You said you didn't know him well.'

'None of your bus—'

'I hear you were going out with Dean Crawshaw at that time. Setting your standards as low as usual, I see. You do realize he'll be sitting on that same bar stool in the Victoria twenty years from now, just like he was sat on it twenty years ago!'

Elizabeth closed her eyes against the shame of him knowing about Dean, and noisily started getting some cups out of the super-neat cupboard. John looked around the kitchen: the sparkling worktops, the polished floor, the oven hob so shiny it looked brand new. She used to clean her house until her hands were raw and bleeding because she couldn't clean out the mess in her head.

'It isn't his,' she said. 'And yes, I'm sure before you ask.'

'What is it all about, Elizabeth? Another way of hurting yourself?'

'How bloody dare you? It wasn't like that at all!' she yelled at him.

'Then what was it like, Elizabeth?'

'It . . . it . . .' *She nearly told him.* She very nearly told him, but he knew too much about her already and that made him dangerous.

As if he was reading her thoughts at that moment, he said, 'Do you think I'd tell anyone if you told me? Think I've told anyone at all any of that stuff I know about you?'

'There's nothing to tell. I made a mistake and I'm paying for it, so just get lost, will you!' she said, and then her eyes started squirting again.

'Oh, come here, you daft beggar,' he said, and he opened his big arms and forced a quick, safe hug on her just before she pushed him off, before she let herself savour that feeling. She knew he would never try anything on with her, she knew he would not pretend to like her only to get her upstairs, and that is where John Silkstone had always confused her. John Silkstone was a 'giver'; the takers in life were so much easier to deal with.

'Don't push me away, Elizabeth,' he said. 'Just let me in a little bit, eh? I never wanted us to fall out. I know it was my fault last time – I pushed it, I scared you off and I am sorrier than you could ever know for that, but it's in the past. This is seven years on and I'm back, so please let us at least get on. I don't want to dredge up faults and recrimination and blame. I always thought too much about you for all this to have happened and spoiled everything. Can we *please* just start again, being friends?'

She nodded and blew her nose on the hankie he snapped out of the tissue box, which stood on the shelf of her Auntie Elsie's old kitchen dresser. It had been sanded and waxed, sanded and waxed until it was as smooth as the knotty wood would allow. There was a hook on the side; Sam's dog lead still hung from it that Elizabeth would touch out of habit sometimes when she passed it. They drank their differently flavoured teas quietly and after it, he said goodbye and that he'd see her soon, no doubt, and she hoped that he would, although she didn't say that aloud. Satisfied by that for now, he went.

For a long time after he had gone, Elizabeth sat at the table, wiping her leaky eyes on her sleeve, feeling like a snotty kid. Like the snotty, gobby, horrible, rude, unloved, unlovable kid she used to be. Until the day she came for help to the woman whom she hated most in the world; the woman who saved her from the nightmares then. But who was there to save her from them now?

Chapter 20

She was running like in one of those dreams when someone chases you, and even though they are only walking, somehow they manage to catch you up. She brayed on that postbox-red door with the letterbox so shiny she could see her face in it. She didn't have any shoes on and her socks were encrusted with pebbles, but she hadn't felt them cut into her.

'Please open,' she said to the door and it did like magic, and she would have jumped up and kissed her Auntie Elsie who was thin and spiky as a nettle, if she'd had time.

'Who are you running from?' she said, as the child dived past her. 'And you can get out of that dog-basket and stop being so silly!'

'Shut the door, please, Auntie Elsie, please, please,' the child screamed, and Auntie Elsie shut it, just in time as the Yale lock had barely engaged when there was another hard bang on the door.

'Auntie Elsie, don't open it, please!'

'Who is it?'

'It's me dad and he wants me to get in bed wi' him.'

'Eh?'

'He said, I'd not to go to school, I'd to go to bed and give him a cuddle.'

Auntie Elsie ignored the hammering at the door and she marched over to the small girl with the wild curly hair and dragged her out from behind the bemused dog in his big wicker-basket bed.

'Elizabeth Collier, what are you talking about? Are you telling me stories?'

'I'm not, I'm not,' the child sobbed. 'He made me lie on the bed and said . . . and said . . . I'd not to tell.'

'Well, you tell me now. What did your dad do?'

'He . . . told me I'd not to get dressed for school because I wasn't going in that day. Then he called me into his bedroom and . . . and . . .'

'And what, girl? Speak up!'

'He was lying there on his bed with just his pants and socks on . . .'

It hadn't felt right and it had made her remember what Beverley had said before she ran away from home about not letting him ever 'start on her' but she hadn't understood then. It was only when he started cuddling up to her, that she recognized that this somehow was 'the starting'. He had never cuddled her before, which was why it was funny he had kept her off school to do it, and it wasn't nice, she did not like it at all. His slaver smelled of unbrushed teeth and cigarettes, when his mouth had closed over hers and his tongue pushed into her mouth, slimy and snaking about, looping around her own. She wiped her mouth frantically at the memory of it.

'I tried to push him off, Auntie Elsie 'cos he were making funny noises. You're not supposed to touch children there, are you?'

'Where? Where did he touch you?'

The child felt hot and uncomfortable pointing down below, then she screamed as the door reverberated in its frame from her father's determined attempt to gain entry.

'Never mind outside,' said Auntie Elsie. 'What happened then?'

'I'll get done—'

'What happened?'

'I bit him and ran here.'

Auntie Elsie looked at the child, from her terrified grey eyes down to the blood coming through her dirty-white socks. Her face blackened like a thundercloud wiping out the sun and the child waited for her to start shouting again, but instead she went to the door, opened it and slammed it behind her. The child crept over to the window and peeped through the safety of the decorative holes in the snow-white lacy nets, listening to the voices. Auntie Elsie was really mad, that much she could tell, and she called her dad a nasty B-word, which sounded funny coming from her auntie because she never swore. She was yelling at him, telling him to stay away or she would call the police and have him up for it. He was shouting back that it was all lies, and he screamed at the window, as if he could see her there.

'Lizzie, get out here now!' he bawled, and his finger stabbed at the pavement as if that was where she was to come to. Then his voice suddenly dropped and he was talking all nice again, and panic gripped the child as she thought he might get around her Auntie Elsie who had stopped yelling at him now. Then Auntie Elsie slapped him hard around the head and kept slapping him, and he went flying over the corsey edge and lost his shoe. Auntie Elsie waited for him to get up, ignoring his pleas and shooing him off.

He walked backwards still talking but her auntie stood firm with her arms on her hips until he had gone. Then she knocked on her own door and Elizabeth let her in. She marched straight over to the cupboard and pulled out a carrier bag stuffed full of others.

'Right, come on, we're going home,' she said, sliding her sleeves up her thin arms.

'I'm bloody not and you can't make me!'

'We're just getting your things and then you're coming back here.'

'My dad'll get me!'

'He won't, he'll stay away 'cos he knows what'll happen if he doesn't – and if I hear you swearing again, Elizabeth Collier, it'll be me that's doing the getting. Now come on!'

The little girl did not move. Auntie Elsie huffed impatiently. 'Oh, for goodness' sake, get a lead on the dog if it makes you feel better.'

It did. She pulled Sam's lead off the hook screwed into the side of her auntie's old kitchen dresser and the big black dog stood tail a-wagging whilst she fastened it round his neck. He was soft, was Sam, but she knew he would bite for her if he had to, she just knew he would.

'Are you all right to walk? You better put my slippers on,' said Auntie Elsie, passing over a long tartan pair with a bobble at the toes. 'Come on, look sharp!'

She held out her hand and the child took it for the first time ever. It was thin and bony but the grip was tight, strong and safe, and between her auntie and big, black Sam, she flip-flopped down the street in the direction of that place she would never again call home.

When they came back struggling with bags, Elsie pulled the girl square in front of her and wagged a finger in her face.

'Now listen, I'm putting you in what used to be your grandma's room, and if you don't behave yourself here or at school, she'll come down from heaven and tell you off, do you understand?'

The child nodded and then Auntie Elsie took her upstairs into the back bedroom with the dressing-table with the hair-brushes arranged on top of it and the big bevelled mirror behind it and the high iron bed that she used to sneak in and bounce on whenever she went up to the toilet. They were going to hang her clothes up in the dark wooden wardrobe but her Auntie Elsie said they were all hacky and she'd have to wash them properly again for now but they would go to the School Shop to buy her some more. Auntie Elsie chased Sam downstairs because he wasn't allowed up, but she must have known later that he came up every night and turned his three heavy circles before flumping down on the mat at the side of the child's bed.

Auntie Elsie gave her boiled ham and over-diluted orange juice for tea but this time it tasted like a feast for her stomach and her heart. She asked her questions about Bev and the child told her she thought Bev must have run off to hospital because she kept being sick and was getting fat. Auntie Elsie said, 'Dear God,' a lot and sniffed and was lovely to her after that.

And there they lived, the three of them in Rhymer Street. Then, when Elizabeth was eighteen, Sam died in his sleep and before the month had ended, Auntie Elsie had gone the same way.

Chapter 21

For once Janey and George were fulfilling their stereo-
typical roles. Janey was halfway through the ironing
in the kitchen, George was gardening. He caught sight
of her watching him through the window and he
waved and smiled. He wiped some sweat off his forehead and started digging again and Janey's heart went
as fluttery as it did when he turned up for that first
date wearing the big plastic flower. He was taking
advantage of a fine Sunday and had started to level
out the ground to make a patio for them to enjoy
when the summer came. They had a nice big garden
and he'd built a fence around it so they were as private
as a terraced house could be, although most of the
people on the row were old and it wasn't as if they
needed to be that secluded. The wild parties were thin
on the ground, although there was the occasional
slanging match when someone had over-pruned a tree
that was hanging over their boundary.

George broke off for a cuppa and came into the
kitchen with his old gardening clothes on, big gloves
and smelling of earth, although it might well have
been powdered rhino horn, monkey glands and oysters

for the effect it had on Janey – this same Janey who was supposed to get turned on by clean suits and nice white-collar ties. It was like a switch going on inside her that opened all roads to every part of her body that was even slightly receptive to a sexual hormone.

'Come here, you,' she crooned and he did, but protesting that he was all scruffy and the dirt would come off on her clothes. Like she cared; she wanted to be filthy and most of all, at that moment, she wanted him to run his big, dirty hands all over her. She switched off the iron; she wouldn't be needing it for a bit. He was laughing as he pushed her away for her own good, but she grabbed his gloved hands and stuck them on her fast increasing chest and that was the end of that battle. She hoisted herself up on the kitchen table and they pushed each other's clothes aside because they couldn't wait to take them off. Her hand was in the butter dish at one point and the box of Yorkshire teabags clattered to the floor as both parties orgasmed noisily and fast and together, like they did in films. Then Janey made her husband a cuppa and they fed each other fingers of Kit Kat before he went back to the patio and she carried on with her ironing.

It was touch and go whether the sheets would dry with it being as chilly as it was, but it was a bright day and there was a bit of breeze so Elizabeth decided to risk it. She loved the smell of fresh air on the sheets, and the bed always felt cleaner and softer on those first nights when they were put on. Her washing billowed like sails on a ship and whilst it dried, she got on with making herself a light lunch. She picked out an olive from the jar on the yellow worktop whilst she was buttering the toast, then another and another. She had not known really what possessed her to buy them because she had never bought a jar of olives in her life, but as she was passing down the aisle in the supermarket they seemed to call to her and looked so plump and succulent with their bright red stuffed centres. She had been eating them like crisps ever since and thought maybe this was one of those 'cravings' that she had always presumed was a joke symptom, manufactured by comedy writers so that they could poke fun at how mad women go during pregnancy.

She rang Janey for a quick hello whilst she was scoffing. 'What are you two up to then?'

'I'm just finishing off some ironing, George is in the garden.'

'What do you think of olives?'

'Olive who?' said Janey, who sounded far too breathy for someone who was only supposed to be ironing.

'No, you dummy, olives as in the fruit or vegetable or whatever they are.'

'Oh sorry, olives in jars, you mean?'

'Yes.'

'Yeurch, can't stand them,' said Janey. 'Why are you asking me about olives?'

'I've got a thing for them at the moment.'

'It'll be your body telling you you're deficient in something.'

'Well, it's never told me before that I'm olive

deficient!' Elizabeth replied. 'How come you're all breathless?'

'I'll tell you later,' said Janey, although from her smiley tone of voice it wasn't difficult to work out.

'So you're having "cravings" as well then?' said Elizabeth cheekily.

'Yes, and mine are a bit more exciting than bloody olives, I can tell you that for nothing!' said Janey, watching George digging through the kitchen window, whilst absently licking her lips. 'You excited about tomorrow, chuck?' she went on, turning her attentions back to the telephone. 'First-day nerves setting in yet?'

'I don't know what I feel.' Elizabeth attempted an examination of her emotions, but they were all mixed up as usual. 'What about you, Mrs Manager? How are you feeling about tomorrow? You nervous?'

'Me? I'm raring to go, mate,' said Janey. 'In fact, when I've finished this off, I'm going to start cutting out a couple of very nice maternity suits, seeing as I'll be executive status starting tomorrow. There's hardly any choice in the shops, so I'm back to full-on stitching days again.'

'Clever girl,' said Elizabeth. 'Right, I suppose I better let you get to it then.'

'Well, good luck and enjoy your olives,' said Janey. George's chunky, biteable bottom was sticking up in the air. She thought she might just have to switch off the iron permanently this time.

'I'll ring you at the end of the week to see how you got on 'cos you can't always tell on your first day, can you?' said Elizabeth. 'Then you can tell me how your scan went as well.'

'Yes, we'll compare notes. Have you heard from Helen? She rang me last night to wish me luck for tomorrow but she sounded awful.'

'She rang me as well,' said Elizabeth. 'Poor love. I'll ring her in a bit and see how she is.'

'Good luck, chuck.'

'Knock 'em dead, Fred.'

Elizabeth put another load of washing in. She knew it was ridiculous but she wouldn't lie on the sheets she had shared with Dean until they had been washed and washed and washed, until something inside told her they were finally clean of him. She had scrubbed the house from top to bottom after he had gone, anything and everything that he might have touched had been bleached and sprayed and wiped, but the sheets still felt contaminated, although she reckoned this wash might do it. They had been a birthday present from Helen last year so she didn't want to throw them away. They were thick Egyptian cotton white sheets, pillow-cases and a duvet cover, and Janey had bought her two down-filled pillows and stitched up some small lavender bags to stick in the pillowcases with them. Maybe they hadn't been the most traditional presents but she had mentioned that she hadn't been sleeping too well, and being the sort of people they were, her friends had picked up on it. She decided to ring Helen. It didn't seem fair that she was having such a rough time, seeing as out of the three of them, she was the only one who wanted to get pregnant in the first place.

She took another olive and dialled in her number, but to her dismay Slime-on answered.

'Is Helen there?' said Elizabeth, politely enough but with an obvious tone of displeasure that she had to speak to him and not her friend.

'She's having a lie-down,' he replied. 'Can I help in any way?' he added, far too nicely to be genuine.

'No, I don't think so,' she replied, mirroring his manner, 'but I'd be very grateful if you could tell her I called to see how she was.'

'Certainly,' he said precisely. 'Bye-bye now.'

'Did I hear the phone?' said Helen, emerging from the main white and gold bathroom which had the more powerful shower of the two bathrooms in the house.

'Yes, you did,' said Simon, putting the receiver back down on its cradle in the hallway.

'Who was it?'

'Some customer-survey thing. I gave them short shrift,' said Simon with a smile. He looked at her standing there with just a white bath-sheet wrapped around her body, her shoulders bare and beaded with scented water drops and her eyes impossibly big and blue and begging him to want her. Helen let the towel fall and he came to her and picked it up and wrapped it around her again.

'Don't be silly,' he said, then, 'I'm just going next door to my office; I've got some calls to make.'

Helen said, 'Yes, okay.' Inside, her heart started to bleed.

Chapter 22

The next morning marked Elizabeth's twelfth week of pregnancy and she was happy to find that she didn't feel the slightest bit sick, which was lucky, as she was back on the jiggly train to Leeds for her first day in her new job, an occasion that merited her new navy maternity suit and loose spotty shirt. Her shoes were much lower than she was used to, but she did not want to risk wobbling about in her customary long, pin heels. As a consequence she felt very short waiting with the other commuters for the train, and decidedly plumper than usual, as if she had been given the use of a different body overnight. Not that it was an unpleasant feeling, just very strange.

Nerys came down to collect her from Reception wearing a big welcoming smile then she took her up one flight and over to a lovely dark wooden desk by the window, just outside Terry Lennox's office. She babysat Elizabeth for most of the day, showing her where all the loos were and kitchen areas and coffee and chocolate machines – 'priorities' as she described them. Then she took Elizabeth on a tour of all the departments and gave her the essential rundown on

Terry Lennox's idiosyncrasies: 'has tea with two sugars but no milk, coffee with no sugar and lots of milk, loves Jaffa Cakes, hates Penguins – the foil-covered variety obviously – tends to swear rather loudly at the nearest person when the fire alarm test goes off on Friday mornings . . .'

Then she took Elizabeth to lunch in the very nice underground staff restaurant 'The Sub' and introduced her to a few intrigued faces, before whisking her back up to Security to get her picture taken for her pass. Elizabeth hadn't realized how round her face was becoming until the moment she saw the photo. At this rate, she would look like a Christmas pudding by the end of her pregnancy.

Helen and Janey had sent her a flower display to wish her luck which sat very prettily on her new desk. Terry Lennox buzzed her for coffee at two o'clock to remind her that she had forgotten him and warned her that it was three strikes and out. Elizabeth batted back that it would be his loss then because she had not forgotten him and had actually been on a biscuit search, seeing as there were only Penguins left in the tin. He roared with laughter and said he liked a woman with spirit enough to answer him back and resource good snacks.

The train home arrived punctually, her car started perfectly first time and she climbed into bed that night a tired but contented woman.

There was a bouquet of flowers waiting for Janey at Reception – from Elizabeth and Helen. The card read,

To Janey FF good luck in your new job. She took it up to her new desk in her new department and rang Helen at work to give her a quick thank you, then she rang Elizabeth on her mobile.

'Is that Secretary Extraordinaire for business genius Terry Lennox Esquire?'

'Yes. His that the Manager of Customer Services for Backland Hinternational Cakes and Confectionery?' replied Elizabeth in a mock-posh voice.

'Yes, and she is ringing to say thanks for the flowers,' Janey said.

'Pleasure!' said Elizabeth. 'And thank you for yours as well, they're lovely.'

'An extra thank you for the card, by the way. FF! You pair of sods!'

'We thought it himpolite to write "Fart-Face" in full.'

'Yes, but everybody now thinks that's the size of my chest!'

'You're never only a double F! ZZ Top named their band after your old bras.'

'Bugger off and have a nice first day!' Janey said, not able to keep up the annoyed act then.

'Bugger off yourself, Oh great one,' said Elizabeth, blowing a noisy kiss down the line.

Then Janey set to. She was only surprised they had any customers left at all. There was a constant stream of customers ringing up complaining that they hadn't had a reply to their original complaint sent in an average three months ago, which was doubling the already ridiculous workload. Serve them right for employing a twelve-year-old flibberty-gibbet with a posh degree, thought Janey with some satisfaction, preparing to bring some age and commonsense to the proceedings. She took a couple of girls off data-inputting and put them on those phone calls alone, then she cleared it with Personnel to get some more temps in until they'd dealt with the backlog. They put up a fight and uttered the word 'budget' a lot, but Janey stuck her size nine kitten heels in. She had rolled up her mental and physical sleeves and was suddenly a force to be reckoned with. As she looked down, the sight of her breasts jutting out in front of her seemed to empower her even more. She had seen the effect they had on George. She was a powerful woman – a battleship. She felt bloody marvellous.

Teddy Sanderson leaned over to Helen. 'Can I get you a coffee?' he asked softly.

Helen stole a quick look at the large railway clock on the wall facing her desk and despaired.

'I'm so sorry, Teddy, I didn't notice the time,' she said, struggling to her feet.

'No, really dear, I wasn't pursuing you. I could see you were busy and I do know how to switch a kettle on,' said her boss, gesturing for her to sit back down on her office seat. 'Now, milk and no sugar, am I right?'

'Er, yes,' she said, feeling a little odd at having the senior partner make her a drink, when it was her job to make him one. Teddy Sanderson, however, was not like any of the other solicitors she had worked for.

He was old school: a gentleman and a gentle man. Tall, slim but with nice, broad shoulders and a full head of white hair that made him look instantly older than his forty-seven years, until you studied his almost lineless face. He had a grown-up son reading Medicine at Southampton University, a handsome, good-natured boy who popped in sometimes when he was on holiday.

Teddy became a widower the same month that Helen became a bride, she had recently learned. He lived alone, except for when his son visited, in a huge gabled house secluded by trees that reminded her very much of her parents' Old Rectory, whenever she caught snatches of it through the gates as she drove past. Helen had been his secretary for three years now and he had never treated her with anything but kindness and respect. Kindness was very dangerous to Helen at the moment, though. She felt so tired and limp and nauseous that she just wanted someone to hold her and tell her that everything was going to be all right. She had turned to her mother for comfort and told her she was sick and scared. However, Penelope Luxmore was a harder and completely different animal to her daughter, and her advice had been very succinct: to pull herself together before she made herself any sicker. Oh, and to drink ginger tea, which apparently had cured her own, negligible hiccup of morning sickness.

Helen knew she could always call on Janey and Elizabeth, and that both of them would have been extremely cross to find out she was feeling this way and hadn't rung to talk, but figured they both had quite enough to worry about with new jobs and their own pregnancies, and so she struggled on with her heavy heart alone. More than ever just then, she wished her dad would come through that door and cuddle her.

As she stared at it, willing it to happen, it flew open and Teddy Sanderson came in with a mug of coffee. Helen then burst into tears, giving her 'making a fool of myself in front of the boss' as something else to add to her list of 'how stupid I am's. As if Simon hadn't given her enough.

Chapter 23

Elizabeth felt quite guilty about reminding Terry Lennox that she wouldn't be in on her third day as she had to go to the hospital for a dating scan.

'Well, don't rush back,' said Terry Lennox, lifting up his *I'm The Boss, But Only When My Wife Lets Me* mug. 'That's the worst coffee I've ever tasted.'

'You drank it, didn't you?' Elizabeth threw back.

'I was extremely thirsty,' he said. 'Oh, and if you're not back by after lunch, I'll have your wages docked.'

'I'll call into Starbucks and bring you a slice of their rum and raisin cheesecake if you shut up,' said Elizabeth with a mischievous grin and Terry Lennox shut up, apart from grumbling something under his breath about 'bloody secretaries taking over the world'. Elizabeth sailed out of the building that evening with a big fat smile on her face, feeling as if she had been there for years already.

She had a 9.15 appointment the next morning but was in the hospital car park twenty minutes before that for good measure. She had drunk a full litre of water an hour before, as instructed on her letter, which had been easy enough, but by the time she reached the antenatal waiting room, liquid was almost oozing out of her eyes and she felt as voluminous as a grand piano. There were two women with appointments in front of hers, which made her realize that no way was she going to be on time and would probably have burst by then anyway. The first woman in the queue had a husband who couldn't sit still, saying in a whisper that was tantamount to anyone else's shout, that hospitals made him nervous. The second woman was really a girl in a school uniform who was crying because she couldn't keep the water down. Her boyfriend stood nearby in spots and a baseball cap and a grubby white shell-suit that made his super-skinny body look as if it actually had some meat on it.

By the time they called out her name, Elizabeth was a walking water bomb. She went into a softly darkened room where the white-coated lady sonographer helped her up onto a couch and positioned Elizabeth's maternity trousers so they just about covered her dignity, then she apologized for the gel being cold before she proceeded to squirt it all over Elizabeth's tummy.

Elizabeth gave a startled gasp. Cold? It's so cold it must have been stored up Simon's backside! she thought, which made her want to laugh, and she knew she better not with a bladder that full. She couldn't see what the sonographer was looking at on the screen in front of her but she was studying it intently, whilst moving a probe through the gel on her stomach.

'I think just over twelve weeks is spot on,' she said eventually. 'So, judging by the date of your last period, you're looking at a late September baby, around the twentieth, although it could be as late as two weeks after that.'

'So by mid-October, he'll definitely be out, one way or the other?'

'That's right. Want to see?' said the sonographer, and before Elizabeth could say aye or nay, she had twisted the monitor around to show a screen full of grainy lines. Then, like a magic-eye picture that suddenly makes sense, something moved and Elizabeth realized what she was looking at. Not for one minute did she expect to see something as formed as the vision on the screen. She could make out the clear shape of a baby with the makings of toes and fingers. She also didn't expect to cry out as she did. Her eyes filled up and started spilling warm tears over her cheeks.

'It gets quite a few people, that first sighting,' said the sonographer, snapping out a tissue for her from a ready supply at her side.

Elizabeth could see his little spine and his big head and his little thin legs. The sonographer pointed out his tiny feet and his heart.

'You can take some pictures home,' she said, moving the probe around to show her some more angles.

'Can I?' squeaked Elizabeth, dabbing at her eyes which were clouding her vision of the little bones picked out in white.

That was her baby, nobody else's. Hers.

'You can collect them at the Reception desk outside when you've had a wee,' said the sonographer, wiping the jelly off her stomach a minute or so later. 'I expect you are more than ready for one now!'

It was positively the most rewarding visit to the loo she had ever had in her life and she could easily have given Niagara Falls a run for its money. Then she picked up the pictures of her baby at the desk, paid over her money for them and headed back to her car with the envelope pressed against her heart. Down the corridor a couple of boisterous, flirting teenagers were play-fighting. They would have knocked into her had not something dark and non-negotiable spiralled up in Elizabeth. Her left arm shot out and swept the girl clear of her space.

'Watch it!'

The girl was going to give her some face-saving lip back, but one look at the small woman's glittering eyes made her save the cocky 'stupid cow' comment until she was well clear. Elizabeth wasn't sure if this instinctive protectiveness was love that she felt for the thing growing inside her, but she did think she might have killed anyone who tried to harm it.

'I wish they'd hurry up. I'll burst, I will!' said Janey, in the same waiting room, but four hours later.

'So I suppose tickling you wouldn't be a good idea?' whispered George, clawing up his hands and making a slow menacing move towards her ribcage with them.

'You dare,' she said, edging back from him. 'Maybe later though!' and they both laughed, even though she wanted to cry with discomfort.

'Those boobs of yours are getting bigger by the

hour,' said George, pointing at them as if she didn't know where they were.

'Gerroff my pups, you!' said Janey, batting his hand away.

'Pups? Pups, you say? They aren't pups. They're fully grown Alsatians!' said George. 'Bloody hell, Janey, I'll have to get some Polaroids of them before they go down again.'

'Dirty bugger,' she said, whilst hoping they wouldn't go down that much. She had forgotten how much fun they used to have with them in the pre-diet days.

'Excuse me,' Janey said, grabbing the attention of a passing nurse. 'I'm not one for moaning, but I can't hang on much longer.'

The nurse gave her a sympathetic look. 'We are running very late,' she smiled. 'Look, go and let a little out just to take some of the pressure off your bladder. Sometimes they do get so full they interfere with the quality of the picture anyway. Just a little one, mind!'

Easier said than done, for once she had started, Janey couldn't stop. She reckoned that when she finally managed to squeal the brakes on, she must have built up a pelvic-floor muscle like Schwarzenegger's arm. She had just come out of the loo when her name was called and with a, 'Thank God,' Janey followed the lady in the white coat down the corridor. George helped his wife up onto the couch by holding her bottom which made the sonographer laugh. The gel squirted on Janey's stomach was not as cold as the ice-cubes from Saturday night, but a bit chillier than the squirty cream from Sunday afternoon. She lay there still with George holding her hand in the quiet, dark little room with the bunny curtains. Then, when the checks had been completed, the sonographer turned the screen around and George burst into tears as Janey went into shock.

She could not move, she was so overcome with guilt that she hadn't wanted this child as much as her career; this wonderful tiny living thing inside her that made her catch her breath and instantly added another dimension to her life with a free batch of new never-felt-before emotions thrown in. She had read what it would look like at twelve weeks but never thought for one minute that today she would be seeing a baby-shaped baby inside her. *Their baby.* She would never know how it had happened as they were so careful about contraception, but it didn't matter any more. Seeing her own baby growing inside her, feeling George's joy impact upon her heart was powerful and magic, and humbled her. It was the moment Janey fell in love with her baby. It was also the moment that she realized how much she loved the big, hairy lump blowing his big nose on his big hankie next to her. How could she have thought there was a life out there for her without him?

Helen hadn't taken the car to work because Simon was supposed to be picking her up and together they were going to the hospital. Then he rang to say that his meeting had overrun and she would have to get a taxi and go alone.

'But it's my scan!' she cried.

'Don't you think I don't know that,' he hissed down the line, his voice muffled as if he was covering up his mouth so others wouldn't hear. 'I can't do anything about it. Don't you think I would if I could?'

Teddy Sanderson caught her ringing for a taxi and made her cancel it, and then he insisted on driving Helen to the hospital in his Bentley, even though she protested. Thanks to Simon and the crushing discomfort of all the water she had drunk, she was not in the mood for small talk and Teddy was sensitive to this and hummed along to the radio without trying to engage her in banal conversation. He deposited her at the front entrance to the small private hospital on the outskirts of Wakefield and she declined his offer to wait with her, saying she would get a taxi home. She was not sure that she could keep the water in or down; it was making her feel ill and she had embarrassed herself quite enough in front of Teddy Sanderson recently with her crying fit, even though he had been very kind to her.

Luckily for Helen, she was shown straight to the sonographer as the appointment before hers had been cancelled at the last minute. She was helped up onto the couch and yelped at the icy hit of gel on her skin, but her reaction to the first sight of her baby was very much different to how she imagined it would be. She felt her heart almost stop. It was as if time stood still as she stared at her baby growing and moving inside her. She had thought she would cry or scream with joy at this moment that she had waited so long for, but she only smiled. She felt as if her whole being had been filled up with calm, warm sunshine that threw the sickness and tiredness and those stupid rows with Simon into dark shadows. It was the most thrilling thing she had ever seen, *her baby inside her.* She felt fulfilled, beatific, in harmony with life.

She looked at the blur of little fingers and toes, attempting to count them.

'He'll have nails on those,' said the sonographer.

'Her,' said Helen. 'I just know it's a her.'

This moment was theirs, mother and child, a moment she would carry with her for ever because it imprinted itself upon her and became part of her. Everything outside it was immaterial, of no consequence. For one wonderful minute, nothing else in the universe mattered but them.

Chapter 24

'So how did you get on?' said Elizabeth down the phone, as her first working week at Just the Job HQ came to an end.

'Job or baby?' said Janey.

'Job.'

'Amazing.'

'And your scan?'

'Amazing.'

'What did George think?'

'Amazing.'

'Haven't you got a *Thesaurus* in your house?'

Janey laughed. 'What date have they given you?'

'September the twentieth, and yourself?'

'Thirtieth, so we're all about the same then, aren't we? I'll ring Hels and see how she is in a bit. Have you heard from her?'

'Well, I rang on Sunday and spoke to Simon because she was having a lie-down, but she didn't ring back,' said Elizabeth, who wouldn't have put it past the oily tosser not to have passed her message on.

'What about you then? What did you think when you first saw the baby?' asked Janey.

'It's still sinking in,' said Elizabeth. 'Unbelievable, I suppose.'

'So come on, how's the new job?'

'It's great, I really like it, lovely people, Terry Lennox is ace and I've got a desk overlooking the canal. So how's being a whip handler?'

'I love it,' said Janey with relish. 'The Department was so bad I couldn't have made it worse if I tried, which helped.'

'Don't be so modest,' said Elizabeth. 'You're good at what you do and we all know it.'

'Bloody hell, Elizabeth, don't start giving me compliments – this week has been weird enough as it is without *that* happening.'

Elizabeth rang Helen after she had spent a good half an hour, and a good half jar of olives, on the phone with Janey. They did not talk for long though. From the edgy way Helen was speaking, it was obvious Slimy was hovering in the background so they did a brief summary of the main events and agreed to catch up properly later. Helen was going out for a meal with some of Simon's friends and was just in the middle of getting ready so Elizabeth left her to it. She herself was only set for a night in with the fire on and a battered cod supper, but she wouldn't have swapped social lives with Helen in a million years.

She was just pouring out some raspberry tea, hoping to shift a few acidy burps, when there was a distinctively heavy knock on the door.

'I was just passing,' John said, when she opened it to him.

'Liar,' she replied and moved aside to let him in. 'I suppose you want a cuppa?'

'Aye please, but not that fruity stuff,' he said, sniffing up and wrinkling his nose.

Cleef had got up, for once, and started purring and wrapping his silky, black tail around John's boots.

'I'm going to tread on this cat one of these days,' he said, lifting him up.

'You won't be here that often,' she said, and then felt immediately annoyed at herself. 'Sorry, I didn't mean that the way it came out,' she said.

Blimey, she apologized! he thought and looked at her as if she had gone insane.

'What?' she questioned.

'Nothing.' He sat down in the usual seat at the table and shrugged off his coat. 'There was a reason I called in,' he went on. 'I can get some paint – it's the best stuff, look,' and he handed over a paint chart. 'I wondered if you wanted some for the bairn's room.'

'What colour?' said Elizabeth, getting out a cup for him.

'Any colour you want, straight off that chart.'

'Not off the back of a lorry, is it?' she said suspiciously.

'Back of a . . . you cheeky mare! Is it hell! It's an insurance write-off for smoke-damaged stock. Well, the tins are – the paint inside them is okay. People are always trying to sell or swap things on building sites.'

'I can get paint cheap anyway with my staff discount.'

'You can't get it cheaper than free, can you?'

'Free? How come they're giving it away?'

'Oh, for goodness' sake!' said John, throwing his hands up in exasperation. 'I'm getting it for free because the bloke who's flogging it is trying to get on my good side. He'll want a favour later, no doubt. That answer your question?'

'I'll have a look,' she said. 'I hadn't thought about a nursery yet,' although he alerted her to the fact that she really should start.

She supposed the baby would go in her auntie's old room, which was a lot bigger than hers was, as she shared the back half of the house with the bathroom. She had never moved herself into the larger room because she always felt safe and secure where she was and sometimes, in the middle of the night, she was sure she could hear those three circles and a flop that Sam always did. She wanted him to haunt her; it was a nice feeling knowing he was still around, looking out for her.

'You eaten?' he asked, after he had drained his cup.

'Not yet. I was going to get a fish supper from Les,' she said.

'I haven't eaten either. What if I go for them and you get an extra plate out? It's bitter cold out there, you don't want to be going out in it in your condition.'

'It's only a bit of cold. This is Barnsley not Siberia!'

'Just get the kettle on again, you,' he said, not giving her room to argue further because he then slid back into his expensive-looking jacket, flicked up the collar and swanned out of the house.

She stood at the window and watched his broad,

leather-clad back disappear down the street. At least his clothes sense is better now than it was back then, she thought, remembering that first sight of the black-garbed cowboy sauntering towards her in the bus station like he was going to ask her where the nearest gold mine was. And thank goodness he saw sense to shave off that stupid moustache! She smiled, then realized she was smiling and stopped and went to get the table ready. She made some fresh tea, buttered some bread and put an extra setting out. Whilst she waited for him to return, she took a quick look at the paint chart. There was a lovely pale lemon that caught her eye and, as yellow had been her Auntie Elsie's favourite colour, it seemed a good choice for the large front bedroom.

Her tummy rumbled although she knew she wasn't in for a long wait as the chip shop was just at the bottom of the snicket. It was locally known as 'Les Miserable's', but not in the French way. Les Shaw, who had run the place since Elizabeth was a girl, was the most miserable-tempered human being on the planet – but his batter was the best in the area and his chips were superb. John came back soon with enough food to sink the *Bismarck*.

'Well, you're eating for two,' he explained.

'Me and a three-inch baby, not two giant starving hippos!' she said. 'There must be half of Ireland in chips here!'

'Get stuck in then and stop mithering.'

'I don't eat chips.'

'That's what I liked about you, Elizabeth, you were

always such a grateful beggar,' he said, and plonked a handful of chips on her plate anyway. He remembered how she used to eat the equivalent of her own body weight in them every week, not that it ever made her put any weight on.

'I won't even make a hole in this!' she said.

'Well, eat what you can and leave the rest on the side of your plate,' he said, and she smiled involuntarily because that's what her Auntie Elsie used to say.

She made more of an impact on the feast than she had thought possible.

'Remember sitting on the seafront at Blackpool with fish and chips, trying to spot the biggest bottom that walked past us?' he grinned as he sat back and stroked his full stomach. 'I said that whoever won was going to buy the ice creams . . .'

'That's right, and you won,' she said. 'That bloke with the vest and the braces! Then you said that it should have been the loser that bought them.'

'Yes, but I honoured it, didn't I?' he laughed.

'Aye, but you moaned about it.' The memory came running to the front of her mind as if it was showing off how clear it still was.

'And that fat kid fell off the donkey and his dad came rushing over . . .'

'. . . And fell in the donkey crap,' she finished off for him. 'Oh God, that was so funny!'

'We bought a bucket and spade and made sand-castles, and that old bloke thought we were bonkers.'

'Well, you had your shorts on and a leather jacket.

I thought you were bonkers, never mind him!'

'And I won that teddy bear for throwing darts. I don't suppose you still have it?'

An alarm went off; things were starting to get too cosy.

'No,' she said flatly, 'of course I don't. It's all years ago,' and she started to clear up the plates.

Those days were gone and they had no business going back to them, especially to that day in Blackpool. They had gone there on a mad sunny whim and somewhere in the hours that followed she had started looking at him in a different light. The big guy with his hair getting ruffled by the sea breezes and his face turning brown in the sun and his dark chocolate eyes sparkling with fun, laughter and some other ingredient she was scared she recognized as they twirled around on the Waltzers. He'd taken her hand, they had run down the prom like kids, and she did not want him to let go of it when they slowed down, but she pulled it away all the same. Then she had made up some stupid argument when they got home because she knew he was starting to take root in a forbidden place in her heart. She made him storm off and the next time she saw him, that Lisa was all over him like a rash at Janey's cousin's wedding and she forced herself to totally blank him. He got drunk and pulled her outside and he kissed her with soft but insistent lips and said he loved her. She shoved him off and wiped the taste of him from her mouth and told him to piss off. *Hadn't he got the message? She didn't love him, she hated him.* She felled him like a tree. She would always remember how he looked at her then, love and hurt and confusion all vying with each other for supremacy.

Elizabeth shook the memory away and forced out a yawn. 'I'll have to get to bed soon, I've had a hard week at work.'

'Nice place? You enjoying it?'

'Smashing and yes. I suppose you'll be going out, it being Friday an' all.'

'No, I'm not going out,' he said, but took the hint and got up.

'Thanks for tea, John,' she said.

'It's all right. Here,' and he pulled out of his back jeans pocket a business card. 'Just in case you didn't keep my number last time. Ring me if you're ever stuck,' and he went to pin it up on the noticeboard behind the door, where she had put up one of the scan pictures.

'This him then?' he said, after taking it off and looking at it for a long time.

'Yes, that's him.'

'That's amazing. Look, fingers and everything!' He pinned it back up after he had looked at it some more. 'I could have come with you, you know, if you'd asked.'

'Whatever for?'

'Just in case you felt a bit "single". I could have pretended to be your other half.'

'John Silkstone, what age are you living in? There are more single mothers than couples out there these days.'

'I still think a kid needs a father though,' he said,

and instantly regretted it as her face clouded over.

'Well, I didn't, did I? Anyway, thanks again and goodnight.'

'Maybe if you'd had a right dad, Elizabeth, you wouldn't be so bloody closed up,' he said, as he went out of the door. He was barely out of it before he heard her lock it behind him. Just like she had locked him out of her heart.

Chapter 25

The Fox Inn was attracting so many office types since the new owners took over, that it was known locally as 'the Fax Inn'. It had become quickly famous for its opulent décor, ridiculous prices and exclusive clientèle. The food was bettered in many minor establishments, not that it mattered because at the Fox, appearance was everything. It suited Simon down to the ground. At the very second that Elizabeth's door was closed on John Silkstone, Simon was pushing the Fox's oak portal open for his business associate Con, and his horsey wife Melia. Con was actually nice, something Helen could not say about many of his friends. Melia was okay but not exactly good, girly company. She always seemed bored, unless the conversation turned equestrian.

'You look nice,' said Con, leaning over and kissing Helen as they walked over to the table.

'Thank you,' she said, knowing he was lying through his back teeth, but she appreciated his gallantry. She felt totally washed out and looked it, and wondered when the legendary 'blooming' was supposed to start, because she felt very much as if she might have blinked and missed it. Janey was looking more fantastic than ever before; her eyes were shining and she was bouncing with energy. Elizabeth suited the extra weight, it made her face look younger and cheekier, but Helen's only intimation that she was in glowing pregnancy was the growing bulge around her middle. Her breasts were still flat and her hair was lank and greasy, however many times she washed it. Her skin had not cleared up either and was rough and so spotty that Simon told her to go back and put more make-up on when she presented herself earlier for his approval.

'And don't you have anything smarter than that dress?' he threw after her as she was about to walk tearfully into the en-suite.

'Yes, of course I do, but nothing that doesn't press on my stomach,' she said, 'and if you don't want me to vomit all over Con and Melia, I suggest I had better wear loose clothing.'

He cast her a look as if he was unsure what species she was and then stomped off to get his jacket from the wooden valet next to his Benetton neat wardrobes.

Simon was giving Melia the sort of full-beamed attention Helen wished he would give her and she felt herself growing green, but not from nausea this time. Melia had four-year-old twins and her stomach had snapped straight back into her original size eight, which gave Helen some hope that afterwards her body would sort itself out too. Maybe then Simon would see her as attractive again. Sexually attractive as well, for despite having just reached the long-awaited twelve-week marker when the baby was 'bedded in', Simon still would not touch her intimately. He was now saying that knowing the baby was in there totally put him off and he rolled away from her and slept as near to the edge of the bed as was possible. Janey hadn't helped, talking about how Elvis never saw Priscilla as an object of desire again after she got pregnant, although it had been part of a general conversation and not in any way directed at her. Helen had not told her friends that Simon and she were experiencing problems; everyone continued to be blinded by the illusion that they were the golden couple.

'Well, I'm not Priscilla and Simon isn't Elvis!' she had told herself after the Janey conversation. That would not happen to them – she would make damn sure it didn't. Plus it was perfectly understandable that some guys were put off by pregnancy fat, only to be loving husbands and fathers when the baby finally came along, she rationalized. She had wondered if Simon felt excluded from what was happening – she had read that some men did – and so tried to involve him at every stage, but that had only served to annoy him more. Her only hope was to bide her time and wait until September when her baby came into the world and things would fall naturally into place again.

As she was about to order, Simon stepped in and asked if she would like him to do it for her. She accepted his offer, beaming at his chivalry, only to watch the others tuck into duck pâté and fried cheeses whilst she chomped her way through a boring melon salad. He poured her half a glass of the South African Pinotage, when it arrived, for which she managed to smile convincingly gratefully. She suddenly wished she could get totally blasted and have a merry evening, make a total fool of herself, anything but endure this crippling, conversational desert she was sharing with Melia. Con and Simon talked business for most of the meal, whilst their wives had a banal and strained interchange. It was hard work as it was fairly obvious Melia would rather be joining in with the boys than talking babies. Melia had a fulltime nanny and Helen doubted that she ever saw her children long enough to be able to recognize them in a line-up. If she wasn't at the gym, she was having hot stone massages, doing Pilates classes or playing at her stables.

'Simon tells me you're going to be busy decorating after the weekend!' said Con.

'Did he?' Helen looked at Simon for clues as she really had no idea what Con was talking about.

'We're starting the nursery on Monday – well, the decorators are, anyway,' said Simon, putting his hand down over hers and Con smiled indulgently. No doubt he and Melia subscribed to the theory that the Cadberrys were the perfect loving couple too, who would make upper-middle-class love when they got home, with a half-time break for champers and canapés.

'Yes, that's right,' Helen affirmed blindly.

'Who's doing it for you?' asked Melia with slitty-eyed curiosity.

'Chansons,' said Simon, delighted with the opportunity to swank the name of the 'in' decorators up North. It was a mutually beneficial agreement – he got a top name quickly and cheaply; they got a big fat discount on their advertising bill.

'Bloody hell!' said Melia with admiration. 'We couldn't get them for months for Barcelona's room' – she pronounced the name *Bar-the-luuu-na*, lingering over the vowels like Julio Iglesias might in a love serenade. 'So, what colour scheme are you going for then?'

'Well, I was thinking . . .' began Helen.

'White,' Simon said, smiling beautifully.

'You'd be better with an off-white,' said Con. 'We did Salvador's room in white at first and had to redecorate. Far too bloody cold for a baby.'

'It's classic and neutral. The house theme is white,' said Simon with icy explanation.

White? Helen's first thought was disappointment, but her second was more comforting; with lots of pink or blue accessories, it would not look cold at all when she had finished with it.

'We'd better clear the room out quick then!' laughed Helen to Con. 'It's absolutely full of Simon's junk.' Whereas she was thrilled that Simon was thinking about the baby, she wished he had given her slightly more notice. It would take forever to shift all that stuff out.

'Which room are you talking about, Helen?' Simon said to her slowly and deliberately, as if she were slightly retarded.

'The guest room, of course.' Her smile withered as his head began to move wearily from side to side.

'No, we're putting the baby in the little room.'

'We can't do that, it's far too poky!' she protested.

'The guest room isn't appropriate – besides, I have plans for it. The little room is far more sensible and, as it's more or less empty, it can be done quickly.'

'I'll clear it out, I don't mind!' said Helen, a little more loudly than she had intended, biting back the temptation to ask where he would go to sulk if the little room was occupied. Maybe that's what his secret plans for the guest room were.

'We've gone through all this before. Honestly, you and your hormones, darling, you can't remember a thing at the moment, can you? The small room is perfectly adequate for a tiny baby,' he said, and gave her hand a hard squeeze whilst smiling softly. Helen heeded the warning and she quickly moved onto a less controversial subject.

Janey woke up late on Sunday morning to the smell of paint. She weaved a yawning path down the hallway to the spare room earmarked for the little one to find George in some old clothes, halfway up a ladder finishing off wall number two with lilac emulsion.

'Oh, flaming hell, I wanted it to be a surprise for you!' he said, hearing the door creak open. 'I didn't want you to see it until I'd finished.'

'Wow, it's going to look really bonny, isn't it?' she said, visualizing some nice lilac curtains with swags and tails framing the pretty picture of the quiet back gardens. Obviously she would make them herself.

'Only the best for Hobson junior!' said George.

'We'll have to start thinking about names, won't we?' said Janey.

'Whitney or Brad, I was thinking.'

'Hmm, I fancy Keanu or Sinitta.'

'Eric or Hilda?'

'We can't call it the same name as the goldfish. I might get confused and start feeding it mealworms!'

'Or stick your boob in the aquarium!'

They both laughed; it was a tinkly sweet sound that left them smiling at each other.

'I'll get us some toast and come and help you,' she said.

'Naw, get back to bed for a bit, you shouldn't be climbing ladders and stuff,' said George.

'George, I feel as fit as a flea. Let me help you!'

That was the truth of it, too. Janey felt better than she had done in the whole of her twenties and early thirties put together. There was no worrying about dieting, no frustrations about her career, and her sexlife was better than a rabbit's in a Viagra-testing laboratory.

'I've got two things to show you,' said George, stepping off the ladder.

'Oh yes?' said Janey saucily.

'Give over, you minx!' He dragged over something that lay under a dust sheet. He whipped this off, to reveal a dainty little crib carved out of wood. Janey dropped to her knees to examine it.

'George, when the hell did you do this?'

'Ah, hang on, not finished yet.' He flicked a switch on at the side which made the crib start to slowly rock.

'You really are a clever sod, aren't you?' said Janey with admiration.

'I'll carve the bairn's name at the top when we decide,' said George, thrilled that she liked it. It was the way he was wired; he just got pleasure from making her happy.

'And what was the other thing?' said Janey.

'Close your eyes.'

'Closed.'

She heard scuffling.

'Now open them,' said George.

Janey flashed her eyes open to find George standing beside her with a massive plastic Viking helmet on. Her libido roared into life, firing up instantly on all cylinders. She swaggered over, her nightie already half off and, for now, George abandoned trying to please her with his paintbrush and satisfied her with his longboat instead.

The surprise decorators came first thing Monday morning to Helen's house and decorated the poky spare room at the end of the hallway plain white. It was to be a cold, small nursery for their baby.

Chapter 26

At Elizabeth's fourteenth-week antenatal appointment, she heard her baby's heartbeat for the first time. It was going like a racehorse in the last furlong of the National and she panicked immediately and said, 'What's up with him?'

Sue, the midwife, laughed kindly and replied, 'That's a good strong heartbeat, nice and normal. A baby's heartbeat is faster than yours or mine.'

Satisfied then that he was all right, Elizabeth lay back and listened to him, totally unconscious of the width of the smile on her face. She had looked at the scan pictures so many times, but hearing him inside her, thriving, *living*, was indescribable. It was so loud, so positive. At least she must be growing him right.

She came home from the surgery to find three tins of Lemon Sunshine emulsion and some white gloss and brushes on the back doorstep.

John had refused to take any money for the paint he had left. He said that it had not cost him anything in the end and so he couldn't very well charge her for it now, could he? Then the next week he brought her some huge fluffy white towels that one of the blokes on-site was selling off for his wife who worked in a textile factory. They were supposed to be seconds, although Elizabeth couldn't see anything remotely faulty about them. She had ended up with a beautiful stack of baby-soft towels for a fiver. This was followed by baby nappies the week after – again, smoke-damaged stock apparently, although like the paint, there was not a hint of anything smutty about the packaging. He brought her enough to keep the little one in nappies until he was twenty-five.

The morning of Helen's sixteenth week was the anniversary of her daddy's death. April was a queer month; sometimes it countermanded the dictates of March that spring was on its way and froze the air, sending howling winds and cruel showers. Sometimes it was as balmy as summer and permitted the early May bluebells to fill the woods like thick, violet carpets. Today it was as then, bright and bitter, and the night that followed it would be dangerously beautiful. Chips of diamond stars would be peppered across the black skies and it would be so very cold.

She took red flowers to his grave in Maltstone churchyard – long scarlet Asiatic lilies – and arranged them in the pot there. Funny how we fear death so much, but come to these places to sit amongst the dead and find comfort, she thought, taking a place on the nearby bench that was under the budding cherry-blossom tree, and she talked to her father as if he was there beside her and not buried in the ground.

'I still feel so sick all the time, Daddy,' she said. 'I wish you were here to tell me everything is all right. I know it is really, but it would sound so much better coming from you.'

She did not know how long she sat there telling him about her fears, but her bones were stiff when she got up for a badly needed stretch and flex. She was getting hefty around the middle now, her little waist had all but disappeared, but still her breasts stayed disappointingly small. She wasn't greedy – she would have been happy with an extra cup-size. Just so that she could fill a normal bra, for once, without having to pad herself up in special bras stuffed with chicken-fillet gel pouches. Not that there was anyone around to enjoy them even if they filled out as big as water-melons. Simon was not involving himself in the pregnancy at all, despite the glimmer of hope she had felt when he had made the effort to get the decorators in for the nursery. She soon came to realize that that had more to do with bandying famous names about than preparing for their baby's arrival. He had ignored the scan pictures and changed the subject at the mere mention of anything veering towards her condition.

Helen desperately tried to rationalize his reactions and concluded that maybe he just couldn't relate to something he couldn't see properly or hold yet. So she stored the bags of baby things that she so much wanted to show off to him in the cold little room at the end of the hallway instead and bided her time. She hated that room where Simon always slept when they had one of those silly arguments that swamped her like a tidal wave and left her dazed and battered. She did not want her baby sleeping in there and said so to her father's grave.

'*Goodness me, girl, where's your Luxmore backbone!*' She heard her father's voice as clear as day, even though she knew she was imagining it. It was what he always said to her when she needed that extra spur, like when Carmen Varley started to call her 'posh cow' names at school and she came home crying. Her father sat her down and talked it through with her; he told her how bullies functioned, and that standing up to Miss Varley would be a far better option in the long run, because bullies did not let go of weaker meat. So Helen had gone into school the next morning, armed with a Luxmore backbone full of iron, only to find Carmen Varley sobbing from a split lip and a triumphant Elizabeth there to greet her with a: 'I've brayed her up for you' as she put it.

'*Stand up to bullies, darling, don't ever let them walk all over you,*' that's what her father had said, and he had been right then and was still right now. Helen decided there and then that she was not going to put her baby in that horrible room. She would clear out the large, sunny guest room and somehow she would get her own way on this.

'I love you, Daddy – sweet dreams,' she said to him in death as she had in life, always, every night. Even on the night nineteen years ago, when she killed him.

'You okay for baby towels?' Elizabeth asked as she climbed into Janey's Volvo. Her seventeenth-week appointment to see the consultant was only half an hour before Janey's, so they had decided to go up together and have some lunch afterwards in the hospital café.

'Am I okay for baby towels?' said Janey with a sigh. 'I've got about three hundred, thanks to Joyce. I was going to ask you if you wanted some. Why? Where've you got yours from?'

'Oh, er . . . a sale on the market,' said Elizabeth. If she told her the truth, Janey would regard that as tantamount to an engagement.

'Got your sample?' checked Janey. 'And your notes?'

'Affirmative,' said Elizabeth. 'Do you think Mr Greer will give us an internal?'

'You should be so lucky!' said Janey, but Elizabeth didn't laugh for once and Janey adjusted her tone. 'You're not scared, are you?'

'Well, I'm a bit nervous,' said Elizabeth.

'You'll be okay, you daft bat. You won't have anything he hasn't seen before.'

'I know that,' said Elizabeth, although that did not make her welcome the prospect any the more.

The hospital was less than a ten-minute drive away, but finding a parking space was the difficult part. Luck was on their side that day though and they slotted into a nice vacancy right by the door. They reported their arrivals to the Antenatal receptionist and then took a seat as instructed, amongst a room full of other women with varying-sized bumps.

'Well, we're never going to be seen on time, here!' said Janey with a huff. 'I can't see why they bother putting a time on your card if you're going to be seen two hours later,' and with that she picked up a magazine and started reading about Tantric Sex, although she could not see what all the fuss was about. Who wanted to wait seven hours for an orgasm when George could give her three or four in that time, as last Saturday night proved? She had made a note on the Sunday morning to let him have chilli con carne followed by apple crumble more often.

Eventually, Elizabeth's name was called and she moved to another queue outside the consultant's room, to be joined ten minutes later by a moaning Janey.

'Where do you think we'll be queuing next?' she asked, wearily flopping down next to Elizabeth, who did not have time to answer as the consultant's door opened and it was her turn to go in.

She liked Mr Greer instantly. He reminded her of Alex Luxmore: tall, lean, quiet and courteous. He scanned through her notes whilst a nurse in the background took her sample and tested it. Then she had her blood pressure taken and the results noted and Mr Greer asked if she had any problems, which she hadn't. He smiled and said, 'Good, that's what I like to hear,' then he helped her up onto the couch, and she lay down stiffly, her muscles tight and tense, dreading the moment when he would slip on a glove and ask her to part her legs. She wasn't sure if she could.

He had warmed up his hands and felt around her stomach with his head cocked to one side as if filling in a mental checklist. Then he crooked his arm for her to take and he pulled her up by it and said,

'Everything seems fine. We'll see you again around thirty-four weeks, Ms Collier.'

'Is that it?' she asked.

'Yes, that's it,' said Mr Greer and went over to the sink to wash his hands.

'No internal?' Elizabeth said quietly to the nurse.

'It's not necessary,' she replied. 'They don't give them these days at this stage. Not unless there's a problem.'

When Mr Greer had finished with Janey, they both went up to 'Phlebs' to have their bloods taken. Elizabeth had elusive veins and the midwife would prod and poke at her arm taking bloods, so it was a relief to have the experts on the case. The older the pregnant woman, the greater the risk of the baby having Down's syndrome, so their blood was to be screened to assess the risks.

'What if it's high?' asked Elizabeth.

'Well, you'll be offered an amniocentesis,' said the blood nurse, 'but that's got its own risks. Why don't you cross that bridge if and when you come to it? The blood results are taking about two to three weeks to come through at the moment.'

'Three weeks?'

'Try and put it out of your mind until then. I know it's hard, but the radiographers take very thorough scans.' The nurse stuck a plaster on Elizabeth's arm and declared, 'All done!'

'The woman who scanned me said she had done a really thorough check and couldn't see any abnormalities,' said Janey to Elizabeth, getting out of the chair next to her.

'Scanned you? You sound like a bag of peas!'

'Don't you of all people talk to me about peas, missus! Anyway, whilst we're on the subject of grub, let's hit the baked spuds. I think we deserve one – what do you think?' said Janey, and marched her off in the direction of food without waiting for an answer.

Helen picked up the phone to Elizabeth's chirpy, 'Hello.'

'Hello, yourself,' she said back.

'What are you doing? You sound puffed out,' said Elizabeth.

'Oh, I'm just clearing a few bits and pieces out of the guest room.'

'Well, don't overdo it,' said Elizabeth. 'How are you feeling?'

'Oh, fine,' Helen lied, because she had just been sick again. She had mentioned her endless vomiting to her consultant last week at her seventeen-week appointment and he had offered her some drugs that would help, but the thought of them entering her baby made her decline. He said that prolonged nausea was unfortunately normal in some cases and suggested a few alternative remedies and she listened, without telling him that she had tried them all already.

'It's just a quickie because I'm at work, but I wanted to see if you were okay.'

'I'm absolutely fine. Thank you for worrying about me,' said Helen, who felt over-sensitive to sympathy in her weakened state and had to gulp back some tears fast.

'Well, look after yourself,' said Elizabeth. 'Don't go doing too much hard work. Go and have a wander around the shops instead and spend some of your millions.'

'I went shopping this morning with my mother for some fresh air,' said Helen.

'Did you buy any?'

'Ha, ha. Guess who I saw? Your friend!'

'I don't have any friends except you two,' said Elizabeth. 'Everyone hates me.'

'Oh, shut up. I saw John Silkstone.'

Elizabeth tried not to be interested but failed dismally. 'Oh? Where did you see him then?'

'Babyworld, can you believe? He was looking at a lovely blue rocking chair and a footstool.'

'Really?' said Elizabeth, whose nostrils were suddenly full of the smell of a big, fat, lying rat. Especially when the rat in question turned up with a cargo of furniture that very same evening in the back of a large van and tried to tell her they were from a fire-damaged warehouse. Both chair and stool were, *by startling co-incidence*, in a complementary shade of blue to the décor of her lounge. He was as strong as an ox and carried them both in, putting them *in situ* whilst she stood there smouldering and waiting for his big, fat, lying rat mouth to open.

'This will be just the job, excuse the pun, for you to relax in before the baby's born. Then when he's here, you can both rock yourselves to sleep in it,' John said, beaming proudly and nodding with approval at how good the two pieces looked by the window.

'Lot of fire-damaged warehouses about these days, aren't there?'

His smile withered when he saw how narrowed her eyes were.

'Er . . . well, yes, I suppose there are.'

'You bloody liar!' she snarled at him. 'You were spotted in Babyworld buying this earlier on today. What the hell are you up to, John Silkstone?'

He sighed and held up his hands in resigned defeat. At least he did not try to keep on lying.

'Okay, I'll come clean. I just wanted to help you.'

'Help? *Help*, is it? I don't need your sodding charity!'

'Charity?' he said, blocking out the light from the window and looking like a big black shadow. 'This isn't charity, Elizabeth. They're gifts, you know – the stuff that people give you and don't expect anything back for. But you, you haven't got the capacity to understand that. You're so hard to give anything to.'

'I don't *want* anything given to me!' she said, turning half-feral.

'So this is how you're going to bring up your baby, is it then, Elizabeth?' he said. 'Never learning to accept anything, never letting anyone be nice to him, and being that flaming hard he'll never recognize a bit of kindness when it happens? You'll teach him to push folks away all the time and not trust a soul? Is that what you want for him, eh, Elizabeth? To be as big a block of ice as you are?'

She stared at him, not able to bat anything back because she was in shock. His words had got right through to the core of her and made it listen. She had not thought of it before – that she would be her baby's point of reference and that he would pick up on how she was with people: the way she could not let her defences fall ever and found it so hard to trust even those who had never let her down. John had hurt her with what he had just said and she knew she'd hurt him too, that was obvious from the way he was shaking his head at her.

'I'll leave it here. If you really don't want it, ring me and I'll pick it up and take it back by the end of the week,' he said, wounded but riding it. Then he went, trying not to slam the door behind him, but he was a big bloke and how it shut was a definite statement on how he felt about her at that time.

Chapter 27

It had been the police who came to inform her that they had found her father dead at home; he had lain there for four days. The pub landlady at the Miner's Rest had rung them to find out why he had not turned up as usual, knowing that the February snow would never have been enough to keep Grahame Collier away from his tipple and the camaraderie, and they had broken the door down and found him upstairs in the bathroom. The cause of death was a heart-attack apparently, but cirrhosis of the liver was also written on the death certificate. He must have been in consi-derable pain, a fact that neither upset nor pleased Elizabeth. She had thought she might feel relief if she should ever see this day, but there was only numbness and disbelief, and she rang John for help when the police had gone, even though she couldn't remember doing it.

It had been he who had arranged the undertaker and the vicar. Later, he would talk to the solicitor and sort out the clearance of the house and the sale of it for Elizabeth too. And when the undertaker needed a suit in which to dress the late Mr Collier, John said he would get one from the house for him, but then Elizabeth announced he had done enough for her and she would go for it. She was adamant, but there was no way he would let her go alone and so they went together. She didn't know why she felt the compulsion to confront her fears after all those years, but the feeling was so strong that she knew she had to go with it. After all, it was just a house, an empty house, bricks and mortar, there was nothing there to frighten her, but she was shaking when her foot landed over the threshold and straight into the front room, in the absence of a hallway in those houses.

It was so much smaller than she remembered, but other than that, it was almost exactly as it had been on the day she had run from it, down the road to her Auntie Elsie's in her stockinged feet. It even smelled the same − a mix of cigarettes and dank air − a smell that made his presence feel very strong in the room. There was a thick layer of grime on the windows and the skirting boards were furry with dust; the nicotine had stained the wallpaper over the years and stencilled lighter squares where pictures had once been hung, then removed. The nets at the window were filthy and torn, and the tops of the big heavy brown velour curtains were grey with cobwebs. A print of an Indian woman with her hair over one shoulder was aslant, and Elizabeth remembered that it had always been that way. It added to the feel that time had not moved on and nothing had changed. Except it had − because she was a grown woman and no longer a scared and confused little girl. So why did she feel like one inside?

She wandered through to the kitchen. The walls behind the oven were thick with splashed grease, and the sink was piled high with mugs and plates. The bin in the corner was overflowing, and bottles and beer cans were defying gravity at the angle they were hanging out. There was a smell of something rotting, sour like milk but with a faint sweetness that made her want to retch.

'Come on,' said John, pulling her by the hand up stairs that had not seen a vacuum in years, by the look of it. They passed the bathroom door; thankfully it was shut. They had found him in there, hanging over the toilet bowl; a suitably undignified end to his undignified life. She hesitated in the doorway of her mam and dad's room. It was the same bed he had rolled her onto that day and most likely the same sheets too, judging from the stink of the place. She stood and stared at it, not knowing why she was mentally putting herself back there, letting him stroke her hair all over again and telling her what a big girl she was getting now and that she had to cuddle her dad and let him kiss her and show him that she loved him. She could still conjure up the feel of his tongue, hard and slimy as it wormed into her mouth, his hands moving up her leg . . . until she shook her head and sent the thoughts back to that dark place in the corner of her head again. She shivered, partly from the freezing temperature but mostly from the chill of stagnant memories trapped within these walls.

The big walnut wardrobe door opened with a creak behind her. There was not much in there to search through.

'This'll do,' said John, wanting to get her out of there as soon as possible.

'Do they want socks and shoes as well?' said Elizabeth flatly, her eyes still on the bed where Bev had suffered things she couldn't bear to think about.

'We'll get some just to make sure,' said John, hunting through drawers and looking around, although the best pair of shoes he could find were battered and scuffed.

'I'll polish them up,' he said. Elizabeth nodded and he took her arm and steered her out of the house. He locked the patched-up door, but the stench of the place followed her.

She didn't tell John until much later that she went to see her dad in the chapel of rest. He lay there looking death-bloated in a suit that was obviously too big for him with a made-up face looking more wax than flesh. His hands were placed together and they had done their best to get all the nicotine stains out but failed at the last. His nails were clipped, she had noticed that. Nice and neat like a daddy who took care of himself. She had not known why she'd come. She thought maybe she would say to his shell what had been in her heart all these years waiting to say to the man, but this was not a place for hate and he was dead and rotting before her eyes and could not answer her questions even if she had asked them. Then, when she saw the old shoes that John had polished and buffed up proud for him, a flood of unexpected and uncontrollable tears burst from her. She grieved for a dad that wasn't hers; one who protected her and took an interest in her and loved her appropriately like Janey's and Helen's dads had loved them. She found herself missing a dad she had never had and the pain was terrible.

There were few mourners at the service and no one she recognized. She had sat with John in church, listening to the vicar's eulogy about how Grahame Collier loved a pint and a bet on the horses and that he was a good worker and that he would be sorely missed by his friends at the Miner's Rest. Then, what a shame it was that he had died so relatively young and alone, but he was in God's arms now and in *eternal peace. There was no mention that he fiddled with his daughters.*

The mourners lingered by the grave in the frosted church-yard, hovering for invites to any refreshments that were going until John, politely, put them straight that there would be none. They kept their comments to themselves but there were mutterings of disgust that his own daughter could not do right by him, and they went to rectify that at his local where they would hold their pints up to heaven and toast a sadly missed drinking companion.

Elizabeth was not there to hear them, she was still in the church, staring up at the great stained-glass window of Jesus on the Cross. 'Why have You forsaken me?' He said to God, didn't He? Elizabeth knew what He meant. She sometimes felt God had forgotten her too.

Chapter 28

Janey and Helen called in at Elizabeth's for a Saturday-morning drink, bringing with them fresh cream cakes from the Lamb Street Bakery, which made the fattest éclairs in town. The first thing they saw when they walked into the front room was that big rocking chair and the stool, still wrapped in plastic, and Helen, *'Ooooooooh-ed,'* knowingly. She explained for a confused Janey's benefit that she had espied John Silkstone looking at this very same chair on Thursday, whilst she was out shopping.

'Well, well, well, you *are* a dark horse, aren't you, Miss Collier,' Janey said and Elizabeth looked at her in that way she had, shrugging a bit as if she didn't know quite what you meant, even though it was stark staringly obvious.

'Are you seeing John again then?' asked Helen hopefully, her big blue eyes wide with anticipation.

'Am I heck,' said Elizabeth, with a face that could have refrozen a cooked Christmas turkey. 'I met him a few weeks back. He gave me a lift somewhere and he's been round a couple of times when passing, that's all.'

'And he just happened to be passing with a chair that cost six hundred pounds?' asked Helen.

'*How much?*' said Elizabeth, deciding it really was going back now. What was his game, spending all that money on a flaming chair? Was he barmy?

'Well, thanks for telling us!' said Janey, huffing and taking up residence in the big wing leather chair by the side of Elizabeth's fire.

'What's to tell? He turned up with it, saying he'd got it cheap from someone. He thinks I'm a frigging charity case.'

'I don't think that's it at all, Elizabeth,' said Janey, who wasn't in the habit of dressing things up in cottonwool to spare feelings. 'He knows how flaming hard you are to give stuff to and it was probably his way of getting you to take it without you flinging it back at him and telling him that you aren't a charity case.'

Elizabeth gulped. *His words coming out of her mouth.*

'I think it's an incredibly thoughtful thing for him to do,' said Helen in her soft voice, and christened it by sitting in it and starting to rock on it. 'Oh, this is lovely. Haven't you tried it, Elizabeth?'

'No, I haven't tried it and I'm not going to, either. It's going back.'

'God, you're a hard cow,' Janey said, suddenly impatient with her. 'I thought you would have grown up by now. I wonder why he bothered at all, knowing what you're like.'

'I'd be taking it under false pretences,' said Elizabeth with a sniff.

'What do you mean, "false pretences"?' said Janey.

'Well, I'd be leading him on.'

'How do you work that out?' said Janey in a much-raised voice. 'How do you know he's the slightest bit interested in you other than as a friend? Has he said? Why can't the bloke just be giving you a present?'

'A six-hundred-quid present, Janey? Come on!'

'He can afford it from the change in his arse pocket these days.'

Elizabeth dropped a big sarcastic, 'Ha!' which sent Janey's blood to boiling point. If she had been a kettle, she would have been whistling by now.

'So, when George came around and gave you that cat-litter tray he got from work, he was after you, was he?'

'No, but—'

'And when my dad gave you that trout he'd caught—'

'That's different. This is six hundred quid, not a flaming fish or a cat bog, so please don't be stupid.'

Janey erupted. 'It's no different at all in principle, and it's not me that's stupid. But I tell you this, Elizabeth Collier, I'd rather be stupid than hard. You're lucky the bloke even wants to talk to you after how you treated him last time, have you thought about that?'

'I'm not hard!' Elizabeth cried indignantly, feeling that she was fighting *him* again as well as Janey. 'I'm not hard,' she said again, sounding anything but hard.

'I wish someone would go to all that trouble for me,' Janey went on. 'Look at it, it's absolutely gorgeous!'

'You have it then!'

Janey groaned and threw her hands up in despair. 'I could happily throttle you sometimes. You're hard as granite and twice as thick!'

'Do you think I'm hard?' Elizabeth said to Helen, still rocking in the chair.

'I'm afraid I do, Elizabeth, sometimes,' said Helen, without any of her customary cushioning. 'The guy has done a really sweet thing and you've spoiled it for him.'

'So you're all on *his* side then, are you?' Elizabeth said, her voice spiralling.

'Yes. In this, I think we are,' Janey said firmly. 'It's about time you started letting people in before you twist up that baby inside you to be as bad as you are.'

'Janey, for goodness' sake!' said Helen crossly.

'Oh, so I'm twisted now, am I?'

'Come on, Elizabeth, you're not right as far as emotions go. You didn't even cry at your auntie's funeral, for God's sake.'

Elizabeth gasped. 'You think I wasn't upset when my Auntie Elsie died?' she said in disbelief.

'Ladies . . .' came Helen's referee-like voice. She had stopped rocking and decided that this all needed to stop before it got out of hand.

'Who can tell with you? Then when your dad passed away . . . huh!' said Janey. 'You never even told us until, what was it, three weeks after his funeral, and I've seen more emotion on our bloody goldfish. Your own dad an' all!'

'That's because I didn't give a toss about him!' she screamed back.

'See?' Janey turned to Helen for support, who started

to say again that they needed to cool this now, but her voice was drowned out by Elizabeth's.

'Not everyone's dad is like yours, Janey, so just leave it.'

'Ten years he's been dead and you haven't once visited his grave.'

'So?'

'It's not right. How can that be right?'

'Okay,' said Helen. 'Enough is enough.'

'Look, just because you idolize your dad, doesn't mean to say—'

'I could always understand you going to live at your auntie's because he couldn't cope.'

'What?'

'That must have hurt you, but surely he deserved a bit of respect when he died.'

'You don't know what you're talking about,' Elizabeth gasped.

'Don't I? How much easier can it be to understand? He was your bloody father, for God's sake!'

'A father that got his own daughter pregnant!' screamed Elizabeth. 'Is that the sort of father you'd miss, is it? That the sort of man you'd want to grieve for? That sound anything like *your* nice daddy, Janey, does it?'

A pin-drop silence followed in which the only sound was Elizabeth's post-tirade heavy breathing. She slumped to the sofa, giving out three nuclear power stations' worth of radiation vibes that no one should in any way approach her/touch her/attempt to hug her.

As she sat down, Helen stood up, as if they were on a seesaw. 'You?' she croaked. 'Was it you?'

'No, not me,' said Elizabeth. 'Our Bev.'

Janey and Helen both breathed a sigh of relief, then realized the revelation was no less terrible.

'Why on earth didn't you tell us before?' Helen said in a voice one notch up from a whisper.

'Because I didn't want you ever looking at me like you're doing now,' she said. The compassion in their eyes was terrible, burning her with its purity.

'Is that why you really lived with your Auntie Elsie?' Helen asked, patting her chest as if to steady her heartbeat.

Elizabeth nodded but she couldn't speak; the words could not have got past the hard ball of tears in her throat. At that moment, she looked so wee, so fragile to the others, and Janey came to sit beside her on the sofa and hugged her, and for the first time ever, Elizabeth let her without protest.

'That why your Bev ran off then?' said Janey, and felt her nod against her shoulder.

'I heard so much in that house and I never knew then what was going on. Of course, now it all makes perfect sense,' Elizabeth said. 'I can hardly let myself think what our Bev must have had to put up with after our mam left. He were a dirty . . . *dirty* . . . bastard. I hated him when I realized what he'd done to her. I was so terrified my Auntie Elsie would die and I'd have to go back to him, I was sick every time she got a cough or a cold. She used to promise me that she wouldn't die before I was eighteen and she didn't, she cleared it by nine months.' Then she laughed, but it was an empty sound without any mirth at all in it.

'Has your Bev ever been in contact with you since?' asked Helen, coming to sit at the other side of her friend.

'Naw, and it's twenty odd years now, so I don't think she will be. My Auntie Elsie told the police she'd run off and they checked the hospitals but she never turned up at any of them.'

'Why didn't she tell them about your bloody dad an' all?' said Janey.

'I don't know. Maybe she didn't know what to do for the best. It's not as easy as you might think, holding the power to decide a man's fate. Whatever he might have done.'

'Looks easy enough from where I'm standing!'

'Janey, for God's sake, pipe down,' said Helen.

'Sorry,' said Janey, biting her lip. 'So, didn't the police find anything at all?'

'Not a dicky bird. I've tried to trace her through her National Insurance number, but it's never been used. I can understand why she went and I never blamed her for it – she needed to get away and start afresh. She had to forget about all of us to be able to do that.'

'Was she really . . . you know . . . when she left?'

'Pregnant? Yes, I'm as sure as I can be that she was pregnant. She stopped going to school, she was so sick and her stomach was getting really big . . . and her chest . . . I used to tease her about that getting huge. I was rotten to her, calling her fat names all the time until one day, she stopped fighting and just sat down and cried in front of me, and I walked off and left her because I wanted a bag of crisps from downstairs. I can even remember the flavour – KP beef, can you believe that? That was the night she left, two days before her sixteenth birthday. I was eating KP beef crisps and she was going through hell.'

'You weren't to know,' said Helen. 'You were a little girl. You can't possibly feel guilty – how can any of this be your fault? You must never think it was!'

'That, my friend, is so much easier said than done.'

'I just can't imagine . . . Did he ever . . . you, Elizabeth?' said Janey, not able to say all the words.

'It started, but I managed to run away,' she replied, her voice increasingly trembling, 'to my Auntie Elsie's. I don't know what would have happened to me, if I hadn't had her. I still lie awake at night and think, What if she'd been out that day? Or, What if she'd not believed me?'

'What ifs can drive you insane,' said Helen, who knew. 'She *was* in and she *did* believe you, that's all you should remember.'

Elizabeth was crying now, great big round blobs that landed on her cardi and she couldn't wipe them away with the back of her hand fast enough, then Janey handed her a tissue.

'And I'm carrying a bairn with those rotten genes in it!' wept Elizabeth.

'I don't know – you didn't turn out so bad.' Janey nudged her, smiling, but she needed a tissue herself.

'That's funny, 'cos you've just spent the last God-knows-how-long telling me I'm a hard cow,' said Elizabeth.

'You are!' said Janey, who had no intention of letting her off with anything because she had spoken for her own good. 'But you're also my best mate and I love you to bits even though you drive me crackers.'

Elizabeth half-laughed, half-cried and let her head stay on Janey's shoulder.

'Oh Elizabeth, you should have told us, love, you stupid daft mare,' Janey sighed, wiping her own eyes. *Dear God, they'd never even suspected that's why she was so mixed up.*

'Yes, I think I am stupid sometimes.'

'Well, now it's all out, you can stop being stupid, can't you?' said Janey.

'Start by telling John you'll take the chair,' said Helen. 'Stop punishing yourself and let people be nice to you, Elizabeth. Let him buy you this. I have one and I love mine. Course, it's old now, it was my da—' She stopped and cursed herself.

'Don't do that, please,' said Elizabeth. 'Don't be doing stupid stuff like not mentioning the word "dad" in front of me. Alex and Bob – they were always both so lovely to me.'

For years she had watched both men for that look in their eyes – predatory, unsafe, unclean – but had never ever seen even a trace of it.

'They were good blokes, both of them. You were lucky.'

'Make it up with John,' Janey said, passing her a fresh handful of tissues. 'He's another good bloke.'

Elizabeth shuffled and nodded and grumbled in her usual Elizabeth non-committing way.

'I'll put the kettle on, shall I?' said Helen, who could always be relied on for a good old British solution.

Chapter 29

After her friends had gone, Elizabeth had a wash and re-applied her cried-off make-up because turning up like Alice Cooper was not the best face she wanted to present for what she had to do. Then she grabbed her handbag and car keys and drove off in the general direction of where John said his building site was, although Oxworth was not exactly a huge place and he would surely be easy enough to find.

Her task was more straightforward than anticipated, for when she got to the village boundary, there was a big sign directing would-be buyers to *Silkstone Properties* and a telephone number for enquiries. There was an even bigger sign at the actual site, which was on the far outskirts. Oxworth was semi-rural, pretending to be nothing other than what it was – a small quiet village at the side of a pretty stream six miles away from the town centre. It had a lovely Italian restaurant, a few shops, a kindergarten and an old-fashioned cinema that had about three seats and where the film stopped halfway through for an ice-cream break. Elizabeth had been there with John a few times in the past, when it was an unwritten rule that whoever had the seat nearest the aisle went up for the tubs.

As she got out of the car, she saw John chatting to a twenty-something, slim woman at the bottom of the steps to a temporary pre-fab building. Despite the surrounding mud, she had clippety heels on and was doing all the flirty things like pushing her hair back, laughing at what he said, sticking her small Wonderbra-ed breasts out to indicate that she fancied him. Not that it was a surprise, for John Silkstone was a good-looking bloke, even in those big boots and that hefty jacket and with the dark waves of his hair just poking out from under his hard hat at the back.

His generous lips were curved into a smile for his eyelash-batting audience, who was caught in the soft gaze of his big toffee-coloured eyes. He had always been handsome, although his clothes sense had been slightly dyslexic in his Spaghetti Western phase. He could have had any woman he wanted, except he never seriously looked at anyone but her, the mad fool. Lisa must have wet her pants when his spotlight came round onto her, although she had just about set fire to herself to get him to notice her.

At the moment, John was listening to what Miss Frilly Drawers had to say and the crinkles at his eye corners made him appear more attractive than Elizabeth had ever seen him looking before, even when he was younger and line-free. Okay, she made the grudging admission to herself that she was jealous to see him talking to another woman and smiling at her like an enamoured pup. Especially a slim, pretty, blonde, young, responsive, unpregnant woman. She started walking back to the car again, grumbling under her breath words to the effect of, 'Oh, what's the use?' when she heard him call her name. When she turned he was coming over, clearing the distance between them in big, heavy-booted strides.

'I presume you want me?' he said, without smiling. 'I suppose you're here because you want me to come over and take that chair away. Don't worry; I'll pick it up when I've finished work. Right, I've said it for you and saved you the trouble. See you later.' Then he started to go.

'Er . . . no, wait,' she said, and he stopped and turned back to her.

God, this was difficult.

'I'd . . . er . . . like to keep it, if that's okay with you?'

'Oh, really?' he said, folding his arms across his vast expanse of chest. 'Well, there's a turn-up. And . . . ?'

'And?'

'Well, you could have rung me to tell me that!'

Elizabeth took a big, fortifying breath and said, 'And . . . I'm sorry.'

'For?'

'For? Okay, for being ungrateful. Thank you, it's lovely and so was all the other stuff.'

'And?'

This was not just difficult, it was excruciating.

She huffed. 'Not making this very easy for me, are you?'

'No,' he said, 'and why should I? You hurt my feelings.'

'Yes, I know. I'm s . . . sorry.'

'Apology accepted. And . . . ?'

Oh, flaming hell, I'm going to tell him to shove it in a minute.

'Okay, I'll answer for you, shall I?' he said. 'And . . . you're going to cook me my tea tonight to make up for it.'

'Am I, indeed?'

'Yes, you are, *indeed*,' he said, expecting her to argue. He could see her biting down on her lip, fighting the urge to tell him to go to hell and he chuckled inwardly, wondering how far he could push it.

'All right then,' she said, with a smile that nearly burned her lips off. 'So what would you like to eat?'

'My favourite.' His eyes twinkled at her.

'Okay,' she said, managing to stuff the word with both humility and murderous intent.

She remembers, he thought, hanging onto his best poker face.

'Right, I'll see you later then, Elizabeth. Now, if you'll excuse me . . . This isn't the weekend for me, unlike some. I've still lots of work to do,' and off he stomped, splashing through the mud, back to the half-finished buildings and burring machines and other men in big boots and lumberjack shirts. He did not look behind him but she was still very much on his mind.

Well, well, well. Miracles *do* happen in South Yorkshire then, thought John Silkstone, who grinned all the way to tea-time.

Elizabeth went home and took all the plastic off the chair and the stool, and then almost ceremoniously she sat down in it, bolt upright, before she softened her spine against the cushion and tried her best to relax.

When Helen drove home from the supermarket that afternoon, she had to stop the car to vomit at the side of the road, unfortunately having to suffer the indignity of being seen by others driving past. When she first read the list of adverse symptoms one gets in pregnancy, she did not, for one moment, expect to get them all. Her gums were always bleeding, she sounded like she had a permanent cold and was totally debilitated by the relentless waves of nausea. It was a long journey home and all she wanted to do when she got there was snuggle into Simon and to draw some comfort from him.

She found him reading in the lounge and he kissed her on the head in greeting, then recoiled immediately, saying she smelled of sick and should go and brush her teeth. When she came back from the bathroom, he had disappeared into his office next door to the house. She would have taken him tea, just to see him, just to be with him, but she was not allowed in there – even though she had put down the 60 per cent cash deposit to purchase the house in the first place. The house, like his heart, had strong boundaries within it.

Teddy Sanderson had been so sweet when she was especially grey the previous morning. He said that his wife Mary had suffered likewise with Tim: dreadful sickness, hair like a grease factory and she had slept more than their old cat, but it had all been worth it in the end. As soon as she had that little boy in her arms, all that misery and discomfort had instantly become a distant memory. He promised the same for Helen.

She tried to focus on the positive. When her daughter arrived into the world, everything would be good and normal again; her sickness, Simon's indifference, her fears and insecurities would all fade to nothing. That is what would happen, because she did not think she could face it being otherwise.

When Janey and George were courting, they didn't have a great deal of money, but invited Elizabeth around for tea one night – just a cheapie, they said, with eggs, chips and peas. Then Janey got a strange feeling that there was one type of pea that Elizabeth didn't like so she bought in processed, garden, mange-tout and a tub of frozen mushy peas and some beans, just in case she hated all sorts of peas. Then whilst she was unpacking the shopping, she dropped the full box of twelve eggs on the floor, and there were no survivors. George had had to dash out and buy another dozen. It turned out to be one of the most expensive, cheap egg, chips and peas meals in history.

'Why didn't you just ask me? I'd have told you straight there and then that I didn't like garden peas!' Elizabeth had scolded Janey.

'I felt bad enough about only inviting you for flaming egg and chips, without quibbling over the side order!' Janey had retorted, and then they had both laughed and feasted on an Alp of chips and fried eggs and tea and bread and butter and all manner of peas and beans.

Elizabeth had recounted the story to John a few days after. He listened patiently and at the end announced that it had to be the most boring story he had ever heard, which made her snort with laughter. However, he admitted that he was starting to slaver over the idea of egg and chips and beans, which he said had to be his favourite comfort meal of all time and the one he'd have as a last request, if he ever ended up on Death Row. He got Elizabeth lusting over them again as well, so they cooked them up in her little kitchen, drenched them in salt and vinegar, cut big slices from a new white loaf of bread and buttered them thickly, opened up a cheap bottle of plonk and sat on the sofa giggling at *Blazing Saddles*. It had been a good night.

John arrived at seven o'clock, washed and brushed up with a pair of jeans that showed off his very nice bottom and a Paul Smith pink shirt that made the best of his broad shoulders.

'Is it ready?' were his words of greeting.

'No!' said Elizabeth indignantly. 'How the hell did I know what time you were coming?'

'Best get on with it then, hadn't you? This is my treat and, I tell you, I'm going to savour every flaming minute of it,' and with that he sat in the new cover-free rocking chair with his feet up, read the newspaper and flicked through the television stations on the remote whilst she disappeared into the kitchen to cook. When it was ready, she served him with a tray with a sarcastic plastic flower in an eggcup and then got her own and sat on the sofa with it. Every so often, he would look up at her whilst chewing and winking, and she endured him silently, smoke blowing out of her ears.

When he had finished, she took the tray from him, only to drop it with a cry as she bent over double. He jumped up and pushed her gently down onto his vacant seat in the rocking chair. She was rigid, leaning forward like a seated statue in an awkward pose.

'What's up? You all right? Elizabeth, what's the matter?' he said, kneeling at the side of her.

'I don't know,' she said, rubbing her stomach. 'I think I felt him move.'

'Did it hurt?'

'No, it was just the shock of it.'

It was a weird feeling, like a load of bubbles going off inside her, like an inside-out burp. John cleared up the dropped plates and poured her some more of her fruity tea, whilst she sat stiff-limbed in the chair waiting for the next sensation.

'You okay?' he said.

'I think so,' she said. Something inside her rippled. 'Oh my, oh my, there it goes again!'

She froze and let it happen to her. It was a gentle but odd, scary sensation and would be until she got a handle on the fact that what she was feeling was actually another human being move around inside her. Naively, she hadn't even considered it would.

'Can I have a go?' he said, only to immediately withdraw that and apologize, but Elizabeth tentatively took his hand and placed it on her very rounding stomach because she so much wanted to share this moment with someone and halve the fear. His hand lay lightly on her stomach, hers on top of it, guiding it and he said he felt the slightest shift inside her. She didn't know if he did but he said it at the same time that she felt it for herself, so it was possible.

'Feeling better now?' he asked.

'Yes. I think that's what it is – it must be the baby starting to move.'

They looked up at each other, smiling. It was the perfect moment for him to lean over and kiss her if he was ever going to, but he took his hand away and sat down on the sofa and handed her the mug of tea, telling her to take it easy for a bit.

He thanked her for the meal when he left and she let him kiss her softly on the cheek. It was a small sweet kiss from a big sweet bloke, and she knew that if she were normal, she would never have let him go home.

There was a hideously early phone call on Monday morning, which set Elizabeth's heart boom-booming a little. No one phoned at this hour unless it was serious.

'Hi, it's me,' said Janey, sounding out of breath, which made Elizabeth's senses all switch to alert.

'You all right? God, Janey, what's up?'

'No, I'm not,' said Janey in some distress. 'Look, I

know you're off to work but have you got one of those Just the Job paint charts handy that you gave us?'

'Crikey, I thought you'd got your blood test back or something serious!' said Elizabeth, annoyed with relief.

'It *is* serious!' said Janey. 'Go and get it.'

'I'm getting it,' said Elizabeth, hunting in the odds and sods drawer. 'Right, I'm back with you, and now what do I do with it?'

'Bottom left, Brazilian Wonder.'

'Got it. What about it?'

'That's what colour my nipples are.'

'Oh, for God's sake, Janey, I haven't had my breakfast yet!' said Elizabeth in despair.

'I'm not joking, they used to be pink! I've just noticed them in the mirror. What colour are yours?'

'Pink.'

'What shade?'

'Janey, I'm not comparing them to a paint chart! Oh flaming hell, hang on then.' Elizabeth indulged her friend. 'They haven't got all that much darker . . . Cameo Rose.'

'Where's tha . . . Hang on – Cameo Rose – that's still pink! I'm Brazilian Wonder and you're Cameo Rose!'

'I think they're supposed to turn a bit browner, Janey.'

'A bit! Will they go back to normal?'

'I haven't a clue,' said Elizabeth, who hadn't.

'They look like holes through my bra! I don't want dark brown nipples!'

'Oh go to work, you sad mental bag! I'll see you later,' said Elizabeth and put the phone down. She'd tell Janey about the baby moving later, when she was *compos mentis*.

Janey was genuinely upset; she really did not want nipples that colour. She ripped off her bra and showed them to George, but he just went googly-eyed and it was obvious he didn't care if they were Brazilian Wonder or sky-blue pink with yellow dots on. They looked fine to him and they felt even better. Janey was late for work, but lied and blamed the traffic.

Dirty old man, she thought with a smile as wide and juicy as a watermelon as she logged onto her computer, feeling totally energized for the hard day's work ahead. Who needed stimulant drugs when you could have a George? Now that was true ecstasy.

Chapter 30

When Elizabeth got the date for her second scan at twenty weeks, John offered to go with her – merely as a support, he said casually. She had been going to pull up her drawbridge and say, 'No, sod off,' when Janey's, Helen's and his own words came back at her about the baby turning out like her if she did not learn to let people near. Not that she hadn't known love, because her Auntie Elsie was lovely to her, but she was not what anyone would call a demonstrative woman, as far as feelings were concerned. She was almost twenty years older than Elizabeth's father, and they didn't do hugs and kisses in Granny's family, although it hadn't warped Elsie like it had *him*. Sometimes she knew her Auntie Elsie wanted to cuddle her, especially when she had those nightmares that even had Sam whimpering in confusion, and Elsie's hands would come out, only to end up patting the quilt around her instead. She never blamed her auntie, who showed her love in so many other ways, but that would not do for her own baby. Elizabeth didn't want him to be an emotional island; she wanted him to bask in that sunshine feeling of being loved and not bat it back because his system couldn't cope with it, as she had, when a big love eventually came along.

Elizabeth stuck her neck out and practised being less independent. She said to John, 'You can come if you want.'

And he did want and he picked her up at nine on the Thursday morning.

By nine-forty, Elizabeth was fidgeting desperately with the pain of holding all that water in. Thank goodness the appointment only overshot by ten minutes, because any longer and she would have flooded the place.

She didn't expect John to come in with her, but the sonographer said, 'Come on, Dad!' and they both froze, then it seemed less complicated for them to play the game than explain that he was merely her escort.

It hit Elizabeth as ironic that here she was with no bloke in tow being accepted as half of a couple, and there was very-married Helen, who was having to go through this by herself for a second time, because Simon was busy being an aspiring top-management exec in his swanky Leeds office again. Helen had been trying to justify him on the phone the previous day and Elizabeth sympathized and, 'Hmed' in all the right places whilst thinking, Thoughtless wanker. Helen, it appeared, was even more alone than she was.

She forgot they pulled your trousers down to smear the gel on, and the sonographer did not spare any of her blushes, seeing as 'Hubby' would have seen it all before. Gallantly John kept his gaze averted, for which she was pretty grateful, as she suspected the top line of her pubic hair was on display, and she could not see it properly to trim it these days. Any worries on that score were needless though as John's eyes remained fixed on the screen, and Elizabeth could tell the exact moment he saw the baby for the first time by his re-action. His eyes rounded into dinner-plates and his face broke into the sort of amazed smile usually reserved for a first UFO spotting. The little one looked like a real baby now, an agile cherub wriggling to get himself comfortable and content within her.

'Do you want to know the sex?' asked the sonog-rapher.

'No,' said Elizabeth. 'I want that "it's a boy" or "it's a girl" moment at the end of it.'

John nodded as if he understood that completely.

'Will you have a really good look, please?' asked Elizabeth. 'I got my blood tests back yesterday and they've given the baby's chances of having Down's syndrome as one in seven hundred and fifty.'

'Is that high?' said John, the smile closing up.

'It's higher than Helen and Janey got on their results.'

'It's still relatively low,' said the sonographer. 'Don't worry though, I'm very thorough.'

'I rang the midwife up in a bit of a panic,' said Elizabeth. 'She said you would be.'

Struggled through it alone again, Miss Bloody Independent, thought John with a little shake of his head, but he didn't say anything aloud.

'Is everything okay?' said Elizabeth eventually.

'I've had a very good look and he or she looks fine to me,' said the sonographer, giving nothing away on the baby's sex, just as the new mum-to-be had asked.

Helen had always felt hers was a girl, although she would not have cared if she had been wrong. At the second scan they asked if she wanted to know for definite and she replied that she would. When they told her she was carrying a daughter, she burst into tears. Big, fat, happy tears that were issued straight from her heart.

Now she would have the empty guest room decorated in pale pinks, in readiness for the arrival of the little girl whom she could now feel fluttering inside her. Whatever Simon said.

George started crying as soon as he saw the baby appear on the monitor, and he set Janey off.

'That's my baby in there,' he said, sounding a bit like a sobbing Orville the Duck. 'It's got my feet.'

He handed Janey a tissue. She was as moved as he was by the sight of her fast-developing baby on the screen. Like Elizabeth, they didn't want to know what sex it was.

'So long as it's a healthy son or a healthy daughter, I really don't mind which,' George had said, before blowing his nose on his hankie. That more or less summed it up for Janey too. She wished he could feel the baby moving inside her, as she could now. He deserved more than her to feel it. He was so happy, and when she thought of how close she came to breaking his heart she could have kicked herself, with

George's great big feet. She would have to carry the guilt with her for the rest of her life, like a yoke on her shoulders and her shoulders alone. It was her burden, the price she had to pay.

John sat holding a coffee in one hand, the pictures of the baby in the other, staring at it with unblinking intensity.

'That was the most amazing thing I've ever seen,' he said.

'What, my big belly covered in gel?'

'I was a gentleman, I didn't look.'

'Good job, it would have put you off blancmange for life.'

'Not me, you know how I like my grub,' he said and smiled.

They were sitting in the hospital café, which was very nice, scrubbed and the air was full of toast smells. They looked to the entire world like a couple celebrating the forthcoming arrival of their baby, conceived in a loving relationship, which made her feel a bit odd – nice odd, though. She pushed half of the toasted teacake towards him but he waved it back.

'You have it,' he said. 'I don't want to get your picture greasy.'

'There is a solution. You can put it down, you know,' she replied.

'I don't want to. It's just . . . gorgeous. I mean, this is inside a woman,' he said with a catch in his voice. 'You'll have it inside you for nine months; it'll have nothing but you to rely on. You'll grow it like a seed, feed it, protect it, love it . . . you couldn't let it go, could you? After all that, you'd not want to, would you? Ever?'

His eyes were shiny as autumn chestnuts as she shook her head in answer to his question. No, she couldn't let it go. She had presumed he meant her.

Chapter 31

Terry Lennox buzzed through to Elizabeth with his usual reverence, charm and respect.

'Oy, Fats, get yourself and me a coffee and waddle through here, please, will you? I want you a minute.'

She groaned and headed off for the kettle, waddling indeed because in the five weeks since the second scan she felt as if she had doubled in size. Not that she considered it a chore, pandering to the whims of the great executive. She secretly loved the banter that batted between them like a highly charged ping-pong match, and it was all far more fun than the insipid, colourless days working for Beelzebub and his demonic monobrow. Minutes later, she swaggered through his door, which he held open for her, and dropped into the big leather swivel chair opposite his own.

'Fancy a night in a posh hotel – all expenses paid?' he asked.

Elizabeth looked blank. Sometimes it was hard to know when he was joking and when he wasn't.

'I've one of these work things to go to,' he answered her bemused face. 'I've to give an after-dinner speech about inspiration. Apparently I'm inspirational, did you know that?'

'Fancy!' said Elizabeth, deadpan, which made him roar with laughter.

'Irene won't go, she hates that sort of thing anyway, plus she's promised to babysit whilst our lad takes his missus out for their anniversary. So it would be just you and me.'

He mistook Elizabeth's immediate look of reticence and defensiveness for something else.

'Oh, don't worry, your mate Laurence won't be there. I have it on good authority that he'll be in Holland, although no doubt Handi-Save will be sending some representative – whilst they're still surviving. I'll have them soon, you mark my words.'

Terry had long since explained that the over-rated talents of Laurence could not rescue Handi-Save; the sharks were clustering around the bleeding animal, waiting for the kill. Admittedly, he was one of them – a Great White Shark, not like the benign Whale Sharks spectating and the more placid Basking ones that were sniffing around, hoping for scraps. Terry Lennox wanted to own Handi-Save, build it up and then sell it on for an enormous profit, and the stupid bloody-mindedness of Laurence Stewart-Smith, puffing himself up and still trying to convince him that he was operating from a position of power, was not going to stop him. Only a fool would take on Terry Lennox when he was running at full pelt. He was feared and hated but always admired. Or 'inspirational', as was his mantle.

'I can't get out of it,' Terry Lennox went on. 'It'll be

excruciating, but I'll have to do it. Will you come? I'll drive you down there and back, and you'll be paid over-time for it. Lovely hotel, great food, minibar on expenses, although I can't see you two costing me that much in booze.' He indicated her twenty-five-week-old bump.

She relaxed a little, berating herself for having suspected his motives back there.

'When is it?' she asked.

'Couple of weeks. You do my diary, woman – when's the Ocean View thing?'

'Thirtieth of June, which is three weeks today,' she said, without even blinking.

He looked at her in amazement. 'You're a walking Filofax, aren't you?'

'It's my job,' she said, clicking her tongue at him.

'I'll take that as a yes then,' he said.

'If I must,' she sighed.

'Yes, you must,' he said, and sent her out for Hobnobs.

Helen thought that when she rang Simon from the hospital to tell him he was going to have a daughter, some miracle would have occurred and he would have softened immediately – daddies and daughters and that sort of thing. He punctured that little hopeful balloon immediately by snarling that he would have to go and she had just dragged him out of a very important video conference to tell him something she could have told him four hours later at home. Her heart had felt as heavy as a stone inside her still non-increasing chest, and she hadn't mentioned anything about the baby in the weeks since.

She knew it was the coward's way out, but since visiting her father's grave, she had been secretly orchestrating the major renovation of the guest room, planning it to take place when Simon was away on business for a few days. The room was full of detritus that his parents had brought over when they moved from their large house in the affluent outskirts of York to a smaller cottage in the Cotswolds – things that Simon hadn't really wanted to receive and most of which was immediately planned for the dump, except they just got too comfortable in their space.

The baby was moving within her now, spurring her on, and within an hour of Simon leaving for his meeting in Frankfurt, a skip had arrived on the drive with the name *Tom Broom* and a telephone number painted on the side. She had actually spoken to the man himself when she had ordered it on the phone. When she told him she was clearing a room for a nursery, he had offered her two labourers to lift out the stuff for her, at a very reasonable cash rate. She was more grateful than he could know and intended to tip them well.

All this tat whilst my lovely things languish in the garage, she thought, watching the two strong wiry lads carry a broken football net and posts outside. Three hours later, local decorators were hard at work, painting and doing easily as good a job as the ridiculously priced Chanson's. She had picked a delicate Shell Pink for the walls and Old Cream for the paintwork and the floorboards. Then, when they had left two days later, a beautiful deep rose, longpile rug was put in place. The two men who delivered it were sweet and indulged her by moving the crib and the changing station from the cold little north-facing room at the end of the hallway into the new sunny space. The hand-made curtains were hung that afternoon and cast a soft, warm light into the room. Her baby was twenty-five weeks old now inside her and she was getting ready to say hello to her mum. In the next couple of weeks, she will be able to breathe for herself, Helen thought with a joyous thrill as she busied herself around the new nursery. She ferried in little trinkets from her secret stash in the garage – teddy bears and ornaments, and then she put a photo of her father in a silver frame upon the baby's chest of drawers. He'll watch over my daughter, she thought, like he watches over me.

The few days in which Simon were away were a tranquil oasis in her life, that she knew would be at an end as soon as he saw what she had done in his absence. On hearing his car crunch into the drive, she ran out to greet him, hugging him hello with gusto, hoping to soften him up for the scene she knew was around the corner. As she suspected, as soon as he entered the house he could smell the paint and, with the olfactory senses of an expert wine taster, he followed his nose down the hallway to the source of it. Helen waited with trepidation – it was all she could do. He glared at her silently, threw open the door of the guest room and blinked disbelievingly at the sea of froth and pink facing him.

'I know what you're going to say,' said Helen.

'How could you?' he asked, in almost breathless shock. Not only was the colour an affront to his vision, but it was full of hideous tat – stupid teddy bears and photos of dead people.

'How could I?' said Helen, with her courage mounting. 'Because my baby is not sleeping in that horrible, cold, designer white room, that's how I could!'

The baby fidgeted inside her, as if she knew she was being talked about.

'Helen, I really don't need this. I've been travelling for hours,' he said, shaking his head at her with tired impatience though he still had plenty of energy to jab his finger at her and throw commands about. 'Ring those decorators in the morning and tell them to paint it back to how it was. And get the people who moved the furniture out of the spare room to move it back again. Then get all that pink rubbish out of my house!'

My house? thought Helen, with a prickle of annoyance. *My* house?

'I most certainly will not,' said Helen, which shocked him like a surprise slap because he had expected her to back down as always and say meekly, '*Yes, Simon, of course, Simon, three bags full, Simon . . .*' but this time there were two of them facing him.

She took in a long, deep breath as if she was about to parachute off a plane and continued, 'Every time I think of that room, all I can see is you sulking in there. I hate that room and our daughter is *not* going in there.'

'It will be changed back, Helen, trust me.'

He made a grab for Helen's arm and manoeuvred her out of the baby-pink room. She was not sure where the strength came for her to do it, but she shook him off and with a force that surprised her more than him as he crashed back against the wall.

'Don't you EVER hit me again,' she said, with a voice as hard as Helen's voicebox was able to achieve.

'Hit you?' he countered, but a little thrown still by the change in her. 'When have I ever hit you?'

'All those sly nips and shoves and pushes and you shouting and swearing at me won't happen again, do you hear me, Simon? They are abuse, too – *abuse, do you hear* – and I won't take them from you any more, do you understand? No more!' she said with quiet conviction. 'No more.'

He looked back at her with as much disgust as if it was Elizabeth in the room with him, not mild, gentle Helen who wouldn't say boo to a goose, but Elizabeth who would, and tell it to stuff itself as well. The shock of his domestic worm turning knocked him off course and he did not come back at her with his usual sarcastic and hurtful retorts. He merely waved his hand dismissively to indicate that he had had enough of this nonsense for now and he disappeared outside, striding off in the direction of his car, snarling that he was so pleased she was glad to see him back and how happy he was to be home again.

Helen leaned against the wall and gathered her thoughts and her breath. *I did it! I stood up to the bully!* It was the moment she should have had all those years ago with Carmen Varley. She was proud of herself; she felt her father would be proud of her too. It was then she realized that she had not been sick for over twenty-four hours.

Chapter 32

Elizabeth's mobile went off and her stomach did a hopeful little flip, but the number display said it was Helen at work. She felt hideously guilty for being so disappointed it was not John phoning. There had been a couple of phone calls since he had come with her for the second scan six weeks ago, but they were very quick ones. He enquired how she was and then would tell her how hard he was working to finish his houses in double-quick time. A couple of the lads were on holiday and he apparently was having to work around the clock, he said. He promised to call in and see her as soon as he had the chance, and made her promise to phone him if she needed anything and she said she would, but she didn't ring.

'Hi,' she said to Helen, as cheerily as possible. 'And what can I do for you this fine Monday morning?'

'Elizabeth, when are you leaving work?'

'What do you mean – today?'

'No, for your maternity leave.'

'Er . . .' said Elizabeth, who hadn't really decided yet, but with fourteen weeks to go before blast-off, it was something she really should start thinking about. 'Dunno yet, what about you?'

'I think I'm going to work as long as possible,' came the reply, 'but I just wondered what you and Janey were going to do.'

'I haven't really thought about it,' said Elizabeth, 'although I suppose I had better make up my mind soon, hadn't I?' It appeared the list of things to think about with babies was endless.

'Well, I've got a meeting with Teddy about my date in five minutes.'

'You sound like Andy Pandy,' said Elizabeth.

Helen laughed.

'Sorry, I've been useless as usual,' said Elizabeth.

'See you later, Useless.'

'See you later, Andy!'

When Helen put the phone down, she went through to Teddy Sanderson's office for her meeting. He had a lovely old room with floor-to-ceiling oak panelling on the walls, a massive black iron and tile fireplace feature, and knotty polished boards on the floor. It was saved from being over-dark by a huge sash window, which overlooked a small east-facing grassy area with benches that were always full of pensioners feeding pigeons.

He held the chair for her as she sat down and she smiled at his gallantry. He belonged to a different era, one of moonlight and roses and Noël Coward and long cigarettes in holders. Teddy Sanderson was Mr Art Deco; he even had a Clarice Cliff-style coffee mug.

'Now, Helen,' he began, 'we need to have a little

chat about your leaving date and your future plans when the baby arrives. I do so hope you are going to return to us after your maternity period. You're a very integral part of our team and I rely on you far too much for you to leave me.'

'Thank you,' she said, beaming. She was aware of lapping up any kind words these days with the zeal of a starving child. 'I think I'd like to work right up to my due date, if that's all right with you.'

'Of course it is, of course it is,' but he sounded doubtful. 'The thing is, my dear, I think you underestimate how tired you will feel towards the end of your pregnancy – and we are heading for a hot summer, by all accounts. Tim was a September baby and I remember just how exhausted Mary was with the heat. Anyway, I just want you to know that at any point you feel you've been a tad ambitious in that decision, I'm entirely flexible.'

'Thank you, Teddy,' she said, and smiled gratefully at him. He smiled back and their eyes lingered for longer than either of them had intended. Long enough for something surprisingly intimate to pass between them, which Helen had not been prepared for. She felt her cheeks heating and she dropped her eyes away from him, hoping he didn't think her a hussy. She thought Teddy Sanderson a very handsome man, but in a totally different way to Simon with his perfect features. Teddy's face was – she searched for the word and found it – *noble*, and the aura he carried about him was gentler and kinder than her husband's was. His eyes weren't beautiful like Simon's with their long lashes, but they were soft grey and they seemed to warm her whenever they touched her. And he was so much like her father in the way that he never had to raise his voice to make himself heard. He did not use force to get his point across, but got it across all the same.

'How are you feeling now?' said Teddy. 'You've had quite a rough ride, haven't you, dear girl?'

'I'm much better, thank you,' she said truthfully. She had not had a moment's nausea since it had suddenly stopped in the middle of last week, and in that time, her skin had cleared up beautifully. It seemed her spots had eloped with her sickness to torture some other poor girl in her first throes of pregnancy.

'Well, you let me know about dates and intentions,' Teddy said again, and Helen affirmed that she would and went out to make some coffee.

She really must think in detail about the mechanics of what would happen after her maternity leave had expired. She had hoped to speak to Simon about it, but he walked away from any baby conversation and she quickly came to realize that if *she* did not make decisions, then no one else would. Her mother had offered to look after the baby occasionally, but her life was so busy these days with bridge, friends and all sorts of committees and clubs, that any arrangement would have to be a very casual one. She did not want to leave her baby with a childminder, and the idea of a live-in nanny was not exactly thrilling her. She wanted to stay with her baby, but she loved working at the solicitor's office so much. The people there were so lovely, although she sometimes felt that she was outside a great glass bubble, merely able to look in where she had really wanted to be a part of it all.

Her first year at Exeter University studying Law had been wonderful. Then her father became ill and she could not bear to be so many miles away from him, even though she always intended to go back to Law, truly she did. She had limped along for the first couple of years after his death, existing, trying to get on with things, presenting a hard shell to the world that belied its brittleness and fragility. Then, when everyone thought she was finally getting her life back together again, some stupid television programme about hypothermia triggered off a major flip and she fell headfirst into some dark place that she thought she would never be able to climb out of again. Then Simon found her. He rode into her life, like a beautiful knight in shining armour, strong, capable and commanding, just what the lost, lonely part of her so badly needed. Loving him gave her the confidence to face the world. Until he started to take it away again.

Twenty-six weeks – I'm six months' pregnant! thought Elizabeth and, to amuse herself, sat down at the kitchen table with her diary and started to work out how many days she had to go if hers was a regular pregnancy. Someone knocked at the door and she did not for one minute think it would be John, but it was, and he was bearing a bunch of flowers.

'They're smoke-damaged stock. My mate's wife—'

'Oh, shut up,' said Elizabeth, beating back the grin that was bursting her lips open, and she let him in.

He handed over the flowers without fuss nor cere-
mony and she said, 'Thank you,' not, 'What are you
bringing me flowers for?' which he had expected her
to say and so had prepared an answer for.

'I thought they might go with your rocking chair,'
he said, trying to justify their presence anyway.

'These are pink, the chair is blue.'

'Oh, hellfire! That's colour-blind builders for you.
The woman told me they were blue – wait till I see
her!'

She laughed, more pleased to see him than she
could let on. She had not realized how much she had
missed the sight of him over the past weeks until she
was seeing him again, now, in her house, big and smiling
and exuding warmth, although the evidence of over-
work was there in his eyes: he looked tired out.

'There's a little flower van down the road from the
site,' he said with a slightly nervous gabble. 'They always
look that nice in their buckets when you're passing.
They're not expensive.' He felt the need instantly to
correct that. 'They're not cheap ones either, though.'

She cut him off, before he drowned himself. 'Cup
of tea? Sandwich?'

'Oh, both if you're offering, please. I'm starving,' he
said.

'Didn't you take your snapbox to work?'

'Snap? I've no time for food!' said John. 'No joking,
Elizabeth, I really haven't.'

'So what are you doing here then?'

'Well, I haven't seen you for weeks and I was just
passing . . .'

'Liar!'

'Okay, I wanted to see you and I've just been round the corner to get an electrician so I could hardly pass you by, could I?' he said, not getting eye-contact, then he asked to use her loo and she made him a big doorstep tuna sandwich whilst he was upstairs. He scoffed it as if he hadn't been fed for a fortnight, so she made him another, joking that he was unfillable.

'So how's things in the world of Silkstone Properties?' she said, joining him at the table with a fork and a jar of olives.

'Great. I've sold all of them but one already, and that's before the roofs are on. Thanks to the rising house prices and a buyers' market, I'm more in pocket than I bargained for so I'll be able to finance most of the next ones myself, when I can find some decent enough land. I dropped lucky with The Horseshoes; it's a bonny spot, all right.'

'Horseshoes? That what you're calling them then?'

'Aye, there used to be a blacksmith's there years ago.'

'I'm sure someone will want the other one soon enough,' she added encouragingly.

'I sincerely hope so,' he said, wrinkling his nose up at her as she speared another olive. 'Do you actually like those horrible green things?'

'Not as much as the horrible black ones, but I've run out.'

'Where's my tea?' He winked at her.

'Oy!' she said. 'Mr Bringing-a-two-quid-bunch-of-flowers-and-getting-fifteen-quids'-worth-of-sandwiches-in-return!' Then she added quickly, 'Only joking about the two quid, by the way.'

'Two quid! They weren't that much – do you think I'm made of money!' he said, thinking, God, when did handing a bunch of flowers over become such a minefield?

He couldn't hook his big finger through the handle of the pretty little black cat china cup and it took three of them before he had even dampened down his thirst. Then he wiped his mouth, stood up and said, 'Right, thank you for that. I best get back to it.'

'Oh, you've not finished working?' she said. 'At this time?'

'Yes, I've finished, for once. I'm taking the lads out for a couple of pints because I've driven them into the ground and I owe them.'

'Oh, okay then,' she said, surprising herself by how disappointed she felt that his visit was up. She was going to suggest they retire to the lounge with a packet of plain chocolate Digestives, one of his old favourites which had managed to find their way into her shopping basket recently. He turned to her at the door.

'By, Elizabeth, you are bonny fat,' he said.

'Piss off,' she said, and he grinned and he went.

She could not tell if the feeling inside her was baby or butterflies.

Janey was craving Marmite desperately.

'Go and get me some.' She elbowed George in bed and disturbed him from a good bit in his Stephen King.

'Go and get it yourself, you lazy mare,' he said.

'I'm six months' pregnant, it'll take me for ever.'

'Give over! You've more energy than Linda bloody Lovelace on speed,' said George.

'You would get me it if you loved me,' she wheedled, knowing of course that he would.

He groaned aloud and slipped on his dressing-gown, and five minutes later he was back empty-handed.

'Don't tell me we've run out!' she said. The craving was so strong, she might have to get up and drive to the all-night garage if that was the case.

'No, we've not run out.'

'Oh, thank God,' she sighed in relief. 'Well, where is it then?'

George flashed open his dressing-gown and his naked body was smeared from neck to thighs with it.

That night Janey found that being six months' pregnant and roughly the size of a humpback whale in no way interfered in her newfound sexlife.

Chapter 33

Elizabeth was sure one of the odd side-effects of her pregnancy must be sharpened intuition because recently, she felt people had started to look at her slightly differently at work. It was not in the nice benign way that people looked at pregnant women, either, but one that gave her cold prickles at the back of her neck. It crackled in her psychic airspace that she was somehow the subject of gossip; she caught just one too many stares lingering in her direction followed by covered whispers for it all to be down to an over-active imagination.

Nerys was her usual sweet self, but when Elizabeth casually asked her, 'Is there something I should know about me?' Nerys shook her head and pretended a little bit too hard that she didn't know what Elizabeth could be talking about. Elizabeth did not press her too hard. Nerys was not the malicious type and whatever was being said, this gentle young woman with the sweetheart face and big smile was unlikely to be the source of it. Not that Elizabeth had ever been one to be bothered by what other people thought of her, but it niggled at her all the same in her sensitive state.

Two days before the Norfolk conference, Elizabeth

had just taken a document over to the other end of the building when she found she needed the loo. These days when her bladder spoke, she listened immediately and she slipped into the nearest Ladies. She did not suppose anyone expected to find her there, which is why the women spoke so freely at the other side of the door when they came in mid-bitch.

'. . . Apparently she's a right old slapper. Got drunk at a party and doesn't even know who the father of the sprog is,' and the owner of that voice entered the next cubicle to Elizabeth and started to urinate noisily.

'Well, there's a rumour that Terry Lennox is the father, which would explain why she was fast-tracked to being his secretary.' This from another younger voice, who seemed to be standing waiting for Cubicle Woman by the sinks.

'Possibly, but she looks dog rough enough to me to have been shagged on a pile of coats at a party. At her age as well – ugh! Julia Powell says she told her and the MD to stick their job. Then she lands up in a plum job here. Now if that isn't fishy, what is?'

The loo flushed.

'Old slag!'

'Fancy having a mother like that. It's got no chance, has it? Kids should be taken off women like that, in my opinion. Poor little bastard.'

That was the pivotal moment when Elizabeth decided that she was not going to let this go. She had been called far worse than an 'old slag' but that was not what had infuriated her. She marched out of the cubicle, and if she could have bottled that look on their faces, she would have kept it for ever and looked at it when she needed cheering up. She didn't shout or scream or swear. She went calmly over to the sink, pumped some soap from the dispenser and nudged on the tap lever to wash her hands.

'Not that it is any of your business, but I know exactly who the father of my baby is and it isn't Terry Lennox, although I'm pretty sure he'll be interested to hear that he is on your shortlist.'

She knew the gobbier of the women now that she had seen their faces. She was Sue Barrington, a jumped-up, mealy-mouthed secretary who hung around coffee machines with her arms folded talking to anyone who would give her the time of day. She usually had more colour in her cheeks than she did now though, because she was corpse pale.

The other one was just an impressionable office junior who was at the other end of the embarrassment colour spectrum with a face working through red and romping towards puce and looking very much as if she was about to cry when Elizabeth said to her, 'And as for fast-tracking – I was a secretary working my backside off when *you* weren't even born.' She snapped off a paper towel. 'I've never been the slightest bit affected by petty-minded, lazy office bitches and I'm not starting now, but never NEVER' – her voice galvanized to iron – 'talk about my child with your foul mouths again. *Is that understood?*'

The women kept their heads down, hoping she would go away but Elizabeth stood her ground.

'WELL, IS IT?'

Her voice bounced off the wall tiles and left an equally threatening echo in its wake. There was an embarrassed muttering by response, which satisfied her enough to sweep past them and out of the door with a flourish before she asphyxiated on the atmosphere in there, which seemed to have every bit of oxygen sucked out of it. It was only when she got back up to her office and sat down, exhausted from the effort of trying to keep the waddle out of her dignified, purposeful exit that she asked herself, 'How did Julia know that? How the hell did Julia know?'

The waiting times for a letter from Customer Services were down to three weeks, something that no one had ever managed before Janey came on the scene. She had streamlined the staff, got rid of a couple of the ones who preferred making personal calls to customer ones, which had a warning ripple effect on the others who thought the new boss might be a soft touch because she was pregnant. Those who were expecting the 'new broom' to leave them to it whilst she killed time until her maternity leave had been in for a big shock.

Janey had the old (useless) broom's desk moved out of the little box of an office so she was in the thick of the action. She had never felt so full of determination, bounce and energy in her whole life. The good sex might have had something to do with it, though the Marmite was starting to give her terrible heartburn. George was certainly full of beans too. He was working all hours to get as much overtime in as he could and they were squirrelling away every penny because no one was going to come along and give them a nice fat cheque for £10,000, like Penelope Luxmore had just given Helen to start off the baby's savings fund.

A couple of temps were good girls and Janey set them on permanently. One of them had been a supervisor in her last job and Janey quickly earmarked her to be her temporary cover whilst she was on leave, although one of the old guard – Barbara Evans – had something to say about that. She had presumed the position would come automatically to her because she was the longest-serving advisor there. Janey disagreed because she knew that Barbara, brilliant as she was with customers, would not have been able to produce all the stats and reports that were a daily part of her job.

She noticed from Barbara's personnel record that her grade didn't reflect her acumen or her long service, and she had a word with Barry Parrish who agreed to bump up Barbara's wage as a consolation prize. Barbara was more than happy with that, because she had only really wanted the extra money anyway, not all that responsibility. Even before Janey had explained to her why she was not in line to be her temporary cover, she knew deep down that she could not do all the complicated paperwork stuff.

She extolled Janey's virtues to anyone who would listen, and lots of people listened to Barbara. There weren't many bosses who would care enough to do that for you, she had said. Janey Hobson had known her capabilities better than she had known them herself. She was quite the best boss Barbara Evans had ever worked under, and no one disagreed with her.

Yep, Janey had most definitely found her niche.

'There's a story going round that you're the father of my baby,' Elizabeth said to Terry as she took in his morning coffee.

'Well, I'm more flattered than you probably are, Elizabeth,' he said, and she hooted with laughter.

'It might be as well if I don't go to Norfolk on Wednesday with rumours like this floating about though,' she said.

'I don't give an arse for rumours,' said Terry Lennox, bashing his fist down on the table and crushing an unsuspecting Jammy Dodger. 'You're going and that's that. And if I find out who's spreading these stories . . .'

He left the threat hanging in the air, his face icing over enough to cause fatal damage to any passing *Titanic*. He no longer looked the archetypal figure of a benign, joking boss, and for the first time Elizabeth saw him as the feared shark he was reported to be in the business world. She pitied anyone, even Laurence, who got on the wrong side of him. It occurred to her then that she didn't know Terry Lennox half as well as she thought she did.

Chapter 34

It was like Elizabeth always said: you did not get to be where Terry Lennox was with a ball of cottonwool for a heart, though at least he proved that he didn't have to have his ruthless button switched on twenty-four seven like certain people to be a force. He saw no need to treat people like muck or lower beings just because he was a rich and clever bloke, plus he was infinitely more of a gentleman than Laurence Stewart-Smith could ever be. He picked her up mid-morning from her front door in his Jaguar on the day of his speech in Norfolk. She had only been on one Away Day with Laurence and he had made her get the train (economy ticket) whilst his chauffeur drove him down south in a Rolls Royce. Terry, she was pleased to find, was a nice steady driver, despite the car having an engine capability only a couple of horses short of a Ferrari.

En route, he asked her if she had heard any more rumours and she had answered a truthful 'no'. The sly looks had stopped as if they had been cut off with a sharpened scythe after that close encounter in the loos. She had actually travelled with Gobby Corpse Face in the lift the previous day, and the woman had been more or less tap dancing with tension. Elizabeth didn't suppose she had ever had a longer journey up to the fourth floor. She could have dropped her in it, but why make a martyr of her? She had been fighting her own battles for as long as she could remember; she didn't need a Terry Lennox to do it for her.

It was a boiling hot day, and Elizabeth was in desperate need of a lie-down when they eventually saw the signs indicating that Ocean View was the next turning right. The journey from the main road, down a tree-shaded drive to the charming castle-like hotel, felt like half the trip again. Terry, typical male driver that he was, did not believe in taking coffee or loo stops, and had to disappear in the direction of the Gents as soon as they landed in the Reception foyer, leaving Elizabeth to check them in.

'Mr Lennox is in the Garden Suite,' confirmed the receptionist, 'and you, Miss Collier, are in Crystal – that's our Honeymoon Suite.'

'No, there must be some mistake,' said Elizabeth, foraging for the confirmation letter in her handbag and finding it. 'Look, I'm in Harlequin.' Blimey, Expenses would have a fit if she didn't sort this out!

'I had you upgraded,' said Terry, appearing at her shoulder.

'Oh, right,' she replied, immediately wondering why. Somewhere in her head, a warning flag started to rise.

The porter wasn't around so Terry said he would carry their bags upstairs himself. Elizabeth was very quiet in the lift as they headed up to her bedroom first. She knew it had all been too good to be true. A bloke couldn't help but misuse power; it was hard-wired into his genes.

She opened up the door of the Crystal Suite to a room flooded with sunlight that bounced off all the crystal lights and ornaments and made pretty rainbows on the walls. There were two huge glass doors open to a balcony that gave a magnificent view of the sea in the distance. With its airy lightness and long chiffony drapes, it was just like Rebecca's bedroom in the black and white film they made of the book, and it would have been Elizabeth's ideal room, give or take Mrs Danvers trying to shove her out of the window. She had always wanted to live near water – ideally the sea, but the beach didn't stretch to Barnsley. Once John and she had drawn their dream houses for a laugh. His was quite practical, except for the huge basement cinema and snooker room, whilst hers was a labyrinth perched precariously on rocks overhanging violent, crashing waves. It was one of the few million occasions that he had said she was completely barking, but in a nice way because John Silkstone had never been unkind to her.

There was a bathroom off to the left that was like something out of *Dynasty*, and the focal point of the room – the bed – was wide enough to have contained the honeymoon couple, the bridesmaids, best man, ushers and the vicar, if he was lucky.

Did he want to sleep in it with her? Is that why she was there? All that rubbish about his wife babysitting – who was he kidding? They were all the same, really . . . didn't she know that by now?

She did not want those thoughts in her head, but

nevertheless they were landing there, thick and fast, and wouldn't budge. She recalled his anger about the gossip, how much of a stranger he had seemed then; her realization that she could not possibly know all his depths and capabilities in such a short time. She felt suddenly unsafe and froze as he called out her name softly.

'Elizabeth . . .'

Here we go, she thought, forecasting a difficult scene which would no doubt end in her having to get a train home and then start a job-hunt again tomorrow. He came over, put his hands on her shoulders and looked down into her face.

'I hope you didn't mind me and Nerys plotting behind your back,' he said. 'I thought you deserved a little surprise. Me and the wife have stayed in this room before and it's a real treat. There's a gym downstairs, although you'd break the equipment if you went on anything, the size of you, lovely gardens outside, nice coffee lounge with big cakes, or you can just go out on the verandah there and read. Get room service to bring you up some sandwiches and charge it to your room. I'll expect your moral support at seven-thirty in the bar to the left of the stairs at the bottom. Oh, and if you're going for a shower, watch out because the force of it will blow your bloody head off!' He pinched her cheek, as if she were his favourite niece, picked up his bag and left her in wide-open-mouthed silence, shame stifling her with its heat.

She realized when she went downstairs at seven-fifteen why he needed someone along. He was trying very hard not to shake. He looked like an executive jelly.

'I hate these bloody Captain of Industry speech things,' he said, glugging away on a Perrier and wishing it was a brandy. 'Your calming influence will be greatly appreciated. How was your afternoon?'

'Lovely,' she said, and meaning it. 'I had a nap in the sunshine, sent down for a sandwich and a scone with clotted cream, had a bath and here I am.'

'And looking very nice as well,' he said, indicating her long navy gown. She had to admit, she was starting to feel pretty formidable. The baby bump gave her extra presence, and she had noticed how much smilier and nicer people were to her, unless she was in the alien toilets at work, of course. She felt quite the lady that night, especially in that posh frock. Not that she'd ever have occasion to wear it again, of course.

There were lots of suits, bow-ties and ballgowns around. She clung to a corner, glad that she wasn't expected to hang onto Terry's shirt-sleeves. He was busy circulating and a lot happier knowing that he had at least one friendly face in the crowd of Brutuses, or was it Bruti? She thought of Miss Ramsay, and how the teacher could never have known the impact her shaking up of the class seating arrangements would have on their lives. If it had not happened, she might still have been best friends with Shirley Cronk and Julie Williamson, who, if the local rag was to be believed, had clocked up between them more charges than the whole of the Great Train Robbers. She wondered if Miss Ramsay was still alive. Probably not; she was giving

Methuselah a run for his money when they were twelve. Did she die a spinster with no one to mourn her but an old cat – like Elizabeth herself probably would?

A gong sounded and everyone started to filter through into a huge dining room, ornately decorated in white, gold and silver. According to the seating-plan, she was not placed next to Terry at dinner; he was annoyed by this, but Elizabeth told him not to make a fuss. Secretly, she did not relish being in the lime-light and inviting rumours from even more directions that she was his mistress. Instead, she was seated between two very nice and bumptious men: one a potato farmer from Doncaster, the other a poop-scoop manufacturer from Cornwall. They were both merry and down to earth, and she was happily entertained by them during a 300-course meal which still left her hungry, mainly because most of the dishes consisted of little more than a grape or a mushroom. People were filling up on drink instead and, through her very sober eyes, she could see there were going to be quite a few red faces in the morning. The woman in the scarlet dress, for instance, who had arrived looking cool and distant, was now eating strawberries from some Tuxedo's lips, and there was a very loud young Suit talking rather aggres-sive politics to someone who was trying desperately to ignore him and eat his roulade.

There were four speeches – the so-called warm up in which she would have nodded off, had it not been lent some interest from Politics Boy heckling. Then there was Potato Man's rival, which made for some very acidic but amusing side comments from her dinner companion during the self-inflating monologue. As the fill-up of coffee arrived, a lady with a voice as plummy as Mrs Plum's plum jam took the stand, but she was surprisingly witty and made everyone laugh. Then there was the *pièce de résistance*, the man they had all come to hear – Terry Lennox. He began his speech after the long bout of applause had died down. There was not the slightest hint of nerves in his very funny, intelligent delivery in a voice with both boots in South Yorkshire; Elizabeth could have listened to him for hours. He got a tumultuous round of applause and a standing ovation, and both were well deserved.

'How was I?' he asked as the crowd started to wander out, mainly in the direction of the bar.

'Inspirational! But don't tell you I told you so,' she said.

'Thanks for being here, Elizabeth,' he said. 'Half these bastards would stick their cheese-knives in my back if I turned round. It really helped having someone on my side in the room.'

'Well, there was a Potato Man and a Poop-Scoop Man next to me who both thought you were the bee's knees,' she said.

'Ah well then, three of you, out of what, two hundred? Not bad odds for me.'

'That's at least fourteen thousand more than Laurence. He's way into minus figures,' she whispered, and they both chuckled.

'Look, come through to the bar or bugger off up to bed. I'll not hold you fast to any more duties, but I need a very large brandy,' he said.

'Well, I wouldn't mind going up if you can do without me,' said Elizabeth, as a yawn popped out. She felt tired and very heavy. It seemed that she was putting on weight by the day, and all the rich food had not helped what she presumed was her first taste of heartburn.

'Okay, off you go then,' he said. 'We'll have breakfast about nine. Ring my room number when you're up. It's er . . .'

'Seventeen,' she said.

'Memory like an elephant!'

'Goodnight, Captain, have a brandy for me,' she said, saluting him, then heaved herself up the staircase in the welcome direction of her room.

Tired as she was, it was too beautiful a night not to sit out on the balcony and watch the moon over the sea. She got a glass of orange from the minibar and the warm breeze ruffled the waves and played with her hair. It would be a gorgeous place to spend a honeymoon, not that she would ever get to find out – an old tart on the cusp of forty with a baby to an unknown father – boy, she could see them starting to form an orderly queue already! She needed to get real – that much was true after being actually vain enough to think that very-married multi-millionaire Terry Lennox might have wanted to bed her. There were decent blokes out there as well as rats, although the most decent of them all was not interested in her any more.

John Silkstone hadn't come back into her life to reclaim her. The truth of it was, he had come home for his parents and if she hadn't bumped into him in a DIY store, then their paths might never have crossed again. John was a friend, a good friend who once got very drunk and told her he loved her but had recovered sufficiently to marry someone else within three months. Seven years later he might be back in her life – helping her out, enjoying her company, drinking her tea, eating her Jaffa Cakes . . . but he was not a fool who would make the same mistake twice. Normal people moved on; no one stayed frozen in time as she did. He was a good bloke and all he wanted was her friendship, and that would have to be enough. Sitting there in that beautiful room meant for lovers, she felt incredibly alone and sad that friendship was all there could ever be between them now.

At three in the morning, Elizabeth was to discover that the perfect Honeymoon Suite had one fatal flaw; the wall behind the bed was paper-thin. Although, to be fair to the architect, the couple in the next room were making a huge amount of racket – and their own porn movie, by the sounds of it. She managed to drift back to sleep, but the sounds of their obvious enjoyment of each other awoke her again half an hour before her alarm went off. She escaped to the bathroom and enjoyed a powerful shower, wondering if it was Lady in Red and Strawberry Gob Man, or maybe Politics Boy got lucky. She rang Terry Lennox and told him she was up and about, then she heard the rampant couple open their door to leave. She had to know who it was, so she grabbed her bag and mischievously timed her exit to coincide exactly with theirs. She stepped out into the corridor – smack into her ex-boss's assistant and her best friend's husband.

She had a few moments of disorientation that occur when people from the different worlds in life are seen out of their normal contexts and the brain struggles to make sense of the situation. Elizabeth, Julia and Simon stood in a stunned triangle, none of them really knowing what to do. Well, actually Elizabeth knew what she wanted to do – she wanted to hit them both. She wanted to protect Helen's lovely, beautiful heart from this disgusting pair. However loose Elizabeth's morals might have once appeared, she had never touched a married bloke, and certainly not one with a substantially pregnant wife at home. Elizabeth drew in two big angry lungfuls of air, too furious to do anything but charge through them and go down the stairs to breakfast. She didn't know what she would do with this information. She didn't know what she *could* do with this information.

It was a lot easier in the old days, when you could protect your friend by smashing someone else's face in.

Chapter 35

From the start, something had niggled Janey about the way Elizabeth had explained the conception of her baby. Even though her friend hadn't exactly got the reputation of an angel, Janey didn't buy the 'drunken bonk at a New Year's party' story one bit. There had been more than a few undesirables in Elizabeth's life, and far more than her fair share of casual and careless relationships – starting with creepy Wayne Sheffield and ending with scraggy Dean Crawshaw – but Elizabeth had always been meticulous about contraception; she just did not take chances or do accidents. Nor would she have played around behind Dean's back, Janey was sure of it; she was very moral like that, was Elizabeth. No, none of it added up. It was like peering through a dirty window, knowing all was not well inside but being unable to make out what was going on in there. Then she found the slit of an opening and the little she saw through it was enough to make Janey feel sick.

She had called around to Helen's to show off the new classy blue company car she had just picked up and noticed the souvenir key ring on the work surface.

'Ocean View?' she asked with an immediate huff,

presuming Elizabeth had brought it back for Helen, and if that was the case, where was hers, seeing as *she* had been the one feeding Cleef whilst Elizabeth was away?

'Yes, Simon went there last Wednesday. Some business dinner function thing, no partners allowed.' Not that she had wanted to go anyway, and be ignored all night. 'Have you heard from Elizabeth? Did she enjoy her night away? Where was it she went again?'

'I forget,' lied Janey, thinking on her toes. 'Some place in Somerset, I think.'

As she drove the fifteen-minute journey home from Helen's, Janey's mind was busy forcing pieces together in a mad jigsaw puzzle that was starting to give her a very weird picture. She thought about how vague and distracted Elizabeth had been when she had rung to say she was back, and to thank Janey for looking after Cleef. In fact, her answers had been virtually monosyllabic when Janey asked all the normal things. Had the place had been nice and did she have a good time? Did she see anyone she fancied . . . ho ho? She hadn't mentioned seeing Simon at all, but surely she would have done, if they were at the same function. Why did she seem to dislike him so much anyway? *Who was this bloody mysterious father of her child?*

Then the day after, as she was driving home from work, Janey saw them together – Simon and Elizabeth – those two adversaries who always acted so coldly towards each other, meeting furtively and befittingly in the Old Mill pub car park where Elizabeth had once bonked Wayne Sheffield when they were nineteen.

Elizabeth had not said anything to Janey about Simon's affair. Janey could be a bit of a loose cannon with her mouth sometimes and she did not want this going any further than it had to. Janey would only go straight away and tell George, then there would be twice the chance of the information getting out. So, for a full week, she struggled alone with it, eventually coming to the conclusion that she could not just sit back and pretend it was not happening. She would at least have a go at sorting this out before any more damage was done.

For once she took her car all the way to work, then rang Simon's office, lied about who she was to bypass his Rottweiler of a PA, then as soon as she heard his voice, she told him to be at the Old Mill car park at six that evening. Then she slammed the phone down before he had the chance to refuse her.

She picked the place because it was just at the side of the motorway, two minutes away from the penultimate slip road before their junction, and both of them would pass by it to get home. The fact that Janey passed it too on her way back from Wakefield hadn't even entered Elizabeth's head, but then this was no well-thought-out plan because, beyond getting Simon to the venue, she hadn't a clue what to say or do. This was one she would have to play by ear.

In the beginning, she had thought Simon was quite nice and just what Helen needed. Her friend had coped with the loss of her father bravely and was getting on with her life, she and Janey had both thought, but because they had been distracted by George and John, they didn't see the big breakdown coming until their friend was lost in the middle of it. Simon could not have timed his arrival into her heart more perfectly. Successful, handsome, authoritative . . . they all thought she had landed Prince Charming. That was, until the wedding reception, when Elizabeth saw a very different side of him that too much bally champers could not have been wholly responsible for. She had always felt guilty that she had not spotted what he was really like until he was safely down the aisle, wedded to a considerable Luxmore fortune to come. Well, she had sat back long enough. Her smashing-faces-in days might have gone, but her protective feelings towards her friends were still in place and as strong as they ever were.

She got there ten minutes early and was shaking so hard she wished for the first time in ages that she had a cigarette handy to hang onto. There was no sign of him, but that was to be expected – he would not have wanted her to have too much control. Six o'clock came and went, five past, ten past . . . She decided to give it until half past but a few minutes later, a black BMW with his personalized reg plate pulled into the car park and came to a stop a good thirty yards from her bright yellow car as if it were afraid of contamination. Simon got out of it, looking extremely bored and as if he wanted to get whatever this was out of the way quickly so he could get on with the rest of his life.

'*He wouldn't be here, if he wasn't rattled,*' Elizabeth said to herself, and she tried to focus on it. '*What I know could lose him access to all that lovely Luxmore money.*'

Although no one would have suspected that Simon

was the slightest bit agitated, from the smug look on his face as he said, 'Elizabeth, how lovely to see you! Should we embrace?'

'Let's not. We both know why we're here.'

He sighed and got out his chequebook. 'Okay, how much?' he asked wearily.

'How much?' She wanted to smack that oily smile off with a weighted right hook. 'How much for what?'

'You know what.'

'What's the matter, can't you say it? Too ashamed to admit you're screwing a tart behind your wife's back, Simon? So you bloody well should be, as well.'

'Come on, cut the crap, your sort always has a price,' and he tapped his pen impatiently on the chequebook cover.

'My sort? And how would you classify *your* sort, Simon? I won't ask if bonking Julia Powell was a one-off. I wondered how the gossips seemed to know more about me than I knew about myself.'

She didn't blame Helen for telling Simon the little she had told her about the baby's father. Wives talked to husbands; they just did not expect they would pass on the pillow-talk to their mistresses, and for those mistresses to gossip with their business contacts.

'I really haven't a clue what you're talking about,' said Simon, looking highly amused now by it all.

'What is it with you?' said Elizabeth. 'You have someone as lovely as Helen at home and yet you have to chase the likes of *Julia*? What's up, Simon? Can you only get it up with tarts?'

Simon's self-satisfied smile dropped enough for

Elizabeth to realize that her wild shot had landed surprisingly near the bull's-eye.

'Why are we here then?' he snapped. 'Surely you can't be jealous – is that it?'

'Ambitious little slags like Julia Powell might make you feel you're irresistible, Simon, but trust me, you aren't.'

'Really?' He licked his lips.

Elizabeth ignored it. 'Are you going to leave Helen?'

He threw back his head and laughed then as if she had just told him the funniest joke in the world.

'Why on earth should I leave Helen? She loves me!'

'Because you're a lying, cheating scumbag?'

'And you'd tell her, would you?'

Would I? thought Elizabeth. They both knew she wouldn't and that's why he laughed.

Then he leaned down to her ear and said quietly, 'Do both try not to die in childbirth, won't you?' and he patted her stomach before she had time to avoid it. Then he climbed back into his car and zoomed off, squealing his tyres, leaving Elizabeth shivering in his wake, as if he had just delivered a curse.

Janey had spotted the daft-coloured car when she was on her way home down the motorway, and it was unmistakably Elizabeth's. There might have been other bright yellow cars on the road, but none with a big pink flower on the back.

What on earth is she doing in an empty pub car park? Janey thought, and pulled off at the next exit and headed back towards the pub down the B road, thinking she might have broken down.

By the time she had got there, Simon's car with the easily recognizable registration plate had just arrived, and she saw Elizabeth walking over to it. Janey drove quickly past, she was in her new car so Elizabeth wouldn't have spotted her. She did a full circle at the roundabout and came back for a second surreptitious peek to see Simon leaning back on his car talking to her, casual as you like, and laughing. They looked nothing like a couple who hated the mortal sight of each other, that was for sure. Then again, maybe all that false-smile stuff was an act to throw her and *his wife* off the scent. It wasn't impossible; she'd read far worse in magazines like *Women by Women*: daughters bonking fathers-in-law, sisters bonking brothers-in-law, friends doing the dirty on each other . . . and Elizabeth's emotions were off-kilter to say the least.

Janey sped up the bypass and turned around again, waiting for the Benny Hill music to start up and accompany her, but by that time they had gone and luckily for them too, because Janey was in confrontational mode. There was absolutely no legitimate reason that she could think of in a million years why Elizabeth and Simon should be meeting in private behind Helen's back. As such, it didn't take an Einstein to add this particular two and two up.

Elizabeth rang her that night, but when Janey saw her number flash up on the caller display she let George take it instead and told him to tell Elizabeth that she was in bed. She wondered if Elizabeth had somehow spotted her and was trying to head her off at the pass. Well, it would do her good to be worried, if she was doing what Janey suspected she was doing with Simon. Let her sweat it out until the morning, until I'm ready for her, she thought.

'What's up with you not wanting to natter?' said George, after he had put down the phone.

'I'm just tired,' said Janey, and it wasn't a lie. Twenty-four hours' worth of angry thoughts had worn her down and she badly wanted the oblivion of sleep before she tackled it all head on tomorrow.

Elizabeth had not even considered the possibility of dying in childbirth, but since Simon's parting shot, she could think of nothing else. She rang Janey in a blind panic but George said she had gone to bed. She could not face talking to Helen at the moment but she was desperate to hear someone else's voice, for someone to tell her that she was getting things out of perspective. In tears, she started to dial John's number, but on the last one, she put it down. How could she start turning needy on him now?

So instead, she curled up in bed and mentally tortured herself with a mind video of what would happen to her baby if she died, and how she would feel if *he* died. She saw herself following a tiny white coffin out of the church, knowing he was going to be tucked up in a cold earth grave where she could not hold him. And the more she tried to stop the thoughts, the stronger the tormenting images forced themselves upon her.

A six o'clock alarm awoke Simon as he lay in bed close to his wife. Golden-haired and pale-skinned, Helen was everything a man should be proud of in a wife, but he felt no stirring in his loins at all. His finger traced down over her long neck, to her small pointy breasts and further down to the swelling in her stomach that made him instantly recoil. Suddenly he felt suffocated, resentful. He had to get away from her. From *'it'*.

Helen's looks had attracted him at first, of course, and together they made a striking couple, as he knew they would. But she was never intended to be the keeper of his heart; her purpose would always be to embellish *his* essential executive image. She was attractive, wealthy – thanks to a legacy from her father – and she would be even richer when her widowed mother died, something he hoped would be sooner rather than later. Helen was so vulnerable when they first met, easy to charm and to seduce, and she adored him. Together they had almost everything that was important to him.

The yin that Simon presented to the world was proficient, successful, in control. His yang, however, was a darker being who desired women with ridiculously sized breasts who could purr like wildcats and talk dirty to him. There was no reason he could think of for this quirk – it was just how he was. Only with these women could he reach sexual ecstasy, but afterwards the self-loathing was waiting to envelop him like a heavy, dirty blanket. Then, and only then, would he try to force his wayward persona back into 'respectable Simon'. He would buy presents for his wife, fuss over her, even occasionally make love to her, until the urge to break free from his domestic repression came upon him again, making him kick out at the life he had to be seen to be living – an unfulfilling, banal, frustrating existence. He ricocheted between the two poles of his character, projecting the self-hatred for his weakness towards the soft target of his wife, and that dirty slut of a friend of hers, whom he despised even more because she *was* able to stir that animal inside him.

He didn't want children. He had acquired the perfect image without them. Look how they had softened his friend Con, made him lose his bite. Simon didn't want snotty-nosed brats with sticky fingers making him lose his focus, draining his time, piling on even more guilt.

Elizabeth worried and cried all night, and in the morning her eyes were red and puffed-up and she looked awful when she answered the door after a knock that was worthy of a drugs raid. In stormed Janey, who'd had a restless night herself building up to this moment. She pushed past Elizabeth to get in, then stood in the middle of her front room, swaying with barely contained rage.

'I *know*. How could you?'

'Know what?' said Elizabeth, worn out from crying and now confused as well.

'About you and him, so you might as well tell me.'

'What?' said Elizabeth, who really looked as if she did not know what Janey was talking about, which poured more petrol all over her flames.

'Don't you dare look at me like I'm nuts! I know

you spent the night at that posh hotel together and . . . and . . . I saw you both yesterday, in the Old Mill car park – that ring any bells?'

The wind fell from Janey's sails a little because Elizabeth really did look terrible. She was shivering as if she was cold, despite the morning being full of promise of a warm day to come, but then the hard part of Janey reasoned that she was probably that way because of the weight of her guilt. That thought made the wind rise and billow up the sails again.

'Me and Simon?' Elizabeth said quietly.

Janey laughed grimly, taking this as some kind of admission. 'Ah! I see you know who I'm bloody talking about then!'

'Us together? You're off your head.'

'I know he was in Norfolk in the same hotel as you on the same night, and I SAW YOU TOGETHER in a flaming pub car park. So you tell me what that was all about, if it isn't the obvious!'

'It isn't the way it looked.'

Janey laughed hard. 'People always say that when it's *exactly* as it looked.'

'Trust me.'

'That's a good one! I'm not blind; I went round a few times to make sure I wasn't dreaming what I was seeing. Don't treat me like an idiot, Elizabeth. For a start you look as guilty as sin. You can't look me in the face, can you? Go on, I dare you!'

Then Janey gasped as a new notion presented itself to her overworking brain. She pointed out at Elizabeth's stomach.

'Please don't tell me that's his in there!'

Elizabeth flopped down on her rocking chair and wearily put her head in her hands. 'Oh God, what a mess,' she said. 'It'd be funny if it wasn't so tragic. Me and Simon? It's enough to bring my morning sickness back!'

'There's nothing funny about someone shagging a pregnant woman's husband!' Janey screamed at her.

'No, you're right there,' said Elizabeth. She lifted her head, stared Janey straight in the face and realized she would have to tell her the full story after all.

A ready-for-work Simon leaned over the bed and kissed a sleepy Helen on the cheek and she smiled at his sweet, 'Good morning.' She listened to his footfalls down the hall, the door open, his car drive away, then she mulled over the events of the previous night. He had brought in some non-alcoholic wine for her, then he had made supper – pasta and chicken and asparagus – and they had relaxed quietly in the lounge, listening to mellow music. He had drunk rather a lot of scotch, she silently noted, but then stress was coming off him in waves. She rubbed his shoulders and then, after a while, he took her hand in his and led her to bed. They had not made love, but it did not matter for she had woken in the night at one point and felt his arm around her. They were at a turning-point, she was sure of it. There was hope.

'Why didn't you say something before?' Janey almost snarled when Elizabeth had finished talking. Her aggression was masking a deep shame. She had handled this so wrong and was only glad she hadn't gone storming off to Helen first, as it had crossed her mind to.

'I'd hoped to try and sort it, and I thought the fewer people that knew about it the better,' said Elizabeth. 'You'd go and tell George and then that would be ano-ther person who might open their gob, mistakenly or otherwise.'

Janey did not argue with that, she knew Elizabeth was right.

'Okay. So how come you've never liked him?' she asked. 'Proper answer this time, none of your mumblings that it's just a clash of personalities.'

She had to press her a bit; Elizabeth wasn't keen to tell her.

'Okay, if you must know, he came onto me at the wedding. His own wedding,' she said eventually. 'He was standing outside by himself and I'd gone out to have a fag so I walked over to him and starting chat-ting – you know, "Have you had a good day?" – all that sort of stuff you say. He lunged at me and no, he wasn't that drunk before you ask. He said he'd seen the way I'd been looking at him. I thought he was joking at first. I mean, it was his wedding, for God's sake, and I was one of his wife's bridesmaids. His hands were . . . all over me.' Elizabeth shuddered at the memory of him pawing at her.

'In the end I had to knee him in the spuds to get him off and, well, you can imagine the names he called me. Not exactly the gent I thought he was.' She sighed and it was a deep, tired sound. 'I don't know, Janey.

Maybe it *is* my fault. Maybe I'm just one of those people who give out signals . . .' She gulped a few times and Janey wanted to hug her, but felt she didn't have the right to.

'You don't do anything wrong,' she said softly. 'It's them that see what they want to see.'

'You were quick enough to believe it.'

'I'm sorry. I feel terrible, if it's any consolation.'

'It's okay, forget it now.'

Elizabeth being gracious about it made Janey feel even more of a cow. A big, fat, bovine hypocrite going on about infidelity as if she was the Virgin Mary. Her, of all people! Now that was a joke and a half.

'So what did you ring me about last night then?' asked the cow, sheepishly.

'About dying in childbirth,' Elizabeth said in a very wobbly voice. 'I got myself in a loop about it after what Simon said. All I could think about was me dying and my baby having nobody, or the baby dying and having a white coffin . . .' Her voice dissolved on the word and her head tipped forward into her hands and she couldn't get it together again.

'Oh, Elizabeth,' said Janey, and opened up her Big Momma arms and pulled her friend up from her seat and into them. Elizabeth only came up to her shoulder. She used to be taller than me once: did I grow or did she shrink? thought Janey with an overwhelming fondness for her little friend. However could I have thought all those things about her – Elizabeth Collier? It had been like having their own personal minder at school. Her mind rewound to that bitch Carmen

Varley who made Helen's life hell, and boz-eyed Miriam Sutton who used to call Janey 'Fatty Arbuckle'. That was, until Elizabeth waded in like a Tasmanian Devil with her fists flying and without a care for the resulting detention or the bruises she sustained, because Carmen and Miriam were tough, meaty girls and got a few hits in before Elizabeth obliterated them. Funny how Elizabeth always thought she was twisted, but where friends were concerned she was as straight as a die, thought Janey. Whereas she . . .

'Anyway, never mind about me, what about Hels? I've driven myself nuts trying to work out what to do, and I can't think of anything. I'm damned if I tell her and damned if I don't,' Elizabeth said, with a loaded sigh.

'I don't see there's anything we can do, Elizabeth,' said Janey, and that was the sad truth of it. As far as either of them could see, all they could do was sit back and wait for the crash.

And sit back and wait they did, but nothing happened and certainly, for the next week and a half anyway, life outwardly carried on as normal for the Golden Cadberrys. Helen had her friends over for tea on an evening when Simon was doing an overnight in London to show them the beautiful completed nursery, which made Elizabeth doubly wish she had done hers earlier because she had really left it too late to do now. Janey told her to ask John to help – he and George together would have it done in a couple of days, but Elizabeth didn't ask favours and Janey knew better than to push her on it. Then Helen made her feel a little better by saying that the baby would probably be in with her in the 'womb room' for a few months so there really was no rush.

Helen was looking so pretty and lovely at thirty-one weeks, still maintaining her air of delicacy despite her fast-growing girth, although she would have traded anything for a bigger chest, like the others had. She had not put on nearly as much weight as either of them. Elizabeth was turning into a small football and her already generously proportioned bust had ballooned, much to Helen's envy. Janey was starting to resemble some formidable horned-hat warrior queen from a Wagner opera. Her breasts were growing so much that each one would have a different post-code soon. Her face looked like a full moon and she had splashed out and gone to Antony Fawkes, the posh hairdresser in town, for a complete restyle as her straight, shoulder-length hair only accentuated the roundness. Their top stylist had cut her hair in a fringe, given her a swishy little bob and put some choppy dark streaks in it to add interest to the red; it was the best hundred quid she had spent in a long time.

They all sat in Helen's surgery-like kitchen, taking alternate swigs from their cups of raspberry-leaf tea, which apparently aided a smooth delivery, and bottles of Gaviscon, totally ignoring the 'one teaspoon every three months' instruction. It was a standing joke at the doctor's surgery how much of it Elizabeth was going through. Dr Gilhooley said she was practically an addict.

'Should I be drinking stout for the iron?' she had asked him. Being Irish, he was bound to extol its dark and creamy benefits.

'What the hell do you want to drink that foul stuff for?' he had said, and told her to eat lots of sprouts instead.

Helen took a long guzzle of Gaviscon and shuddered as it went down.

'Hubby back tomorrow?' asked Janey politely, without any of her drooling. Simon had well and truly fallen from grace now in her eyes.

'Yep – and guess what? I'm going away for a couple of days on Friday myself,' Helen announced.

'Anywhere nice?' asked Janey, swinging her hair as it was still a novelty.

'Mum's taking me to a health spa to rejuvenate me.'

'Oh, that'll be lovely for you,' Elizabeth said, knowing that it would be, too – only the best was good enough for Mrs Luxmore. It hurt her to see how much Helen smiled then, how much she thought everything in her garden was lovely. Still, a nice weekend relaxing away from that toxic dickhead she was married to could only do her the world of good.

And so off Helen went to her fancy health spa, little realizing just how rejuvenated she would actually be when the end of that weekend came.

Chapter 36

The Luxmore ladies arrived at 'The Retreat' just in time for lunch. After a harvest festival of a salad, Helen had a long swim, a yoga class, a light supper and an hour's massage just before bed, and still she tossed and turned in between the cool, white sheets, ring-roading the city of sleep. How could she think of enjoying herself there whilst her marriage lay in little more than tatters at home? Simon was going to be alone in their house all weekend – surely she should be there instead, spending the time with him. So, early in the morning, she left a note for her mother at Reception to say she was getting the train back; she would explain later and told her not to worry. Penelope Luxmore would be disappointed, but she would still enjoy her time at the spa. She had been there many times before and was no stranger to the facilities. Helen, however, knew her priority was to go home and work on her relationship, before it was too late. She and Simon might have recently reached a turning-point, but there was still a long way to go. She had to fight for her marriage for the sake of their baby.

As the taxi pulled up on the main road, Helen noticed that Simon's car was out in the driveway, which was unusual, and even odder, it was blocking in a snazzy red Mini. She trod over the gravel as slowly and as quietly as she could without fully understanding why she needed to act like that – call it instinct, call it panic.

She unlocked the back door and crept in, discovering just how stealthily a heavily pregnant woman could move. Gliding like a cat through the kitchen and into the lounge, she was immediately alerted to the trail of clothes across the carpet there – a G-string, a bra that she could have carried a hundredweight of melons in, shoes, a pair of black stockings. She scooped them up and stuffed them in a cupboard out of sight, along with the alien handbag on the sofa. Her heart felt dry, each beat a loud and painful throb; her throat was so parched she felt sure it was on the verge of cracking.

She stole like a whisper down the hallway, picking through the silence for evidence of what was going on, and then stopped outside her own bedroom door when she heard her husband's voice from within it say, 'Look, I'll ring her in a minute to see what time she's coming back tomorrow if you're that worried.'

Then a female voice answered, 'I wish you would. I've just got this funny feeling, that's all. I don't want to bump into her in the hallway.'

They both laughed at that.

'I love your tits.'

'I know.'

'They're huge.'

'Are they as good as your wife's?'

'You're joking, aren't you? They're like mosquito bites!'

They laughed again. At Helen.

'Come here, you,' he said smokily. Just as he used to say at the beginning, when Helen thought she was the luckiest woman alive. Just as he said to Helen before rolling her beneath him and kissing her that sex-charged night when together they made the beautiful daughter who was growing inside her; the child who was being as betrayed as she was.

Helen's trembling hand sought out the door handle; she braced herself, then charged into her bedroom to see a scrawny shape with enormous bobbling breasts riding her husband, whose hands were handcuffed to the wrought-iron bedhead with something covered in pink feathers. They all froze in a tableau of *Pregnant Wife Discovers Cheating Husband With Tart*; even the clock seemed to hold its breath. The naked couple were in the bed in which Simon had taken his wife's virginity, and where they had made their child. *Their bed, their child.*

Helen felt the agony of tears make their barbed way up to her ducts, and just as she was about to collapse into them, she heard that voice again: *'Come on, girl, where's that Luxmore backbone!'* and the tears stopped their passage and were driven back. It was as if her father was inside her, propping her up, straightening her spine, and in the few moments that followed his words in her head, all hell broke loose.

'Helen, look . . . ' said Simon, rattling uselessly against the pink fluff and metal.

'I'm looking,' she said, sounding remarkably calm considering her heart was booming as loud in her ears as a Status Quo concert.

'It's not what you think.'

Yes, he actually said that. Miss Handcuff-administrator was attempting to cover her bulbous-like growths with two tiny doll-like hands, whilst trying to work out how to get round the tall, blonde woman to escape to her clothes.

'I just needed some sex and I didn't want to hurt the baby,' Simon went on.

As if it wasn't bad enough, he's actually using the baby as an excuse for his behaviour, thought Helen with disgust.

Big Boobs did not look very happy at that and started raining expletives on him whilst slapping him. Her hands were so occupied that she did not notice Helen coming up behind her – a Helen who was no longer a gentle, fluffy thing, especially with the advantage of the extra weight behind her. This was a Helen who was boiling with adrenaline and rage for herself, but most of all for her unborn child. Growling like a savage, she lifted the naked woman up by the back of her hair and propelled her down the hallway with hardly an effort. She left *him* wriggling away on the bed trying to get free and looking remarkably as if he was having an epileptic fit. Helen picked off his keys from the hook as she passed: she did not want this *thing* in her own car. She stormed out of the front door and down the path towards Simon's BMW, not loosening her grip for one nano-second.

'Ow, ow, ow!' the woman cried as the stones cut into her bare feet. Helen zapped the car doors open and threw her onto the back seat.

'Time to drive you home, I think,' she said.

'My h . . . h . . . handbag, p . . . please,' the woman stuttered.

'I'll have it sent on,' said Helen.

'It's got my door keys in it!'

'Tough.'

The woman tried to get out as Helen fired up the ignition, but the childproof locks made that an impossibility.

'Could I at least have my clothes?' she said, rather snottily, whilst trying to cover herself with an ancient torn *A to Z* that disintegrated upon unfolding.

'No, you can't. You shouldn't have taken them off, should you?' hissed Helen, spraying gravel as she squealed out of the drive, accelerating away like Ralph Schumacher from a pitstop.

The woman, whoever she was, then started sobbing her apologies, not that Helen was in the slightest bit softened by them. She was thinking about all those times that Simon told her he was too tired to make love, how disinterested he had been in her and her baby, and in the back of her car was the reason why – because he was spending his executive energies on *her*. The woman had squeezed herself into a small pink ball on the car floor, trying to cover herself up with her hands as Helen roared through the prestigious little village of six-figure salaries, double garages and remote-controlled gates.

'Where do you live?' said Helen, realizing she had not a clue where she was supposed to be driving to and was presently on automatic pilot for the centre of town.

'Er . . . Horsforth,' came the meek answer.

Helen had not a clue how to get there – M1 and follow the signs when she got near Leeds, she supposed. She had better do a double-back through town then and head for the motorway in that case.

It was Saturday afternoon and the town's main market-day. Crowds were everywhere, but luckily for the woman crouching in the back, every traffic-light seemed to turn to green on approach. Helen could not see her at all in the rearview mirror; she was successfully managing to avoid public humiliation by being so skinny that she could sink into the footwell, although the sight of her naked astride her husband was branded on Helen's brain. Their laughter rang in her ears like a severe attack of tinnitus and their scoffing words were playing on a continuous loop. *I don't want to bump into her in the hallway . . . ha, ha, ha . . . mosquito bites . . . I don't want to bump into her in the hallway . . . ha, ha, ha . . .*

Lava started to spill out of Helen's veins just as she braked for the red traffic-light in the epicentre of the town, and in an impetuous moment of devilment, she pressed down the electric window switches, ignoring the yelp from the back, then twisted the key in the ignition until it gave a satisfying snap. It took almost superhuman strength to do it, but at that moment, Helen *was* superhuman – a good Angel of Justice fused with a dark

Angel of Vengeance. She sprang off her seat-belt and got out of the car.

'What are you doing?' cried Boob Woman with a desperate sob.

'I'm going home,' said Helen, leaving the car door wide open and walking off triumphantly towards the taxi rank. Behind her, drivers started to honk at the abandoned vehicle, and an interested crowd started to gather around what appeared to be a well-stacked naked woman in the middle of Barnsley on a Saturday afternoon.

Simon was still struggling against the handcuffs when she got home.

'Where the hell have you been?' he screamed. 'Just get me out of these things. The key must have fallen on the floor here, this side,' and he butted his head towards her bedside cabinet. '*Now*, Helen!'

Helen noted that there was no courteous enquiry about where his companion was, even though he must have known that a return trip to her house could not have been possible in twenty minutes. She picked up the keys from the carpet and saw the relief wash over his face.

'Now unlock . . . what are you doing?'

She put the handcuff keys in her pocket. He then watched her take out a digital camera from her drawer and start to photograph him. She had always meant to renew her old pastime. What better occasion than this to pick it up?

'You crazy mad bitch! Stop that! I mean it, Helen!'

'Smile,' said Helen, actually enjoying herself, feeding from his frenzied attempts to escape the tight metal cuffs. This temporary sadistic possession was holding off the other feelings that she knew were only round the corner – ones of hurt and betrayal and sadness that her marriage was over because there could be no recovery from this. He had not wounded their relationship, he had killed it with one clean blow. Their marriage was history, and their future family life with their child was history, and for the latter she hated him most of all and kept on snapping because of it. He sneezed. The air seemed full of bits of escapee feathers.

'By the time I come back in four hours, you will have left,' she said eventually. 'Or you have no idea what I'll do with these pictures.'

'Has it crossed your stupid, tiny brain that if I'm to leave, you will have to get me out of these things?'

He was furious now, red-faced like a restrained demon that needed exorcizing, not releasing. He called her the worst names he could think of, names that her unborn child was hearing, and she was not going to let them go by unpunished.

'You really shouldn't swear at me like that, Simon,' she said with a tired sigh. Then she picked up the bedroom phone and dialled in a number after finding it in the *Thomson Local*.

'Hello, is that Phoenix Locksmiths? . . . Yes, sorry, my husband's managed to get himself in a bit of a pickle with his mistress. Could you send someone round to release a lock? . . . Yes, I'll give you the address . . .

I've got to go out but I'll leave the door open. Just go straight through to the bedroom – you'll find him in there naked and handcuffed to the bedpost . . . No, you can't miss him, he's covered in pink feathers . . . Thirty minutes? Good, thank you.'

She turned to the snarling, spitting creature writhing on the bed and screaming out commands and terrible expletives. She was calm as a millpond, detached, indifferent to the terrible embarrassment he was about to undergo, even though less than an hour ago she loved him so much that she could not wait to get back to him to repair their damaged marriage. Now she felt nothing.

'Four hours,' she repeated, and with that, Helen took the last-ever look at her husband on their marital bed and went out to the garage, past the tarty red Mini to drive to the Old Rectory, where she would sit on the swing in her mother and father's garden and plan the first stage of her newly single life.

Chapter 37

Terry Lennox bounced in from his early-morning meeting at Handi-Save, threw his jacket successfully onto one of the hooked arms of the old-fashioned coat-stand in the corner of his office with the ease of a Harlem Globetrotter and buzzed Elizabeth to get her enormous backside in there as quickly as she could with two hot chocolates and a packet of anything but Penguins.

'Sit down, woman, you're blocking all the light!' he said, when she bumped open the door with her bottom because her hands were full. For once, Elizabeth did as she was told without a clever retort because a) he was obviously champing at the bit to release what-ever news he had and b) she was carrying the packet of biscuits in by her teeth.

'Guess what I've just heard.'

'I can't imagine.'

He was going to make her guess for a bit, but it was too good to dither over.

'Your mate Julia Powell—' he began, before Elizabeth interrupted him.

'She's no mate of mine!'

'Will you shush! As I was saying before I was so rudely interrupted, *your mate Julia Powell* was found naked in the middle of Barnsley on Saturday.'

'Yeah, right,' said Elizabeth, pulling open the packet of mint Viscounts and offering them over.

'No, honestly, and Laurence, by all accounts, is furious. Personally, I think she's kept it quiet that she was seeing someone, wanted to keep Laurence dangling, and then she's had to come crawling to him to sort all the mess out. He's pulled a mighty lot of strings to keep it out of the newspapers for her, but he isn't happy about it at all because everyone knows anyway and it doesn't land him in a good light trying to manipulate the press, especially with his political aspirations!'

'No!' said Elizabeth, who was starting to believe him now. 'Straight up?'

'As straight up as a levitating poker,' said Terry, and began at the beginning.

'Apparently she's been seeing some married bigwig advertising bloke. His wife comes home, finds them at it in the marital bed; she throws Julia, naked, in the car and drives her to the middle of town where she dumps the car, jams the key in the ignition and gets a taxi home. Anyway, someone eventually gives Miss Powell a blanket and drives her home, but there was a hell of a crowd by all accounts. Laurence is not a happy bloke, I can tell you. He could hardly look at her in the meeting. There's been innuendo flying about all morning, then she eventually twigged that all the sniggering was directed at her and ran out crying. Silly little girl. As if poor Laurence hasn't got enough on his plate, with me breathing on his jugular. Anyway,' he took a swig of chocolate and nodded with approval, 'I thought you might like to know.'

'Oh, you can't imagine how glad I am you told me,' said Elizabeth with a delighted smirk. 'Though I wouldn't have had you down as a gossip, Mr Lennox.'

'I'm not,' said Terry Lennox, 'but I can't abide marriage-wreckers. They deserve every bloody thing they get in my book. I'll have another of those biscuits. Nice, aren't they?'

Well, well, well, thought Elizabeth, passing him the packet of biscuits again. Helen said to wait for karma and here it is, making its arrival in its top hat and tails. Or in the buff, whichever way you look at it.

Helen . . .

Oh bloody hell – *Helen!*

Elizabeth rang Helen on her mobile to find she was at work as usual. It obviously wasn't Slimy found *in flagrante delicto* then because Helen would have been in pieces if it had, and would surely have told them, needing their support.

'Oh, hi,' said Elizabeth. 'I was . . . er . . . just ringing . . . er . . . no reason, really. Just to see if you were okay.'

'I'm fine,' said Helen, who sounded finer than she had in a long time. 'In fact, I've never felt better. I was going to ring you at lunchtime actually, with an invitation.'

'Oh, were you? What's up?'

'Well, I've thrown Simon out and I've got myself a new man and I'd like you and Janey to come over. Let's make it tonight, shall we? Come for tea, then you can meet him. Will you ring her or shall I?'

This wasn't Helen, she was obviously in that mad stage that sounded like euphoria but was actually hysteria with a mask on. Any minute now and she would break down and start wailing like a banshee crossed with Celine Dion.

'Er . . . I'll ring her. Are you really all right?'

'Elizabeth, really I am, apart from the heartburn – but I think I might have just got rid of the biggest pain in my pregnancy. We'll talk later and I'll tell you everything. I'll see you at six.'

She left Elizabeth staring down at the receiver as if she expected to hear it cry, 'April Fool!'

They looked down at the sofa where the new male in Helen's life lay sleeping.

'Gorgeous, isn't he?' she said, with an indulgent smile.

'Never thought you'd go for a ginger fella,' said Elizabeth.

'Oy!' said Janey, making a stand for redheads. 'I think he's very handsome, Hels, well done.'

'What's his name?'

'Brian,' said Helen.

'Well, he's a good sleeper!'

'He had a huge dinner, I expect that tired him out.'

'He looks content, bless him.'

'Big lad, isn't he?' commented Janey.

'He'll bugger up your leather sofa,' said Elizabeth.

Helen stroked the big ginger cat's fur and he responded to her touch in sleep with a long claw-showing stretch.

'Yes,' she said, sweetly but dangerously. 'I hope he rips it to shreds.'

They ate prawn cocktails, scampi and chips, and a home-made Black Forest gâteau that stood about six inches tall, and Janey had two portions of it with cream and was in seventh heaven. Mind you, she was burning up so much raw energy at work and in bed with George that she needed the extra calories.

The centrepiece of the dining table was Elizabeth's vase filled with pink flowers, like the ones Janey had bought for her birthday. The big abstract, boring pictures had gone and Helen's cat paintings, which had been stored in the garage, now graced the walls. Little feminine knick-knacks had appeared everywhere and the house had a gentler, softer feel already.

Helen relayed the events of the past few days without tears, without emotion as if it was the story of someone else and not part of her recent past. The others had not dared to as much as smile because at the heart of it all was a friend who had got hurt and deceived, but when she got to the bit about the locksmith, despite everything, they couldn't hold the laughter back and exploded like round giggling bombs until they were spent.

'Will you cope all right on your own?' asked Elizabeth.

'Well, *you* do,' said Helen.

'Yes, but I'm *hard*,' she replied, casting a look at Janey who flicked a middle finger up in her direction.

'Mum's been wonderful. I thought she'd try and make us get back together, but she didn't. I told her everything and we talked like we never have done before,' said Helen. 'Anyway, I wouldn't go back if the whole world was trying to persuade me to.'

The others didn't ask why she had not shared her unhappiness before. They knew there were some things they would always have to keep to themselves.

'I hope he doesn't give you a hard time,' said Janey.

'He wouldn't dare,' said Helen, thinking about her little insurance policy, dually lodged in her mother's and Teddy Sanderson's safes.

When her friends left and the hot lemon sun started to drop down on the fine summer evening, Helen started to feel jittery at the hour that Simon usually returned home. She realized, with some sadness, how conditioned she had become to that tense, nervous state. She had great joy in telling herself that he was not going to come through the door. There would be none of his moods to contend with ever again, no tip-toeing around him on eggshells in case his hair-trigger temper went off, no going to bed wondering what she had done to send him off in a sulk. Never again would he sleep in the cold little room at the end of the hallway to teach her a lesson or call her those names or push her around. She had so much wanted to share his life, but now, suddenly after all these years, she knew he would always have been

incapable of letting her do that. All he wanted of a
wife was someone to sit decoratively in the background until needed – and she knew she deserved so
much more.

Helen had thought that she and Simon were so
happy, but with this newly found perspective, she
could see now that she had lost sight of her own
happiness long ago and had strived only for his. So
long as she stayed slim and beautiful, he paid her
attention; so long as she did not dare have opinions,
she was assured of his kisses. Kisses that were not
exclusive to her, it seemed. Once all these realizations
had hit home, she felt different, as if she had been let
out of a dark, cramped cage. She also knew that she
would not stay in that house longer than was necessary. She wanted her baby brought up in a place as
she had been, full of love and bright colours. Her
mother had asked her to move back into the Old
Rectory, and the next day the two of them would
start to pack up her belongings and move them across
to her old home.

It hurt her to think of his deception, because not
only was he unfaithful, but he respected her so little
that he brought another woman into their bed. To
think of *them*, together there, brought an actual physical pain to her gut that she hoped the baby couldn't
feel. By coincidence, the baby booted it a direct hit.

'That's my girl,' Helen said.

Just like her dad used to say to her. Just like he said
to her that last night of his life.

She felt strongly that Alex Luxmore was there in

that room with her; but he would come back with her to the Old Rectory. He would always be with her; he was her father, a beloved part of her, as she would always be part of him. She had her child, her two dear friends, her mother and now Brian too. The tears made a short reappearance then left. She was not alone; in fact, Helen had never felt less alone than in all the time she was married.

Chapter 38

There was no reason for Helen to jolt awake in the middle of that freezing April night, but she did and, not able to get back to sleep, she went downstairs with the intention of revisiting her bedtime routine, which she had heard helped a restless sleeper. She padded down the long hallway, past the library, her father's study and the morning room, which he used now for a bedroom, and there became aware of a distinct draught coming from the direction of the kitchen. She opened the door to that room to find it icy, which was very unusual because the central heating was never switched off for her father felt the cold so very much these days. She checked the back door and it was unlocked, which was even stranger, because she had locked it herself before going up to bed. Tentatively she opened it and saw her father there on the terrace and realized it must have taken him a monumental effort to turn the key and wheel the chair out there by himself. There was a long glass on the small wrought-iron table and some straws and he was trying to unscrew the top off a bottle of brandy.

'Daddy, what are you doing? How did you get out here?'

'Oh, dear God, go back in,' he said. 'Please go away, leave me alone, Helen.' He struggled with the words, for his speech had started to go by then.

'Daddy, let me take you back ins—'

He stilled her arm on his chair with the little remaining strength in his bony hand.

'Let me go, Helen. I've seen what this disease does to the body and I don't want it any more. I don't want to suffer and I don't want your mother and you to suffer watching me. I don't want you to remember me like that.'

'Daddy . . .'

'It has to be tonight. I've been watching the forecast and it would be cold enough. The weather will change soon. I want to go here, in my garden, Helen. I want to fall asleep and just let go . . . Oh dear God, why did you have to come out?'

'Please, Daddy! I can't just walk away and let you do this!'

'The insurance won't cover me for suicide, Helen; it has to be this way – accidental death. They'll say I was an old soak and you will agree.'

'But you aren't – you hardly—'

'YES, Helen, and you will tell them that if asked,' said her father. 'I have been drinking recently, building up to this night, just in case they perform a post-mortem.'

Helen started to sob.

'You have to be strong, my love. I realize how much I'm asking of you. Now help me get the top off this bottle.'

'I can't!' she cried.

'Please, Helen, remember that Luxmore backbone! You have to, my darling, darling girl. I need you. Go and get some gloves – don't leave your fingerprints.'

Alex Luxmore was trapped in the grip of the disease he feared more than any other; it was his own living nightmare. Almost blindly, Helen got some woolly gloves from the kitchen drawer, took the bottle and, with shaking hands, poured him a brandy that filled and ran over the top of the glass. Then, as he asked, she put the straws in it for him, as if he were a child.

'Goodnight, Helen. Say it, my love, as we always do and then go to bed. Leave me; you'll need your strength for the morning.'

'Daddy, please don't do this.'

'My darling girl, I love you so much and I know you love me enough to do this one thing for me. It's what I want. Please, Helen, please . . . I can't take any more.'

She did not want to see him cry. She did not want to see her tall, brilliant, strong, gentle dad reduced to begging. He had given her everything and never asked anything of her, but this. What cruel coins they were that would now repay the debt. She dropped to the ground and cried on his lap and he stroked her hair, his lovely girl's beautiful, golden hair.

'Yes, Daddy, I will do this for you.'

'That's my girl. I love you. May God forgive me for putting you through this.'

She wiped away the tears that were rolling from his bright, grey eyes. Then she put the large glass of brandy into his hands.

'Try to forgive me, Helen. Now go. Say goodnight, my love.'

'Goodnight, Daddy, sweet dreams, I love you so much, so very much, always . . .' and she kissed his warm cheek for the last time. Then she walked into the house with a straight Luxmore backbone – and left him to die.

Chapter 39

The weather was boiling flower heads that penultimate day of July. It was far too hot even for people whose spines were supporting the equivalent of a hundred-weight of spuds. Janey and Helen waddled towards the agreed rendezvous point in the park where Elizabeth was waiting for them with Cornettos.

'I've only walked from the car and I'm totally knack-ered!' said Janey, struggling to breathe.

Helen nodded in agreement, although she did not want to moan about anything because the pregnancy fairy was coming through for her at last and she was starting to notice a definite increase in the size of her chest. She had never had proper breasts before and it felt very nice to jut them out like loaded machine guns. To her abject shame, she had found herself sticking them out a bit further at work when Teddy Sanderson made an appearance. She really had no business aiming them in another man's direction, considering she had only been estranged from her husband for less than a week, but her heart appeared to have closed the door after him, locked it, bolted it and then concreted over it. There had been one day of minor depression and tears that came and went like a small, air-clearing shower, but she realized she had done most of her crying in the years past.

Of course, Simon had called to enquire how she was – and the baby, he added as an afterthought. In other words, he was asking if she had calmed down yet and come to her senses. She was not in the slightest bit fooled by his apparent concern and surely enough, seconds later, he tried to come to some sort of financial arrangement about the photos. When she refused, he told her that he wouldn't play fair about any future settlement then.

'In which case I won't play fair about the photos,' she had retorted, and put the phone down on him.

He rang back immediately in thinly covered panic to re-open negotiations, but Helen had no intention of complying with his wishes; she was calling the shots now and it felt marvellous. All she had to do was think of how he had betrayed their child and she stayed impervious to his mind-twists. For a control freak to be not in control was torture for Simon, and he was reduced to snarling and spitting like a vampire in a crucifix factory, but Helen would never relinquish any of her power to a man again. It fired up her energy levels no end to be in charge of decisions and her own life. Add to that a discernible bosom and she was indomitable.

She was seriously considering going back to university and completing her Law studies when the baby was older. Her mother had been incredibly supportive and had volunteered babysitting services whenever she might need them. Penelope Luxmore was getting into 'Nana mode', much to her daughter's surprise and delight, though she was more likely to shop in House of Fraser for bootees than get the knitting needles out – she was never going to be *that* sort of Nana.

'Eeeh, that's what I like to see . . .' said an old bloke, walking a stiff dog along the path in front of them. He stopped and smiled at the three rotund women eating ice creams on the park bench.

'. . . Three grand-looking lasses all in the Pudding Club.'

'Aye, and we're not just any old Pudding Club,' said Elizabeth. 'We're the Yorkshire Pudding Club,' which made them all laugh.

'Well, I tell you, you're bonny pieces looking like that,' he said, beaming a three-toothed smile and raising his cap to them. 'Good luck to you all,' then off he, and the grey-faced dog, went on their way.

'Aw bless,' said Janey, suddenly cloudy-eyed. The old guy reminded her of her granddad. He would have loved to have seen her like this.

'Think they're smiling on us?' said Helen, hijacking her thoughts.

'Who?' said Elizabeth.

'Janey's granddad, your Auntie Elsie and my dad,' said Helen, cocking her Cornetto skyward.

'I imagine so,' said Janey, blowing a kiss up to heaven. 'I tell you what, he'll enjoy watching me have this ice cream. I could feel him shaking his head and tutting every time I so much as looked at a lettuce.'

'Come on, girlies,' said Helen, pulling her friends to their feet. Elizabeth was looking particularly resplendent in a big, cool orange kaftan top.

'You know, you look like a space-hopper in that!' said Janey, dodging the ensuing slap, and together they walked off in the direction of St Jude's Church hall for their first Parentcraft class.

George met them at the door, tapping his watch. 'It's past six o'clock, we'll be late! Where've you all been?'

'Oh, shut up before you start,' said Janey.

'They'll think I've a harem if I walk all three of you in,' he said.

'We'll tell them you got all of us up the duff,' said Elizabeth, sidling suggestively up to him.

'Give over,' said George. 'I haven't got the strength to service more than her. You should see some of the things she's had me doing!'

'Get in, Casanova, before I make you do them all over again tonight. Twice. With the snorkel,' said Janey, giving him a push through the door.

George only hoped she was joking.

The church hall was large and echoey, with a stage and a black upright piano at one end and lots of kids' paintings of the Disciples in fishermen mode at the other. Strangely, one of them appeared to be holding the directional sign for the toilets, which felt a bit irreverent. There were twelve women assembled already and one other brother-in-arms who did a male bob-of-the-head thing over to George that signified both 'hello' and 'help'; they were both slightly nervous to see so many women resembling Peggy Mount in the same room.

Everyone took up their seats, which were set up in a central crescent around a whiteboard with a toy box underneath it; the latter was full of videos and books, a worrying part of a skeleton and a full-term baby-sized doll. The sessions were run every couple of months by one of the local midwives. Sue Chimes said they were very useful for all those little last-minute unanswered questions and socially it was quite fun too when there was a good bunch of women attending, so Elizabeth had stuck all their names down on the list and here they were.

Looking around, she was quite surprised to see that most of the ladies in the group were on the same side of thirty as she was, because she had been sure that she and her friends would be grossly outnumbered by gymslips in this day and age. The 'teacher' Mandy made her introductions, welcomed everyone, and gave them all a badge on which to write their names. Meanwhile she wrote *What To Buy* on the whiteboard, and then listed a few essential items of shopping for the early days.

Helen was okay on that front – the baby's nursery in the bungalow was equipped like a Boots superstore, not that the room would ever be utilized now. Her mother had started to take things across to the Old Rectory and put them in Helen's old nursery. Janey too had been buying bits in for a long time, but her parents and her in-laws were causing a world shortage in baby powder. It was starting to give her dreams about the Sorcerer's Apprentice. Elizabeth hadn't a clue if what she had been buying for the baby were the right things. She had bought powder and oil in and lotion and Vaseline and some vests and sleep suits, but she knew hardly anything about babies – she had never even changed a nappy in her life, and when did they start eating real food? She scribbled down notes almost desperately, reminders of things to get: cottonwool, baby shampoo (she hadn't thought they would have enough hair to soap up), a baby bath . . .

One of the other girls, 'Carol' according to the name on her badge, was on her fifth baby and already at loggerheads with the midwife, who was extolling the saintly virtues of breastfeeding to the others when 'Vanessa' was asking about the various types of bottled milk.

'Oh, you don't want bottled milk when you've got two big boobs full of natural breastmilk! It's convenient, easy—'

'Can I just say that it isn't as easy as Mandy is trying to make out sometimes, and I'd recommend getting some nipple-shields in,' Carol interrupted. 'It can be bloody agonizing for a while and, personally, I've no qualms about bottle-feeding this time, seeing as I'll have to get back to work as soon as possible.'

'It's not always agony,' said Mandy, afraid that she was losing her captive audience already. She was, after all, the appointed authority in this class, not this Supergob Carol.

'Very true, but it doesn't come that natural for a lot of women either, and if you're going to feed, make sure you ask them to stick the bairn on your boob as soon as they can. They didn't do that with my first and I went through hell trying to get him to work at me once he'd had an easy feed from a bottle. I felt I was a right let-down to him and tortured myself that I was a total failure, even though he absolutely thrived on Farleys!'

'But—'

'With the second bairn I was determined to do it and I did manage it, but it was hard work. I couldn't produce enough milk and it was agony, especially when I got mastitis . . .'

A terrified murmur started up. *'What the hell is mastitis?'*

'Bloody painful, that's what mastitis is. Don't let anyone pressure you, girls, into believing that a bottle equals failure,' said Carol, exchanging militant glances with Mandy, who had just been about to deliver the message that bottled milk was tantamount to Satan's juice.

'Scientific research has shown that breastfeeding a child significantly reduces the chance of breast cancer . . .' began Mandy.

'Yes, but scaring people like that isn't going to help if they can't feed their baby. I'm not saying mum's milk isn't good stuff,' Carol went on, 'but getting yourself all stressed and stressing out the babby because you can't feed it doesn't do either of you a right lot of good.'

Elizabeth felt sick; she had not even started thinking about the politics of breast or bottle, and judging from

Janey's face, she hadn't either. Carol, thankfully for the others, was not the type to be cowed by Mandy's biases. Motherhood had been her main achievement in life and she knew what she was talking about.

'Get a changing station if you can afford it,' said Carol. 'You've no idea how much pressure it'll take off yer back.'

Pens started to scribble wildly.

'. . . Sudocrem – top of the list, better than Vaseline in my opinion. And a papoose – it's lovely to feel the baby all snuggled up next to you whilst they're little.'

'No! If you fall, you'll fall on the baby!' Mandy protested, not that it stopped any pens adding it to their shopping lists.

'. . . And don't let any of your relatives buy fancy suits for the bairn with no poppers on the crotch.'

Scribble scribble.

'. . . Get one of those bouncy things in that hang from the door-frame; you'll have a right laugh and babies love 'em . . . Oh, and beg, steal or borrow a rocking chair!'

Janey and Helen nudged Elizabeth and gave her a smug look, and she stuck her tongue out at them both.

'Right – about nappies,' began Mandy, wafting away a very red, angry flush from her neck.

'If you think you've got time for terries, you're fooling yourself!' piped up Carol, who wished she'd had someone like herself in her first class all those years ago, after Miss Idealistic the Midwife had frightened her to death and made her spend an ill-afforded fortune on so many wrong things. *Terries are better for baby and hardly any extra work, my arse!*

'In your overnight bag you need some nappies, cottonwool and baby lotion,' began Mandy. 'A few Babygros, some money for the hospital trolley, a dressing-gown and slippers, maternity sanitary towels . . .'

'. . . And two of the biggest T-shirts you can find for nighties. Get disposable maternity knickers – they aren't sexy, mind – baby wipes and nappy sacks, some juice, the cooler the better, a massive bar of fruit and nut, a Jackie Collins and your nipple-shields just in case,' took over Carol.

At the end of the session, Mandy told the girls there was a big box of books and child birth videos available to borrow. She was exhausted from battling her wits against that walking brood mare and could not wait to get in the house, kick her shoes off, put *EastEnders* on and get a big gin down her neck. Thank God she had no bloody kids to go home to.

'Don't borrow 'em,' Carol whispered to Helen, who had picked up a video. 'You'll shit yourself with fear.'

Helen did not like to think about that image. They had all watched a film of a birth at school in which a Frenchwoman had poohed whilst giving birth. It would be her worst nightmare if that happened.

Except for Carol, who bounced off down the road stuffed with springs like Tigger, they all came out of the meeting as meek as lambs.

'I've hardly got any of the right stuff in,' said Elizabeth, who looked especially dazed.

'Well, look, at least it's the weekend tomorrow – you can go get your stuff then, now you know what you're missing,' said Janey, feeling a bit sorry for Elizabeth. At least she could send George out if she was short on anything. He would be a fulltime househusband soon; she was going to draft his letter of resignation this weekend.

'What if I've left it too late and give birth tonight?' Elizabeth replied in a bit of a panic.

'Do you think we'd not help?' said George, giving her a big hug, and was surprised that she let him. She did not do her usual pulling-away thing that he always teased her about.

Elizabeth smiled gratefully, but knew she wasn't ready for this by a long chalk. She wasn't ready at all.

John was waiting in the car outside her house when she got home; he was in his builder's gear so it looked like another flying visit.

'You're lucky,' he said. 'I was just waiting another five minutes then I was off. I thought I'd pop by to see how your class went.'

'How did you know I was going to a class?'

'I met George for a pint in the week.'

'Oh.'

He followed her into the house. She was so stressed she didn't even put the kettle on and sank on the sofa staring trance-like at the carpet.

'Well, are you going to answer me or do I have to put it down to one of life's mysteries, like the pyramids?'

'It was frightening,' she said. 'I realized I haven't got enough stuff in.'

'Like what?'

She got the list out of her pocket. 'Sudocrem, nappies, pram . . . Can you believe, I forgot I'd need to buy a pram?'

'*I* got you nappies!'

'But have I got the right size? I need to get some of the really tiny ones just in case he comes early. I haven't got my bag sorted. I haven't even got a bag to sort! I haven't got sanit . . . er . . . things.'

'Then go and get them tomorrow. It's Saturday, you've got all day to shop,' he said gently, trying to stop her panicking. 'Anything I can get for you?'

He snatched the list out of her hand and she tried to get it back because she didn't want him seeing she needed big sanitary towels and disposable pants, but he was about twelve foot bigger than her and she got it back only when he had committed most of it to memory.

'I can manage,' she said indignantly and embarrassed, and he laughed. She was reforming, but she was still Elizabeth, bloody-minded obstinate independent Collier.

His Elizabeth.

Chapter 40

Janey was tossing and turning.

'What's up? Can't sleep, love?' George asked.

'No, I can't get comfortable,' groaned Janey from her nest of twelve pillows. They were resting under her bump, in between her legs, under her boobs, behind her bottom, you name it and Janey had a pillow stuck there. George got out the baby oil, lifted up her nightie, clicked on the bedside lamp and began to rub her back.

'My sexual days are over,' she said wearily. 'Please tell me this isn't your idea of foreplay.'

'*My* sexual days are over!' said George. 'You've worn my todger off!'

They both smiled tenderly, both hoping their sexual days were most categorically *not* over by a long chalk; not now they had discovered them again and improved on them three millionfold.

Who would have thought my life would be this changed but this good, this time last year? Janey thought, enjoying the sensation of George kneading her back. The massaging was every bit as intimate as the expression of their love in sex. He rubbed her with his big hands until he heard her breathing in that way that told him she was asleep. For an hour or so, until she had to be winched to her feet for the first of her five nocturnal trips to the loo.

Elizabeth put her foot on the stair and realized she couldn't lift the other one far enough up to climb to the next, for the pain down the middle of her thigh was excruciating. She tried again.

This is ridiculous, she thought. I can't get up the sodding staircase.

She needed the loo badly, so she attempted the leg-lift again, slowly, but, nope, the pain would not let her. She stood there looking up at the stairs and suddenly understood why so many old people moved to bungalows.

'This is crazy,' she said, gritted her teeth and tried again, but as her leg got to that same certain point, the pain shot through her, forcing her to admit defeat. It was so ludicrous she laughed.

'You!' she said to the baby, scrunching up a fist and shaking it at him.

She sat on the step and tried to bump up backwards. It took her ages but after a few hundred hours, she managed it.

I don't believe I've just had to do this! she thought, and then, How the hell am I going to get downstairs again? She decided not to even try; the doors were locked and there was just the one light on downstairs that would have to wait until morning to be turned off now. She went straight to bed instead and like Janey, she had cushions and pillows positioned everywhere.

She lay on top of the quilt because it was far too warm a night for covers. The window was open and a cooling breeze from outside fanned her to sleep.

Helen woke her up the next morning with a phone call.

'Do you know how long it's taken me to get my pants on?' she said, as soon as it connected.

'Well, if you think that's bad, I could hardly get upstairs last night. It was mad. I couldn't lift my leg up and I had a terrible pain right down the back of my thigh. I ended up having to go backwards upstairs on my bum,' said Elizabeth.

'Ah – that's actually happened to me. The thing to do is kneel forward with your hands on the floor and rock backwards and forwards,' said Helen. 'The baby will be lying on a nerve so rub your tum till he or she moves.'

'If it doesn't work, you do realize that I could be trapped upstairs for ever,' said Elizabeth. 'You'll read about me in the *Chronicle* – "local woman discovered, eaten by pigeons".'

There wasn't a chapter about *that* in her Miriam Stoppard.

'How does it feel when you stretch?' Helen asked.

Elizabeth lifted up her leg. 'It still aches but not as much as it did last night, thank goodness. I think I'll be able to get downstairs without having to call the Fire Brigade, anyway. God help their backs if they have to give me a fireman's lift out of the window!'

'Good, because I'm taking you shopping,' said Helen. 'Please be ready in half an hour.'

'Shopping?' said Elizabeth.

'You don't think I am going to leave you in the state you were in yesterday, do you?' said Helen. 'I'm going with you to get supplies.'

When Elizabeth came off the phone, she rocked on the floor and rubbed her stomach as instructed by the new Dr Luxmore. It helped lots.

They bought a few of the smaller things on the list that Elizabeth had made in the class, and whilst they were in the queue for the till with a baby bath, a well-timed text came through from John to say, WHERE R U??? HV CHNGING STATION, BATH & PRAM 4 U IN VAN. She showed the text to Helen, who looked at her expectantly.

'What?' snapped Elizabeth.

'Nothing,' said Helen, with her eyebrows lifted and a sly smile twisting one corner of her mouth.

'I wish he'd keep his nose out,' Elizabeth said, about to text him to say as much, but then she stopped. She would tell him off to his face instead.

The assistant in Mothercare measured them both for nursing bras and Helen was thrilled that her 32AAs were now 34Bs, but she was sure she was still growing so she didn't buy one yet. Elizabeth was thrown into total disbelief on learning that her once 34Bs were now 40Es, and decided there and then that she might as well give breastfeeding her best shot with those Sten-guns *in situ*. Christ, 40E qualified her for a career as a Bond villain! Either that or she could open a dairy. She bought the nipple-shields at the same time, although she mistakenly asked the assistant for nipple-clamps, which sent Helen into a fit of giggles. They looked like Mexican hats for a mouse fancy-dress party. She had just thought you stuck a baby on your breast and it fed. It was supposed to be natural, wasn't it, so how complicated could it be? Or so she had naively thought, until Carol had enlightened them on that score and added another heap onto her worry pile.

Janey rang her on the mobile just as they were coming out of the bra department.

'Do you want to go shopping?' she asked. 'You looked in such a state yesterday, I could hardly sleep for thinking about you. Well, you and the backache and the fact that my bladder has shrunk to the size of a walnut.'

'I'm out with Helen shopping as we speak,' Elizabeth replied. 'I think I've just about got it all now, but thanks – you're a diamond.'

'S'okay, chuck. Right then, if you're sorted, I'll start my cleaning.'

'Eh? Cleaning – *you*?' Elizabeth turned to Helen. 'Hey, Helen, Janey's cleaning!'

'Oy, you cheeky sods!' said Janey. She had heard about 'nesting' but thought she was the last person who would experience *that* phenomenon. She had her Marigolds at the ready and was actually raring to go and clean the bathroom. She hoped it would last because it was quite thrilling, although she was not going to make herself look sad and admit that she was getting excited about bleaching some porcelain. She had a reputation as a complete slattern to maintain.

Elizabeth fell to sleep in her rocking chair in the afternoon. It was a nice, relaxed sleep because she had just finished packing her bag for the hospital and she felt more prepared now if the baby put in an early appearance. Then Father Christmas arrived. A big, black-haired Father Christmas with a *Silkstone Properties* T-shirt and steel-capped boots, in a Transit van sleigh.

Elizabeth rocked up to her feet and sleepily answered the door to John, who moved her quickly aside and directed two big lads to carry a changing station past her and into the far corner of the sitting room.

'If you've got any of this stuff already, tell me and I'll take it back to the shop,' he said, carrying a Moses basket in and plonking it on the sofa whilst she stood there with her mouth agape. Then he wheeled in a sweet little pram full of a stack of blankets and a tiny sheepskin rug, an armful of Fisher Price toys in boxes, a baby bath, something else in a big box, a massive bar of fruit and nut and, to her absolute cringing horror, a carrier-bagful of disposable maternity knickers and sanitary towels.

'I . . .' was all she got out before he strode out past her.

'Can't stop,' he said gruffly. 'I've wasted enough time coming up earlier on when you weren't in and I've stuff to do. I'll see you later,' and with that he was off before she could protest that she didn't want his presents or his charity. Or his friendship. Or his love.

Chapter 41

'Ready, Tiger?'

'I think so!'

'Got your letter?'

George patted his back jeans pocket. Janey kissed him and hugged him because today he was giving up his job for her. He said it wasn't a sacrifice really, but she knew different because letting his wife win the bread would filter down and jar on his Northern male ego somehow. She knew he would be the subject of mick-taking for his new status of 'Househusband', even though some of those he worked with thought the presence of testosterone in their systems gave them the right to spend all the mortgage money down the pub and chase other women. She knew who was more of a man in her book.

Even their parents had been a bit shocked by the arrangement, and she could tell Cyril wouldn't be bragging down the pub about his son's new career move. *'Even though you should be!'* she had wanted to shout. *'You should be proud and shouting it from the bloody rooftops.'* He was doing more for his family than processing pieces of plastic from a machine ever would.

She would never find a better bloke than George, ever. Even though she had ended up in someone else's bed, thinking she wanted to try.

Three years ago, when she got down to her target weight – a stick size nine with no wobbly bits – she really thought she was something. She had gone on a course to Bristol and it was the first time she'd ever been away with a nice figure to show off and with executive blokes flicking their eyes over *her* slim-fitting dark-blue suit for a change. It made her feel sexy and powerful.

'He' had been a Finance Manager from Watford, cocky and arrogant, Hugh Grant floppy hairstyle, plummy voice and an Armani suit; he had reminded her of Simon initially. She got stuck on her computer – well, not really – she pretended she had so he would come to her rescue, which he did. No one had ever fancied her for her body before but it was obvious he was flirting with her, the air was baked with all those smouldering, smokey looks he passed to her and it would have needed a chainsaw to cut through the sexual tension arcing between them.

She knew exactly what the act of adultery was going to be like before they gravitated up to the room. She'd played the scene out in a million of her fantasies – him: powerful man in a suit – her: sexual dynamite just waiting for her fuse to be lit. And now she was going to be living it instead of dreaming it. She could be completely abandoned – she wouldn't have to worry about any fat blobbing out of her clothes now and she wouldn't throw a fit if he left the lights on.

However, 'Hugh Grant' didn't play to the script she had written for him. He was so carried away that his touch was as rough as sandpaper. He went straight in there without all the wonderful show of slow foreplay she had imagined – the words 'bull' and 'china shop' came to mind. At the crucial point she had stopped him and asked, 'Aren't you going to put a condom on?'

'What do you want me to use one of those for?' had been his reply. She thought being an executive he'd have had some brains. He had a wedding ring on as well. Didn't he care about his wife? At least she cared enough about George to protect herself – which was so very big of her, she had told herself later, when it was done. He sighed but got up, went to his jacket and took one out of the inside pocket. What was he doing with condoms in his pocket if he was away from home? she had thought, with a twisted sense of morality.

He came quickly, she felt nothing, then he said he shouldn't have done that and should go. She didn't try to stop him. He sat on the edge of the bed and started to put his pants back on. He had Y-fronts, and not the trendy ones that were all the rage recently either. Unforgettable Paisley and purple, she could identify them in a police line-up tomorrow if she had to. Then he put on some really long black socks with beige diamonds up the side. He had lots of spots on his back, his shirt was stained on the sleeve, and it had gone a bit at the cuffs. She felt sick with disgust at him and herself and had a bath and a shower before falling into an unrefreshing, guilty sleep.

He did not look anything like a figure of romance the next day, just a seedy, cheating, selfish bloke who happened to be wearing a good suit, musky aftershave and drove a flash car. She couldn't get his horrible pants out of her head, and the sight of him made her feel cheap and uglier than she had ever been at four stones heavier. She could not wait to get home and never see him again.

All the way back up to Yorkshire she beat herself up with questions like: Why the hell hadn't she kept her fantasy behind the line? How could she have done that to George? He had been so pleased to see her when she got back too, hugged her and told her how much he had missed her; and he had cooked something really special and decorated the dining room with balloons and *Welcome Home* banners for her, and she had cried. He'd been touched at how happy she was to see him, although he hadn't known that it was guilt pushing most of those tears out.

She nearly told him once what she had done but she knew it would destroy him. The past was set in stone, it could not be undone. All she could do was make it up to him, and she bought the privilege to do that with her silence.

There was a weird atmosphere at the factory. The machines were whirring and chugging the same but something was definitely different. George could feel it and so could all the others, who gathered in little clusters throughout the morning to ask each other what was going on. George was less concerned with that and more with trying to have a word with his foreman so he could hand over his letter.

'Not now, lad,' said his foreman, even though he was three years younger than George was – but looking a good fifteen years older today. George being George, he didn't push it and stuck the letter back in his pocket for a more conducive time.

Janey came out of the consultant's room smiling. He had said that the next time they met, she would probably have her little baby in her arms. It was unlikely he would be delivering it himself though, Mr Greer told her, which disappointed her slightly because she liked him. He had the same gently efficient manner as Alex Luxmore, and she trusted him on sight. He said he would see her on his rounds afterwards though, which would be nice. It was a good job George wasn't delivering her baby, she thought. It would take him a fortnight, although the baby would come out perfect at the end. She'd bet anything he had not given his resignation letter in.

John Silkstone had worked hard in Germany and had earned himself quite a name over there for good quality work, which was a compliment, considering some of the craftsmen he had been up against. It had been a useful seven years and he had picked up many new skills from the German plasterers and the Italian tilers. He did a lot of overtime. He had realized almost immediately that his marriage had been a huge mistake. Lisa was pretty but she didn't excite him or interest him at all. He knew why he had married her and it shamed him. Then she started the affair with Herman to get his attention – though he was just grateful for the escape route it gave him. They had both thrown themselves into their work to plug the emptiness; she had started importing underwear and had a thriving business in Germany now and he had worked all the hours God sent him to avoid going home to be bickered and nagged at in her frustration at not reaching a heart that was closed to her. Maybe if they hadn't been so unhappy with each other, they would not have been as successful as they both were now in their careers. It was his only consolatory thought about the past years.

He had not called after playing Santa's advocate, so Elizabeth phoned him on Monday and left a message that if he cared to bob in when he was free she would thank him in person for the stuff, though they both knew it was because she wanted to give him a piece of her mind. He bravely turned up that same evening, as she was rounding off a phone call to Janey about her visit to the hospital. She offered him a beer and he thought, She's got these in for me, and he accepted one gratefully.

'You shouldn't have spent all that, you know,' she said, but a lot more gently than he had anticipated. 'I can afford to kit my baby out myself, I'm not skint.'

'I know you can,' he said, 'and before you say anything else, no, I don't feel sorry for you because you're by yourself and no, it's not charity – it's just a gift, for the baby, not you. Well, the big pants were and the sanitary things. Some gift, huh?'

She turned away, embarrassed that he was even mentioning those.

'Did I get the right size? It's not a subject I'm up on.'

'Oh, for goodness' sake!' she said, trying to shake the subject away and he smiled at her discomfort.

'Okay. I promise I won't buy any more stuff if you don't want.'

'There's nothing left to buy!' she said. 'And even if there were, you'll be bankrupt if you get anything else.'

'Oh, will you shut up, Elizabeth. I'm not exactly skint myself. I did more than okay in Germany.'

'You won't be well off any more if you keep throwing your money about,' Elizabeth grumbled and he huffed impatiently.

'Don't you worry about me. Besides, I've nothing as nice to spend my money on. My dad will go into the best home I can find when it's time, my mam's well set up and she'll never want for anything, and actually, Miss Collier, it was really good fun going out and buying your bairn stuff. I think I've finally got in touch with my feminine side – I can understand now what you women see in shopping.'

She laughed. *Feminine side? Him with his hairy arms and stubble, standing there as tall and solid as Blackpool Tower?*

'You didn't use that paint I got you then? You didn't get your nursery done?'

'No,' she said. 'I'll have my money back, please.'

He laughed then and she went on, 'Well, there's no rush, the baby will be in with me for a bit. I left it too late, anyway, and I don't think I could get up a ladder to paint the ceiling now.'

'I'd do it for you myself, Elizabeth, but I'm run off my feet with these hou—'

'I'm not hinting for you to do it, you know!'

John made a move to strangle her and growled, 'I give up with you! Why not get a decorator to do it? Use that money from the house because I bet you haven't touched it yet.'

She looked at him, horrified that he had even mentioned it.

'I couldn't use it.'

'Yes, you can.'

'Well, half of it's our Bev's, for a start.'

'The other half isn't.'

'I told you at the time the house sale went through that I'd never touch it. You wasted your time setting up that bank account.'

'I bet you don't even know how much is in there, do you?'

'No, I haven't a clue,' she said proudly.

'It was your grandmother's old house before your mam and dad bought it from her – think of it that way. You liked your grandma, didn't you?' he reminded her, but that argument hadn't convinced her then and it didn't convince her now.

'It was *his* money, whatever way you want to put it.' Her voice softened suddenly. 'I know you sorted it all out for me with the solicitors, John. I don't mean to sound ungrateful.'

'There was thirty thousand there at least, Elizabeth. Add all your interest payments over ten years and . . . well, it's a fair whack,' he said. 'The money itself isn't evil, Elizabeth, and you may need it when the bairn comes along.'

'I can't see me ever being that desperate that I touch it,' said Elizabeth, and especially not for decorating her baby's room. Oh, flaming hell, why didn't I get the room organized before! she thought. There might not have been a rush to get it finished but it would have been nice to have it done. She felt so out of control, with not a clue how to look after a little baby. She had been bad enough when the cat arrived! She was scared stiff she wouldn't love her baby and be one of those mums who didn't bond with her newborn and looked blankly at it, just wanting it to go away.

'Suppose you'll be off out with your mates on your birthday then?' said John casually.

'Dunno, hadn't thought about it yet,' she said.

'Don't you fancy a nice meal out or the Odeon or something?'

'I don't think we can sit still long enough for a film and I'm not sure any of us would want to face a big meal by then. We've all got cracking heartburn.'

'Right,' he said, with a slow nod, and something in the way he did it made her think, Bugger, I bet he didn't mean with the girls, he meant with him!

'Anyway, I suppose I best get off . . .'

How the heck do I recover this?

'I . . . er . . . egg fried rice?' she blurted out.

'What?'

'I could murder some egg fried rice and Chinese chips. Want some?'

'I thought you didn't eat chips.'

'Yes – well, I fancy some now. If you want to stay and have some I'll pay. Sort of a thank you, you know, for all the stuff you bought.'

'You? Say thank you? Twice in one lifetime?' he said, putting his hands on his chest and feigning a cardiac arrest.

'Look, do you want a Chinese or not?' she said impatiently.

'Seeing as you put it so charmingly, how can I refuse? You got a takeaway menu then?'

'Or' – *gulp* – 'we could eat out. The bookies around the corner is the Golden Dragon now. Apparently it's not bad.'

He stared at her as if she had just grown another head, then thought, Well, I never! and rubbed his hands together.

'Okay then, but if you're paying, I'm going to town, lady, because I am one hungry beast.'

'Just as long as you don't expect to share my rice, mate.'

'Your rice will be your rice alone, I promise.'

Elizabeth grabbed her jacket and her keys and, together, they walked down the road to the Golden Dragon, both wanting, but not quite daring, to link arms.

Chapter 42

'Ready again?'

'As I'll ever be!' George tapped the letter in his pocket and came over all *déjà vu*.

'Right, this morning it is then,' said Janey decisively, trying not to nag but failing. 'I mean, how flaming difficult can it be to hand a letter over, love?'

'I'm not just going to slam it in someone's hand, Janey. I've worked there a long time, I owe them more than that.'

George operated one of the most financially important machines in the factory – a big, reliable German piece of equipment that pressed out tiny plastic cogs. It was also the most boring job in the whole place and he was the only bloke who had ever stuck it for longer than a month without being dragged off in a shirt with sleeves that tied behind the back towards a waiting white van. Day in, day out, George patiently worked on it though, and no one was envious that he actually got paid a bit more on his hourly rate because it was such a brain-dead job. He knew he would be hard to replace.

Janey shook her head impatiently at him. Yes, he

was sure-footed and always got there in the end, but he was so *flaming slow*! She just wished sometimes a freak stick of dynamite would lodge itself up his backside and detonate. At this rate, he'd still be working his notice when her legs were up in stirrups and she was bearing down to push.

That was the fourth morning on the trot George had set off with his letter in his pocket but no one had the time to let him book even two minutes in with the Personnel bloke. The management were buzzing around like mad bees looking all serious and intense; it was like working in a very stressed hive. If he had been a pushy sort like Chris Fretwell, he could have insisted on seeing someone and made lots of noise until they took notice, but George reckoned he would get to speak to someone in the end, when they had time to listen to him without forcing the issue and getting people's backs up.

He clocked on, then made his way down the factory floor past the big tool shop and the massive machine that made coat-hangers for Marks & Spencer, past the ones that churned out cat-litter trays and right to the far end to his own, anything but cosy, corner. He had just sat down at this machine, noting how much the lazy swine on the night shift hadn't managed to do, when he noticed his foreman taking Chris Fretwell off his machine and leading him away. Then a little later on he came for Fred Hines, then Johnny Skelly. None of them came back, either. It was like being in an Agatha Christie. Then the foreman came for him.

'George, mate, Gary Hedley'd like to see you in his

office,' and he gave him a strange soft clap on his back, that felt almost like an apology.

At last, he thought, and stuck his machine on idle.

He was just outside the Personnel office, getting his resignation out, when he suddenly realized that he had not yet had the chance to tell anyone that he wanted to see Gary Hedley – which either meant that Gary Hedley was Mystic Meg in disguise or that summat else was up. George wisely stuck the letter back in his pocket, for now, and knocked.

'Come in!'

Then he was in, being told to have a seat.

'George, mate, I'll come straight to the point with no beating about the bush,' said Gary Hedley, Personnel Manager of Clayton's Plastic Injection Mouldings. 'We're having to make everyone redundant. You're one of the two longest-serving blokes here and it galls me to say we've to close the factory with immediate effect. A Japanese firm have bought it lock, stock and barrel and they're gutting the place.'

George paled with automatic panic, and then he remembered he'd been jacking his job in anyway.

'I'm sorry, Georgy lad. Obviously, you'll get the best references but this Japanese lot – they like to pick their own workforce, although someone like you they'll set on again in a snap, so I wouldn't worry too much. You'll get a redundancy pay of . . .' he referred to his sheet '. . . fifteen thousand seven hundred and forty-nine pounds, twenty-eight pee. I'm sorry it couldn't be more. It's not a lot, considering how long you've been here.'

'Tw . . . twenty-eight pee?' was all George could say

because he was in shock. He could handle the fact
that he could get twenty-eight pee, the other bit wasn't
sinking in yet.

'It's how these things work out, mate. It includes your
holiday money and your loyalty bonus as well. I hate
doing this, George. I've got forty of these to do this
morning and then come back for the late shift tonight.
You've to get your coat and go home. Once I've told
you, you can't touch your machines, in case anyone tries
to vandalize them out of pique. Not that I for one
minute think you would, lad, let me just say that. I have
to work to a set procedure here. New management
directives and all that. Very specific they are.'

'Tw . . . twenty-eight pee?'

'Do you want a coffee, mate?' said Gary Hedley. He
hadn't ever seen anyone shake that much. Not even
in that documentary about Parkinson's.

'No, I'm all right,' said George.

'Get it in the bank, lad,' said Gary Hedley, handing
him over the cheque, 'and good luck. I'll put a good
word in for you with the Japs when they've refur-
bished. When they move, they move quick, I'll say that
for them.' He shook George's limp, shocked hand firmly.

'What will you do?' asked George.

'Eh?'

'You — about a job? What will happen to you?'

'Redundancy is a great leveller,' said Gary Hedley,
who'd had a brand new Jag delivered last month without
knowing all this was round the corner. 'I'll be sticking
around for a bit to tie up ends and officially hand over
to the Japanese lot, and then if they don't set me on

or I haven't found another job, I'll be meeting a few of you in the dole queue. Car'll have to go, of course.' He looked wistfully outside at his parking space.

George took the cheque and slipped it into his pocket with the undelivered letter of resignation.

'Well, good luck yourself, Mr Hedley,' said George.

'Thanks, George, I'll need it at my age,' said Gary Hedley – too young for retirement, too old to set up his stock against the younger market whizzkids with their fancy business degrees. He appreciated George's consideration; he doubted anyone else would think to wish him luck. Gary Hedley expected to hear nothing but more sentiments ending in 'off' over the next sixteen hours.

By the time George had got outside, it had just about sunk in that he'd got forty-nine pounds as well. The other lads were waiting by the gate in a conspiratorial cluster.

'We're going down the pub, George, are you coming?'

'Nay, it's only half ten!'

'So? I think we deserve one after this, don't you?'

That was typical of Chris Fretwell. His lass wouldn't see much of his redundancy, not unless she worked in the Engineers as a barmaid anyway.

'What else are you going to do?'

'Go home,' said George.

'Japs won't be set up for another three months at least,' said Fred Hines.

'I'm not going for a job with them,' said George.

'Oh aye, what are you going to do then?' asked Chris Fretwell, wondering if George had inside info about any other jobs. He didn't fancy working for the Japs either. His more relaxed working methods might clash with their military efficiency, and he was already on the look-out for a softer option.

'Stay at home, look after the house and my bairn when it arrives,' said George.

'Eh?'

'You heard.'

Chris Fretwell's face split into a slow grin. 'Oy, lads, Georgy Hobson's turning poofter!' he said. Then, turning back to George: 'You batting for the other side now, mate?'

He soon shut his mouth though when big George Hobson took a step forward, gathered up a fistful of his jumper and lifted him up with it. That way, at least, he was able to speak to the little squirt at eye-level.

'I'll be looking after my kid, and being at home just like I've always wanted to,' said George, not raising his voice, not snarling or spitting but hammering the point home all the same. 'And then when my wife comes in from her well-worked-for big executive job in Leeds, I'll be sitting down wi' her to a nice tea and a good bottle of wine in a house that's well on its way to being bought and paid for. If that makes me a poof then so sodding be it. *Mate.*'

With that, George Hobson let Chris Fretwell fall to the floor in a crumpled heap of testosterone and, without looking back, he went home.

He cooked fillet steak and mushrooms, sweetcorn and big fat chips, and had a bottle of Moët in the mop bucket filled with ice on the floor when Janey walked through the front door at six that evening.

'Did you do it then?' she said, her eyes rounding at the table set-up, thinking, This is either a celebration or a big apology.

'Didn't have a chance,' he said.

'Oh George, flaming hell . . .' Apology then.

'Hang on, hang on, missus. Want to know *why* I didn't have a chance?'

Janey thought it wiser not to open her mouth and nodded her head instead.

'Okay, I'll tell you then, because they only made me redundant. They made me BLOODY REDUNDANT!' and he handed over the cheque to his wife.

She looked at it. Twenty-eight pee, she thought. Then she looked at him. Then they started bouncing around the kitchen.

If he'd handed that letter in at the beginning of the week he'd have got nothing! she thought, and came over all faint at the near miss of it. He popped open the champagne and poured her out a glass and she drank it because she didn't think the baby would mind her having one or two, not after this shocker.

How's he got that twenty-eight pee? her shocked brain fixed on, but the champagne bubbles raced up to that thought and knocked it out to make way for another: never again to berate her husband for being the big slow thing that he was. They weren't exactly the Speedy Gonzaleses of life, but – between them – they were doing okay, thank you very much.

Chapter 43

Elizabeth picked up Helen from her mum and dad's large old house. It was a lovely place and she had always liked going there when they were kids. The house always seemed to be filled with new baking smells when their housekeeper Mother Hubbard was there. Dr Luxmore would potter around in the garden or emerge from his study to distribute toffees from his pocket, and Mrs Luxmore would make them posh tea in china cups and proper saucers that Elizabeth was always terrified of breaking. It was the sort of house she would have loved to bring a bairn up in – lots of rooms and a beautiful garden with a little brook running past the bottom of it.

The Old Rectory had a truly serene feeling to it and was much nicer than Helen's marital home, the impressive bungalow that was currently sporting a For Sale sign on the black iron gates. Brian was asleep in the garden hammock that was strung between two apple trees, one paw dangling over the side, and he was most definitely snoring. He had landed well and truly on his feet here.

Helen manoeuvred herself into Elizabeth's car. She

felt three tons heavier than last week, not counting the extra half a ton that had landed on her chest, which she thought was fantastic.

'Hels, do you think you love your baby yet?' asked Elizabeth, dropping it casually into the conversation as they approached their destination.

'Yes, of course,' said Helen, immediately stroking her stomach in confirmation of it. The baby was asleep, she felt; the more active she was, the quieter her daughter was and vice versa.

'How do you know you do?'

'I just do,' said Helen. 'Why are you asking?'

'Nothing, just making conversation,' said Elizabeth, before parking up in time for their second Parentcraft class.

The midwife smiled them all into the room, although it got a bit strained when she saw Carol coming in. *Pain Relief* was written on the whiteboard. Mandy wished she could get some relief from that gobby pain.

'Breathing,' started Mandy, when everyone was settled.

'Helps a bit,' Carol sniffed.

Mandy ignored her and went on to demonstrate how one breathes through a contraction.

'How do you know when it's a contraction?' asked someone.

'O-o-o-o-h, you'll know!' said Carol, with a knowing, scary laugh.

'I've been getting these tightenings,' said Janey. 'My stomach goes rock hard.'

A few women nodded and leaned forward to hear the answer to that one, Elizabeth included.

'Any pain?' Mandy asked.

'No.'

'Braxton Hicks,' said Carol and the midwife together.

'You have them all the way through your pregnancy, but only really feel them at the end. They are perfectly natural, but not "contraction" contractions that spell the start of your labour,' said Mandy, feeling she needed to add a little extra explanation.

After demonstrating the various shallow- and deep-breathing techniques for the different stages of labour, and letting them all have a practice, Mandy took out some TENS machines.

'Anyone know what TENS stands for?' She smiled smugly when Carol looked dense for once. 'Transcutaneous Electrical Nerve Stimulation,' said Mandy, holding one up like a hostess on *Sale of the Century*. 'Anyone know what it does?'

'Bugger all,' grumbled Carol.

'It blocks pain with an electric current,' said Mandy, through gritted teeth. 'Developed from research by Dr Norman Shealy . . .' She launched into a history that no one was particularly interested in.

'Might have known it would be a bloke,' said Carol, leaning into Elizabeth and doing a bad job of a whisper. 'Only a man would think of taking a woman's pain at being split in half away by electrocuting her in the back.'

Mandy ignored the sniggerings Carol's over-loud observation had inspired by completing her background knowledge, then she sent them off in pairs and showed everyone how to fasten the pads onto their partner's back. There were a couple more husbands this time, one very loud one with *Marc* on his name badge (with a 'c', Elizabeth noticed). She would bet her life savings he wasn't born with a 'c'. He listened very intently to everything Mandy said with much expression of facial muscles.

Helen fastened the pads onto Elizabeth's back and switched the machine on; apparently it felt weird, prickly, like a cross between pins and needles and a light electric shock. There was a dial on the small control box that Helen turned slowly up to max, but Elizabeth didn't like the sensation at all; it annoyed her too much and she ended her turn prematurely. Helen didn't mind it though, and thought it might be quite useful at the start of the contractions. She decided she would go into Boots and hire one, as Mandy said they could.

'Entonox!' said Mandy next. 'Otherwise known as gas and air. You inhale it just before your contraction peaks to help you crest it.'

'I slapped it on my gob and didn't take it off for six hours with my second,' said Carol, with her alternative experience. 'Can make you very sick though, so it's not for everyone.'

'No, maybe not,' said Mandy tightly, 'but these methods of pain-relief cause no harmful effects on your baby, unlike pethidine and epidurals.'

She sounded like a spitting snake trying to get rid of a horrible-flavoured toffee when she said those two names.

'*We're* going to try for a natural birth,' said Marc,

squeezing his wife Pam's hand. '*We've* been to see the water bath at the hospital. Pam's very keen on that, aren't you, dear?'

'*We?*' scoffed Carol, nudging up her bosom, Les Dawson-style. 'We'll see!'

'Now we come to pethidine,' said Mandy, scrunching up her nose as if she was about to tell them all something very distasteful. 'Let me just warn you that there is scientific evidence to link pethidine administered at birth with drug addiction in late teenage life.'

Carol shook her head in barely cloaked despair. She remembered being in labour the first time, terrified to take anything that might endanger the life of her baby, thanks to the indoctrination of a midwife like this at her classes, even though she felt she had eaten a tiger and was being ripped apart as he fought his way out. After struggling on for four hours and being told she was only about half a centimetre dilated and still had a long hard slog ahead of her, she was persuaded to have a half shot of pethidine by a concerned midwife, who had been absolutely fuming about the advice her fellow nurse had been giving out.

The drug worked like a dream. At last, Carol found her feet resting on a plateau that gave her the ability and considerable breathing space to cope with what was going on. She felt the relaxation filter down to her unborn and she knew they were *both* less stressed than either had been ten minutes ago. Now the baby was twenty-three, and despite doing English at Manchester University, showed no propensity to getting high on anything stronger than Bacardi Breezers. Carol mentally rolled up her sleeves and prepared to commence battle.

'You can have a half shot of peth to start off with,' Carol said. 'It made my friend very spaced-out and sick, but I was just dandy on it. Just nipped the edge off the pain a treat during my first birth. My daughter was in perfect health when she was born, no troubles, and the only thing she's addicted to is Robbie Williams.' She smiled victoriously at Mandy.

'Not for us, I don't think,' said Marc, who was obviously in Mandy's team and probably got thrown in the nettles at school for being a suck-up. Pam nodded in support when he prompted her with an elbow. Elizabeth thought she might need a triple shot of pethidine in a minute just to put up with him until the end of the Parentcraft session.

Mandy was dreading even mentioning epidurals and hoped to skirt over them very quickly.

'Best thing ever!' said Carol, wrecking her plan. 'Takes the pain away totally. I was sitting watching Jerry Springer with the monitor on, picking up contractions that registered on the Richter scale with my fourth and I never felt a thing, even if it is a bit weird feeling like Chris Tate.'

'There is the danger of permanent spinal injury with an epidural,' said Clever Marc.

'You won't give a sod if it causes your head to fall off if you need one,' said Carol, who had enough practical experience behind her not to be cowed by Textbook Kid.

'Yes, but when it wears off you won't have built

up any resistance to the labour pain and it will hit you like a sledgehammer,' said Mandy, going very red.

'When it wears off, they top you up!' Carol came back at her. 'I don't get this. Why are you trying to frighten everyone?'

'I am not! I'm trying to give you the best advice I can for the safe delivery of your babies!' said Mandy indignantly, crossing over quickly to her model of a pelvis and a lifesize baby doll, and demonstrating a birth with them. The women who hadn't fainted by the time she got to episiotomies, made a mental note to have any drug, legal or illegal, during labour and to buy a possessive Alsatian for afterwards to stop a man coming anywhere near them ever again.

As they walked out of the lesson, Elizabeth fell behind the others, hoping to grab a word with Carol. The chance came when Carol dropped her bag and Elizabeth picked it up for her.

'Ta, love,' Carol said. 'First baby?'

'Yes, it's my first, I'm a late starter,' said Elizabeth.

'I tell you, it's a lot easier having them when you're younger. I'm forty-six on my due date and I'm chuffing knackered. Thought this one was menopause symptoms!'

'Got long to go?'

'Three weeks, but you mark my words I won't last that long,' she said, huffing and puffing as they walked out. 'Don't let Stalin there frighten you either,' she said, thumbing back at Mandy the midwife who was gathering all her stuff together.

'I am a bit scared,' admitted Elizabeth. 'I don't know what to expect.'

'No one does until they have one, kiddo,' said Carol with a kind laugh. 'You can read all the textbooks you want but nothing prepares you for that first bairn coming out. You'll learn as you go on.'

'Can I ask you – why do you come to the classes if you're so experienced?'

Carol gave Elizabeth's cheek a gentle nip and shake. 'I like meeting new mums. Especially the sort like you, that remind me of when I was first pregnant. I wish I'd been in a class then with a rough old bird who could have put me in touch with a few of the realities, I can tell you. Plus it's nice to see who I'll probably end up at playgroup and nursery and school chatting with. There's some strong friendships formed at the school gates, my love.'

'Carol, can . . .'

'I'll have to whizz, flower. I'll see you next week, if I make it that far. I've got a son to get off to Scout Camp and I'm late.' She gave Elizabeth a sisterly squeeze on the arm and did a wobbly run towards a hairy man and a little boy in a peaked cap sitting in a very cherished old blue Ford Capri with a black vinyl roof.

Janey was waiting for her to catch up along the road as Helen and George walked on in front. Janey was desperate to talk some more about George's surprise redundancy. They were going to buy some Premium Bonds for the baby with some of the money, she said, seeing as the bank interest rates were so bad at the moment for savings.

'Do you think you love your baby yet?' Elizabeth asked her.

'Course I do! I think I loved it the first time I saw it on the screen at the scan,' said Janey.

'How did you know?'

'What do you mean, how did I know? I just did, like I did when I first realized I loved George. You know when you love something, don't you?'

When she got home, Elizabeth went up to her bedroom where all the lovely baby stuff was: the Moses basket, all made up ready at the side of her bed, the teddy bears and rattles that had taken over the top of her shelves, the basket of tiny socks and all the snow-white Babygros she had washed and ironed and put in the drawers. It all felt so unreal; she couldn't imagine that soon there would be a baby using them. Her baby.

'Please let me love it, God,' she prayed, kneeling at the side of the bed like a child with her eyes tight shut and her hands clamped together. Because she wasn't sure if she knew how.

Chapter 44

It had been a week and a half since Elizabeth had last seen John, when they had gone out for a Chinese and he had cost her a fortune, albeit nothing compared to what he had spent on the baby. He had even ordered a double portion of banana fritters for afters whilst she sat with a jasmine tea in one hand and her Gaviscon bottle in the other, although even anti-heartburn medicine was giving her heartburn these days. He had walked her to the door and then said he was not coming in for a coffee.

'I haven't asked you in for a coffee,' she had tutted, and he'd laughed like the school Santa had when she'd sat on his knee as a little girl, and when he'd asked her what she wanted for Christmas, had said, 'Tony Curtis.' Then John had ruffled up her hair as if she was his kid sister and driven off home. All that insisting she had done that she didn't want him, and there she was heavy with disappointment that he'd not even tried to hug her, or kiss her. He had backed off, just like she had wanted. So why did she feel so painfully dejected?

A couple of nights ago he had rung to ask how she was and to say again that he was really busy with the last house. He was slightly behind schedule, he explained, and was working like a madman to get it ready for the new owner.

'Oh, you've sold it then. Well done!' said Elizabeth.

'Aye well, with craftsmanship like mine, what do you expect?' he said. 'You'll have to come and have a look around when it's ready.'

'I will,' she had replied. 'I'll come and check that you've done it right.'

'You cheeky little beggar! I'll give you "done it right"!'

She doubted she would be able to climb all the stairs though, as his houses had a second floor, and going up one flight to the loo was wearing her out these days. She wished she had a downstairs bathroom like Janey and Helen because she seemed to want to go every two minutes, just like she did in the beginning, but the midwife said that was perfectly normal. She was going every week for her antenatal appointments now and on the last one she had written out her birthplan, which had looked very different to the mental one she had composed prior to her last Parentcraft class. It read: *Drugs to be decided at the time, averse to nothing that helps* as opposed to the first draft: *As natural a delivery as possible, gas and air possibly.*

There was still a blank on the birth partner section. She reckoned that if Helen and Janey had not beaten her to it, they would probably be too tired to go through a birth with her. They had about six – eight, max – weeks to go and were all slowly grinding to a halt. It was knocking them all out taking the top off their Gaviscon bottles, what with the weight they were all piling on by the second and the vicious heat of a summer that made 1976 look like an Ice Age. The only good thing about the weather was that it was too warm to wear tights, because Elizabeth could not have got into them in a million years. Shaving her legs was a nightmare, even trying to get her drawers on in a morning was like a Houdini act in reverse. At least after today she could swan about in a dressing-gown from dawn to dusk if she wanted to, because she was so tired that she had pulled her date forward in line with that of the other two heifers.

This time tomorrow, they would all be on the first day of their maternity leave.

'I'd like, from us all, to wish Janey good luck, good health and a very happy maternity leave,' said Barry Parrish, and everyone applauded and yelled, 'Speech, speech!'

Janey's desk was undetectable below a huge pile of presents and it felt like the whole building had formed a circle around her. A smiling, happy circle that radiated warmth and lots of good feeling.

'Well, I'd just like to say that I'll miss you all very much, but as the great man himself said, "I'll be back"' – and she did a weighty impression of big Arnie that made them all laugh. 'I'd like to say as well, thank you for the lovely presents. I'm truly touched,' and this she said with genuine gratitude too. Her team had done a lot of crafty homework, finding out the things she didn't have so they would not duplicate. They had also bought her the biggest pair of ugliest pants they could find on Wakefield market, to discourage George from going near her afterwards. They had drawn a No Entry sign on them and written *for 6 years* underneath, which had made her crease over. People only do daft things like that for someone they like, she thought, and felt like crying.

Barry Parrish had given her the last hug and pushed an envelope into her hand. 'This is an extra little something from me, Janey. I knew you could do this job and you've done me proud.'

Janey beamed, just as much as if her dad or her granddad had said that to her.

'I'd like to raise a toast to Helen: good health and good luck,' said Teddy Sanderson, raising a glass of champagne in her direction, and everyone repeated, 'To Helen, good health and good luck,' and took a sip.

'Thank you so much, everyone,' said Helen, savouring the cool taste, knowing the heartburn would take its revenge on her pleasure later.

'Helen, please come back to us, we shall all miss you terribly,' said her boss, tipping his glass to her in an extra, fond toast, and some of the other solicitors joined in a chorus of 'Hear! Hear!' behind him, then drifted off back to their offices when the champagne had been drunk. The band of secretaries scurried around clearing up the pink wrapping paper and the ribbons and bows that had dressed a Steiff teddy bear, some beautiful little pink baby outfits and a thick furry pink pram blanket.

Teddy Sanderson helped Helen carry out the presents to her car, which was parked in one of their reserved spaces outside the back door exit. She nervously over-arranged them in the boot because the air was crackling with a strange tension and she wasn't sure how this particular goodbye was going to be performed.

'And this is from me, for you,' he said, taking a package out of his inner suit pocket. 'Because everyone forgets the mother, so this is to redress the balance.'

'Oh, I didn't expect . . .' said Helen, silencing herself and hoping the butterflies flipping about in her tum weren't going to suddenly come flying out of her mouth and waft Teddy Sanderson to death. She opened up the exquisitely wrapped box to find a locket in white gold, engraved on the back with *To H from T*, along with a small horseshoe.

'It's beautiful, Teddy, thank you so much,' she whispered, battling with some very sudden tears.

'To wish you luck, dear Helen,' he said, and he bent to kiss her cheek. His lips lingered slightly longer than a simple, platonic goodbye merited, but Helen did not mind that one bit.

'. . . And she's been bloody useless and I'll be glad to see the back of her. Good riddance!' said Terry Lennox as Nerys and the girls in the office shook their heads in despair and Elizabeth looked at him with mock weariness.

'All right,' he began again, 'I'll be serious for a minute. Elizabeth, you've been a breath of fresh air and an absolute joy to work with, and you make a cracking cup of coffee, despite what I usually say about it. I think I speak for all of us when I say, "Good luck, old bird and come back to us safe and sound with a lovely little healthy baby in your life",' and he gave her a kiss and then everyone else gave her a kiss and little Nerys started crying because Elizabeth *was* lovely and she *would* miss her. She had always felt awful about not being able to stop those horrible rumours that had been circulating about her. Luckily, all that business was now over. There had been a post-script of gossip though, that Sue Barrington had had her long-overdue come-uppance from Elizabeth in a loo at the other end of the building. Lots of people who had fallen foul of Sue Barrington had cheered at that. Anyway, Sue had not so much as mentioned her name since, and she talked about *everyone*.

'Back to flaming temps then again. I hope you aren't going to be one of these women who only comes back for about five minutes, just to get her maternity pay and then buggers off for good!' said Terry Lennox, delivering her a coffee as Elizabeth tidied off some loose ends at her desk when the throng around it had dispersed. She looked at the cup and then at him as if he was an alien and had just given her a rock from his planet.

'What's up with you? I can boil a kettle, you know!' he said.

'I'll come back, even if it's just to make your life a misery.'

'You don't make my life a misery, lass,' he said in a

voice that punched her in the gut with its unexpected tenderness. 'Here, by the way,' and he shoved a folded-up cheque unceremoniously into her hand.

'Terry! Five hundred quid? God . . .'

'Buy yourself some gin and chips,' he said. 'It was the only thing that kept our Irene going and sane. Trust me, you'll need all the strength you can get. I should know, we have three of the buggers. Look after yourself, Elizabeth, you're a good girl,' and he gave her a nice kiss on the cheek that was appreciative and giving, and did not ask for anything back from her. Nerys appeared at her side to help her carry her presents down to the car.

'Don't be going soft, Adolf, I'm not used to it and I'll start blubbing,' she said, as he helped her on with her jacket. She would make a fool of herself in a minute if she didn't get away. She and Nerys started to walk out.

'Oy, you,' he called after her. 'I lied about the coffee. You *are* bloody useless at making it.'

Chapter 45

They met that evening for their third and final Parentcraft class, as usual, in the car spaces at the back of the park. There was a nice cool breeze, for which they were all grateful as it was like carrying a central-heating boiler around, having a little baby inside. They bought an ice cream from the van and excitedly swapped stories about their last day at work and all the presents they had received. The giddy sensation in their stomachs made it feel as if they were back at Barnsley Girls' School and had just broken up for the six-week holiday. Then they all set off for the church hall; it was only a short walk away, but it was as much as they could manage in their thirty-fourth week.

Carol was conspicuous by her absence. Apparently she'd had her baby three days before at home – a little girl called Palma. Mandy smilingly delivered the news, whilst secretly hoping she'd had enough stitches to keep her at home sat on a rubber ring and away from the last of her three classes. Elizabeth was happy for her, but disappointed that she had never got the chance to ask her if she had bonded with all her babies straight away. She was starting to get fixated about it, having dreams that she was looking at her baby and feeling nothing, even though she wanted to, as if a wall stood between them.

It was to be a mixed bag of a lesson that week. *Any Questions* was the subject on the whiteboard, although Elizabeth couldn't bring herself to ask the one that was torturing her most of all – they would all look at her as if she was a freak if she did.

'How likely is a Caesarean delivery?' asked Marc with a 'c', after the subjects of babies mixing with dogs and cats, sleep, the best first toys and cutting baby nails had been exhausted.

'Well, the odds are that one of you in this room will have one,' said Mandy. Elizabeth's jaw dropped open because she thought only actresses and Posh Spice had those – weren't they more of a cosmetic thing?

'Sometimes, if the baby is breech or goes into distress – basically starts poohing inside you – then a Caesarean will be performed, or c-sections, as they are sometimes called. Emergency Caesareans can be quite scary as the room will suddenly fill with surgical staff, but that's a good thing in a way because they just want to get your baby out without any fuss or nonsense,' said Mandy with a beatific smile. 'They'll make a slit just here,' she indicated a low-down horizontal slash, 'and you can be awake or asleep during this procedure.'

'*Awake?*' said Pam, so loudly that the echo returned to her from the back of the stage.

'Oh, don't worry. You're all numbed up and there's a screen there so you won't be able to see a thing. Then you're stapled . . .'

'*Stapled?*' said someone else even louder, and with panic vibrating their voice to full-on falsetto.

'Or stitched, depending on the surgeon. They all have their preferred methods.'

Helen noticed that Mandy's voice seemed to jolly up the more she panicked people, thereby allowing her to move in and give comfort. She wondered if she had some form of Munchausen's.

Then they all gratefully left that subject for 'hazards in the home'. Apparently, everyone's house was a lethal death-trap for a child, and Janey wondered how she had ever made it to adulthood with all the sharp edges in her parents' house, especially with her mum's penchant for fancy glass tables. Thinking back, though, the only domestic accident she could remember having was when she cut her face open on the zipper of a cushion whilst doing illegal roly-polys on the sofa.

'A health visitor will come round to your houses to make sure everything is okay in the days when you get back from hospital,' said Mandy, summing up. 'No one expects you to have a sparkling home, but try and keep on top of the kitchen and the bathroom. Be firm with visitors as well because they will all want to come and see the new baby, most likely when you just want to sleep. Remember, when the baby sleeps, you sleep. Don't try and catch up with the ironing – you need your rest. The best friends will be the ones that come and vacuum up for you, not sit there for hours with the baby *you* want to cuddle. Get your partners to pull their fingers out and look after *you* for a change.'

That would have been nice, thought Elizabeth, being

looked after when I got home. As it was, she would have nothing but an empty house to come back to – no Penelope Luxmore fussing around her, no George shoving a meat and potato pie on a tray for her.

I can't do this.

You'll have to, countered another voice, a robust no-nonsense voice. It sounded like her Auntie Elsie's.

You'll have to . . .

They all made plans then to convene on Tuesday evening at the hospital for their 'Stork Walk', a look around the Labour Suite and the wards to acclimatize them for the big one to come. Janey braved the video box and took out *Four Births*.

'Look, come round to mine one day next week – let's make it Wednesday,' she said. 'I'll cook and we'll watch it.'

'You'll what?'

'Okay, okay, we'll get a takeaway in.'

'That Carol told us not to watch anything like this.'

'Well, we're all going to be doing it soon,' said Janey, 'so, personally, I think it will help to see what we have to face.'

Within the next eight weeks max she would have had her baby and she was impatient for it to happen. She was fed up with pregnancy now; she had got used to the extra energy her first two trimesters had given her and she wasn't enjoying feeling like a wound-down clock. She had read that some mothers felt what sex child they were carrying – like Helen had – but she herself did not have a clue. Some nights she had strong dreams it was a little girl, only to dream the next night that she had a baby boy, but she didn't care; she just wanted it healthy. And she wanted it out.

Elizabeth lay back in the bath looking like, she supposed, a giant half-submerged hippo. Although, stick a palm tree on her stomach as it rose out of the water and she could do a jolly good impression of a cartoon desert island. Thank God there's no one here to see me looking like this, she thought, and then she remembered how George looked at Janey, who was fourteen times bigger and rounder than she was. Her friend really had never been as pretty ever. *Radiant* – that was the word they used to describe mums-to-be who looked like Janey did.

Elizabeth's stomach suddenly rose and shifted like someone wriggling under a pink tent. She had come to enjoy the sensation of the baby jiggling around inside her. He usually started his main gyrations when she had settled down at night in her snuggle of cushions and supporting pillows and had got as comfortable in bed as she was likely to. She let herself go with the sensation of lying there, feeling him twizzle inside her to get comfortable, like Sam used to do on the rug. She would miss this more than anything, knowing he was safe inside her and that no one could ever hurt him whilst he was there, nestled up near to her heart.

How could her mam have gone through all this and then left her?

The weekend was full of terrific thunderstorms that gave everyone some cool respite from the unrelenting

August heat, but on Monday the rested sun fired up again with a vengeance. Elizabeth set off to the hospital for her last visit to the consultant, puffing like an old tired train. She parked in the nice wide mother and toddler spots in the hospital car park and plodded across to the high square building in her flat ballet pumps. For someone who had power walked everywhere on heels since she was sixteen, it was nice to be forced not to rush. Even if she had wanted to, snail's pace was all she could manage these days.

The appointments were running over half an hour late, but she was quite happy sitting with a bottle of orange and a *Women by Women*, which apparently was the magazine for the 'woman of today', whatever that meant. Am I a woman of today? she mused, concluding that she probably wasn't. Her thoughts had been too firmly in the past for too many years than was good for her. Now she should not only move forwards, but make up some time too.

'Elizabeth Collier,' called a nurse eventually, and Elizabeth put down the magazine, scooped up her bag and went straight through to Mr Greer, clutching her notes and her urine sample.

'So, how are you keeping then?' he said, as she tried to make a dignified climb onto the couch after her blood pressure had been taken.

'I'm tired, I know that much,' she replied, and he nodded sympathetically. She had only gone up two steps and it felt like she had just scaled Everest.

'Yes, the weather we've been having doesn't do ladies like you many favours, does it? I expect you enjoyed the rain at the weekend as much as the ducks did.'

'I feel like a duck the way I'm waddling these days,' she replied, but Mr Greer was concentrating too hard to laugh. He felt around and manipulated her stomach gently, then he said, 'Hmmmm,' in a way that made her immediately start to worry.

'You're presenting breech,' he said.

'Am I?' she said, a cold sweat breaking out at the back of her neck. The word 'breech' had a strong association with 'Caesarean', which led onto 'emergency', which led onto the sorts of fears she didn't want to think about in detail.

'There's nothing to worry about,' said Mr Greer, 'but you'll probably find that his position might cause you quite a lot of heartburn.'

'It does already,' said Elizabeth. The baby's head was like a coconut under her breast.

They listened to the baby's strong heartbeat and Mr Greer addressed Elizabeth's fear balance with a few 'excellent' comments.

'I think I'll see you again in two weeks, just to make sure. The nurse will make an appointment for you,' said Mr Greer eventually, with a gentle smile as he helped her off the couch. 'Have you anything you'd like to ask me in the meantime?'

'No, I don't think so,' said Elizabeth, who had, but she suspected even nice Mr Greer, with his vast experience, would not be able to answer how to guarantee that she would love her baby. And how not to die in childbirth.

Chapter 46

Thank the Lord I ended work when I did, thought Elizabeth, who checked her watch and pictured herself getting off the train from Leeds at this time and heading back to her car for home. Unless, that is, a leaf had landed on the track at Carlisle and disrupted the whole country's network.

Instead, she was sitting out in the garden, basking in the mid-August sun, and had been doing some small sketches with watercolour pencils that she would later frame for the baby's room. There was a cat, a rabbit, and a duck, all of them bright and colourful with not a thick black line in sight. Elizabeth loved the sun and she thought the baby just might be enjoying it too. She felt that he was content, in his warm, watery cocoon; she was imagining that he was sleeping and dreaming of growing up to be a footballer, which at least would explain why his leg kept shooting out.

The back garden at Rhymer Street was small but perfectly formed. There was a little stone-flagged patio with a table and chairs, where she had spent many a pleasant sunny afternoon after school with her Auntie Elsie, soaking up the day's last rays and tucking into a glass of Ribena and a Golden Syrup sandwich. Roses flanked either side of a little ragged path, which cut through the flowerbeds to a second shaded area where Elizabeth had bought her auntie a swinging seat in the sales with her first wages. They had put it at the top of the garden where Sam was now buried and where her Auntie Elsie's ashes had been scattered too, and where Cleef always sat, strangely enough. He was there now, motionless in sleep, except for his snake-like black tail periodically tapping as if in impatience. There was nothing to the back of the house but allotments and, give or take the distant sounds of the odd car in the neighbouring streets, it was usually peaceful and quiet.

She was just dropping off, savouring the warm feeling of the baby squiggling inside her, when she had the weirdest feeling that she was being watched, and it sent her catapulting back into full consciousness. She jerked up as she saw the large figure looming at the back gate.

'What are you – some mad stalker?' she shouted, shielding her eyes from the strong light.

'I was just working out if you were asleep or just resting your eyes. I didn't want to wake you,' said John.

'You did wake me,' she said.

'I knocked at the front.'

'I was here, falling asleep, in the back.'

'Sorry,' he said, mock contritely. He didn't tell her that he'd been watching her, savouring how serene she looked, sitting there with her face raised to the sun and her hand resting lightly on her tummy.

'Come in if you're coming then,' she said. 'I'll get you a drink, there's some beers in the frid . . .' She tried to get up but fell back again, cursing. 'Hang on, I'll give it another go!'

'I'll go, Miss Weeble,' he said, coming in and pushing her gently back down. 'What's that?' and he indicated the jug on the table.

'Lemonade,' she said.

'Fancy a shandy?' he said.

'Shandy drinker? You?' she teased.

'It's very refreshing on a day like this. By heck, it's hot; I bet you're glad you've finished work.'

'I was just lying here thinking the same,' she said, stretching her legs out and putting them up on the chair. She looked like she had elephantitis, judging by her ankles. Did celebrities get all these unglamorous symptoms, she thought, or was it just normal people? She couldn't imagine Demi Moore giving interviews about her piles, although so far so good, she had escaped that particular symptom – unlike Janey, who was suffering and imparting too many details for the others ever to enjoy a bunch of grapes again.

Boobs like watermelons, swollen fingers, battery acid heartburn . . . she didn't think her body could ever go back to normal after all these changes. There was even a weird brown line that had appeared on her stomach, from her navel down, that made her wonder if she had started to split in half until Helen told her it was a normal *linea nigra* – a simple, bog standard 'black line'. At least Miss Ramsay's lessons had come in useful for translating the language of pregnancy if not for conversing with any Roman soldiers who happened to be touring the area. She only hoped she could say a big fat goodbye to the chronic backache after the baby's birth. She didn't half envy Janey when she said George gave her those lovely back-rubs every night.

'How you feeling then?' John said, bringing two half-glasses of beer out, topping them up with lemonade and setting them on the little wrought-iron table.

'Fat, lumpy and kicked to death. I think I've got Pele in here.'

'Can I?' he said, stretching his hand out tentatively.

'Be my guest!' said Elizabeth. Even a woman in the market had asked that question and she had found, oddly for her, that she had been proud to show him off. John put his hand down carefully on her stomach and the baby wriggled underneath it.

'He's saying hello,' said Elizabeth, grinning.

'Wow!' he said, smiling with fascination; he could actually see her tummy changing shape, lifting and shifting. 'Look at him go!'

'Tell me about it!'

'Is everything all right with you? You know, blood pressure and all that?'

'I think so, but I went to see the consultant this morning and he wants me back in a fortnight 'cos the baby is the wrong way round.'

'So what does that mean?'

'I don't know really, only that it would be better if he was the right way round. He said I hadn't to worry, so I'm trying not to think about it.' She shrugged and swallowed and he could see that she was worried, despite the bravado act. She shifted his hand to a higher place on her stomach. 'Look, see this hard bit? That's his head.'

'Crikey, that's solid!' he said, feeling it. 'Can't believe you've got a little baby in there. Really, it's amazing.'

'I know. I still can't quite believe it myself yet.'

'So when are you seeing Bubble and Trouble again then?' he said, taking his hand away before it outstayed its welcome.

'Well, I'm seeing Janey tomorrow night,' she said. 'We're going to the hospital for a walk around.'

'What time?'

'Half past five.'

'Want me to come?'

'What do you want to walk round a hospital for?'

'Company for you.'

She thought about it for a second. Where was the harm in it? Janey was taking George. Helen was not going; she had already been with her mother to the posh private hospital.

'Okay then, if you're that desperate for something to do with your spare time,' she found herself saying.

'What time shall I pick you up?'

'I've to be there at five thirty.'

'Yes, you said and I was listening, you know. Say five past then, that'll give us plenty of time to get parked up.'

'Okay,' she said, smiling far more than she intended to.

At exactly five past five the next evening, the horn tooted outside Elizabeth's house. She noticed that John was all dressed up when she got into the car and smelled of a delicate but manly aftershave. He scrubbed up quite well out of his builder's garb. Very well, actually, and it was nice of him to make the effort. It made her feel quite special and a bit fluttery in the stomach area.

They met Janey and George in the main foyer. Janey gave her a knowing wink.

'Bringing your *boyfriend*, I see?' she said as the two blokes were talking together in front of them.

'Get stuffed,' said Elizabeth. 'He's just saving me from being a raspberry.'

'Gooseberry,' corrected Janey. 'He's a bit dressed up, isn't he?'

'Can't say as I'd noticed,' sniffed Elizabeth.

'Anyway, come on. Mandy "Just Say No" is here already.'

They all wandered over to the rest who were congregated by the lifts. After a couple more arrivals, Mandy clapped her hands and welcomed them all. Marc with a c and Pam were still wearing their name badges, and Elizabeth wondered if they had one ready for the baby when it arrived – *Ffreddy* with two fs, probably. They all waddled off behind Mandy to the Labour Suite. Elizabeth had been imagining something a lot more archaic than the softly painted room with the serene pictures on the wall and beanbags and big cushions all over the floor.

'Some women like to move about in labour and work with gravity,' Mandy said, then demonstrated how they might use the beanbag, which was much the same position Janey conceived in, if she remembered correctly.

'. . . Although obviously you can't get up and do that if you've had an *epidural*,' Mandy continued, managing to imbue the word with all the qualities of the anti-Christ. She then took them just to the door of the Special Baby Unit and explained that if a baby was premature or needed some intensive treatment, this was where the nursing staff would bring him or her. There was a mother in there gazing at a baby, but luckily she looked quite smiley. Janey was glad they didn't go in there; she had not let thoughts in of either herself or her baby being poorly, not even when Elizabeth went through that funny phase about dying in childbirth – and she did not want to start entertaining them now.

Following this, they had a look around the ward. There were some individual rooms with televisions in, as Helen was likely to have – that, and a butler – but most had four beds in them with baby stations at the side that looked like rectangular goldfish tanks.

'They're alarmed,' said Mandy. 'You'll have a unique key to deactivate it when you want to lift up your baby. Very security conscious we are at Barnsley.'

They clustered around a mum with her ten-hour-old baby asleep in a tank at her side. He was wrapped up in a pistachio-coloured blanket and he looked like he was peeping out of a perfectly iced little cake. The new mum looked totally knackered but sublimely happy. Elizabeth put her hand on her stomach, trying to reconcile the fact that a baby as big as *that* was in her tummy, and it freaked her out a little and she came over a little woozy. John saw her rock and his hands closed on her arms to hold her up.

'You all right?' he bent to her ear and whispered.

'Yes, I'm fine, just a bit hot,' she said, not wanting to draw attention to herself; but she wasn't fine, not really. She felt totally shell-shocked.

Janey was even more excited now. The hospital visit just made her realize how close she was to the big day. She couldn't wait to meet her little baby and, almost more than that, she couldn't wait to see the baby in George's arms. They had actually started talking sensibly about names now but she did not want it set it stone, just in case the baby did not suit the name when she saw it. Her parents, apparently, had been going to call *her* Bonnie – except she arrived into the world all red hair and snarls and looking anything but.

George was not enthusing so much on the subject of the baby at the moment. Yes, he was excited, but he did not want to see Janey in all that pain. He'd had a sneak look at *Four Births* when she had gone to bed and had had to switch it off and swig a big brandy.

Janey asked the others back to the house for a drink after the visit was over, but John said immediately that he couldn't as he had somewhere to go, and apologized.

That's why he was all dressed up, Elizabeth thought. It wasn't for me, it was for afterwards. She knew immediately what the 'afterwards' was – it had to be a date. That would explain the nice aftershave and the smart shirt. She was an unexploded bomb of hormones, fears and insecurities and went quiet and had to concentrate hard to stop tears flooding her eyeballs. The drive home seemed so very long.

'You feeling okay?' he said.

'Yes, I'm fine. It's just that there's a lot to think about.'

'Aye, well, you'll be forty in just over a year. No wonder you're getting worried,' he teased gently, trying to make light of things.

'You'll be forty in just over a year yourself,' she tried to joke back, but it didn't work and came out flat.

'Aye, but I'll always be younger than you!'

Not if I die in childbirth.

She didn't mean to think that. It just slipped into her head again, as strong as the day when Simon first put the thought there. John braked outside her front door and turned around to take a long hard look at her, because there was definitely something up with her.

'Want me to come in with you for' – he checked his watch – 'five minutes?'

That slight action wasn't lost on her.

'No, I'm fine. I'm just done in,' she clipped. 'Thanks for coming with me but I don't need your five minutes.'

'I'll see—'

However, she had shut the car door and was gone into the house before he could get the rest of his words out, and it was more than obvious to him that she would not let herself be followed in.

Once inside, she threw herself into her chair and rocked vigorously, listening to his car drive off, following the sound of it, wondering where he was going, who he was seeing.

What did you expect him to do? she thought. Hang around for ever? Put his life on hold for you?

Elizabeth didn't know. She didn't know anything any more, except that she was alone and confused and very, very scared.

Chapter 47

It was probably the stupidest thing they had ever done, even stupider than Elizabeth copping off with the disgusting Wayne Sheffield, even stupider than Helen's first Saturday job in a florist with her pollen intolerance, even stupider than Janey's penchant for puffball skirts in the 1980s with legs like hers. Watching a video about four real births outranked all those stupid things, especially whilst eating a Deep Pan pizza that was looking more and more like a placenta by the minute.

The water birth had looked very calming at first, until the woman started screaming in agony, and not even the wondrously happy look on her face when the baby arrived about five years later could make up for the full horror of what they had just witnessed. The 'normal' birth, woman on table, legs splayed, pushing and groaning a lot, featured a ventouse and then a forceps delivery. The baby arrived with a pointy head like an alien from Planet Ugly and a bruised swollen face, screaming the narrator into second volume place.

'I think I'd scream if I had a chuffing Dyson sucking me out as well,' said Janey, who was most categorically not looking forward to the birth experience now as much as she had been. She kept reminding herself to keep focusing on the beautiful little baby she would have at the end of all the pain, but the picture kept slipping away from her as if it was coated with mind grease. She tried to tell herself that she might be one of the lucky ones who only did two pushes and a shove anyway. It had been known, her midwife had said at the last antenatal; not everyone had long drawn-out labours, and she cited some welcome examples.

Helen was okay until the home birth, when the woman poohed on the carpet as the baby emerged. The midwife just scooped it up without a fuss, but the Frenchwoman's image from that school day Biology lesson was re-burned in Helen's mind bigger and brighter than ever, like a digitally remastered film.

They thought there was nothing left to see until the Caesarean-section delivery of a breech baby, which looked like an explosion in a mince factory. Helen screamed and hid her face behind a cushion, saying she could not watch any more, and Janey turned it off and put *Emmerdale* on instead.

'I think we've seen enough now,' she said. 'Whose bloody idea was this?'

'Yours,' said Helen, still from behind the cushion. 'Why didn't we listen to Carol?'

Elizabeth couldn't say anything; she continued to sit there looking stunned and rather grey. No one could go through *that* and live!

'Look,' said Janey, about to spread her 'end justifies the means' theory. 'You have to keep your eye on what we'll have at the end of it all – a lovely little baby.'

'But to get from this' – Helen pointed at her massive fundus – 'to that stage, we have to go through one of *those*.' And she pointed at the video.

'Well, it's going to have to come out somehow!' said Janey, sounding far braver than she felt.

'I don't think I can,' said Elizabeth.

'You'll have to, love – we all will,' said Janey, patting her bump. 'Put it this way, it's a bit late for us to back out now!'

Still traumatized, Elizabeth slotted the key in the door and walked into the cold silence. This is what it will be like coming home with my new baby, she thought. There would be no welcoming committee popping champagne corks, no mum pushing her down onto the sofa and getting her a nice cup of tea, and no one to have switched the fire on if the weather had turned.

Cleef stretched up and yowled a sleepy hello and she smiled gratefully. She sat down in the rocking chair and he jumped up and perched comically on the top of her bump.

'At least you'll be here for us, sweetie,' she said, and gave him a good old scratch under his chin that had him purring like a Mercedes engine. She needed to ask John if he would feed him for her when she went into hospital. She wondered, too, if she dare ask him if he would pick her up and bring her home after-wards, so she wouldn't have to take the baby's car seat in with her. She did not want to ask him this favour, but she was going to have to, because there was no one else – she couldn't exactly ask Janey or Helen.

Her head fell forwards into her hands as if weighed down by her thoughts. There were so many little things still to orchestrate and gadgets to unpack and work out how they operated – the baby surveillance monitor that John had brought in his Santa visit, for instance, and the steriliser – and how the hell did you strap a car seat in anyway? It had taken her an hour to work out how to collapse the pram to get it into the car (even following the instruction leaflet) because she and the baby would need to go shopping together not long after they came out of hospital. The enormity of a simple bit of shopping in the future seemed as big as organizing a military operation to invade Australia. She had stocked the freezer up until it was groaning, but she would need fresh milk, and vegetables, and some fruit . . . Her brain was bursting with it all but at least she could make sure Cleef was covered.

John's mobile clicked onto answerphone when she rang. *Probably out with his bird.*

'Please leave a message . . .'

'Hello, John,' she said, trying to master the unwanted waver in her voice, 'it's Elizabeth. I'm just trying to get organized and I wondered if you would do me a favour when I go into hospital. Will you call in and feed Cleef for me? Once a day will be fine if you leave him some biscuits out as well and change his water. I'll give you a key when I see you next, if that's okay. Thanks, bye.'

She knew he would help, but then a thought infested that surety. Suppose he was going away on holiday somewhere – with his new woman? He must be ready for one, with all that hard work he had been doing, and that's what couples in love did in summer. What would she do then? The questions just got too big for her head and she didn't fight back the tears when they came. She wondered if they would ever stop.

She met Janey and Helen the next day for herby tea and a laboured look around the shops to make sure there was nothing any of them had forgotten to buy. However, considering they had more or less bought up Mothercare, Babyworld and Sanitary Towels 'R Us between them, it was hardly likely.

'Teddy Sanderson sent me some flowers yesterday,' said Helen, picking the angelica diamond off her meringue.

Four giant owls' eyes rounded at her as if they were on a diet and she was a mouse covered in clotted cream.

'What did it say on the card?'

'*Hope you're feeling well, would you mind if I called you?*' She was smiling like a happy lunatic with no cares in the world except what to smile at next.

'You like him, you do,' said Janey.

'You're right, I do,' said Helen.

'What – like as in fancy?' asked Elizabeth.

Helen mused for a few seconds. 'Yes, I think I do. He's been on my mind more than I imagined he would.'

'Could you snog him?'

'Oh, most definitely,' said Helen, with no hesitation whatsoever.

She had imagined that scenario already and found it a very pleasant one. It had gone quite a bit further than kissing in her fantasies but she was not going to admit it to anyone. Sometimes friends were too close to tell everything to – she had discovered that fact a long time ago. She had got too used to holding her secrets close.

'Ooooooooooo,' said Janey.

'Oh, come on. It can't go anywhere, can it, really?' said Helen, dismissing their excitement with a wave.

'Why not?' said Elizabeth. 'You're both single, you're gorgeous, he's rich, you're not a gold-digger, you're the perfect age for each other, he's handsome . . . I think he's exactly your type and you have to be his; he'd be mad not to fancy you. Need I go on?'

'Oh, stop it,' said Helen, whilst inwardly agreeing that, yes, he *was* her type, far more than Simon ever was. She could see that now with the wonderful gift of hindsight.

'You heard from you-know-who?' asked Janey, right on cue.

'The barest communication via his solicitor,' said Helen. 'We have a buyer for the house. I'm getting the deposit back and eighty per cent of the equity.'

'Wow, that's good, isn't it?' said Elizabeth.

'I haven't asked him for maintenance and he hasn't asked for access to the baby.'

'Oh sod, that's not so good.'

'He never did want the baby. I know that now, so

I'm not shocked,' said Helen with a loaded sigh, 'but I feel so incredibly sad that my little girl will never share the sort of wonderful days with her father that I did with mine.'

Life with Simon seemed a million light years away, almost as if they had happened to someone else. She had not realized how cold and unhappy her marriage to him had been until she stepped out of his shadow and into the sunshine once again.

'I still think you and Teddy might get together,' said Elizabeth, hoping this was an appropriate thing to say in the circumstances. 'Why do you say it can't go anywhere?'

'The reason why it can't really go anywhere is because I'm heavily pregnant with someone else's child, if you hadn't noticed,' said Helen, with a little laugh.

'Not all blokes are pregnant-women-hating bastards,' said Elizabeth. 'I can see him and you with a little daughter walking in the park. He'd make a lovely step-daddy. He's even called Teddy, for God's sake. If that isn't the most perfect name for a husband for you, I don't know what is.'

Janey laughed and had a big bite of bun. Her torturous indigestion had gone and her bump had seemed to drop three feet overnight, which took the pressure off her digestive organs and transferred it to her pelvis. Win some, lose some, she had thought at that, with a smile of resignation.

'What about you and John then?' Helen threw back.

'What about me and John?'

'Well, you seem very friendly. I mean, he went to the hospital with you, didn't he, so I hear?'

'Oh aye, has Mouth Almighty there been gossiping?'

'Yep!' said Janey.

'Well?'

'He's a friend,' said Elizabeth. 'He was only ever a friend.'

Janey and Helen threw each other a colluding glance, which Elizabeth caught.

'What?' she demanded.

'Rubbish,' said Janey.

'Rubbish what?'

'You were in love with each other. Still are, by my reckoning.'

'You rubbish!'

'*You* rubbish!'

'Oh, come on, children,' said Helen. 'Elizabeth, grow up and listen.'

Elizabeth looked as if Helen had just slapped her.

'We read your letter, so you see, we *know*,' said Helen, adding a limp, 'Sorry, but we did.'

'What letter? Know what?'

'The one you wrote after you sent John away at that wedding all those years ago.'

Elizabeth coloured. 'You went snooping in my house?'

'No,' corrected Janey. 'You left it out on the table – well, under a tea-towel. It wasn't like it was in a drawer. We thought it was your drawings, so you see, we opened it for a look and then discovered it by accident.'

'You didn't chuffing read it by accident!' said

Elizabeth, feeling as if she had just been emotionally stripped naked in front of her friends.

'We tried to head him off at the pass,' said Janey, 'to tell him for you, but he'd upped and gone with that fluffy gonk.'

'You what?'

'We chased him to the airport,' said Helen. 'I think we missed him by half an hour.'

Elizabeth was open-mouthed with annoyance or shame or indignity or what, she wasn't sure. 'I can't believe you read my letter!' she said.

'I can't believe you felt that about John Silkstone and let him go,' said Janey.

'If you've got a second chance with John, you should take it,' said Helen. 'You would be a fool to let him go again.'

'Listen, that was then and this is now,' said Elizabeth, still red-faced. 'Anyway, he's seeing someone.'

'Who?'

'I don't know who she is! I haven't asked him.'

'What makes you think that?'

'I just know.' Elizabeth stiffened up her spine bravely and tried to look unbothered. 'Good luck to him anyway, he deserves someone.'

Janey and Helen both gave a sympathetic sigh.

'You don't really feel like that, do you?'

'Yes, of course I do. We're friends, nothing more. It's too late for anything else.'

'It isn't, Elizabeth.'

'It is, Helen. We've both moved on from those days. We're happy being just good friends.'

'Really?' This from Janey.

'Yes, really. Anyway, you said it yourself when we were arguing about that rocking chair. He isn't going to look at me again, is he, after last time? Friends, that's all either of us wants.' Or can ever hope to be.

'That's a shame,' said Janey. She had become increasingly sure that there was more to it than friendship: all the stuff he had done for Elizabeth and bought her, the way he had looked at her in the hospital. Then how quick he had been to react when she came over a bit wobbly and how genuinely concerned he had been for her. Although he had always been a very caring bloke.

Just a friend? thought Janey and Helen together. Maybe so. Awwww no . . . what a shame!

Seven years on, Elizabeth still had the letter wrapped in tissue in her drawer. She had written it on the night when she had come home from Janey's cousin's wedding, when she could not get his face out of her head after telling him to leave her alone for good. *Why couldn't she just take his love? Why did she have to throw it back at him?* She had taken out her sketch-pad and pen and sat at the kitchen table.

I'm sorry for what I said, I didn't mean it, but you know what I'm like, John. I didn't think I could ever love anyone. I didn't know what these feelings were until I knew I'd lost you tonight, then it was too late. I know you won't have me back and I don't deserve you. I don't know why I did what I did. I'm screwed up, I'm stupid, so bloody stupid . . .

She never sent it, of course. He had a chance to be

happy with someone who adored him and you could tell by the way Lisa looked at him that she thought the absolute world of him. It wouldn't have been fair to wreck that by telling him her heart was still ajar for him, because he would never have left her then. Lisa would be a lot less emotional maintenance for him than she ever would be.

Over the years, she had stamped down so hard on those feelings she'd had for him: how she loved being with him, how much she looked forward to seeing him, how much she wanted him, only to find that it hadn't made the slightest bit of difference. They were all still there. As the letter was preserved in tissue, her feelings were as fresh in her heart as the day she wrote the words down on paper. If only she could have let him know how she felt before it was too late, if only she hadn't been so warped and twisted by her past.

She didn't want her baby to be like her and miss his chances if love came calling. She wanted him to run towards it with open arms and embrace it and feel it fill up his heart and his soul. She would bring her child up with gentleness and affection, learning to trust when it was right to do so. There would be no life of fear and confusion and ridiculously pitched independence for her child, no feeling that he wasn't worthy enough to be loved.

There was a message waiting for Elizabeth when she got home. It was from John saying that of course he would look after Cleef and he had taken it as read anyway that he would be official catsitter. He asked if she was okay because she sounded a bit down and could she give him a ring back and let him know. Then he said had she made any plans for her birthday on Monday because he wanted to pop in and say 'hi' and bring her a card up. He didn't say anything about taking her out for it. It was too late for that to happen now. He had other stuff going on in his life. Other people to think about.

She didn't ring back.

Chapter 48

The baby woke Elizabeth up with a 'Happy Birthday' kick in the spine and he was as active as if he was holding his own celebratory party for her and had invited a few mates around. She tried to get back to sleep but Michael Flatley inside her wasn't having any of it, so she went downstairs for a slice of heavily buttered granary toast and some olives. At least her craving was a pretty low-key affair. She didn't have to embarrass herself with a compulsion to go into McDonald's and ask for a haddock and gorgonzola McFlurry.

Janey and Helen's cards arrived on the doormat; they knew Elizabeth liked getting nice post, so had sent them to her via Royal Mail even though they were meeting for her birthday lunch anyway. She had a card from Terry Lennox and the girls at work too. There was a note in the envelope from Nerys to say that Julia had run off to lose herself in London. Even Laurence had totally distanced himself from her, after pulling one last string to get her a job torturing students in a training centre. No doubt her penchant for married men would eventually kick up another scandal and another well-connected Laurence would bail her out.

It was a shallow existence but that type would always prize stolen shags from bored husbands above the simple pleasures of friendships and real love, of which they, sadly, had no concept.

There was also an offer of a cut-price hearing aid and the thrilling news that she was 'only one of a few special people in her area to be selected for a big money prize draw'. She didn't feel very special; the three cards looked lost on the great big wooden mantelpiece.

She still had not rung John back. It hurt so much to think that he had moved someone else into the space in his heart that she had taken for granted belonged to her. How stupid she was not to have seen it coming! *That's* why his visits had slowed down these past weeks. Not that she blamed him, though; he was a bloke with a lot of love to give out, and she was the fool who had turned it down just once too often.

She had scrubbed away thoughts of him by mopping at the floors and cleaning down the skirting boards with the burst of mad energy that visited her. Elizabeth had always liked cleaning, but this was different; this was not down to her own compulsions, this was Mother Nature stirring up her hormones with a floor mop in preparation for the new arrival in the house. She had got on her hands and knees and cleared out drawers and cupboards; she had even managed to take down all the curtains, wash them, peg them out in the sunshine and put them back up again the same day. They had needed doing as well; there were enough cobwebs trapped in the folds at the top to tart up a haunted house.

She had taken care on the ladders but felt invincible going up them, although she realized later that it was not on her list of 'wisest things to do whilst being thirty-six weeks' pregnant'. She also knew that if she didn't burn up the extra energy she would never get to sleep in a million years. If the baby didn't keep her awake, the tormenting thoughts whirling round in her head of John Silkstone with another woman would.

She slipped on a cotton dress that had looked so enormous when she bought it that she, Helen and Janey could have got in it and danced the Bump, but now it was getting tight on the bust and the ties at the side were let out to their loosest. Not that she felt blobby fat, for her stomach was as hard as iron, the skin drum-tight across it, not at all the soft, flabby cushion she had once imagined a pregnant tum would feel like. It was an effort to get into the car these days without an enormous shoehorn as the baby protested at being pressed into the steering wheel, but if she moved her seat any further back, her legs would not reach the pedals. Elizabeth kissed her hand and pressed it onto her stomach, hoping he would feel the sentiment filter down.

'Sorry, little one,' she said. She would be holding her baby properly very soon. She had tried to imagine so many times what it would like look. Would it have hair? How much would it weigh? Would it be a boy or a girl? She had always thought of it as a boy; a little boy would be lovely, but a little girl would be equally as nice. She had done the needle test but it had gone up and down and then round and round, and she'd scared herself stupid that it meant it would be a hermaphrodite like the baby on *Footballers' Wives*. She stuck the needle back in the sewing box where it belonged and mentally slapped herself for being so silly and superstitious and for stressing herself out when there was no need.

Janey had reserved a little table so they could dine al fresco, but in the shade because the heat was cracking flags. It was another sun-flooded day and girlies everywhere were flashing flat midriffs below their cropped tops, although Janey was not looking at them enviously any more. She had been there, done that and much preferred the big baggy T-shirt she had replaced it with. She would miss not wearing maternity clothes; she felt quite formidable in her big pinafore. HMS *Pinafore*, George called her – not that he was complaining; she was just more woman to love, in his eyes.

Her friends gave Elizabeth a big kiss and as tight a hug as their portly frames would allow. It was strange cuddling Elizabeth, they both thought together, but nice. It was good she was starting to soften, especially as they had given up hope a long time ago of her ever enjoying the simple pleasure of a hug. They had made her up a hamper in a pretty basket with chocolates and tiny cherry pies and miniature jars of pickles and jams and biscuits and assorted olives, all of which Helen had found in one of her posh food shops, and they had bought her three frames for the pictures she had painted for the baby's room.

'I tried to get you some Gaviscon liqueur chocolates but Thornton's had run out,' said Janey, rubbing a niggle out of her lower back.

'Thanks for the thought, though,' said Elizabeth. 'I just want to start scoffing everything you've brought me now.'

'Even the frames?'

'Especially the frames. They'll be nice and tasty with a crushed olive or two.'

'You poor mental bag,' said Janey. 'Well, thirty-nine, eh? We're all on countdown for the big *four – ohhhhhh* now!'

'You first,' said Helen. 'Three months to go.'

'Yep,' said Janey, watching as Helen passed them all menus then tipped some of the salt pot onto her hand and proceeded to lick it off.

'What on earth are you doing?' said Elizabeth in horror, sounding like an exasperated Billy Connolly.

'Salt and lemons – can't get enough at the moment,' explained Helen. 'You've got your olives, Janey has her Marmite and this is my weirdo craving.'

'Thought "teddies" would be yours,' said Elizabeth cheekily.

'Go away,' said Helen, but she was smiling.

'So, is this where we all thought we'd be then, in the year leading up to forty?' asked Janey.

'What – sitting in a café with you two comparing bizarre food fantasies? Yes, of course I did,' said Helen with a tut.

'No really, come on. Elizabeth?'

'Dunno,' said Elizabeth, whose ideas had changed

on that one over the years. When she was little, all she wanted to do was grow up and be old so her dad wouldn't get her. Then, when she did grow up, she had hoped to find someone to love her, look after her ferociously as she had always tried to look after her friends. Then again, she *had* found someone who wanted to love her and look after her, only to throw him away. Did that constitute success or failure?

'How about . . . married to Liam Neeson and walking permanently like John Wayne when he let me get out of bed,' she said.

'Trust you, you dirty cow!' said Janey.

'Oh, Elizabeth, play the game,' said Helen, with good-humoured frustration.

'Okay, okay.' Elizabeth held up her hands in defeat. 'Well, failing the Boy from the Bogs keeping me as a sex slave, I just wanted a good job, with a nice house, and a decent car and a kind man – you know, the ordinary things most people take for granted.'

'Bet you never thought a kid would be in the equation though?' This from Janey.

'No,' said Elizabeth, 'and I still can't visualize myself as a mother, to be honest.'

'Well, you soon will be, so you'd better start getting used to the idea,' said Helen, with a little laugh.

'I'm trying,' replied Elizabeth, patting the mound of her stomach. Was not *not* wanting the baby the same thing as wanting it? She had driven herself half nuts asking herself questions like that. Her feelings about the baby were still so dreadfully confused.

'What about you, Janey?'

'Well, I wanted to have a super-dynamic job and a bloke I love to bits who treated me like a queen. Oh, and a Yorkshire terrier called Harvey that I could carry around in a basket, like my Auntie Cheryl used to have.'

They chuckled, and then a big jug of water arrived, with plenty of lemon slices in it for Helen to scoop out and encrust with salt.

'And you, Hels?'

'I wanted to be happily married to someone hand-some and successful, with lots of babies and living in a nice big house like Mum and Dad's.'

'I'd rather have the house than . . . ow!'

Janey kicked Elizabeth under the table. *Let's not bring his name up and spoil the atmosphere*, was her intimation. Elizabeth rubbed her leg. Janey had feet like skateboards.

'It's okay to talk about him,' said Helen. 'It doesn't hurt at all.'

'It does if her boot lands on you for saying it,' said Elizabeth, pointing at Janey. 'Jeez, are you wearing steel toe-caps?'

'In fact, I met him yesterday,' Helen announced.

'Did you?' the others said in unison.

'Yes. He was coming from his solicitor's office.'

'And?'

Helen released a tinkly little laugh. 'He was with a woman.'

Neither Elizabeth nor Janey knew what to say to that.

'Go on, then. You're dying to ask me: "what did she look like?"'

'I am dying to ask, I've got to admit,' said Janey.

Helen leaned over the table with a big beaming smile. 'She looked like me. Pre-baby, obviously. Long blonde hair, skinny, blue eyes. It was weird – I saw them coming down the street and I thought, Lord, they look like Simon and me! Then I realized that the man really was Simon.'

'It wasn't that Julia then?' asked Janey.

'No, this one had positively inverse breasts,' said Helen with glee.

'What did he do when he saw you?' asked Elizabeth tentatively.

'He looked a little startled, to be honest.'

'And what did you do?'

'I stuck out my C-cups and walked past him.'

'Just like that?'

'Elizabeth, I swear to you, my heart didn't even miss a beat. It was as if I was looking at a stranger.'

'Funny, that,' said Janey. 'Him going for another Helen.'

'A pale imitation of Helen,' amended Elizabeth. She would bet her life savings there would be a succession of pseudo-Helens to come, whilst he was young and handsome enough to tempt them, anyway. Sweet, fragile women with no complications, whom he would control and bully to compensate for his innate weaknesses. Trophy women he could show off in public, who befitted his picture of an executive ideal, yet in private he could probably only do the business with a bit of rough, sporting massive gazongas. He really was a tortured soul. Good.

'I bet it made you feel bloody marvellous, didn't it?'

'Oh yes,' said Helen with a face-splitting grin. 'It most certainly did.'

They ordered food and it arrived nice and quickly: lemon chicken for Helen, lasagne for Janey, and Stilton-topped pork tenderloin for Elizabeth.

'My boobs are like two big Stiltons,' said Janey, just as Elizabeth was about to take her first mouthful.

'Oh, flaming hell,' said Elizabeth. 'It's a good job I'm not put off my food easily.'

'I mean, where the hell do all those veins come from?'

'Will you give over?'

'I'm just saying, that's all.'

'I don't think I'll ever look attractive again,' said Elizabeth.

'Did you ever?'

'Bog off!'

'Well, wait until you're floppy and fifty and you've grown a beard, then you can go abroad and find a gorgeous young nineteen-year-old Turk on the make,' said Helen.

'Then you can get yourself an extra three hundred quid by selling your story to *Women by Women*, about how you got married and he left you three seconds after cutting your cake,' said Janey. 'You wouldn't have any life savings left, but you'd have some really great memories of his seduction techniques.'

'Eat your lasagne and belt up,' said Elizabeth, and pinched the olive from Janey's side salad at the same time as Helen nicked her lemon.

'So what are you planning for your fortieth birthday bash then?' asked Elizabeth when the bill had been paid and they were wobbling back to their cars.

'A big sleep, if the rumours are true. Apparently we'll be selling our souls for a few hours' kip when the babies come,' said Janey.

'I can't see what the fuss is about sleeping, I mean, surely babies sleep loads, don't they?' said Elizabeth. She had hardly thought about what was to happen in the months after the birth. Her head wouldn't let her get much further than coming home from hospital and getting through her first shopping expedition with car seats and prams to negotiate. Everything after that was a big fuddled cloud.

'Don't think it's quite that straightforward,' said Helen. 'We fit in with them, not the other way round, and sleep when they do, otherwise we might not get any!'

They kissed and went on their way.

There's so much to know, thought Elizabeth, with a heavy heart as she followed the others out of the village. And I feel I know less every day . . .

When Elizabeth got home, she made straight for the big blue chair by the window and drew comfort from being rocked in it. She dropped seamlessly into a vivid dream that the baby was born with a grown man's face with adult teeth, and then she woke up suddenly, realizing that she must have been sobbing in her sleep because her cheeks were wet. There was a heavy knock on the door just as she had got up to find some tissues in the kitchen. She wiped away her tears quickly and opened it to find John on the doorstep.

'Hello there, Happy Birthday,' he said, striding in, handing her a card and then giving her a brotherly squeeze on the shoulder. She looked up at him like a little stunned rabbit lost, disorientated and scared and as if she had been crying because her mascara was smudged, although he didn't draw attention to it and embarrass her.

'Thank you,' she said, holding the envelope stiffly.

She felt awkward, uncomfortable; she didn't know how to act around him now and it was clear that he didn't know how to act around her either because he was keeping his distance.

It hurt to see him in her house, knowing there was someone else on his mind, and when he said, 'I'm not staying, I've somewhere to go,' it was as if he had rubbed salt into a big open cut somewhere very deep inside her.

'I thought I'd just bob up and take a chance you were in, seeing as you never rang me back,' he added, 'so don't put the kettle on for me.'

'Oh, okay. Well, thanks for this.'

'Aren't you going to open it?'

'Oh yes . . . yes, of course.'

She opened up the card; it had a nice verse, a 'dear friend' verse.

I've lost him.

She kept her head bowed, trying to read it, and battled with some mutinous tears. She felt as if she had cried an ocean since the day she told Laurence to stick his job. It was hard work being emotional and letting people in, although she had let them in too late and had only a gaping wound in her heart to show for it.

'I'll be off then,' he said.

'Okay,' she said, managing a small smile that accentuated the sadness in her watery grey eyes. 'Well, thanks for the card. See you, John.'

She expected him to turn and go then, but he didn't. He just stood there, waiting for something.

'Come on, then. Get your coat if you need it.'

'What?'

'Get your coat,' he repeated.

'What do I want my coat for?'

'You're going with me, that's why.'

'Where?' she said.

'I've got something to show you,' he said, grabbing her little summer jacket from the peg near the door, because the day was cooling and he had seen enough of her shivering to last him a lifetime.

Helen gently rocked on the swing by the little babbling stream at the bottom of the garden and lifted her face to the sun. It was wonderful to be able to enjoy the summer without itchy eyes and sneezing every two minutes because her hay fever seemed to have been chased away by her pregnancy.

It was so peaceful there in the grounds of the Old Rectory, especially because she wasn't being relentlessly fussed over by her mother, who was away at a wedding in Oslo for a few days. She had been reluctant to go, but Helen had made her. First babies were notoriously late, she told her mother, she could easily last another five weeks.

She had quite enjoyed being by herself there, padding around her old home and remembering all the wonderful times they'd had in it. The study still smelled as it had done when her father was alive – of old books and polished leather – and his presence was so warm and dear in it. Even the patio where she had found him the morning after he had died held no bad memories for her any more. The years had gently edited out the ugliness and guilt from the scene and finally she could remember him as looking peaceful and released from the pain that had depressed and frightened him so much.

Her mother's dressing-table was still busy with the lotions and potions that Helen used to dab at and poke into as a girl, and in the kitchen lingered the spirit of their old housekeeper, Mother Hubbard, in her voluminous housecoat leaping on any speck of dust with an aggressive cloth and filling the air with the wonderful aromas of her baking. Helen would steal the cooling scones, throw butter at them and smuggle them upstairs to her two friends, splayed over her floor cushions as they savoured the problem pages of *My Guy* and *Oh Boy* whilst Mother Hubbard pretended not to notice.

She so wanted to bring her child up in a happy home like this one had been for her. A wonderful feeling of elation flooded like sunlight through her. It was so sharp it was almost a pain.

Chapter 49

'Where are we going?' Elizabeth said as he drove off.

'Shut up and wait and see.'

'You shouldn't speak to your elders like that!'

'You're only older by two weeks.'

'I'm still older.'

'Like I say, shut up and wait and see.'

So she shut up and waited, whilst he drove out of town, into the surrounding countryside and turned into his building plot at Oxworth. It was eerily different to the last time she had been there, as if a magic wand had been waved over it, for now there were four complete houses, two on each side of a small road that went up and round a corner to a further destination. They were large, double-fronted constructions, two with turf already laid at the front, and each with a weighty millstone set in the garden bearing the number of their address.

'You wanted to check I'd done 'em right,' he said, 'so now's your chance.'

'I hadn't imagined them as nice as this though,' she said.

'Oh, charming!'

She punched his arm, not that he felt it, it was like hitting a brick wall. He helped her out of the car and she followed him down the path to the first house. Then he opened the door and turned off the burglar alarm. She came in behind him and nosed around at the large, light rooms.

'They cram houses into estates these days, don't give any space between them and hardly let you have any room inside either. Well, I didn't want to be known as a builder that did those sorts of homes. I want my buyers to be able to breathe,' he explained to her as her shoes echoed around the oak floors of a very generous kitchen.

'You could have built a lot more houses here, John, surely? Made yourself more profit.'

'Aye, I could have, if I'd wanted,' he said.

There was a long sitting room that went front to back of the house, a study downstairs and a utility room. Upstairs were four bedrooms, one en-suite, one with a vanity sink, and a lovely separate bathroom. There was a boxroom as well for storage, although it would have been big enough to sleep in at a push, and outside she could see there was a good-sized back garden and a double garage. She noticed the roof of the fifth house out of the upstairs window.

'What's that?' she said, pointing to it.

'That's the one I've been working flat out on to get finished these past weeks. Come on – I'll show you,' he said.

They walked out and round a corner of thick hedges and trees that looked as if they had been there years already. The fifth house was different to the others, much larger and set apart in a very grand plot.

'Bloody hell,' was Elizabeth's immediate verdict. 'Which rich sod bought this then?'

'Come in and see it before the owners move in,' he said, finding the keys for it on his big jailer's keyring. They walked into a wide hallway with rooms leading off everywhere and an imposing oak staircase going up the middle of it with an arched stained-glass window of summer flowers at the top through which light flooded and tinted the walls with soft pastel shades.

'Wow,' she said, twirling a full circle and looking up at the galleried landing. 'This is lovely, John.'

It was, too, just like the dream house she had drawn for him a long time ago. *I'd have doors going everywhere . . . like a labyrinth . . .*

'Come on.' He led her into a square sitting room. There was a study leading off, cosy but decent-sized enough to have a big desk, lots of bookshelves and a sofa under the pretty picture window that framed a view of a landscape garden in the making. There was a sweet little downstairs loo that she would have killed for in her pregnant state and a huge country kitchen area with knotty beams above her head, and a Belfast sink set in one of the thick wooden work-tops, a walk-in pantry and a utility room just like the sort she had always thought would be really handy to have. There was a breakfast area round the corner of the L, and a couple of steps down to a separate dining room, leading out to a lovely light conservatory.

Whoever was moving in here would be lucky, Elizabeth thought, because they would never be able to leave it and find another better. It was the sort of house she hoped Bev was living in now. In peace, in the country, with a kind man who could make her forget her nightmares. She went back for a second look at the kitchen because it was so nice.

'That's lovely. Where did you get it?' she said, examining the solid pine table that must have weighed more than she did – i.e. a ton and a half.

. . . I'd have a big heavy table that I wouldn't ever be scared of scratching, that people would want to sit at and talk around . . .

'I made it,' he mumbled modestly. 'Come on, there's upstairs to see yet.'

She struggled up the wider than average staircase, having made enough complimentary vowel sounds downstairs. There was a bathroom facing her, then three sizeable bedrooms to one side. A spiral staircase led up to a vast loft area that was almost all windows. She was puffed out at the top of it, but it had been worth the climb. It would have been her fantasy room, her folly.

. . . I would have a room that caught the sunlight all day just for painting in . . .

The fourth bedroom had its own bathroom and a spacious dressing-room, just as she had drawn on her house, all those years ago. The windows looked out onto the stream, and when she unlocked one of them and opened it, she could hear the water shushing past and a duck laughing like Sid James. She had always wanted to live by water. Give or take the sea, this would have been her perfect house.

Her perfect house . . .

Then she knew.

He's built this for me, she thought. He *has* been working flat out all these weeks, on this . . . for me. Her body locked, she stood there, looking at the stream as it danced past over the stones. He saw her back stiffen and he knew she had worked out why he had brought her here. His voice cracked when he started to speak.

'There was only ever you, Elizabeth,' he said, coming up behind her. 'I never wanted anyone else but you. Every time I tried to put you out of my mind, you came back stronger than ever. No one even came close.'

She couldn't answer him. There was a heartbeat in her throat that no words could get past.

'I want you and the baby,' he said softly. 'I want you both so much.'

'You can't take on another man's child, John,' she said at last, dropping her head.

'Why? Why can't I? I've watched that bairn grow, I've seen it with you before it's been born, I've felt it moving inside you. Don't you think I've not come to love it as well? As much?'

'But you're not its dad and you never would be,' she said, wishing he was. Wishing this was her bairn's dad with all her heart.

'Your dad isn't always the one who started you off,' he said.

'Of course he is. How can you say that? You don't know . . .'

'I can, and I do know, because my dad isn't my real dad.'

Elizabeth turned to face him. 'Your dad isn't what?'

'I'm adopted. I never knew my real father.'

'You're making it up! You and him . . . for a start, you look so much alike!'

'I'm not making it up, Elizabeth. I know, everyone says we look alike, but he's still not my real father.'

He cleared his throat then he told her the two memories that had dominated his childhood. The first was his mam telling him to pick three toys to show to this smart-looking woman that was visiting. Then, when he'd rushed upstairs to pick out his best, he had his coat put on and buttoned up, and the woman took him away for a little ride with a suitcase in her car, but they didn't go back home. Instead he found himself in a bleak, cold house with lots of other kids, bewildered and crying and not knowing what he'd done wrong or where he was, and desperate to get home to his mam. He'd only have been about three.

The second was just before he was five and a nice lady and big strapping man took him for a walk around the garden and said that they were looking for a little boy to come home with them that they could be a mam and dad to. He had to be a really special little boy though because they were really choosy, but they had thought he was very special and would he like to come to their house with them and be their son.

He had said he couldn't because he was waiting for his real mam to come for him but she must have got lost. He sat at the window every night, still waiting for her, watching for her . . . and the lady's eyes had filled up with tears and she had given him a big cuddle and it felt lovely because he hadn't been cuddled before. She smelled sweet, like flowers, and she said he could come and try them out as a mam and dad if he liked. They had a big sloppy dog and a cat and a budgie called Whistle that sat on your finger and they'd got a swing in their garden.

Then the man had dropped to his haunches and said that if he were his lad they could go fishing together and his new mam would make them a picnic up and they could go and kick a football in the park and would he like that? He had always wanted his own swing because the big lads never let him play on the one in the Home and he would love a budgie that sat on your finger. The man had a kind smiling face and he really wanted to kick a football about with a dad and someone to cuddle him like the lady had just done, and so John had gone with them and he recovered most of the faith in grown-ups that he'd lost too early on. But not all of it, because there was a scar in his heart that ran deep and would never quite heal, and he saw the same scar in Elizabeth. She too knew what it was like to have been so little and lost in the dark woods that ran along-side the happy sunlit path of other people's childhoods.

'Oh John, love,' said Elizabeth, watching the tears

run down the big man's face as he let her into that terrified little-boy place that lived on inside him where a part of him would always be sitting at a window waiting for his mam. He would never try and trace her though, there was no point. He could not face a woman who had put a child through that.

'I didn't tell you about it because there was no reason to, till now, and I don't like to think back to how it was before them. Trevor and Margaret Silkstone are my real mam and dad as far as I'm concerned, and I couldn't have wished for more love from any person I came from. I couldn't have had better than them.'

She reached out tentatively to put a comforting hand on his arm, but he hijacked it en route and placed a tender kiss on its palm.

'I love you and this bairn so much; you'd want for nowt,' he said, sniffing back his tears.

Elizabeth's heart was pounding in her chest. 'John . . .'

'Please, Elizabeth, just give me a chance to show you. I'm begging you . . .'

She pulled her hand slowly away. She couldn't; there was stuff he didn't know. She ripped herself away from his space. Life was so bloody cruel. However much she wished she could, she just couldn't . . .

Damned stress incontinence, thought Helen, feeling very wet down below, although it was her own fault for drinking the equivalent of the Irish Sea in lemonade as she sat in the hot sunshine. Dismounting from the swing, she daintily picked her way back to the house like a ballet-dancing crab. She padded across the kitchen as fast as she could towards the downstairs loo, to find that she was actually leaving a trail across the kitchen floor. It was then she realized that this was not stress incontinence, after all.

Oh help! My waters are breaking!

Chapter 50

Elizabeth got to the top of the staircase, and then every brake in her body slammed on hard.

'What are you doing?' asked some deep-buried part of her that was tired of running away from all she most wanted to run *to*. She could feel his pain heavy in the air; it mingled with her own and she knew this must stop, one way or another. There could be no more loose ends, no more not-knowing.

But would he still want me if he knew? she thought. How is this fair on him?

'How fair is it if he doesn't know?' argued a clearer, stronger voice.

She owed him the truth but she was so frightened of seeing disgust for her in his eyes, she knew she would crumble to dust if he turned his back on her. But she did not want to, *could not, would not*, hurt this man any more. Whatever telling the truth of it all might do to her.

John stared out of the window at the peaceful scene of the countryside whilst the inside of him screamed with raw pain and confusion and wanted to close down and go to sleep for ever. *'What now?'* his whole being seemed to cry, because he didn't know where he would go from here or what he would do. He felt destroyed, numb, and not sure he could ever recover from losing her again. Not only her, because there had been the baby, too – a life he had watched grow within her and he had bonded with it as surely as if he was the bairn's own blood. Then he heard the echo of slow footsteps. He lifted his head and looked at her as if she was a phantom that his mind had tricked him into seeing.

'About the baby,' she said, struggling with the words. 'I want to tell you how it came about.'

'I don't need to know, I don't care about that, Elizabeth. It doesn't matter how—' He started to come forward but she held her hand up and stopped his passage.

'Please, John. I don't want to have any secrets from you . . . I need you to hear this now.'

She took the deepest breath her lungs would allow her to, then she told him.

Chapter 51

She had not wanted to go to the damned stupid party in the first place, but Dean had insisted it would be a right laugh. It was in a mate of a mate of a mate's huge shabby house, but there would be loads of beer and food and lots of people he knew were going. So he said.

'What would you do instead – sit in and be miserable and bring New Year in on your own with your cat?' he had scoffed. He had gone on and on so much that in the end she had said yes to shut him up. He told her he was just meeting the lads first in their local for one – one pint, he emphasized – so she had to get a taxi and meet him there.

When she got to the house, she found it was full of students and loud music, and some seedy older blokes in even louder shirts trying to cop off with the young scantily clad female gyrators. She was so cross at herself for agreeing to come when she could have been at home in the warmth and the quiet – and yes, bringing in New Year by herself with a cat. She had tried to ring Dean but she could hardly hear what he was saying because of the loud noise of the pub music in the background, although she got the feeling he had heard more than he was letting on. He would be on his way in five minutes, he said, and she was to stay there. She had come off the phone knowing he was lying and tried to ring a return taxi only to find there was a two-hour wait. She booked one anyway, then went inside and got a drink from a sticky table, and out of anger drank it too fast, and it went straight to her head because she hadn't had any tea.

She had another as well before the tall, fair-haired bloke came up and started talking to her. He had seemed nice, friendly – mature, despite being so young, and as much out of sorts as she was. He said he was waiting for a friend who hadn't turned up yet, and he was going to give it another half an hour and then he was leaving.

'You'll be lucky,' she said. 'There's a two-hour wait for taxis. Have you far to go?'

'Miles,' he said, and groaned and went to get himself a consolatory lager. Then he came back to her and she found it was better talking to him than standing there fuming by herself, plus it would help the time pass more quickly. He was doing History at some university down south, he said, although she could hardly hear him for the music. Then he laughed that she was far too lovely to be waiting around for a man and Elizabeth had pretended to be flattered. He was attractive, she remembered thinking, but it was very dark and she didn't get a proper look at his face.

When she went up to the loo, he was waiting outside for her when she emerged. He had found a quieter place where they could sit and talk if she wanted, he said; kill the time until her taxi came, away from all that banging noise and booze and drugs. He didn't do drugs, he said, they were for idiots. He led her to a little bedroom at the end of the upstairs corridor and jammed a chair up against the door so they wouldn't be disturbed by anyone. It was nice just to sit down and kick off those stupid high heels she had put on, because her feet were killing her. Plus she had felt like someone's granny in a dress amongst all those skimpy bra-tops and mini-skirts. He had brought her a drink up, although he had been a bit heavy-handed on the vodka, she noted.

They had just been talking, then it progressed seamlessly to flirting, then he had leaned over and kissed her. He'd been very gentle, and stupidly she had let him, not wanting to insult him by shoving him off. Then he eased her back on the bed and began touching her, and by then he had taken her polite small resistance as a green light. It was then she started to try and push him off. It wasn't right, plus this student was less than half her age, for God's sake. He was aroused though, and knew she wasn't serious when she starting saying no because she wasn't exactly beating him off with a stick. His drink-filled thought processes reasoned that she probably felt guilty for complying and so preferred to be over-powered a little. Some older women said 'no' when they meant 'yes' — to override their embarrassment at being with a young fit bloke.

He was strong and pinned her down with his long limbs and she couldn't move, could hardly breathe, and she yelped when he unzipped himself and entered her. He was proudly well-endowed and rock hard, and he knew that was every woman's fantasy and pushed harder and harder, pounding into her, encouraged by her cries. Then he caught sight of her frightened face by the half-light of the streetlamp shining through the curtains and he knew immediately that he had got it terribly wrong. He threw himself backwards away from her.

'*I'm sorry,*' *he said, sobering up in a flash.* '*God, I'm sorry. I thought you wanted it.*'

'*Well, I didn't,*' *said Elizabeth. She hurt, inside and out.*

He was pacing up and down, his voice shaking as much as his body, and he started sobbing.

'*Please don't get the police. I truly didn't mean to hurt you . . . I really thought you wanted me. I'm clean – I don't have any diseases or anything . . . Oh God, I'm so sorry.*'

He tried to help her adjust her clothing but she thrashed out at him, hands clawed, nails bared like a feral cat, and he backed off to show her that he meant her no harm.

'*Please, I . . . I'm sorry . . . I got it so wrong. I'm not a . . .*' *The unsaid word frightened him and he tore the chair away from the door and ran from it in a blind panic.*

She sat there until her mobile rang. It was Dean telling her that he'd be there in half an hour, although the jolly backdrop told her it was a lie. He had been caught up in a round, he explained. She switched him off mid-flow, wiped her face and straightened her clothes. Then she stiffened her back, went down the stairs, out of the front door and, with her shoes in her hand, Elizabeth walked the three miles home.

Chapter 52

John stared at her unblinkingly and she didn't know what that look was in his eyes – disgust . . . pity? She couldn't tell, for the part of her brain that deciphered body language had closed off in a panic to protect her.

'You should have gone to the police,' he said quietly, his voice croaky.

'I did go the next day,' she said, 'but what could I say? I got drunk with a stranger and then went into a bedroom with him of my own free will? Me at thirty-eight and him at nineteen or whatever?'

She had walked into the police station and waited in the queue. There were two receptionists there, a nice friendly one dealing with an old lady, and a snotty one who had Receptionist's Syndrome, which gave some people behind a front desk the illusion that they ruled the world and that everyone else was scum under their feet. Maybe if the other receptionist had been free, things might have been different, but she got the pinched-face one who looked at Elizabeth in a way that suggested if she was here to report something that had happened to her, she probably had only herself to blame for it.

'Can I help you?' she said.

She had hard, unpitying eyes, and just as Elizabeth's mouth opened, she saw Sergeant Wayne Sheffield come out of an office behind the glass partition looking for something. He'd thickened out and lost half his hair, but his lips were still as thin, his eyes small, piggy and set closer together than had always seemed right. She stumbled backwards before he caught sight of her and crashed out of the door into the street.

The receptionist sighed disparagingly and called, 'Next!'

Outside, Elizabeth calmed herself and thought about going back in and trying again. Then she pictured Wayne Sheffield being the one to rake over her details, whilst knowing her history, remembering their sordid encounter all those years ago; the words 'leopards' and 'spots' playing in his brain, because even though her wild days were long behind her, she would always be that same slag to him. Then if her case did stumble to court, all those past mistakes she had made would lift themselves out of their shallow graves and present themselves to the prosecuting counsel to colour exactly what sort of person she was, to stop a young man's life from being ruined. She couldn't ever let her past come back. She didn't want her baby tainted by it.

'I haven't said anything because I didn't want anyone to know how the baby was made. I didn't want him growing up and finding out that's how his little life started off,' she said. 'And what I am.'

'And you think I wouldn't love the baby because of that?' said John, his face a mask of hurt and anger.

'I'm not sure even *I* can love it!' cried Elizabeth,

dropping her head in shame. Her greatest fear was out and it hung in the air like poisonous gas.

A distressed and desperate whimper escaped her and she reached out for John. He came forward and pressed her into his chest, closed his great long arms around her and sighed from his core at the feel of her against him. Not love her baby? he thought, and smiled with great tenderness. She didn't know herself at all and that was such a shame, because she was such a beautiful person to know. Crazy, damaged, mixed-up kid that she was, but he had learned the hard way that his heart was made only for her.

'Elizabeth Collier, if only you could see what I see now. Don't tell me you can't love your bairn, and don't tell me I can't.'

She nestled into him, glorying in the wonderful sensations of his touch and his smell. Together, the essences of John Silkstone swirled inside her, easily knocking down those strongholds of resistance that had stood against him for too long. She wanted to let go of everything but him, she wanted to stay against his heartbeat for ever. She lifted her face to him, her feelings for him clear in her great, long-lashed grey eyes. He did not expect to hear the actual words, but she said them aloud – not to herself, not in a letter, but at last aloud to him.

'I love you, John Silkstone.'

And he said back, 'I love you, Elizabeth Collier, always have and always will.'

His head lowered by minute degrees, scared that this was some dreadful illusion that would evaporate when his lips touched hers. And when they finally made contact, his kiss was delicate and sweet, although he struggled against himself not to crush her to bits in his arms. He held her face gently in his great big builder's hands and looked at those dear, darling features and smiled. However long it took to let him love her properly he would wait. She was finally his and he would never lose her again.

Elizabeth ignored her mobile the first four times, but when it rang the fifth time it seemed louder, more insistent and demanded she take notice of it. Elizabeth took it out of her bag and saw that it was Helen phoning.

'John, I'm sorry, let me answer this – it's Hels,' she said.

'Answer it then,' said John. She could answer a million phone calls now that he had heard the words he'd wanted to hear from her for nearly fifteen years.

'Elizabeth, please come to the hospital, I'm in labour!'

'But you're too early!'

'Try telling my *dauuuuuuoooouwwwwwwwwwwwwwwwwwwww . . . ghter* that. *Aaarrrgggggghhhhhhhhhhhhhhhhhh.*'

'Barnsley General? Or are you in that posh private one in Wakey?'

'No time . . . I'm in Barnsley General . . . I've rung Janey. Please hurry, I need you.'

'I'm on my way!'

Chapter 53

Janey was already at the hospital when they arrived.

'Where've you been? I've been calling you for months,' she said, and then she noticed John behind. The couple looked like they'd been dragged through an emotional hedge backwards. 'Oh aye? And what the chuff is going on with you two, pray?'

'Tell you later,' said Elizabeth, waving goodbye to John, who waved back and blew a kiss at her.

'Just a friend, my eye!'

'Not any more.'

'Boy, I can't wait to hear this one!'

'Later. Right, where do we go?'

They followed a series of directions to find Helen in a very big designer T-shirt with a teddy bear motif, sitting up in a bed with the gas and air mask clamped over her mouth.

'What happened?' said Elizabeth, giving her a tentative hug.

'My waters broke. Then these pains came from nowhere.'

'If you'd been in Asda when your waters broke you'd have got all your shopping free,' said Janey.

'Wheel me back there then,' said Helen. 'I'll try and hang on whilst you fill up a trolley with alcohol.'

'And chocolates – let's not forget those!' said Janey. 'Oh, and some Marmite. I've run out.'

'And my olives.'

'Oh hell!'

'Where's your TENS machine?' asked Elizabeth, snapping off the humour.

'There,' said Helen, pointing to some tangled wires on the floor in the corner, where she had flung it. 'Useless thing!' Then she bent over double.

'So, what's it feel like to be in labour then?' asked Elizabeth, when Helen had straightened out again.

'Think of a wave of period pain then fourteen-milliontiply it . . . NNNNNNNYYYYYRRRRHH-HHHHHHHHHHHHHHHHHHH!'

'Jesus Christ, can't you get something stronger if it's that bad?' said Elizabeth, suddenly worried.

'It *is* that bad. Do you think I'm putting this on?'

'Aye, I do, you bloody drama queen!'

'Just you wait until it's your turn, Janey Hobson! I'm waiting for the midwife; she's just popped next door with the anaesthetist and another lady.'

Elizabeth bobbed her head out of the door in the hope of hurrying her up, only to find Marc with a 'c' being wheeled in a chair down the corridor by a porter. He appeared to be holding his eye. She came back in, trying not to giggle.

'Oy, guess what? I think the woman next door might be Pam and my guess is she's just splattered Marc with a "c" with an "r" and an "h"!'

'Eh?'

'Right hook.'

Helen half-laughed, half-cried. 'Bloody, sodding hell,' she then said, creasing over again.

'Do you know, I think that's the most you've sworn ever,' said Janey. 'Just because you've got knockers now doesn't mean you have to turn into Elizabeth.'

'Can we get you anything?' said Elizabeth, more sympathetically.

'Yes, unpregnant! I thought contractions were suppo-sed to build up gradually.'

'Not always,' said the midwife, suddenly appearing at the door. 'You must be one of the lucky ones. I'm Sandra, now let's have another look at you, lovey.'

Without further prompting, Helen put her ankles together and dropped open her knees for the midwife. At this stage, she would have opened them to anyone who looked remotely like they worked in a hospital, as all thoughts of holding onto her dignity had gone with the first contraction. She did not care if she poohed over the entire floor in the process either. She just wanted this baby out.

'Over five centimetres dilated,' said Sandra. 'You're doing very well.'

'Can I have something else for the pain, please?' said Helen like a breathless desperate small child, hoping St Mandy was not around to hear and damn her to hell for all eternity.

'The anaesthetist is quite busy at the moment with a queue of ladies requesting epidurals. How about some pethidine to tide you over?'

'Oh yes, please!'

'Would you like a half shot to start off with?'

'No, a nice big fat one!' said Helen, as pleased as if she had just been offered a giant walnut whip. 'Please, please make it now!'

Elizabeth sank to the chair; she was feeling a bit shaky through hunger.

'Why don't you two go and get a cup of coffee and a sandwich whilst I get on with her obs and giving her some medication,' said the midwife. 'It might be the last chance you get.'

She's as calm as a lake of milk, thought Elizabeth. She does this day in, day out. Sandra managed to combine an air of authority with gentleness and consideration, not at all like Mandy would have been; she would probably have spontaneously combusted when Helen asked for some drugs.

'Come on,' said Janey, battleaxe-style, and linked her short friend's arm. 'Be seeing you, we're off for a bacon butty,' she threw back at Helen.

'I hate *youuuuuuuuuuuuuooooowww*,' said Helen. '*Owww-owwowwwwvowww!*'

'God, it's Kate Bush,' said Janey. 'Do "Wuthering Heights" next, that's my favourite.'

'Don't make me laugh, it *hurtsssssssssssss!*'

It was too surreal for words, with Helen in agony and them laughing and joking. It wasn't at all as Elizabeth had expected it to be. Where was the panic and fear? Where was the feeling that the Grim Reaper was lurking at their shoulders? Janey led the way down the corridor towards the hospital coffee-shop.

'Think she'll be okay if we leave her?' said Elizabeth, feeling horribly guilty.

'Could be a long tiring night for all of us,' said Janey. 'It's like the midwife said, it won't do us any harm to have something before the best of the fun starts. I'd just sat down to have my tea myself. I only managed a mouthful of carrot when the phone went, then I rang you about twelve million times just to get fobbed off with your voicemail because you were with Bob the Builder,' she added pointedly. 'So are you going to tell me why you were too busy to answer?'

'John's built me a house,' said Elizabeth, when they sat down at the table with two crispy bacon sandwiches and a big pot of mixed berry tea.

'A house?'

'A house.'

'What?'

'He took me to see a house he'd built. It was just like one I drew when we were mucking about years ago.'

'Never!'

'He wants me and he wants to be the bairn's dad.'

'And you of course said, "No, John," and ran off.'

'Yes.'

'I could clout you, you stupid, stupid—'

'Then I turned back and said, "Yes".'

A chorus of angels appeared from somewhere behind Janey and started singing 'Hallelujah' in her ear-hole.

'Well, thank the Lord!' said Janey with the biggest sigh of relief she had ever mustered. 'Only fifteen years late as well. At least that proves you do have a brain, I was beginning to wonder.'

'Maybe it wouldn't have worked before; maybe this is our time now.'

'That is Mills & Boon bollocks language, Elizabeth, but I forgive you in your loved-up circumstances,' said Janey, tipping a congratulatory mug of tea in her friend's direction, then she put the mug down, almost leaped over the table and gave Elizabeth a hug that nearly squeezed her baby out there and then.

When Janey nipped off to the loo, Elizabeth returned John's text enquiring how things were going. He had gone over to Rhymer Street to feed Cleef. Big John Silkstone. *Her John Silkstone.* She felt warm and runny inside to think of him that way. She didn't know what was so special about her for him, but she was not going to turn his love away again. Not ever.

When they got back to Helen, she was standing up, rotating an imaginary hula-hoop around on her hips and Walkman singing to Beautiful South. She looked happily spaced.

'She's taken to the pethidine very well,' said Sandra with a proud smile.

'She's off her face!' said Elizabeth.

'*Don't marry her, have me . . . Salvete*, girls, you're back!' hailed Helen, Roman-style. She hadn't looked as slaughtered as this since Whitby, 1983, after the Black Russians had reacted with her hay-fever tablets. She was having a contraction but it felt like it was happening to someone else a few miles away – a twin sister in Australia, perhaps. She was actually having her baby now, a beautiful baby girl. She was going to be cuddling her soon. *Ooooh, that quite hurt.* She was going to call her Daisy Buttercup Bluebell Dahlia Tulip Marigold Dandelion. Then she was going to marry Teddy Sanderson. *When were you supposed to do that breathing thing?*

Aaaaaaaaaaaahhhhhhhhhhhhhhhhh!

'Come on, Shirley Bassey,' said the midwife after a while and dragged her over to the bed. Then she checked her internally again.

'You're dilating nice and quick,' said the midwife, 'but as you are a bit early, I'll get the registrar to come down when you're a little nearer.'

'How are you feeling now?' said Elizabeth. 'Scared?'

'Yes,' said Helen, smiling widely. 'This is it, girls.'

She didn't look scared; she looked sweaty, damp, tired and beautiful but she didn't look scared, thought Elizabeth.

'How's the pethidine doing?' said Janey.

'Nice to know you're using me as a guinea pig!' said Helen, thinking, Janey has a purple face. 'Oh my, it's strong stuff all right.'

'Elizabeth's got it together with John at last,' said Janey.

'Hell, it is strong stuff,' slurred Helen.

'No – straight up!' said Janey.

'I didn't dream that last bit?' Helen asked.

'What, about me and John?' said Elizabeth. 'No, you're not dreaming'

'Thank God for that!' said Helen. 'We thought you were going to be a complete idiot all your life.'

'Cheers!'

They sat for a while as Helen got on with puffing and breathing.

'Who'd have thought when we sat on that Chalk Man's bits what we were starting off?' said Janey eventually.

'Sorry, guys,' said Helen, just before another contraction crested.

'Yes, I hope that one bloody hurt,' said Janey. 'It's all *your* fault. In fact, we should sue you. Know a good solicitor?'

They all laughed, then when the next contraction came, things turned a bit serious. They all fell calm and quiet, holding their friend's hands, dabbing her forehead with the cloth, bringing the cup of water to her lips to let her have a sip before she dried into sand. She could murder a cup of tea, she said, and a square of the fruit and nut that was in her maternity bag. When she got home, she would write to the Pope and ask for Carol to be canonized for suggesting that alone.

'I think the peth's wearing off because my contractions are like tidal waves, if you want an update,' said Helen after a while, although she did not know how long that while was because time seemed all distorted. She was starting to reconcile the pain with her own body now. It was not where she thought it would be situated and was actually concentrated mainly in her back. She just felt as if she wanted to go to the loo and do a big pooh.

Sandra gave her another examination.

'She's ready,' she said. 'Right, Helen, the registrar is on his way but everything's looking fine so no need to worry. I'll want you to start pushing in a minute.'

'More pethidine, please,' said Helen, who was starting to look very weary.

'Not now, darling,' said Sandra. 'Come on, girls, hold her hands and watch out for those nails sticking in.'

'Oy, you flaming eagle!' said Janey, as Helen drew blood on a contraction.

Elizabeth smiled. This was scary but lovely too. This was what women all over the world did and every one of them with a different story to tell. She wasn't expecting her turn to be a picnic but she suddenly knew without a shadow of a doubt that she was *not* going to die in childbirth but would be around to dine out with the other two for years on their birth stories, scoffing cream cakes and drinking big pots of tea. This was life in all its bloody, base, wonderful crudity, and out of all this blood and guts and pain-induced profanities would come a fresh, new, precious, beautiful, pure baby. A new start.

'Baaaaaaaaaaaaaaaaalllllllllllllllllllllsssssssssssssss!'

'I never thought anyone could swear more than you,' said Janey to Elizabeth, who stuck up a digital V at her.

The registrar came in – a tall, slim black man in a beautiful pink shirt. Janey's pupils dilated with pleasure.

'Wish he was fiddling about with me,' she whispered to the others.

'Shut up, you sex-mad tart!' said Elizabeth.

'Can I push now?' Helen begged.

'Yes, you can push, sweetheart,' said the midwife.

Helen let her body do what it wanted to – push down. She felt like she was going to split in two.

'*Nnnnnnnnnyyyyyyayaaarrrrrrrgggghhhhhhhhhhhhhhh-hhhh!!!!!!*'

'She's crowning,' said Sandra to the registrar.

'Good girl,' said the registrar. 'Another push, Helen.'

Helen let go of her friends' hands and gripped the bedhead behind her instead. Elizabeth moved down to watch the birth; Janey followed her lead. The baby's head was coming out and it had lots of fair hair, darkened and plastered to its head with the greasy vernix. They could see her creased up little Winston Churchill face.

'Shoulders now, sweetheart, this is the hardest bit. Push now!'

Helen pushed weakly; it was all she had left.

'I can't,' she said with a cry.

'Yes, you can,' said Elizabeth.

'I can't,' said Helen, starting to sob.

'Well, if you can't be bothered, I don't see why I should,' said Sandra, winking conspiratorially at Elizabeth.

'Come on, you lazy cow,' said Janey, joining in on the game, trying to whip up some adrenaline in her friend to get the baby out.

'AAAARRGGGGGHHHHH!' said Helen, pushing down as hard as she could just to show them all, but it wasn't enough by a long way.

'Again!' said Janey.

'Come on, my darling girl, push!'
Dad?

She knew it was the last of the pethidine fooling her, but there he was, large as life, in his grey suit, his little half-moon specs, his snow-white handkerchief poking out of his top pocket and his yellow tie with the Windsor knot, and he was smiling down at her. She could even smell his cologne, then she blinked and he had gone.

'NNNNNNNNNNNNNNNNNNNrrrrrhhhhhhhhh!!!!'
'That's it, that's it, she's here, oh bloody hell, she's out, Helen!'

Elizabeth watched as a baby slithered out into the midwife's hands, yowling a thin, angry protest. Still with the cord attached, Sandra handed her straight to Helen's outstretched arms and the new mum broke out into a huge joyful sob and said, 'It's my baby – look at my daughter. Hello there, little one. I'm your mummy and this is your Auntie Janey and your Auntie Elizabeth . . .' Helen lifted her head towards heaven and mouthed to her father there, *'Look at her, Dad, look at your beautiful granddaughter.'*

'You okay?' asked Elizabeth, thinking she certainly looked okay, laughing like a maniac, with a smile that was splitting her exhausted, perspiring face in two.

'Oh, it's true what Teddy said – it's worth it, it's worth everything. Look at her, look at my baby . . .'

Janey looked and so did Elizabeth, who saw the bloody, ugly, snotty, scrunched-up, gorgeous, wonderful little thing and she thought, If I feel this strongly about my friend's baby, what will I feel about my own?

Helen was crying, Janey was crying and then Elizabeth's own tears started to spill down her cheeks as if they were coming from a never-ending well within. It felt as if a Berlin Wall had crashed down somewhere in the last closed bastion of her heart and she knew – *knew* – that even this beautiful, perfect moment would drop into shadow when they put her own baby in her arms.

She rubbed her tummy and said quietly to the child within, *'I love you.'*

Epilogue

Alexandra Penelope Elizabeth Jane Luxmore was born on 23 August, weighing five pounds two ounces. Her mother did not pooh during delivery. She has no contact with her father although a Mr Edward Sanderson visits with increasing regularity, always with flowers and toys. He and her mother talk a lot by the old swing in the garden.

Alexandra lives at a lovely old Rectory with her mother and granny, who has gone quite loopy over her; in fact, she even knitted her a cardigan – in cashmere.

Her mother has started reading lots of books on the Law and takes them into her late grandfather's study to work on. Her interest in photography has been well and truly resurrected. And she has finally thrown all her Wonderbras away.

Rumour has it that Teddy Sanderson has instructed decorators to paint one of his seven bedrooms ballet-slipper pink with white bunnies.

Robert George Cyril Hobson was born on 30 September, weighing (according to his father's tearful ecstatic phone calls to their friends and relatives) nine stone fourteen pounds. It was a one-hour, forty-five-minute delivery, and gas and air sufficed.

Young Robert has his mum's red hair and his dad's laughing, sparkling eyes. His mum returned to work and his dad is a fulltime house joiner and childminder – when he can get near his son for the grandparents. It is an arrangement that suits everyone perfectly.

His mum stayed at a 38DD.

His parents are buying a chandelier.

Ellis John Silkstone was a breech baby born on 2 October by planned Caesarean section, which went without a hitch. He was seven pounds fourteen ounces with a head full of dark wild hair, just like his dad's, and long, long eyelashes like his mum's, and when he was first put into their arms, their hearts nearly burst with joy.

His mum is a part-time PA for the infamous DIY and supermarket giant Terry Lennox, who is also his godfather. His dad is famous for building lovely big houses for families to be happy in. The little lad can hear Oxworth stream from his nursery window, and sometimes he is sure there is a big dog in the room, flumping down at the side of his cot in the middle of the night. He likes the feeling of having him around. He also has a cat called Cleef who occasionally moves.

His mam and dad love him, the cat and each other to bits.

They are getting married next May.

Acknowledgements

Thanks to the friends who made this story possible, each in their own special way.

To Lucie Whitehouse, who opened the door and let me in from the cold and Suzanne Baboneau, my Fairy Godmother, need I say more? To Nigel Smith, who ripped up my story and made me put it back together again properly. To Tara Wigley, who is a delight to work with and has done so much to get me here. To Joan Deitch, for making me look like I know what I'm doing. To 'my novelist friend' Sue Welfare, for our invaluable no-holds-barred natters. To Chris Douglas-Morris, Tony Spooner and David Greaves who all took a chance on me and changed my life. To Mrs Gunsen, who forced me to sit next to Cath Marklew in Latin and gave me a friend and a sister. To Rachel Hobson, for the turkey sandwiches in her mam's kitchen 'sobre la mesa'. To Maggie 'Penelope' Irwin, for always being there. To Caroline Durham, for keeping me on the right side of sanity. To Paul Sear, Alec Sillifant, Ged and Kaely Backland, for keeping me on the right side of insanity. To Sara Atkinson, for her bottomless heart.

To Karen Towers, for her warmth. To my S.U.N. sisters – Helen Clapham, Pam Oliver and Karen Baker – for all our dramas. To Sue Mahomet, for her straight talking and our secret-sharing. To Debra Mitchell, who knows me so well and is *still* my friend!

Read on for an extract from Milly Johnson's

The Perfectly Imperfect Woman

Chapter 1

'CHEESECAKE? CHEESE. CAKE?'

If the situation hadn't been so dire, Marnie might have laughed at her mother coming across like an uppity Peter Kay.

'Yes, Mum, cheesecake.'

'You are not telling me that you're leaving your job to ...' Judith Salt couldn't finish off the sentence because the words were too ludicrous. Her mouth gave an involuntary spasm as if she had just bitten down on a pastry filled with battery acid.

Marnie might as well have said 'I'm going to be a stripper' or 'I'm working in a brothel' instead of 'I'm making cheesecakes for a living', though illicitly peddling sugar and fats was right up there with those sinful occupations, in the world according to Judith Salt.

Cheesecake was where it all started for Marnie really. Nearly twenty-two years ago, when she had first encountered the word.

Puddings and desserts were not allowed in Salty Towers, as Marnie came to think of both her childhood residences. At least not proper desserts: eclairs, cake with fudgy layers, a knickerbocker glory with a tower of whipped cream. Dessert was a banana, a baked apple, yogurt (low fat) and peaches that set her off gagging when her teeth made contact with their suede-like skins. Marnie's diet at home was micro-managed and that included school packed lunches: no Penguins or Mr Kipling cakes for her in her Tupperware box. She wasn't allowed to go to the birthday events of other children where there might be – drum roll – party food. If Marnie had been asked to give one word which summed up her childhood, she would have replied 'hungry'. Hungry for food, hungry for attention, hungry for love.

Then, in the summer of 1994 old Mrs McMaid with the pronounced limp and the guttural Scottish accent moved in next door and Judith Salt thought it might be a nice gesture if ten-year-old Marnie offered to run errands for her in the six-week holidays. Her eight-year-old younger sister Gabrielle didn't have the spare time, what with her singing, ballet, piano, flute, elocution and Spanish lessons. She had shown a natural propensity in all of these things, so Judith told anyone who cared to listen, therefore they were to be encouraged. Marnie had shown no such talents, which is why she escaped all the extra-curricular activities. She didn't mind; she'd seen Gabrielle dance in a show and decided she had all the lightness of a Yorkshire pudding made with cement and was grounded for a week by her mother for tittering in the performance. And Sarah Brightman certainly had nothing to worry about. So Marnie was sent off to do her Christian duty and be of service to Mrs McMaid, with a firm dictate that she was not to be given any food whilst she was there as she was on a strict diet for health reasons.

It was torture for young Marnie because Mrs McMaid made jam, and lots of it. And she told Marnie how wonderful it tasted slathered on her fresh-from-the-oven white bread and warm scones, with curls of creamy butter that she kept in a big jug of iced water in her fridge. And she let Marnie whisk up bowls of cake mix, which smelled better than the baked end product, and line tins with circles of pastry for fruit tarts. Marnie's stomach growled more that summer than it had in all her previous years put together.

'Och, it's a shame I canna give you any food, hen. What's the matter wi' you?' Mrs McMaid asked her one day, absently handing her a jam spoon to lick before hurriedly snatching it back.

'Nothing,' replied Marnie with a sigh loaded with disappointment. 'Mum just doesn't want me to get any fatter.'

'But you're no' fat,' Mrs McMaid exclaimed, and her grey shaggy eyebrows creased in consternation. 'In fact your mother and your sister could dae with fattening up a wee bit. It's nae good fir you walking roon wi' all your bones on show.'

And she passed the spoon back to Marnie whose hand almost shook with a seismic wave of joy as she reached out to take it and lift it to her lips. Her tongue snaked out in slow motion towards the sugary raspberry jam and when it made contact, her taste buds began to sing soprano. She closed her eyes and savoured the rush of sweetness and then she swallowed with a satisfying gulp.

Then the guilt washed over her like a tsunami.

Her mum would know. An all-seeing camera in the sky would report her sin back and she began to sob and Mrs McMaid enfolded her in a floral-scented cuddle and said over and over again, 'It's no' right. It's no' right at all.'

Then she gave her another spoonful to help her feel better.

Contrary to her belief, her mother could not smell the licks of raspberry preserve on her and the relief that she was not indelibly permeated with it was palpable. That night she dreamt of swimming in a huge lake of jam, like an enormous ball pool filled with red berries instead of plastic spheres. She couldn't wait to run around to Mrs McMaid's the next morning in her cleaning clothes. She decided she was going to risk a mouthful of cake mix next.

But that day, instead of a sponge or scones or biscuits, she found that Mrs McMaid was making a cheesecake. The disappointment fell on Marnie like a hod full of bricks carried by a drunken builder.

'Cheese cake?' Marnie wrinkled up her nose. She envisaged a pile of melted smelly goo in the middle of a sponge and was a little bit sick in her mouth. 'That sounds disgusting.'

'Just you wait and see,' laughed Mrs McMaid, unwrapping a packet of Digestives. She put them in a plastic bag and gave them to Marnie to crush carefully into crumbs with the rolling pin whilst she melted a block of butter in a pan. Then she combined both ingredients until the crumbs were all soaked, then she pressed them flat in the bottom of a round tin with her potato masher before putting it in the fridge.

'That's the base. Now comes the topping,' said Mrs McMaid, taking a tub out of the fridge. 'This is crrream cheese. Mascarrrpone.' It had a wonderful exotic name, especially with all those rich, rolling, Scottish 'r's, far nicer than Edam, thought young Marnie. She beat at the strange white stuff with her wooden spoon, then whipped up some double cream until it stood in soft peaks when the mixer blades were lifted out. She put them both in her blue and white stripey bowl, and added some unholy white sugar which she stored in a jar with odd dried-up bendy brown sticks.

'That's vanilla,' said Mrs McMaid and held up the sugar jar for Marnie to sniff. The little girl felt her nasal receptors sigh with delight. 'All the way frae Madagascarrr'. It sounded somewhere dangerous and dark where spice wars might occur.

'And then there's this,' said the old lady, adding a pinch of something into the mix from an old square tin she brought down from her shelf. 'Ma secret ingrrredient, passed doon frae ma motherrr 'n' her motherrr's motherrr,' she added in a low voice full of drama. Then she whispered what that secret ingredient was and told Marnie never to tell anyone else. A mere nip of it would make her cheesecakes different to anyone else's, promised Mrs McMaid.

Then, with her large spatula, Mrs McMaid plopped the creamy mix onto the cooled crumbs and put it into the fridge for an hour before removing it from the tin and pouring over the raspberries and strawberries and bilberries that she had softened in a pan with a large spoonful of the vanilla sugar. Marnie was mesmerised as she watched the shiny glaze walk across the top and drizzle down the sides onto the plate. Oh my, the cheesecake looked wonderful, the best of all the cakes they had made in the summer.

They cleared up the kitchen, did a bit of dusting and then Mrs McMaid said:

'If you and I were to test oot the cheesecake, would you tell yer mammy?'

Marnie swore on the big bible that Mrs McMaid kept on her sideboard that she wouldn't. So, they set up two deckchairs in the corner of the garden where the pale pink roses smelt of honey, then Mrs McMaid poured out two glasses of her homemade lemonade and passed Marnie a funny fork where the left outer prong was thicker than the others, and a whole equilateral triangle of the very berry cheesecake served up on one of Mrs McMaid's lovely plates with bluebells painted on it.

Nothing could have tasted better. Nothing in the whole wide world was finer than Marnie's first mouthful of that cheesecake. As they sat in the sun Mrs McMaid recounted all the flavours of them that she'd made in her time – and long before the fad came over from America, she said. Some with rum and raisins, others with chopped-up Mars bars in them, lemon and lime ones, salted toffee ones ... And the bases – ginger nuts, crumbled coconut macaroons, minty chocolate biscuits ... so many variations. Marnie wanted to make them all with Mrs McMaid. And the old lady laughed and said that they would – and more.

Mrs McMaid made cakes for fun and for profit. She made them to give to poor old souls who went to the same church as she did and needed a pick-me-up. And she made them for the woman from the big teashop in Ossett who pretended to her customers that she'd baked them herself.

'But that's lying and cheating,' said Marnie, one day when the tea-shop woman with the fat legs and high heels had collected her load.

Mrs McMaid jiggled her old battered purse.

'It is sort of, but I don't mind,' she replied. 'I might as well sell a few because I could never eat all the cakes I love to make.'

'I could,' said Marnie and Mrs McMaid laughed and then asked what they should do that day. Marnie could choose. Anything she liked.

'A rum and raisin cheesecake,' said Marnie. It sounded naughty, illegal and exotic.

'Rum and raisin it is,' agreed Mrs McMaid, who produced from her pantry a jar of raisins which had been soaked in rum and were fat and sticky and smelt wickedly intoxicating.

That late August afternoon, they sat in the garden with a pitcher of Mrs McMaid's blood-orangeade and a slice of rum and raisin cheesecake. It was Saturday and Marnie would be back on school on Monday.

'But I can still come after tea and at weekends and half-term is only six weeks away,' said Marnie, wishing she never had to go back to school again but could stay here with Mrs McMaid making cakes – even if they were for Mrs Fatty-legs.

'Of course you can,' said Mrs McMaid. 'You're always welcome in ma wee hoos.' And Mrs McMaid suddenly put down her plate, lifted up Marnie's face with her small, thin hand and smiled at her.

'If I'd have hed a daughter, I'd've wanted her to be just like you, Miss Marnie.'

And Marnie didn't say it aloud but she wished she had been her daughter and not Judith Salt's. She knew then that she loved Mrs McMaid with her whole heart and knew that Mrs McMaid loved her back as much. Marnie felt as if the sun wasn't only shining outside that day, but inside her too, as if she'd swallowed it.

The next afternoon, Marnie went around to Mrs McMaid's with a cooked chicken leg that her mother had sent, and found the old lady at the bottom of the stairs, cold and lifeless with her body all twisted up. Marnie rang for the ambulance and waited with her old friend until it came and a minute before it pulled up outside, she took

Mrs McMaid's secret ingredient tin from the shelf and put it into her bag. It hadn't felt wrong to do so then, and it never had since. Mrs McMaid would have wanted her to have it. She knew without any doubt she should be its rightful guardian now.

Marnie didn't make any more cheesecakes for years. Not until she had grown up and bought her own house and someone at work asked if she'd donate a cake for a fundraising event. She made a raspberry cheesecake with a sprinkle of the secret ingredient and she remembered that wonderful summer and dear Mrs McMaid and her kindness. Marnie's cheesecake went down a storm. No one had ever tasted anything like it. It had that indefinable . . . mmm, they said. And whatever it was, it was magic.

Chapter 2

Four months before the cheesecake conversation with her mother, Marnie walked into Café Caramba HQ in swanky central Leeds to find the new head of Merchandising in situ in his office. He was certainly a sight to warm up the frosty first working day of the year, her dilating pupils decided: tall, slim, dark hair with an unruly wave, brown-black eyes, sharp suit and a bleached-tooth smile worthy of a Colgate commercial.

If ever a man suited his name, it was Justin Fox, Marnie came to realise over the next fortnight. He was super good-looking with an arrogant swagger in his shoulders that said he was quite aware of his effect on the female workforce – and Glen from accounts. Marnie couldn't stop her heart giving an extra thump of pleasure whenever her eyes came to rest on him, but she had no intention of advertising the fact. It wasn't her fault, she kept telling herself, it was just her body reacting to 'the type' of man it had decided was a match for her. Jez, Robert, Harry, Aaron – all tall, dark, handsome snappy dressers. All tall, dark, handsome, complicated arseholes. And she didn't want another one walking into her heart and stamping all over it with his size twelve lawn aerator spiked shoes – thank you!

She suspected that she was pretty safe from Mr Fox though. She had never felt the warmth of his tobacco-brown eyes coming to rest on her back/bum/tights whenever she passed his desk or when they were in meetings together. No flirty banter bounced between them, no hunting for her attention occurred. She pigeon-holed him as the sort who would go for skinny, leggy, blondes, and she was none of those things. And that could only be good news.

Marnie knew that she functioned much better without a man in her life, corrupting her focus. Whenever she didn't have one of them trying to screw with her head, she could plough her energies into creating, forecasting, delivering. Work made her happier than any man ever had and she loved her job. She'd been at Café Caramba for six years now and worked her socks off for the company. When the last department head – Jerry 'Tosser' Thomson – left two years ago, there had been no one better to inherit the mantle than Marnie, even though HR had a bias towards men for the top jobs. No man wanted Beverage Marketing, though, because it was in a terrible state so the job slid easily to her. But Marnie Salt proved that she could turn a ship around in a force fourteen crosswind. Beverage Marketing was no longer a joke barge but a sleek cruise liner. There was even a waiting list in HR for people who wanted to join its crew and Marnie's reputation, as captain, couldn't have been higher. She was recognised throughout Café Caramba as naturally gifted at organising; an ideas person, an intuitive grafter with foresight who scoffed at comfort zones and a trailblazer for female employees of the company because there had been no other women top execs there – ever. Though Café Caramba, on paper, did most things that a progressive twenty-first-century workplace should be doing, the fat cats liked to see men in their boardroom, give or take the women in wipe-clean aprons pouring out coffees and distributing sandwiches. There wasn't so much a glass ceiling there as a two-foot-thick lead one covered with razor wire.

Three and a half weeks after Justin Fox joined the company, Marnie arrived at work expecting nothing but a normal day. She took the escalator and made a right through the first set of double doors, where the Product Development team sat under the leadership of 'Sweaty' Andrew Jubb, who could only achieve eye contact with women when their pupils were situated on their tits. High on the agenda was a morning executive huddle at one of the tall tables that the superboss Laurence Stewart-Smith had had implemented around the building. Standing meetings got to their point quicker and were over faster was his reasoning, and he was right. Laurence had transformed a number of failing companies into major success stories with streamlining initiatives like this. He was a business genius, adored by shareholders, oiled over by his minions who secretly thought though, beneath their fawning smiles, that as a human being, Laurence was an utter first-class knobhead. But Marnie knew that this morning, thanks to the fabulously shaped mug she'd sourced in the far east, Laurence was going to be a suitably impressed knobhead. They'd carry the company logo much better than the very ordinary ones they used at present. She had the sample in her bag and couldn't wait to present it to him – in front of an audience. She'd had too many of her best ideas pirated in the past, so now she made sure that they all bore a big fat Marnie Salt stamp on them.

As excited as she was about the morning get-together, still her thoughts drifted to Justin when she passed his office. She'd noticed that he didn't wear a wedding ring. But he had to have a partner, she reasoned. He was far too gorgeous to be on a shelf. And he was definitely straight because he flirted heavily with the canteen ladies who brought the refreshments into the boardroom meetings, sending them twittering off like a swarm of sparrows.

Straight on through Merchandising, she took another right into her department: Beverage Marketing, which had once been a merry band of six, but was now a small barrelful of four jolly apples with two rotting, maggoty additions. There was herself, of course; Arthur, a year away from retirement and solid as a rock; Bette, quietly efficient, who did her job and went home and Roisean, the office gopher who was bright and sweet and would end up running the company one day. Then there was Vicky, a twenty-nine-year-old busybody – and the thorn in her side, the stone in her shoe, the hair in her sandwich: Elena. A cocksure graduate eight years her junior who would have garrotted her own mother to get a rung further up the corporate ladder. She was head girl in the 'to get on in anything you have to be a cock' school of life. She'd presented well in her interview for the job and Marnie had since cursed herself for being sucked in by her superficial charm.

'Morning,' Marnie called to them all collectively and as usual received three cheerful echoes, one grumbly mumble and a blank. Within the minute, Roisean had put a coffee on her desk, just as she liked it.

'Thank you, love,' smiled Marnie.

Roisean coughed then gave her front teeth a discreet rub with her finger. It was code for *you've got lipstick on your incisors, boss*. Marnie swept her tongue over them and then test-smiled for Roisean who gave her the thumbs up. Little considerations like that made the day slide on a smoother track, Marnie always thought.

Elena and Vicky were gossiping. Again. And, if the look over the latter's shoulder was anything to go by, Marnie was the subject. Again. Marnie wasn't a hardline boss but Vicky pushed her buttons almost as much as Elena did. They faffed about every morning chatting and drinking coffee between signing in and starting work and now those faffs were getting too long to ignore.

Marnie, on the other hand, had logged on to her iMac and pulled up a report she needed for her meeting before she had even taken her coat off. She took a glug of coffee, pressed print and nothing happened. Her desk printer had been on the blink for a while and this time the usual bang on the side with the flat of her hand technique failed her.

'Elena. I've sent you a file. Could you run it off for me please?' Marnie asked her still-gossiping deputy. 'And Vicky, ring maintenance and get them up here as soon as, to look at my printer.' Her lips were curved upwards but she wasn't smiling as she added pointedly, 'If you have the time.'

'What's Roisean doing?' asked Elena, looking down her thin ski-slope of a nose at her boss.

'Yes they are urgent, thank you, Elena,' replied Marnie with a tone in her voice that sent the folie à deux begrudgingly back to their desks.

Marnie opened her diary and checked what was coming up next week. The yearly job reviews were pending. She would recommend that Roisean, Arthur and Bette be given pay rises and would have no qualms in telling Elena and Vicky that they needed to pull their socks up. Vicky was as slack as a prostitute's elastic. Elena was a much better worker when she wanted to be, but sullen and difficult to get on with. Neither of them felt part of the well-oiled machine the way Linda and Annie had, both happily on maternity leave. Burke and Hare, as Marnie had privately renamed them, were more like people who would nobble the cogs given half the chance. She had an awful foreboding that Linda and Annie wouldn't come back either and she'd be stuck with the terrible twosome.

Five minutes later, Elena strutted across to Marnie's desk in her really tall stilettos. Marnie hadn't been the only one to notice that her clothes had become decidedly more figure-hugging, her heels higher and her lipstick had inched from orchid pink to slapper red since Justin Fox had joined the company. She held her hand out for the report but Elena put it down on her desk instead. Marnie tried not to let the growl inside rush out of her throat as she thanked her, albeit through gritted teeth.

'Pleasure,' replied Elena, sounding as if her duty had been about as pleasurable as cauterising the linings of her nostrils with a red-hot poker. She turned on her ridiculous heel far too fast to keep her balance, stumbled and did a comedy walk that said, *I am going to recover this and not fall flat on my face.* Then she fell flat on her face in a none too graceful way whilst her left shoe flew off her foot, did a perfect double pike back in the air and came to land on the back of her head. Arlene Phillips couldn't have choreographed it better.

'Oh dear,' said a male voice from behind Marnie. She turned to see Justin Fox striding into the department.

'My ankle, my fff . . . bloody ankle,' Elena was crying. A big pink toe bearing chipped purple nail varnish was protruding from her now laddered black tights. Justin rushed forward like a gallant knight although he was hardly crushed in the queue to help.

'Here, lean on me. You came quite a cropper there. I'm surprised you didn't make a crater in the floor.'

Marnie had to turn around to compose herself. Schadenfreude was shameful, but just for once, she allowed herself to savour it.

As if Elena's embarrassment didn't have enough elements to it, her dark blue skirt had collected a million light-coloured fibres from the relatively new carpet and she appeared to have snapped the heel of the shoe that had managed to stay on her foot.

'Is this yours too?' asked Justin, picking up not only the escapee stiletto but a floppy gel Party Feet insert.

If Elena had gone any redder her head would have blown off her shoulders.

He examined the long pin-heel of the shoe, which looked decidedly tatty at close quarters. 'My goodness, no wonder you fell.'

'I think you ought to go straight to the medical room,' said Marnie, in her best concerned boss voice which she knew would feel like a hundred bees stinging Elena's ears. 'Look, your ankle is swelling up terribly.' And it was. Ballooning. It was almost a cankle. On its way to being a thankle.

'I'll take her.' Vicky stepped forward and Elena put her arm around her shoulder. She couldn't have hopped off faster if she'd tried.

'Are you all right?' Justin asked Marnie who was covering up her mouth and really really trying hard to look sympathetic. Had it been anyone else, it would have come naturally but not with Elena and it probably wouldn't have with Vicky either. But then, she was wicked, she'd heard that often enough to believe it might be true.

'I'm fine,' she coughed. 'Just worried about my colleague.'

'I brought these for you to cast your eye over before the meeting in . . .' he consulted his watch. A black-faced Rolex. As classy and striking as he was. '. . . ten minutes.'

'Thank you,' said Marnie, taking hold of the sheets of paper he was proffering, but he didn't let go of them. Then he leaned in to her and said in a whisper: 'Something tells me you rather enjoyed that little floorshow.'

Marnie gulped and gave a demure pat to her chest. 'I think you are very much mistaken, Mr Fox.' It wouldn't have convinced a grand jury.

'See you in . . . nine minutes and counting,' said Justin with a lazy grin and Marnie's heart gave a perfidious kick. *No, no, no.* She heard her brain protest. *Not again.*

Chapter 3

The day ended on a high. Elena and her fat ankle had gone home and, starved of her partner in crime, Vicky was quiet and actually did some work. Everyone in the executive meeting was impressed by the new shaped mug and Marnie received three billion brownie points. And she noticed Justin smiling at her as she talked through the pricings and argued why they should adapt this shape and ditch the old one. He had a flirtatious sparkle in his eyes and her own eyes kept being drawn to his, as if they were twin sparkly light-seeking moths. Her feet almost hovered above the ground as she walked back to her car that day, but the closer she got to home, the more that buoyant, airy feeling began to subside. The weekend loomed drawn-out and depressing in front of her as it had done for too long now. Marnie hated Saturdays and Sundays, for however much she tried to tell herself that she was married to her work and didn't need a man in her life, those two week-end days exposed that statement for the lie it was.

It was a particularly lonely phase as she was both boyfriend-less and best-friend-less and it followed the worst Christmas she'd had for years. She'd intended to spend it sharing a house with her boyfriend of twelve months, Aaron. Her on–off–on–off boyfriend of twelve months that is, who had finally decided in August that she was the one he wanted to spend the rest of his life with. So, she'd sold her furniture and her flat only for Aaron to tell her, on the day of completion, that he'd made a mistake and was still in love with his ex.

Her best friend Caitlin wasn't on hand to pick up the broken pieces as she was besotted by a high-flying city banker called Grigori and she spent all the time she could down in London with him. He was rich and handsome and successful and very posh and Caitlin had changed in the short time they'd been together. She'd become glossier and more groomed and – though Marnie hated to admit this – less fun, more staid and worst of all, distant. She'd denied having elocution lessons, though it was obvious from the slower, more measured way that Caitlin had started to talk and the strange shapes her mouth formed on certain words, that she had. And when Marnie rang her for a chat, Caitlin always seemed to be in the middle of something and said she'd call back. She didn't always. This, the same Caitlin who had had a real go at Marnie for not giving her friendship time when Aaron arrived on the scene.

Caitlin had been single for over two years when she met Grig-ORRR-i, as she'd started to pronounce it. No wonder she'd sucked him up like a dehydrated woman falling face down in an oasis. Marnie couldn't have been happier for her friend – then she'd met him, and she could have been very much happier for her because Grigori was a plank.

He might have been good-looking and clever and super-brainy and drive a Maserati but it was quite obvious that he didn't like Marnie from the off, because the disapproval came off him in waves. She had first met him in person at the night do of an old school-friend's wedding. Caitlin left Grigori and Marnie to 'get acquainted' whilst she nipped off to the loo. Marnie had opened conversation, but Grigori had turned away and wended his way out through the guests instead. Marnie was gobsmacked by his rudeness and she did wonder what Caitlin had told him to provoke that reaction. She had broached the subject once but Caitlin waved it away and said he'd been absolutely whacked with tiredness that night. Marnie hadn't bought it and what she hadn't told Caitlin was that later on, she'd encountered him on the stairs when he was arseholed and he'd been far more friendly. Feeling obliged to give him a second chance to make a first impression, she'd asked him if he was enjoying himself and he'd pulled her towards him and stuck his tongue down her throat before she pushed him firmly off. He'd fallen down two stairs and called her the c-word and though Marnie had tried to forget it and chalk it up to the drink, she never quite had. One thing was for sure – he had come between them and their once-strong vow that no man would ever do that was crushed to dust.

She'd got into the bad habit of drinking too much at weekends to numb that gnawing hunger within her for company, for affection. She recognised she was in trouble when she began to think that sleeping off a hangover was a better alternative than being conscious, and had tried to cut down over the last couple of weeks.

But on this particular Friday, maybe because she'd been so high earlier on from her successful mug presentation and a little male attention from the hottest property on the trading floor, her spirits nosedived and she felt extra sad and pathetic that night. So, unable to satisfy the cravings of her heart, her body tried to compensate by feeding her something else and put her hands in the way of a giant bag of sweet and salty popcorn and a bottle of Tesco's finest Shiraz.

There was nothing on the TV but programmes about house renovations and dream sheds, a crap gameshow and the big film, which was about a man who couldn't forget his first love – far too near the knuckle for her. At times, when she was plastered, she could see herself more clearly than ever and the revelations hurt and bewildered her. Through the clarity that alcohol supplied, she saw that she had been lonely for a long time, far longer than she'd wanted to admit to herself. Even when she'd been with Jez, Robert, Harry and Aaron she'd still been lonely. It took a particular skill to be lonely in a relationship, she had noted. Sometimes she had lain in bed next to a snoozing Aaron after sex and marvelled at how alone she felt. There had been only inches between their bodies but she had never felt as if she were truly part of a couple. Even when they'd been mid-bonk, there had been none of that 'two become one' or 'bodies melting into each other' bollocks. They'd been more like two hard pieces of wood bashing together than two balls of Play-Doh squashing into a single big ball of pliant softness.

None of the men she'd gone out with had made her feel secure, cherished, needed, not after the initial courtship period was over anyway and they had full access to the contents of her underwear. She often wondered if any man ever could. Maybe the men who still held doors open for you after you'd been together for over thirty years only existed in books – written by women fantasising about the same thing. Maybe that's why Midnight Moon romance stories were so popular, because they contained the sort of mythical beings who rubbed your shoulders without thinking that it constituted foreplay, whipped you up a hot chocolate on cold winter nights, made you laugh till your cheeks hurt or set all your nerves jingling like the bells of St Clements simply by placing a hand on your waist.

In books men energised women; in her experience they sapped your energy to below zero level. Give or take the thump to the ego, it was almost a relief when the relationship limped across the finish line, but then she was left with just herself for company. During the week she could work late, plough everything she had into the job but nothing seemed to fill the chasm of emptiness that weekends brought – not even Candy Crush. She couldn't continue as she was, she'd decided, and forced her brain to come up with a rescue plan, and so it did. For years, she'd toyed with the idea of writing a definitive cheesecake recipe book but had never got around to it. Maybe that was what she needed to get her teeth into and transform her weekends into a brighter brace of days.

So, with a notebook at her side, that night Marnie refilled her wine glass, switched on her laptop and typed 'cheesecake' into Google and before long she had been dragged into the deep quark web of baking. Within a few clicks, she'd happened upon an amazing American site which led her to the Sisters of Cheesecake club where fanatics all over the world sent in pictures of their mad creations and recipes or asked for advice. It was a defining moment when Marnie realised that it was nearly 2 a.m. on Saturday morning and she was more than half-pissed and involved in a three-way heated argument with a woman from Calgary and another from Memphis about the base to topping ratio. Sad didn't even come into it. Weren't women of Marnie's age supposed to have wild dirty cybersex, not rows about baking?

The across-the-pond sisterhood were beating Marnie down, forcing her to accept that a thinner base was desirable. Then in stepped a fellow Brit, declaring that thick bases ruled, having Marnie's back all the way. The brave British duo were declared losers of the lowest order but it didn't matter because the connection they made with each other was a winner. And that is how the paths of Misses Lilian Dearman and Marnie Salt first crossed.

Normally Marnie didn't engage with people she didn't know personally on social media. She had no interest in learning about how some woman she didn't know in South Shields had got on at Weightwatchers that week, or viewing some circulated footage of kittens or people's dinners or sharing petitions and patronising inspirational messages. The internet was a nest of fraudulent vipers as far as she was concerned. If they weren't fleeing from Nigeria and needed her bank details to deposit their millions, they were screwed up dickheads on internet dating sites waiting to pounce.

Wine, therefore, had been a strong contributing factor to how she ended up having an in-depth email conversation with someone purporting to be a sixty-six-year-old insomniac, who found the Sisters of Cheesecake site particularly well stocked with 'sanctimonious know-it-all bastards' with whom she enjoyed a good verbal battle. Her sleeps, Lilian Dearman said, though tardy in coming were superbly restful after giving those stuck-up frustrated old crows a pasting. Thin bases indeed.

Marnie opened up another bottle of wine as they messaged back and forth. Somehow the conversation segued from recipes for cheesecakes to recipes of disaster – i.e. Marnie's life. Lubricated by fermented grapes, a dam burst inside her and out it all poured in a torrent. Everything. Starting with Aaron and then reaching back in time to things she hadn't even told Caitlin. And Marnie went past caring if the person she was typing to was a genuine elderly lady, a *Daily Mail* reporter or a serial killer called Darren.

Despite her intentions to clean up her act, Marnie awoke very late on Saturday afternoon with a major hangover, egg on her face and no recollection of getting to bed at all. The last thing she remembered was telling Lilian about reading *Wuthering Heights* at school and having a crush on her English teacher, Mr Trent. Dangerous territory. What a bloody idiot. How could she have blurted out so many secrets to a stranger? Stuff she had locked away in boxes in her head and yet their locks had sprung at the merest tickle and the contents had come spewing out perfectly preserved in brain-aspic.

Marnie was a panicking mess; what else she had said that she couldn't remember?

She switched on her laptop, after taking two ibuprofen and a Red Bull and tried to log on to the Sisters of Cheesecake site but found that, despite being hammered, she'd obviously had the foresight to delete her account before going to sleep, probably to stop herself reading what she'd written to this 'Lilian Dearman' in the private message box. How could she be so thick and rational at the same time? Whilst she was in cringe mode, she also checked that she hadn't sent an embarrassing email to Aaron but no – there was nothing recent in her sent box to her overwhelming relief. What was there in her inbox, though, was an invitation from Miss Dearman to have afternoon tea with her at a mutually convenient time in the near future. She'd suggested the Tea Lady tearoom in Skipperstone, a market town near to the village of Wychwell where she lived. So, Marnie had given Miss Dearman her email address then. And probably her mobile number, house address, bank details, national insurance number, all her PIN codes and passwords as well.

Marnie had a shower and an omelette and, when revived, looked up Wychwell on the internet, because she'd never heard of it and it was probably no wonder as it seemed to be in the middle of a big forest somewhere in the Yorkshire Dales. Photographs of it on 'images' were more complimentary: twee little cottages standing around a village green, an ancient stone church with a crooked spire and a beautiful manor house on a low hill. There were no pictures of Lilian Dearman, though there were plenty of other Dearmans: Montague Dearman, Ebenezer Dearman, Erasmus Dearman, and more. All with very highfalutin names, stiff poses and handlebar moustaches.

And as Marnie had bugger-all entries in her diary and she was inexplicably intrigued now, she emailed back that she would like to meet up. At least that way, they could both see that the other wasn't a serial killer called Darren or a tabloid journo.

Marnie slobbed around in her dressing gown for the rest of the day feeling weak and wobbly. She had planned to go out and buy her sister a birthday card but ordered one from the internet to be sent directly to her instead. They didn't do presents. They never had. Only at Christmas, which was an ordeal in itself because Gabrielle was allergic to soaps, perfumes, wool and animals, didn't eat chocolates, didn't drink, only read certain literary novels, didn't want anyone else to buy her clothes and flowers set her hay fever off. Marnie spent from August onwards trying to source something that showed she'd put a bit of effort in, whereas Gabrielle bought her an M&S talcum and hand cream gift set in a *meh* flower fragrance every year. Gabrielle was brazen about her lack of effort in present-choosing.

Marnie looked again at her diary and found she had filled in some entries, in a looping drunken scrawl, when she'd been off her face. Amongst others she had blocked in a four-hour lunch on Wednesday with Hugh Jackman and a trip to Lanzarote with Justin Fox on Thursday. Saddest of all, she had booked the following Saturday and Sunday for a catch-up, spa and shopping with Caitlin. She was pathetic with a capital 'P' and she'd ruined her diary with the stupid inclusions. She ordered a new one from Amazon and then took out the recycling, noting that she'd put away two full bottles of wine. Usually after two glasses she was comatose. No wonder she'd told a perfect stranger her entire life story and filled her diary with pitiful gobbledygook. Regrettably, she had more chance of having lunch with Hugh Jackman than she did of a whole weekend catch-up with Caitlin or that holiday in Lanzarote with Justin Fox.

FIND OUT MORE ABOUT

milly johnson

Milly Johnson is the queen of feel-good fiction
and bestselling author of fourteen novels.

To find out more about her and her writing,
visit her website at
www.millyjohnson.co.uk

or follow Milly on

twitter @millyjohnson
Instagram @themillyjohnson
facebook @MillyJohnsonAuthor

All of Milly's books are available in print and eBook,
and are available to download in eAudio

Milly Johnson
The Queen of Wishful Thinking

'A glorious, heartfelt novel' Rowan Coleman

When **Lewis Harley** has a health scare in his early forties, he takes it as a wake-up call. He and his wife Charlotte leave behind life in the fast lane and Lewis opens the antique shop he has dreamed of. **Bonnie Brookland** was brought up in the antiques trade and now works for the man who bought out her father's business, but she isn't happy there. So when she walks into Lew's shop, she knows this is the place for her.

As Bonnie and Lew start to work together, they soon realise that there is more to their relationship than either thought. But Bonnie is trapped in an unhappy marriage, and Lew and Charlotte have more problems than they care to admit. Each has secrets in their past which are about to be uncovered . . .

Can they find the happiness they both deserve?

SIMON &
SCHUSTER